INTERNAL AFFAIRS
BY
JESSICA ANDERSEN

AND

PROTECTOR
OF ONE
BY
RACHEL LEE

MILLS &
BOON

"Stay," she said.

He touched a finger beneath her chin and tipped her face up to his.

"You believe in me that much," he murmured, "because of what we were to each other."

He knew touching her was a mistake the moment his fingertip connected with her soft skin. First, because of the warmth that spread up his arm and lodged in his chest, threatening to undo all his best intentions. And second, because her eyes snapped dark with what he thought was fury, but was wiped away before he could be sure, to be replaced by cool, studied indifference. She eased away.

"Despite the impression you might have gotten from my kissing you last night, I'm all too aware of our history. Trusting you got me a broken heart before. This time it could very well put my life in danger."

INTERNAL AFFAIRS

BY
JESSICA ANDERSEN

All the characters in this book have no existence outside the imagination of
the author, and have no relation whatsoever to anyone bearing the same name
or names. They are not even distantly inspired by any individual known or
unknown to the author, and all the incidents are pure invention.

First published in Great Britain 2010
Harlequin Mills & Boon Limited,
Eton House, 18-24 Paradise Road, Richmond, Surrey TW9 1SR

© Dr Jessica S. Andersen 2010

ISBN: 978 0 263 88264 3

46-1010

Harlequin Mills & Boon policy is to use papers that are natural, renewable
and recyclable products and made from wood grown in sustainable forests.
The logging and manufacturing processes conform to the legal environmental
regulations of the country of origin.

Printed and bound in Spain
by Litografia Rosés S.A., Barcelona

Though she's tried out professions ranging from cleaning sea lion cages to cloning glaucoma genes, from patent law to training horses, **Jessica Andersen** is happiest when she's combining all these interests with her first love: writing romances. These days she's delighted to be writing full-time on a farm in rural Connecticut that she shares with a small menagerie and a hero named Brian. She hopes you'll visit her at www.JessicaAndersen.com for info on upcoming books, contests and to say hi!

Chapter One

The pain speared from his shoulder blade to his spine and down—raw, bloody agony that consumed him and made him want to sink back into unconsciousness. But at the same time, urgency beat through him, not letting him return to oblivion.

The mission, the mission, must complete the mission.

But what was the mission? Where was he? What the hell had happened to him?

Cracking his eyes a fraction, careful not to give away his conscious state if he was being watched, he surveyed his immediate surroundings. Tall pine trees reached up to touch the late summer sky on all sides of him, their bases furred with an underlayer of smaller scrub brush. There was no sign of a cabin or a road, no evidence of anyone else nearby, no tracks in the forest litter but his own, leading to where he'd collapsed.

He was wearing heavy hiking boots, dark jeans and a black T-shirt, all of which were spattered with blood. Something told him not all of it was his, though when he moved his arms, the agony in his right shoulder ripped a groan from his lips. He felt the warm, wet bloom of fresh blood, smelled it on the moist air.

Shot in the back, he knew somehow. *Bastards. Cowards.* Except that he didn't know who the bastardly cowards were, or why they'd gone after him. More, he didn't know who the hell *he* was. Or what he'd done.

The realization brought a sick chill rattling through him, a spurt of panic. His brain answered with *I've got to get up, get moving. I can't let them catch me, or I'm dead.*

The words had no sooner whispered in his mind than he heard the sounds of pursuit: the sharp bark of a dog and the terse shouts of men calling to one another.

They weren't close, but they weren't far enough away for comfort, either.

He struggled to his feet cursing with pain, staggering with shock and blood loss. He didn't know who was looking for him, but there was far too much blood for a bar fight, and the pattern was high velocity. Had he killed someone? Been standing nearby when someone was killed? Had he escaped from a bad situation, or had he *been* the bad situation?

He didn't know, damn it. Worse, he didn't know which answer he was hoping for.

The mission. The words seemed to whisper from nowhere and everywhere at once. They came from the trees and the wind high above, and the bark of a second dog, sharper this time, and excited, suggesting that the beast had hit on a scent trail.

One thing was for certain: he needed to get someplace safe. But where? And how?

Knowing he wasn't going to find the answer standing

there, bleeding, he got moving, putting one foot in front of the other, holding his right arm clutched against his chest with his left. The world went gray-brown around the edges and his feet felt very far away, but the scenery moved past him, slow at first, then faster when he hit a downhill slope.

He saw a downed tree with an exposed root ball, thought he recognized it, though he didn't know from when. His feet carried him away from it at an angle, as though his subconscious knew where the hell he was going when his conscious mind didn't have a clue. Urgency propelled him—not just from the continued sounds of pursuit, which was drawing nearer by the minute, but also from the sense that he was supposed to be doing something crucial, critical.

His breath rasped in his lungs and the gray-brown closed in around the edges of his vision. He tripped and staggered, tripped again and went down. But he didn't stay down. He dragged himself up again, levering his body with his good arm and biting his teeth against the pained groans that wanted to rip from his throat.

Instead, staying silent, he forced himself to move faster, until he was running downhill through trees that all looked the same. He saw nothing except forest and more forest. Then, in the distance, there was something else: a rectangular blur that soon resolved itself into the outline of a late-model truck parked in the middle of nowhere.

Excitement slapped through him, driving back some of the gray-brown. He didn't recognize the truck, but he'd run right to it, hadn't he? It stood to reason that was because he'd known it was there. More, when he'd climbed into the driver's seat, he automatically fumbled beneath the dashboard and came up with the keys.

It took him two tries to get the key in the ignition; he was wobbly and weak, and he couldn't lean back into the seat without his shoulder giving him holy hell. But he had wheels. A hope of escape.

He couldn't hear the dogs over the engine's roar, but he knew the searchers were behind him, knew the net was closing fast. More, he knew he didn't have much more time left before he lapsed unconscious again. He'd lost blood, and God only knew what was going on inside him. Every inhalation was like breathing flames; every exhalation a study in misery. He needed a place to crash and he needed it fast.

After that, he thought, glancing in the rearview mirror and seeing piercing green eyes in a stern face, short black hair, and nothing familiar about any of it, *I'm going to need some answers.*

Knowing he was already on borrowed time, he hit the gas and sent the truck thundering downhill. There wasn't any road or track, but he got lucky—or else he knew the way—and didn't hit any big ditches or dead-falls. Within ten minutes, he came to a fire-access road. Instinct—or something more?—had him turning uphill rather than down. A few minutes later, he bypassed a larger road, then took a barely visible dirt trail that par-alleled the main access road.

The not-quite-a-road was bumpy, jolting him back against the seat and wringing curses from him every time he hit his injured shoulder. But the pain kept him conscious, kept him moving. And when he hit a paved road, it reminded him he needed to get someplace he could hide, where he'd be safe when he collapsed.

Animalistic instinct had him turning east. He passed street signs he recognized on some level, but it wasn't until he passed a big billboard that said *Welcome to Bear Claw Creek* that he knew he was in Colorado, and then only because the sign said so.

His hands were starting to shake, warning him that his body was hitting the end of its reserves. But he still had enough sense to ditch the truck at the back of a commuter lot, where it might not be noticed for a while, and hide the keys in the wheel well. Then he searched the vehicle for anything that might clue him in on what the hell was going on—or, failing that, who the hell he was.

All he came up with was a lightweight waterproof jacket wedged beneath the passenger's seat, but that was something, anyway. Though the fading day was still warm with late summer sun, he pulled on the navy blue jacket so if anyone saw him, they wouldn't get a look at his back. A guy wearing dirty jeans and a jacket might be forgotten. A guy bleeding from a bullet wound in his shoulder, not so much.

Cursing under his breath, using the swearwords to let him know he was still up and moving, even as the gray-brown of encroaching unconsciousness narrowed his vision to a tunnel, he stagger-stepped through the commuter car lot and across the main road. Cutting over a couple of streets on legs that were rapidly turning to rubber, he homed in on a corner lot, where a neat stone-faced house sat well back from the road, all but lost behind wild flowering hedges and a rambler-covered picket fence.

It wasn't the relative concealment offered by the big lot and the landscaping that had him turning up the driveway, though. It was the sense of safety. This wasn't his house, he knew somehow, but whose ever it was, instinct said they would shelter him, help him.

Without conscious thought, he reached into the brass, wall-mounted mailbox beside the door, found a small latch and toggled the false bottom, which opened to reveal a spare key.

He was too far gone to wonder how he'd known to do that, too out of it to remember whose house this was. It was all he could do to let himself in and relock the door once he was through. Dropping the key into his pocket, he dragged himself through a pin-neat kitchen that was painted cream and moss with sunny yellow accents and soft, feminine curtains. He found a notepad beside the phone and scrawled a quick message.

His hands were shaking; his whole body was shaking, and where it wasn't shaking it had shut down completely. He couldn't feel his feet, couldn't feel much of anything except the pain and the dizziness that warned he was seconds away from passing out.

Finally, unable to hold it off any longer, he let the gray-brown win, let it wash over his vision and suck him down into the blackness. He was barely aware of staggering into the next room and falling, hardly felt the pain of landing face-first on a carpeted floor. He knew only that, for the moment at least, he was safe.

Chapter Two

Chief Medical Examiner Sara Whitney's day started out badly and plummeted downhill from there.

It wasn't just that her coffeemaker had finally gone belly-up. She'd known it was on its last legs, after all, and simply kept forgetting to upgrade. Sort of like how she kept forgetting to replace her anemic windshield wipers because they only annoyed her when it was raining. Or how she hadn't yet gotten around to having the maintenance crew that served the Bear Claw ME's office fix her office door, which stuck half the time and randomly popped open the other half.

No, it wasn't those petty, mundane, *normal* irritations that had her amber-colored eyes narrowed with frustration as she worked her way through her sixth autopsy of the day, dictating her notes into the voice-activated minirecorder clipped to the lapel of the blue lab coat she wore over neatly tailored, feminine pants and a soft blue-green shirt that accented the golden highlights in her shoulder-length, honey-colored hair.

No, what annoyed her was the memo she'd gotten

from Acting Mayor Proudfoot's people, turning down yet another request to hire new staff, even though she'd only proposed to replace two of the three people she'd lost over the past year—two to the terrorist attacks that had gripped the city in the wake of a nearby jailbreak, one to the FBI's training program. What annoyed her further was the knowledge that she was going to have to work yet another twelve-hour day to catch up with the backlog. It didn't help that her three remaining staffers—receptionist Della Jones, ME Stephen Katz, and their newly promoted assistant, Bradley Brown— were all taking their lunch breaks glued to the TV in the break room, with the police scanner cranked to full volume as they followed the manhunt that was unfolding in Bear Claw Canyon, not half an hour away.

Sara didn't want to think about the manhunt, or the fact that the combined Bear Claw PD/FBI task force had lost two men in an op gone bad, leading to the manhunt. She didn't want to think ahead to those autopsies, and felt guilty for hoping the dead men weren't any of the cops or agents she knew. She also didn't want to think about the fact that until terrorist mastermind al-Jihad and his followers were brought to justice, people in and around Bear Claw were going to keep dying.

She didn't want to think about it, but she had to, because it was happening even as she stood there, elbow-deep in the abdominal cavity of an overweight, chain-smoking sixty-three-year-old man whose badly clogged arteries suggested an all too common cause of death. The autopsy was routine, but the events transpiring outside Sara's familiar cinder block world were anything but.

Bear Claw City was at war.

It had been nearly ten months since al-Jihad had managed to escape from the ARX Supermax Prison north of Bear Claw Creek, gaining freedom along with two of his most trusted lieutenants. Since then, it had become clear that al-Jihad's network was deeply entrenched in Bear Claw, twining through both local and federal law enforcement.

Each time a conspirator was uncovered and neutralized, new evidence surfaced indicating that the internal problems extended even further, and that al-Jihad was continuing to unfold an elaborate, devastating plan that the task force just couldn't seem to get a handle on. The cops and agents had uncovered pieces and hints, but the terrorists' main goal continued to elude them, even as the groundswell of suspicious activity seemed to suggest that an attack was imminent.

Of course, the general population knew only some of what was going on. Sara knew more than most because her office was intimately involved with the BCCPD, and because she was close friends with a tightly knit group of cops and agents, three couples plus her as a spare wheel.

The seven friends had banded together the previous year when FBI trainee Chelsea Swan—though back then she'd been one of Sara's medical examiners—had fallen in with FBI agent Jonah Fairfax. Fax had assisted in the jailbreak in his role as a deep undercover operative, only to learn in the devastating aftermath that his superior was a traitor and he'd been unknowingly working on al-Jihad's behalf. Sara, Chelsea, Fax and the others had managed to foil al-Jihad's next planned attack, but they'd only managed to capture one of the terrorists, Muhammad Feyd, who'd proven to be a loyal soldier and had defied all efforts to get him talking.

Al-Jihad and his remaining lieutenant, Lee Mawadi, along with Fax's former boss, the eponymous Jane Doe, remained at large even now, ten months later. In that interim, there had been other, smaller incidents, along with a deadly riot at the ARX Supermax. Which Sara so wasn't thinking about right now.

She didn't want to remember the men who'd died in the riot, or the one man in particular whose death had hit her far harder than it should have.

Focus, girl, she told herself. *The day's only getting longer the more you stall.*

Concentrating on the innards at hand, Sara went through the process by rote, weighing and sampling, dictating notes as she worked. But although the actions were automatic—they ought to be, after six years on the job, two heading the Bear Claw ME's office—they weren't without compassion. Sara's top-flight surgeon mother might consider her daughter's medical skills wasted on the dead, but Sara knew she worked for the families as much as the corpses, and took satisfaction from providing answers, shedding light onto causes of death that might otherwise be misinterpreted.

Contrary to what some popular TV shows might portray, only a small fraction of the bodies coming through the ME's office were instances of foul play. The vast majority was made up of an almost equal balance between natural causes and accidental fatalities. Her current case fell into the former, i.e., a catastrophic cardiac event brought on by a high-risk lifestyle and inconsistently treated hypertension.

As she stripped off her protective gear and headed for her office to finish up the necessary paperwork, Sara found herself wishing that more of her recent cases had been so straightforward. It wasn't that she wanted her life to be easy or boring, but she'd gone into pathology because she'd grown up a passenger of her parents' roller-coaster ride of emotions, and she hadn't wanted the highs and lows of living medicine.

Little had she known she'd wind up in the middle of a terror threat that had the entire city by the throat, and that she'd be far more enmeshed in the case than she would've preferred. Granted, the investigation had moved away from her office in the months since the prison riot, but her close ties to members of the task force kept her involved, as did the caseload she'd been forced to assume in the face of a serious manpower shortage.

The lack of staff members in the ME's office was yet another of Acting Mayor Proudfoot's unsubtle efforts to get rid of all the young, energetic hires made by his forward-thinking predecessor, who had been disgraced and ousted when damning photographs had surfaced involving the mayor and several girls of questionable age.

That had been too bad as far as Sara was concerned; she didn't condone the former mayor's ethical lapses, but she thought he'd been taking the city in a positive direction by bringing fresh blood into the crime scene unit, the ME's office and several other tech-based divisions of city government. Since the ex-mayor's departure, Proudfoot had been undoing those advances, piece by piece, making no bones about the fact that he intended to return Bear Claw Creek to the "good old days"—i.e., the days of minimal technology and pay-to-play politics.

Proudfoot's efforts had been blunted somewhat by the terrorist threat, but his image lurked at the back of Sara's mind on a daily basis. She knew he was just waiting for her to mess up badly enough that he could get rid of her and return the ME's office to the age of dinosaurs, with his cronies in charge.

"Which is another thing that belongs in the category of 'things I don't want to think about right now,'" she said to herself on a long sigh, pinching the bridge of her nose to stave off the headache that always encroached when she thought about all the things she was trying not to think about these days.

The list was long. And frankly, it didn't leave her much *to* think about.

"Hey, boss." The hail came from Stephen, the sole remaining medical examiner beside herself. He was tall, lean and graying, a good ten years older than her own thirty-five, and had worked in the Bear Claw ME's office for nearly a dozen years. Miraculously, though, he didn't seem to resent that Sara—young, female, relatively inexperienced—had been hired in above him as his boss. If anything, he seemed happy to let her have the headaches that came with the position.

"Hey yourself." Sara didn't ask about the manhunt,

didn't want to know. "You're headed out early today, right?"

He nodded, a soft smile touching his lips, lighting his usual neutral expression. "Celia and I are bringing Chrissy for a checkup." Chrissy was the change-of-life baby, nearly twenty years younger than their eldest, who had surprised Stephen and his wife the year before. By all indications, little Chrissy would grow up dearly beloved by their entire extended family, and most likely spoiled rotten.

The quiet joy on the older man's face squeezed at Sara's heart. She nodded, forcing herself to feel happy for him rather than sorry for herself. "Tell Celia I said hi."

"I'll do that. I can come back after, if you want me to." He glanced at the wipe board that hung in the hallway opposite their office doors, where the pending cases were listed. "Things are backing up."

They were, indeed, and a large part of Sara wanted to keep the office running around the clock until they'd cleared the board and gotten ahead of the looming mountains of paperwork. But logic said that Proudfoot wouldn't be impressed with that show of efficiency. If anything, he'd take it as an indication that she'd manage just fine with an even smaller staff.

She shook her head. "Thanks for the offer, but no. Head on home. I'll clear what I can, and we can start over tomorrow."

He sent her a long look. "Promise me you won't stay past normal human quitting time? It *is* Friday. You know…the weekend?"

She winced. "You got me. We'll start over on Monday." Which didn't mean she wouldn't be in over the next two days. She had abolished the weekend and overnight shifts due to staff constraints, but she still liked to come into the office herself, when everything was relatively quiet.

Two years earlier, it would've been easy to promise Stephen she'd leave for the weekend, because she would've known there was someone waiting for her at home—someone to cook with, eat with, laugh with, love with.

Even a year ago, having more or less recovered from the catastrophic implosion of that relationship, she would've had plans of some sort. She and Chelsea would've hooked up with Cassie Dumont-Varitek and Alyssa McDermott, their friends in the BCCPD crime scene unit, and had a girls' night out. Or maybe they would've "double dated," with Cassie and Alyssa pairing up with their husbands, while Chelsea and Sara hung together.

It wasn't the same these days with Chelsea gone into the FBI training program on the East Coast, though. Sara had tried going out with the others, and had felt like a fifth wheel. Chelsea had been the glue holding them together. Without her, it felt as if the rest of them were trying too hard. Even when Chelsea and Fax came back to the city, they were most often there on task force business, maybe with a little wedding planning snuck in on the side.

Things had changed. The others had moved on, leaving Sara behind.

Summoning a smile, she waved Stephen away. "Go on, get moving. You wouldn't want to keep your women waiting."

But he didn't move. Instead, he gave her a long, intense look. "I'll do the agents when they come in, if you'd like. I can be here tomorrow morning, assuming they release the bodies that early."

He was talking about the manhunt, the men who'd died. She closed her eyes, feeling guilty over the stab of relief brought by the offer. "Have they announced the names?"

"Not yet."

She nodded, knowing that even though she hadn't been paying attention to the reports, the knowledge of the deaths, and the echoes it brought, had permeated her. "I'll let you know." Which was as close as she was going to get to confessing that she couldn't handle how close the terrorists were hitting, and how much it bothered her that things seemed to be ramping up rather than settling down these days. It was hard not to wonder where it would all stop, and how many would die in the attack most of the task force members thought was imminent.

Her mother and father were in rare agreement that she should give notice and get the hell out of Bear Claw Creek. Sara had seriously considered the option…for about thirty seconds before coming to the realization that she couldn't do it. This was her home; she wasn't giving up on it. And what was more, she wasn't walking away from her job or her remaining staff members.

This was her department, damn it. She might be going down, but she was going down fighting.

After another long look, Stephen headed out. Telling herself she appreciated his concern, that it didn't make her feel even lonelier than she had before, Sara completed the necessary paperwork on the cases she'd autopsied so far that day, then suited back up and returned to work.

She processed three more routine cases over the remainder of the day and did her best to tune out the news bulletins when she passed through the break room, or got near Della's desk, where the fiftysomething admin assistant had a police band radio turned low. Still, Sara couldn't avoid knowing that the senior agents had called off the op, that the search dogs had followed two different trails ascribed to the terrorists, both of which had dead-ended in vehicle tracks heading for the main roads.

It seemed that the op had been a quick scramble into the state forest, based on intel that several of al-Jihad's people were holed up in a remote cabin, strategizing. Sara didn't want to know but couldn't help hearing that the two agents had lost their lives in pursuit of a small knot of men who appeared to have been carrying bodies, while a lone man had escaped in the opposite direction, and vanished into the wind. She didn't want to know that the cabin had been stripped bare, and had burst into flames within minutes of the terrorists' escape, torched by a hidden incendiary device.

As usual, al-Jihad's people had been well prepared. Sara wasn't sure what the op had aimed to do, or what the terrorists had planned or accomplished in the forest, but she knew the names of the dead men now, whether she wanted to or not. Both FBI agents, they weren't among her friends or acquaintances, but they'd had their own friends and families, their own loved ones who'd been cruelly left behind. More bereaved to add to the list that had grown over the past ten months.

Sadness beat through Sara as she kept working, starting another case because it wasn't as though she had any pressing reason to go home, Friday night or not.

Della and Bradley clocked out around five-thirty and left arm in arm. Bradley had been mooning after Della—who was a good decade his senior and the mother of two grown children—for as long as he'd been working there. Sara smiled, her heart warming at seeing them so obviously together, though she found herself wondering how she'd missed that change in relationship status. Then she had to remind herself not to dwell on the fact that everyone around her seemed to be pairing up these days. Everyone but her.

Biting back a sigh, she got back to work. By the time she called it a night, around 7:00 p.m., her shoulders, back and neck were burning from the strain. She would've killed for a massage, or at least an hour in a whirlpool, but she couldn't bring herself to hit the gym this late on a Friday.

There was a fine line between being single and being pathetic.

Consoling herself with the thought of a long, hot bath, she collected her hybrid from the parking lot, which was located between the BCCPD's main station house and the connected building that held the ME's office.

The twenty-minute drive home was an easy one, and

the sight of the small stone-faced house eased something inside her, even in the darkness.

She'd fallen in love with the place on her first drive through the city. The cottagelike house had been way out of her budget, but she'd taken an uncharacteristic leap and bought it on an adjustable mortgage, then switched over to a fixed loan as soon as she was able to afford the higher payments. These days she was managing the expenses, though there wasn't much left over at the end of the month for extras or savings. She didn't regret the purchase for a second, though. It was her home, plain and simple.

The house was easily big enough for two people—hell, for a small family—but she'd resisted the option of taking on a roommate because she liked to keep her space the way she liked it, with none of the rapid changes she'd endured during childhood. The one person she'd shared her home with—albeit for only a few months—had fit into her world so seamlessly, despite their obvious differences, that she'd thought it would last. It hadn't, of course. And the final words between them had been angry ones.

"Stop it," she told herself as she parked the hybrid near the house, then gathered her bag and coat to head for the kitchen door.

She didn't know why her ex was so much in her mind lately, but enough was enough. He wasn't coming back, and they hadn't been together for the year prior to the prison riot that had taken his life. His death had been tragic, but it didn't magically erase his sins, didn't erase his betrayal. Not by a long shot.

Muttering under her breath, she fished in her bag for her keys, unlocked the door and let herself through. Two steps into the kitchen, with the door swinging shut at her back, she stopped dead as the smell of blood tickled her nostrils. It was a familiar odor, of course, but it wasn't one that belonged in her house.

She stayed frozen for a moment, adrenaline kicking her heart into overdrive.

Logic said she should get out of the house, get somewhere safe and call for help. But something she couldn't name—anger at the growing suspicion that an intruder had broken in, maybe, or a complete and utter lapse of her usual good judgment—had her flicking on the lights and moving farther into the house.

She didn't see anything out of place in her pretty kitchen, but the back of her neck prickled, warning her that someone had been there who shouldn't have been. Holding her breath, she eased through the doorway connecting the kitchen to the living room. And froze in horror.

A man lay on the floor beside her sofa, blood soaking the carpet beneath him.

Sara stifled a scream, swallowing it in a bubble of hysteria. Her saner self said, *Run! Get the hell out of here!* But something had her stalling in place as her heart hammered in her chest.

Her brain racked up impressions in quick succession: the big man lay motionless, but he was breathing. He wore jeans, a dark blue jacket and boots with soil and gravel embedded in the treads. She could see their bottoms because he lay on his face, hands outstretched, one nearly touching a pen and notepad as though he'd dropped them when he fell.

Her panicked brain replayed info from the radio bulletins: a group of men had disappeared in one direction, carrying a couple of bodies. A single man had gone off alone. Having spent the day listening to snippets about the dead agents and the unsuccessful manhunt in the forests of Bear Claw Canyon State Park, Sara knew damn well she should be running for her life, screaming her head off, doing something, *anything* other than standing there, gaping. But she didn't move. She stayed rooted in place, staring at the notepad.

She knew that writing.

Emotion grabbed her by the throat, choking her and making her heart race even as logic told her it was impossible. That wasn't his writing. Couldn't be. The man lying there, bleeding, was a stranger. A danger. *Get out of the house,* she told herself. *You're imagining things.*

But she didn't run. She edged around the man and leaned down to read the note. It said: *Nobody can know that I'm here. Life or death.*

Sara reached for the notepad, then stopped herself. Her hand was shaking and tears tracked down her cheeks unheeded.

"No," she whispered, the single word hanging longer than it should have in the silence. "He's dead."

But she knew that writing, had seen it on countless notes tucked under her coffee mug, or left beside the phone, telling her where he was going, when he'd be back, or that he'd pick up dinner on the way. Love notes, she'd liked to think them, even though he'd never said those exact words.

Hope battered against what she knew to be true. *He's dead,* she thought. *I went to his funeral.*

Yet she reached out trembling fingers to touch thick, wavy black hair that was suddenly, achingly familiar. And stopped herself.

All rational thought said she should call for help. The note, though, said not to. She wouldn't have hesitated, except for the damn writing. It was shaky, but it was his. She'd swear to it.

She could turn him over and prove it one way or the other. It wasn't as if he was going anywhere fast. He was out cold, his back rising and falling in breaths so shallow they were almost invisible. Blood soaked the rug beneath him; the smell of it surrounded him.

Sara's inner medical professional sent a stab of warning as she dithered on one level, assessed his injuries on another. *He's pale, probably shocky. If you don't do something soon, it won't matter who he is because he'll be dead.*

"Call 9-1-1," she told herself. "Don't be an idiot."

Instead, she reached out and touched him—his stubble-roughened cheek first, then the pulse at his throat. As she did so, she tried to get a sense of his profile, tried to see if it was—

No. It couldn't be.

Yet her heart sped up, her head spun and her breath went thin in her lungs as she debated between checking his spine—which was the proper thing to do before moving him—and turning his face so she could see, so she'd know for sure.

Then he groaned—a low, rough sound—and said something unintelligible in a voice that was achingly familiar. Heat raced through her. Hope.

He moved his right arm and let out another groan of pain. Then, as though sensing that she was there, he shifted, snaking out his left hand to grab her ankle—not hard, more looping his fingers around her, touching but not restricting her.

Sara squeaked and would have jerked away, but once again she was frozen in place, paralyzed by the memory of a lover who'd kept a careful distance between them when awake, but in sleep had always wanted some part of him touching some part of her, as though reassuring himself she was still there.

"Romo?" she whispered. The single word burned her lips and hurt her chest.

Then he shifted again, this time turning his face toward her, so she saw him in profile against the bloodied carpet.

Her throat closed on a noise that might've been a cross between a scream and a moan if it had made it past the lump jamming her windpipe. As it was, the cry reverberated in her head.

She knew that profile—the clean planes of his nose and brow; the dark, elegant eyebrows; the angular jaw. If he was awake and smiling—or snarling, for that matter—at her, she would've known his square, regular teeth and the glint in his dark green eyes. It was really him, she realized, her chest aching with the force of holding back the sobs.

Detective Romo Sampson. Internal affairs investigator. Live-in lover-turned-nemesis. And a dead man back from the dead.

Chapter Three

In that first moment of recognition, Sara's brain threatened to overload with shock and an awful, undeniable sense of hope. She wanted to scream, wanted to laugh, wanted to shriek, "What the hell is going on here? Where have you been? What have you been doing? Why did you let us—let *me*—think you were dead?"

Instead, she forced herself to do what she did best—she buried her emotions, smoothing out the roller coaster.

Clicking over to doctor mode, she shoved her feelings aside, bundling them up along with all the questions that echoed inside her skull. Where had he been for the past four months? What had happened to him? Whose grave had she stood over, dry-eyed but grieving? Whose blood was spattered on his face, arms and hands? It wasn't all his, that was for sure.

He couldn't answer those questions now, though, and might not ever be able to unless she worked fast. Instinct told her he was close to dying a second time.

Sara's heart stuttered a little when she cataloged Romo's injuries and vitals. His breathing was too shallow, the pulse at his throat too slow. And his eyes, when she peeled back his lids, were fixed, the pupils unequal in size, indicating a concussion, or worse.

Shock, she thought, *head injury, and…* She checked him over without rolling him, hissing in a breath when she zeroed in on the wet seep of blood beneath the jacket. *A gunshot wound.*

The hole was ragged at the edges, indicating that the bullet hadn't been going full power when it hit him, and the bruise track suggested it had deflected off his shoulder blade and done more damage to his trapezius muscle than his skeleton. The skin around the injury was inflamed and angry, the blood clotted in some places, still seeping in others. She pressed on his back near the wound, digging into the lax muscles on either side of his spine, hoping the bullet had stayed close to the surface, praying it hadn't fragmented and deflected into vital organs.

He groaned in obvious pain, but didn't move. His hand had fallen away from her ankle, as though having made that effort he'd lapsed more deeply unconscious.

She couldn't find the bullet, but confirmed that his reflexes were decent in his legs, and, having removed his boots, his feet. Her brain spun. The basic exam didn't indicate an immediate spine injury, but the bullet could lie near the vital areas, poised to shift and impinge on the critical nerves if she made a wrong move. She needed more information, needed an X-ray, needed— hell, she needed a doctor who had more experience with living tissue than dead, one who wasn't faintly unnerved to feel warmth beneath her fingertips.

The heat of him, so unlike the refrigerated flesh she touched on a daily basis, unsettled her. More, it wasn't just any living body. It was Romo's living body, which should've been impossible.

Where the hell have you been? she wanted to shout at him. *How could you let everyone think you were dead?*

By "everyone" she meant herself and his parents, because while the funeral had been well attended, and dozens of cops, agents and other staffers had railed against the prison riot that had taken his life, as far as she'd been able to tell, she had been one of the few who had truly mourned his death, one of the few who'd truly considered him a friend, even after everything that had happened between them.

His parents had been there. They'd been shattered and disbelieving, and Sara hadn't had the strength to say anything to them, hadn't wanted to try to define her non-relationship with their son. And maybe she hadn't wanted to admit that she'd been grieving more for what she and Romo'd had in the past, for the man she'd thought him, not the man he'd turned out to be.

Who, apparently, was alive, though not well.

Crouched beside him, one hand on his warm, blood-soaked shoulder, Sara fought an inner battle. She should call for an ambulance, get him to the hospital. The surgeons could deal with the bullet, the cops with his fate. She didn't owe him anything.

But instead of reaching for the phone, she picked up his note and scanned it a second time. *Nobody can know that I'm here.* That was straightforward enough, though difficult under the circumstances, when she needed to get him to an ER. *Life or death.* But whose life or death. Hers? His? A larger threat?

Prior to his death—or what she'd thought was his death—Romo had been working with the BCCPD and occasionally the FBI, using his undeniable computer skills in an effort to ferret out the suspected terrorist conspirators within the BCCPD. Though he'd set his sights on Sara's office as the center of the conspiracy—no doubt thanks in part to Proudfoot's influence—Romo had also been looking at other departments, other cops. Then he'd been killed—supposedly—in the prison riot.

The rumors had said his death had been no accident, that he'd been getting too close to the conspirators and they'd managed to take him out.

From there, Sara realized, it was a short leap to believing that his apparently faked death was related to the case, too. What if he'd used it to drop under deep cover? Chelsea's fiancé, Fax, had pretended to be a killer in order to get himself incarcerated in the ARX Supermax, in an effort to get close to al-Jihad. It was certainly possible that Romo, though a detective rather than an agent, had done something similar. If she assumed he was the lone man who'd escaped the net of the manhunt, then maybe he'd fled the terrorists because they'd found him out, or betrayed him.

But if that were the case, why hadn't he turned himself in to the members of the task force? If not during the chase itself, then why not later? Why had he come to her? Why tell her to keep his presence a secret?

Damn you, she thought as she stared down at him,

trying to figure out if that scenario really made sense, or if she just wanted it to. Her hypothesis did fit the evidence, she decided, but the same evidence would also support the reverse, namely that he'd faked his death so he could drop off the grid entirely and go to work for the terrorists, then got separated from them in the melee of the task force raid on the terrorists' cabin.

Both hypotheses fit, but which was the right one? Or was there yet another explanation she hadn't come up with?

"That doesn't matter right now," she said aloud. "What matters is what you're going to do with him." She glanced at the note, brain spinning.

She knew Romo, knew what he'd been through as a child, and how those experiences had shaped the man he'd become. That, more than anything, told her logic favored the undercover theory. The Romo she'd known had been all about justice, sometimes to the exclusion of all other, softer emotions. She had to believe he'd been working for the good guys. That didn't explain why he wanted to stay in hiding, but it did suggest that if the wrong people found out he was still alive, he could be in very real danger.

Which, if she followed that line of thought to its conclusion, explained why he'd come to her if he felt he couldn't go to whoever he'd been working for. She'd had her full medical training before deciding to specialize in pathology, and kept a small set of supplies on hand in case of emergencies. He would've known that, would've known she could patch him up. And, damn him, he would've known that she'd be unable to turn him away.

Shaking her head, Sara stared down at him. "You're really a bastard, you know that?"

He didn't answer. Didn't even twitch. Which was so not helpful.

She could call an ambulance, then dragoon one of her trusted cop friends to watch over him. There might be suspicions of complicity within the BCCPD and local FBI field office, but she knew for a fact that Chelsea, Fax, Cassie, Seth, Alyssa and Tucker were among the good guys. There was no way any of them were involved with the terrorists. They'd help keep Romo safe.

But Sara stalled, because he'd come to *her*. He'd asked *her* to keep his presence a secret. Maybe, just maybe, it made the most sense to follow his instructions for the moment, and make her decisions once he was conscious and could fill in some of the blanks.

Warning bells chimed at the back of her brain, but she couldn't deal with them just then. She needed to make a decision, and it had better be the right one. Except when she came down to it, she knew she'd made her decision the moment she stepped toward him rather than away; the moment she'd touched his injured shoulder and felt warm skin, and remembered what they'd once been to each other.

"Fine," she said, her words seeming too loud in the silence of her secluded home. "Have it your way. You always did." Reaching for a double handful of his clothing—and steeling herself to be a doctor rather than a woman who still, inexplicably, wanted to weep—she said, "I need to roll you. This is going to hurt."

She doubted he could hear her. The warning was more for her own sake than his, because she wasn't used to dealing with patients who still had their pain responses intact.

Doing her best to minimize the amount she twisted and moved him, in case the bullet had ended up someplace grim, she levered him partway up and checked for an exit wound or other injuries on the front of his body. She didn't find either, which was both good news and bad: good news because his injury seemed localized and treatable, assuming the bullet hadn't punched through to something internal; bad news because she didn't know where the damned thing had gone.

Easing him back down onto his flat stomach, trying not to remember how he'd slept like that, his face smashed into the pillow, his long limbs sprawled toward her, onto her, some part of him always touching some part of her, she rose and headed deeper into the house, through the smallish, oddly arranged rooms that she'd decorated to blend one into the next, with neutral, mossy colors and richly patterned curtains.

She took the stairs leading up to her office and the bedroom, and tried not to remember the night she and Romo had made love on the landing, early in their relationship. They'd been out with her friends, teasing each other with looks and touches, with no question in either of their minds where and how the night would end. They hadn't even made it all the way up the stairs before they'd collapsed, twined together, needing each other so much it had seemed like madness.

Blushing, she stepped into her office, crossing

quickly to the locked gun cabinet in the far corner, where she kept not only the small .22-caliber handgun she'd purchased just after al-Jihad's reign of terror began, but also her medical supplies. The elegant cabinet was far more graceful—and much less expensive—than a safe. She dialed in the combination and popped the door, then stood and stared for a second at the large tackle box she'd outfitted as a field kit.

She'd freshened her supplies regularly over the past year. With al-Jihad hitting targets in and around Bear Claw, she'd wanted to be prepared for emergencies. She'd never actually used the thing, though. Had hoped she'd never have to. She couldn't handle the immediacy of living medicine, the emotions. Now, facing the prospect of working on a man she'd known intimately, a man she'd loved, she quailed. She'd never understood how her mother reveled in the godlike act of cutting into living flesh. Then again, she'd failed to understand a number of her mother's choices over the years.

You can do this, she told herself, squaring her shoulders and reaching for the medical kit. *You* have *to do this.* He'd trusted her enough to put his life and safety in her hands. She would reward that trust by patching him up. *Then, once he's awake, I'll get some answers out of him,* she thought as she returned to his side. Now that she had a plan of sorts, her emotions were starting to shift from dizzying relief at finding him incredibly, impossibly alive…to anger at the deception he'd perpetrated, and his presumption that she'd take him in and treat his wounds on the basis of a note that explained less than nothing.

Leave it to slick, handsome, charming Romo Sampson to assume she'd take care of him after what he'd done to her.

"Bastard," she muttered under her breath, holding on to the anger because it steadied her hands as she cut away his jacket and black T-shirt, revealing the strong lines of his back, the angry bullet wound and the streaks of forming bruises.

She removed the bulk of his clothing, save for his boxers, which were cheap chain-store wear, and nothing like what he would've worn before.

Shoving that thought aside, she piled several blankets over him, then turned up the heat in the living room. She had to get him warm and find a way to get his fluid volume up. But at the same time, she knew she had to be smart, too; she needed to protect herself if things proved more complicated than her more optimistic hypothesis—that he'd been undercover, the blood spatter was from a clean kill of one of the terrorists, and he was in the clear, fully sanctioned for whatever he'd done.

A quiver in her belly warned that the explanation, when she got it, probably wouldn't be that neat. Romo had never been one to make things easy—either on her or on himself.

His clothes were damp with sweat and blood, and streaked with dirt and other substances. His pockets were empty save for her spare key; a quick search revealed that he wasn't carrying any wallet, ID, or weapon. She placed his clothes and boots in a paper bag and taped it shut, signing her name across the tape. Then she locked the bag in the gun cabinet. It wasn't a perfect chain of evidence and probably wouldn't be admissible in court, but it was the best she could do under the circumstances.

It's just in case, she told herself, and worked very hard not to think about what some of those cases might be.

Returning to him, she found that his color was a little better, his flesh a little warmer beneath the blankets. It seemed very strange that her patient's skin was flesh-toned and body temperature, but she shoved aside the oddity, locking it down along with her emotions and telling herself to woman up and do what needed doing.

She set him up on a portable monitor that told her what she already knew: his blood pressure, pulse and respiration were all dangerously depressed. Knowing she needed to get his vitals headed on the upswing, she started him on a saline drip. If it came to it, she'd transfuse him with her own blood. She was a type O, a universal donor. But God help her, she hoped it didn't come to that. She'd already given him everything she intended to of her inner self.

Soon, though, his numbers started coming back up, and his skin and gums pinked, indicating that the shock was fading. Which left her with the bullet wound.

She followed the bruise tracks with her fingers, probing as deeply as she dared. She found three spots where she was pretty sure she felt something. The bullet had fragmented. Damn it.

Doing the best she could, she pulled on sterile gloves, cleaned and numbed the three spots, then chose one and used a scalpel to dissect away the skin and muscle. Without clamps or suction, blood welled immediately, obscuring her working field. She cursed and blotted it with a sterile pad, but gave that up almost immediately as pointless. Instead, she resigned herself to working blind, probing with the scalpel, then forceps.

"Come on…come on…" She was breathing heavily, sweating more from nerves than exertion. Then she felt the forceps lock on to something hard and metallic. "Ah! Gotcha."

She dropped the bloodstained fragment in a specimen jar, used stitches to close the muscle and incision and then repeated the process twice more. By the time she was done, she'd nearly gotten used to the fact that when she cut into him, he bled. Yet although his vitals had stabilized where they needed to be, he hadn't moved or made a sound. He just lay there, breathing. In and out. In and out.

Forcing herself not to watch the rhythmical fall of his back, she returned to her work, stitching up the last of the three cuts before turning her attention to the recovered fragments. When she pieced the ragged bits of metal together in their specimen jar, it looked as though she'd gotten all of the projectile. The metal was deformed, making it impossible for her to be sure, but without an X-ray, there wasn't much more she could do.

She cleaned the entry wound as best she could, then closed it as well, leaving a spot at the bottom for drainage. Finally, she hit her patient with a whopping dose of a broad-spectrum antibiotic. That, plus crossing her fingers, was going to have to be enough. She debated over the painkiller choices she had on-hand, and went with the mildest. He'd be hurting when he awoke—she deliberately thought "when," not "if," as though positive thinking would be enough to pull him out of the deep unconsciousness that continued to hold on to him. But it was that very unconsciousness that meant she couldn't give him one of the stronger painkillers, which had sedative effects.

She needed him to wake up, needed to get a grip on whether the head injury that had blown his pupils to uneven sizes had caused serious damage. If it had, she'd be doing him a major injustice keeping him hidden. But it wasn't as if she had a CAT scan or an MRI handy.

Her training warred with her conscience. She knew she should take him to the ER, where he could be properly cared for. But at the same time, despite what had happened between them, she had to believe that Romo never would have perpetuated a fraud of any sort—never mind faking his own death—if it hadn't been absolutely necessary.

As a child, he'd lived through scandal and a trial when his businessman father had been framed for embezzlement by a coworker. Thanks to solid police work and an ambitious public defender on her way up the political ladder, Romo's father had been acquitted, the other man jailed. Gratitude, and that early exposure to justice, had set Romo on his path to a career in law enforcement.

Sara had heard the story for the first time at his funeral. She also hadn't realized he'd come to Bear Claw via the Las Vegas PD. That it'd taken his funeral for her to learn that much about his past had bothered her. At the same time, it'd made her wish she could have one last chance to confront him. She'd imagined herself demanding to know what had gone wrong between them, why he'd done what he'd done, even knowing about her past and how badly his actions would hurt her.

Now, though, her sketchy knowledge of his childhood only served to reinforce Sara's instinct to follow the instructions in his note. He'd gone into police work looking for justice, undoubtedly moving into internal affairs for the same reason. And though he might leave something to be desired on a personal level, she simply couldn't see him joining the terrorists' cause.

Having done what she could for him, she leaned back on her heels and considered her options. She couldn't lift him by herself, and even if she could, she'd risk tearing the heck out of the stitches. So he'd be staying on the floor for the time being. She did manage, through a combination of leverage and no small amount of tugging, to get a thin camping mattress underneath him, helping keep him warm as well as getting him off the bloodstained floor.

"I'll deal with the cleanup later," she said aloud, wrinkling her nose. But, the immediate issues dealt with, she became aware that she was a mess, and the room didn't smell all that pretty. Maybe she should deal with cleanup sooner than later. This was her home, after all.

Trying not to wonder why he'd come to her rather than whoever he'd been working with since his faked death, she moved around the house, closing the curtains and shutting the blinds, lest a casual—or not so casual—

observer chanced to look in the windows. As she did so, small shivers marched their way along her skin, warning her that she hadn't yet thought through all the ramifications of what she'd done, or the question of what she was planning to do next.

Life or death, he'd written. If the terrorists knew about him, if he feared they would kill him if he surfaced, then wouldn't it stand to reason that they'd be looking for him? But if that were the case, why wouldn't he want Fax, Seth and the few other agents he trusted to know he was alive? Again, why had he come to her?

That made her pause. What if he really *had* been working for—

"No," she said aloud, refusing to go there. The Romo she'd known would never in a million years have switched sides. She knew that for certain. Everything else was just going to have to wait until he woke up.

Still, partly because she didn't want him hurting himself if he started thrashing, partly because her head wasn't quite as sure of him as her heart wanted to be, she pulled a couple of bungee cords from the camping equipment she kept piled in her office closet. Wrapping the cords around his waist and over his wrists, she bound his arms, then did the same with his ankles.

He didn't stir over the next couple of hours, as she showered and changed, made herself a quick dinner and then freshened the living room as best she could. Finally, near midnight, her body drained of the frenetic, nervous energy that had been driving her up to that point, and she sagged with a sudden onslaught of fatigue.

Romo was stable enough for her to detach the monitors and saline as he moved into the recovery phase of his injuries, when she'd need to be watching for infection or other signs that she'd missed something with the relatively crude care she'd been able to provide. Telling herself it only made sense to stay near him, in case problems arose during the night, she clicked on a nightlight in the kitchen to provide a low level of illumination, and bedded down on the couch with a couple of pillows and a thick, soft afghan.

Although she ached with fatigue, her brain kept her restless and wide-awake for far too long. It took almost superhuman effort not to watch him sleep and wonder what had happened to him, what would happen next. It was even harder to keep herself from remembering their times together, both good and bad, all of them tainted with the ache of betrayal and heartache. Eventually, though, she dozed. As she did, she let her hand dangle off the edge of the couch, so her fingertips just brushed the edges of his blanket. Finally, she slipped into a deep sleep.

She awoke hours later, roused by a sound, or maybe just an instinct. Going into doctor mode, she rolled over and moved to rise, opening her eyes as she did so. She froze for a half second at the sight of the empty spot where Romo had been.

Panic sluiced through her and she moved to react, but it was already too late. A man's figure rose above her, silhouetted in the dim light. She saw the glint of his eyes and teeth, and the shadows of his hands as he reached for her, grabbed on to her, his grip hard and hurtful.

Screaming, she exploded from the couch, but it was

already too late. His hands covered her mouth and pressed her back down into the cushions, cutting off her air. Smothering her.

HE BORE DOWN while his enemy grabbed his hands, his wrists, her fingernails digging in as she fought, squirming and bucking against him. And yes, it was a woman, though that didn't make her any less the enemy. Why else had she kept him bound as she slept? She was one of them. One of the ones who hunted him, who wanted him dead. One of the ones whose faces had haunted him in his nightmares and dragged him back to consciousness.

"Who are you?" he said, his voice rasping with the effort his weakened self was expending to hold on to her, as sharp pain flared in his shoulder.

She whiplashed against him, her legs kicking out and meeting nothing but air. *Not a trained fighter,* his brain cataloged, but he already could've guessed that from the way she'd bound him, with cords that had stretched easily under pressure.

He must've been weaker than he'd thought, though, because seconds later she got away from him, clawing and kicking. She hit the floor hard, scrambled up and bolted for the door, screaming.

"Damn it!" Heart hammering—and not just from the fight—he lunged and his legs folded beneath him. Landing hard, he reached out with his good arm, snagged her by an ankle and yanked, bringing her down with him. Strength failing, head pounding with a relentless beat, he went with expediency and lay full length atop her, pinning her with his weight.

She struggled, still screaming, though her screams had turned to words. A name. *Romo*.

He didn't know the name, not really, but he was starting to remember the room. They had fallen halfway into a kitchen; a small night-light was on, allowing him to see more details of the homey, feminine space, and triggering the memory of coming to the house earlier in the day, knowing he'd be safe.

But if he was safe, why the hell had she tied him up? And why the hell was he practically naked?

Scowling, he glared down at his captive. She'd gone still and had stopped screaming, but her face was pale even in the diffuse light, her eyes stark and staring. And a hell of a face it was, too, even terrified.

He couldn't tell the color of her eyes or hair, beyond knowing that they were both light-hued. But the dimness didn't detract from the elegant lines of her face and swanlike neck, the sculpted arches of her eyebrows and the wide bow of her mouth. Beneath him, her body was lithe and strong—he could feel that strength in the sore places on his shin and arms, and the burn of his injured shoulder where she'd yanked against him in her struggles. But although she was strong, she was also wholly feminine, her curves pressing against him, bringing a stir of memory—this one older and more deeply buried.

As he lay atop her, he belatedly realized that he'd come here, to this woman, because he'd trusted her to help him.

Shame washed through him. Guilt. "I'm sorry," he said, though he didn't let her up. "I was dreaming. Nightmare. Then I woke up, not sure where I was, and my arms and legs were tied."

She took a shallow breath and he thought she might scream again. Instead, she said, "Your note didn't give me much to go on. I was trying not to be stupid. Apparently, the bungees were borderline on the stupid factor." He gave her credit for guts, though even as she tried to play it cool, her voice shook.

A roil of memories he couldn't pin down, couldn't place, had him stilling and loosening his hold, then rolling onto his side, taking her with him. She was free to move away, but she didn't. Instead, she lay there facing him, her eyes searching his.

"Where have you been?" she asked, her voice hitching on a suppressed sob. "What happened to you?"

I don't know. I don't even know who I am. Who you are. Who we were together. That was what he should've said. Instead, he found himself staring, filling himself with the sight of her. Though he was no longer touching her, he felt her curves as though they'd been imprinted on his flesh, creating new memories to replace the ones that were gone. A wellspring of loneliness surged from nowhere and everywhere at once—an ache of longing and a deep sense of loss.

He reached for her blindly, moving purely on instinct. Incredibly, she met him halfway in a kiss that started soft and gentle. Then her lips parted on a small moan of surrender and he slipped his tongue inside to touch hers, tangle with hers. He stroked her hair, her face. She cupped his cheek in her palm.

And, for the first time since he'd regained consciousness in the forest, he felt as though he was exactly where he belonged.

Chapter Four

Sara had seen the kiss coming, and could've pulled away if she'd wanted to. Nothing was holding her in place…except her own memories of the two of them together, and the grief she'd felt standing at his graveside. He'd been dead. Now he was alive.

That was why, when he leaned in, she met his kiss. That was why, when he touched his tongue to hers, she returned the move in kind and crowded closer to him so their bodies aligned, though lightly. And that was why, when her blood and body heated at the feel of his bare skin beneath her fingertips and the taste of him on her tongue, she didn't retreat as she knew she should. Instead, she crowded closer, mindful of his injuries but wanting for a moment—just a brief, beautiful moment— to pretend that the past year or so had been a bad dream.

His taste was sharp with pain and fear, but underneath those flavors was that of the man she'd known, deep and complex, rich and multilayered. Her heart kicked in her chest as she soaked in the sensation of touching him and being touched, cherished his soft groan, and the softening of his caress to one of pleasure, and acceptance.

She let herself linger a moment more, then ended the kiss. Regret pierced her as she drew away from him—or had he pulled away first? She didn't know, knew only that now they were lying on her living room floor facing each other, looking into each other's eyes, and he was there, really there after all these months.

And, she realized with a bite of disquiet, he still had the power to make her forget her better intentions, at least for a while.

Damn him.

Fanning the anger because it was a far safer emotion than any of the others he brought out in her, she sat up and glared at him. "If you tore your stitches, I'm going to leave you leaking." Which wasn't the most important issue by far, but was somehow the first thing that had come out of her mouth.

He just looked up at her for a moment, all hard muscles and man, sharp facial angles and clever dark green eyes, with a layer of masculine stubble on his square jaw and the thick dark hair that she'd delighted touching as they'd kissed, as they'd made love. *No,* she told herself, *don't think about that now, don't remember those times. The present is far more important than the past, under the circumstances.*

But before she could demand an explanation of where he'd been for the past several months, he said, "I'm sorry."

It wasn't clear whether he was apologizing a second

time for grabbing her, for disappearing and faking his own death, for kissing her or for potentially having messed up her stitches. Since she wasn't actually sure which she would've preferred, she let it go, asking instead, "What happened to you?"

"I…I'm not sure." He sat up slowly and started climbing to his feet, dragging one of the blankets with him in the absence of clothing. He was clearly feeling his injuries now that his body was draining of the adrenaline spike that must've powered him to this point.

Sara rose and gripped his good arm when he swayed, even though her own legs were far from steady. Forcing herself to focus on the practical stuff when nothing else seemed to make any sense, she said, "Come on. As long as you're on your feet, let's get you to the bedroom." She had a feeling he'd be headed for a collapse once the last of the adrenaline had burned off, and would rather he didn't wind up on the floor again.

He leaned on her heavily as they climbed the stairs to the second floor. She told herself to ignore the fact that he was mostly naked, that her hands gripped the warm, lithe flesh that had brought her such pleasure in the past. She watched his face as they crossed the spot where they'd made love so long ago. When his expression didn't change, she cursed him for being an insensitive ass, and cursed herself for caring when they'd been broken up for more than a year, and he'd been dead—in theory, anyway—for nearly half that time.

He hesitated at her office door, and she urged him past it to her bedroom, where he lay facedown on the bed with a grateful, pained sigh. He stayed obediently still while she checked his wounds, which were inflamed and angry, but showed little sign of additional damage.

"You got lucky," she said, pulling the blanket up over him. "The stitches held." Then, feeling unaccountably jittery, she sat on the edge of the bed they used to share, spinning to face him and perch there, cross-legged. He looked at her, expression unreadable, as she inhaled a deep breath and let it out again in a slow, measured exhale that did little to settle her sudden nerves. "Okay," she said. "Here's the deal. I didn't call an ambulance or the cops, and I didn't tell anyone you were here because of your note, and because we have enough of a history for me to give you the benefit of the doubt. But also considering our history, I think you'll agree that I don't owe you much more than that. So if you want me to keep helping you out, you're going to have to give me a reason and some explanations, starting now."

Although he was lying in her bed, injured and lacking the strength to stand on his own, his expression was intense as he reached out to her with his good hand and gripped her fingers in his. "Thank you for not turning me in."

Something shivered down her spine at his choice of words. "Tell me you're going to call Fax and Seth now, or whoever you've been working for within the PD."

He grimaced. "I'd like to say yes, but…" He trailed off, his expression clouding. After a moment, he said, "Okay, I'm going to tell you the truth because whatever the details, I apparently trust you more than I do anyone else in the area."

She frowned, confused. "I…I don't know what that means."

He tightened his fingers on hers. "It means that I don't know your name. I don't know my own name. I don't know what we were to each other, or why our relationship—judging from what you just said, anyway—ended. And I damn sure don't know who shot me, or why."

Sara felt the blood drain from her face, and imagined she'd just gone very pale. Which was okay, because she had a feeling she was about to faint. "You don't…"

He shook his head. "Not a clue. I've got nothing. Why don't you tell me what you know about what I've been up to lately, and we'll see if anything jogs a memory."

A bubble of near-hysterical laughter pressed on Sara's windpipe. "You…you don't remember any of it?"

He turned one hand palm-up. "Obviously I remember the walking-around skills, like how to drive, and that it was a damn good idea to cover up with the jacket so nobody would see my back. But that's survival stuff. I don't—" He broke off, throat working. "I don't remember the things that make me an individual." He tried for a grin. "The only thing I know is that I've got good taste in beautiful, capable women who deal well in a crisis."

"Good taste, maybe, but also a roving eye," she said quellingly, trying not to let him see how much the words cost her. "But that was more than a year ago. In the interim, you died in a prison riot. I watched your parents bury you."

Whatever he'd been about to say in regards to his

fidelity—or lack thereof—died on his lips, and his face went blank with shock. "You're kidding."

"That's so not something I would kid about."

"Why in the hell would I fake my own death?"

Sara hesitated, trying to sublimate her own swirling emotions to the practicalities demanded by the situation. As a doctor, she knew she should let him rest. Retrograde amnesia, whether from a head injury or mental trauma—or both—could pass quickly…or it could prove permanent. If she bided her time, the memories might start coming back on their own, with less shock than she was likely to cause by telling him about the terrorists, the prison riot and his own disappearance. Unfortunately, she didn't think she had the luxury of time to let him remember on his own. The amnesia fit into her theory that he'd been undercover, explaining why he hadn't gone to whoever had been overseeing the operation. But it also fit into the less-likely-seeming possibility that he'd been with the terrorists voluntarily, then run from them during the chaos of the manhunt. He hadn't known which side he was working for, or even what was going on.

In either case, she realized, the terrorists and cops would both be looking for him. And she couldn't do the logical thing and turn him in to the task force, because al-Jihad's people had infiltrated the official response at almost every level. Until they knew who Romo had been reporting to, and whether he trusted that contact, keeping him hidden could truly be a life-or-death scenario, as his note had said.

She had to tell him about the situation, she decided,

and hope the information would help him remember who he could trust. But that left the question of where to begin the story.

As if reading the question in her face, he said softly, "Start with the two of us. Why did I come here?"

That was easy. "We were lovers. You even lived here for a few months before we broke up. That was about a year ago."

"You said I had a roving eye," he said. "I was unfaithful?"

"Once." Which had been enough for her. She'd made a point never to give second chances in situations like that. She wasn't her mother. "It was a long time ago, though, and not really pertinent to what's going on."

Rather than dragging him through a one-sided postmortem of their yearlong love affair, she told him about how al-Jihad, Lee Mawadi and Muhammad Feyd had orchestrated simultaneous bombings in shopping malls across Colorado just prior to Christmas several years earlier, killing hundreds, including a large number of children who'd been waiting to see the mall Santas.

She described how, after a lengthy trial during which Lee Mawadi's ex-wife, Mariah, was briefly suspected of complicity and then exonerated, the three powerful terrorists were convicted for the Santa Bombings and sent to the ARX Supermax Prison north of Bear Claw City. There, through the sort of clandestine communication network that tended to exist in supermax security prisons despite the inmates' isolation, al-Jihad made contact with Jonah Fairfax, who was supposedly doing life without parole for killing two federal agents during a raid on an antigovernment cult up in Montana. In reality, he was a deep undercover operative tasked with ferreting out al-Jihad's contacts within federal law enforcement. In that guise, his handler encouraged him to help al-Jihad and his lieutenants escape. That same handler, Jane Doe, had been working with the terrorists all along. Fax had turned out to truly be one of the good guys, despite Sara's concerns when her best friend, Chelsea, had fallen for the escaped-convict-maybe-undercover-agent. He and Chelsea's friends had banded together to foil a terror attack on a local concert, recapturing Muhammad Feyd in the process. The others—including Jane Doe—had remained at large, though, and intelligence suggested they had fled the country.

A few months later, Lee Mawadi had reappeared in the Bear Claw area, gunning for his ex-wife, Mariah. Sara was less clear on the details, except to say that the ex was now engaged to one of the FBI agents on the task force. The two had been instrumental in foiling a planned attack on the prison, though they hadn't stopped the riot that had killed—supposedly, anyway—Detective Romo Sampson of the BCCPD's internal affairs department. Who patently wasn't dead.

Finishing up, Sara told him how over the past few weeks the communication monitors had said things were heating up the way they might before another attack. Nobody knew where the next horror would be targeted, though, or when. She paused. "There was a manhunt today. Two federal agents were killed, maybe a couple of the terrorists, too…and then you show up here covered in blood."

His eyes were very dark, though she couldn't read the emotions in them. "I don't know whose blood it was," he grated. "God help me, but I don't know. I don't even know whose side I'm on."

"You're one of the good guys," she said automatically. "You must've been undercover, working for al-Jihad and his people, while reporting back to someone on the local or federal response team."

"You sound very sure of that, considering our history." He paused. "What exactly happened between us?"

Unease was a sluice of cold in her belly. "You sure you want to go there?"

"Yeah." His smile went crooked. "I can't imagine…I don't feel like the kind of guy who would cheat."

Her heart drummed in her chest, with a relentless, aching beat. "Trust me, you did. Then you came to me the next morning and confessed. You said you'd stopped into a bar, had a few, one thing led to another…and you woke up next to your waitress."

He winced, but struggled to lever himself up on an elbow, even though the action must've hurt like fury. His eyes were steady on hers, his gaze deep and probing, making her very aware of his bare collarbones and throat, and the fact that he was all but naked beneath the blanket. "Did I ask you for another chance?"

Her face felt numb, her whole body felt numb. She couldn't believe she was having this conversation with a dead man who didn't even know his own name. "I don't do second chances."

Something flickered in his expression. "Pity. That was a hell of a kiss."

She squared her shoulders as anger guttered. "We were great in bed. In the end, that wasn't enough." He looked as though he wanted to say something more, but she steamrolled over him, snapping, "And is that the only thing you can think about, after what I just told you?"

"Of course not. But it's the elephant in the room, isn't it?"

He was right, of course. They weren't strangers, but in a sense they were, because he didn't remember the things she did—assuming she could believe him about the amnesia. She did believe him, though, because no matter how many times she'd called him a cheat and a liar inside her own head, the truth was that he'd never lied. He'd told her about the waitress the next morning. If he hadn't lied about that, she couldn't believe he was lying now. Which left them—where?

She shook her head, not sure what came next. "You should get some sleep, let some of this gel."

"Actually, what I should do is leave," he said bluntly. "I shouldn't have come here. I just... It was instinct."

The fact that she found that even the slightest bit flattering just went to show how thoroughly she'd been into him. And also that she was her mother's daughter.

"If you leave, I doubt you'll get far," she said dryly.

His eyes went to the window, even though she'd drawn the curtain earlier, blocking out the night. "You're probably right. I've endangered you by coming here. Whether I leave or not, you'll still be a target."

A chill swept over her. "I was talking about the fact that I doubt you'd make it far without collapsing, given the concussion, bullet wound and blood loss." But he was right about the other, too, she knew. People were looking for him. Regardless of who found him first, she was going to be in serious trouble. If the task force found out she'd hidden him, Percy would have his excuse to fire her. If the terrorists found him, they were both dead.

She should turn him in, to Fax or someone she trusted. But what if the blood on his clothing had come from the dead agents? Even Fax was on a witch hunt to cull all the conspirators from the federal ranks, and none of her friends had thought much of Romo in the wake of the breakup. Could she truly trust them to believe in him the way she did?

Damn it, she didn't know what to do, and she hated not knowing what came next. She'd grown up in a family that had been in a constant state of flux, with her father coming and going depending on where her parents had been in the cycle of him cheating, her kicking him out, him repenting and her forgiving him. Over and over again.

"You're a doctor?" Romo asked, no doubt because she'd just predicted he'd fall on his face if he tried to leave now.

"I'm—" She broke off, struck anew by just how odd it was for him to be meeting her for the first time all over again, after they'd been as intimate as two people could possibly be. Or at least as intimate as he'd let them be. "I'm the chief ME of Bear Claw City," she said, and even she heard the quiet ring of pride in the words. And why not? The job might not be hers for much longer, but for now she could claim the prestigious title.

He whistled. "Impressive." He frowned for a moment, thinking.

"What?"

"Nothing." He shook his head. "It's just that it's true, you know. You're in danger now because I came here."

"I have friends who could help."

Romo's expression went instantly shuttered. "Don't tell any of them that I'm here. Don't even hint it. Promise me."

His sudden intensity sent a spear of worry through her. "Why not?"

"I don't want to endanger them the same way I've endangered you," he said, but she had a feeling there was more to it than that.

"They're all cops and agents, Romo. They can handle themselves." She wasn't as sure as she sounded, though. The memory of his funeral was too close to the surface. She couldn't bear to think of reliving the experience for Chelsea, Fax or any of the others.

"Promise me," he repeated, reaching out as though he wanted to touch her, though they were a room apart. "Promise you'll give me the night to remember. Promise me we'll talk again before you do anything."

They stared at each other for a long moment while the air thickened with things said and unsaid, and with too many questions. Finally, unable to deal with the pressure that gathered in her chest and made her want impossible things, she turned away. "Get some rest.

I'm going to call Tucker. He's a homicide detective with the BCCPD. If I tell him the manhunt has me freaked out, he'll send a patrol past here every hour or so." It didn't seem like nearly enough, but it was all she could think to do just then. She couldn't leave her patient, couldn't move him, couldn't kick him out… and she'd just promised not to turn him in until at least morning.

"And one other thing."

"What?" she asked, but the word came out weakly, as exhaustion rushed over her, swamping her. Her brain was full, her heart heavy. She just wanted to shut it all off for a little while.

"You called me Romo."

She stilled, her heart cracking a little, bleeding for what he'd lost, for the uncertainty of when—or even if—he'd get it all back. "That's your name. Detective Romo Sampson, Internal Affairs, Bear Claw Creek."

"And you?"

"Sara Whitney."

He said her name back to himself. "Pretty name."

The offhand comment shouldn't have touched her as deeply as it did. Because of that, because of the weakness it indicated, she backed out the door. "I'm going now. Sleep. And don't stress your stitches."

She closed the door firmly at her back, not to keep him in, but to remind herself to keep out. Romo wasn't hers anymore. He hadn't been for a long, long time.

AS THE DOOR SHUT, he lay still, staring after her, trying on his own name. *Romo Sampson*. It was a good enough handle, he supposed, ignoring the lick of panic that came when he realized he didn't know what "Romo" was short for, if anything. He didn't remember the name, didn't remember the parents who'd given it to him, or the woman he'd instinctively come to for help.

An ex-girlfriend, he thought, trying to align that information with his almost overwhelming desire to roll across the big bed with her, and do something to blunt the roiling, churning lust that had gripped him low in the gut the moment he'd pressed his body against hers, the moment he'd kissed her.

Mine, his entire being had said at that moment. And she had cooperated fully, making it something of a shock to learn that they weren't together, hadn't been for some time. Somewhere in his banged-up head, he'd been sure they were a couple. Apparently, he'd forgotten their breakup. He'd forgotten a whole lot of things, and he had a feeling lots of what he'd forgotten wasn't at all pleasant.

Sara seemed convinced he'd been undercover. He wasn't so sure. But as he lay there, trying to remember something—anything—the gray-brown crept in on the edges of his vision, taking over everything. Willing or not, he slept.

Hours later, he awoke stiff and sore, with an excessively foul taste in his mouth. A dim light shone from the bathroom, and when he made it in there, he found a couple of pain pills and a glass for tap water. He downed the pills and water, and stood there, braced against the sink with his head hanging and his shoulder on fire.

He should go back to bed and give his body more healing time, he knew, but his half-remembered dreams kept him on his feet.

His head throbbed, tangling the present with occasional flashes of what he could only assume were things from his past. They weren't in any sort of order, though, didn't have any context. He hoped to hell the flashes themselves were evidence that his memory would come back quickly, as whatever swelling he had going on inside his skull came back down to a dull roar. Problem was, a part of him wasn't sure he wanted those memories back—they were starting to show him some seriously grim scenes, ones suggesting he hadn't been quite the nice guy Sara seemed to believe.

He saw blood and heard a man's screams, saw a computer with a set of schematics on it. And he had an overwhelming sense that he needed to be doing something, performing some sort of mission, but he was damned if he knew what he was supposed to be doing.

Panic stirred. He was unarmed, unprotected. And he wasn't sure the thought of the local cops doubling their patrols was much of a comfort; first, because from the sounds of it, the terrorists had been running rings around them for months; and second, because for all he knew, the cops were the ones looking for him.

He should leave, he knew. Unfortunately, he was realistic enough to admit that he wouldn't get far. He was too damned weak to run. What was more, he'd been there too long already. Whoever was looking for him might've found him already. If so, he couldn't very well leave Sara, knowing she was in danger. He owed her better than running away. He owed her protection, through the morning, at least.

Pushing away from the sink, he headed for the bedroom door, remembering that he'd glimpsed a gun cabinet in the office next door to the bedroom. Almost as an afterthought, he realized he was wearing cheapo skivvies and nothing else. Detouring to her wardrobe, he unearthed a pair of navy blue drawstring sweatpants and a plain black T-shirt that probably swam on Sara's slender frame, but fit snugly across his chest.

The clothing was soft and smelled of her, of laundry detergent and springtime, though he couldn't help noticing the faint odor of blood that came from his own skin, tainting the moment.

Once he was dressed, he slipped out of the bedroom and down the hall to Sara's office. He crossed to the gun cabinet, alert for any noise from the first floor, assuming she'd bunked down on the couch. The gun cabinet was unlocked, which had him muttering about her lack of security. When he got the cabinet open, though, and saw that it was most of the way full with first aid supplies that looked hastily rifled, he figured that explained it. She'd left the cabinet unlocked in her haste to deal with his injuries.

Either that, or there was no gun in there, just medical supplies.

For a moment he thought he was out of luck. Then he caught sight of a small handgun on the top shelf, shoved most of the way to the back next to a box of ammo. Gritting his teeth against a bit of pain, he dug the weapon out and loaded the little .22. Once he had it tucked into his waistband, he felt far better about the situation, and his ability to deal with anyone who tracked him to pretty Sara Whitney's home.

Granted, a .22 wasn't much in the way of firepower, but it was something.

He was about to close up the cabinet when he spied a crumpled paper bag that looked completely out of place amid the sterile first aid supplies. Beside it were his boots. A quick recon showed that the bag held what he suspected were his clothes, packaged as if for evidence. He left the bag alone, but took the boots, carrying them rather than putting him on because he didn't want to wake Sara as he descended the stairs.

Halfway down, on a small, carpeted landing, he paused as a touch of heat feathered across his skin, accompanied by a flare of longing. He grabbed for the memory but it refused to come clear, leaving him feeling hollow. Lonely.

"She's your ex-girlfriend," he reminded himself. "*Ex*. And you're sure as hell not in a position to be thinking about changing her mind on that one." He'd endangered her by his presence. He wouldn't compound that by trying to seduce her.

He wasn't clear on what had happened between them. He didn't think he was the kind of man who cheated; he'd felt a deeply rooted twist of guilt and self-loathing when she'd mentioned it, along with something else that made him think things had been far from simple between them. But complicated or not, he'd reacted to her. And, injured or not, he wanted her.

Still, though, she'd been very clear: no second

chances. And although he didn't know her well—at least not in this incarnation of himself—he had a feeling she didn't make statements like that lightly.

But while logic and rationality said he should leave her alone, when he reached the first floor and found her lying asleep on the sofa where she'd been before— where she'd been when he grabbed her, kissed her—he had to damp down the almost irresistible urge to cross to her, go down on his knees beside the couch and pick up where they'd broken off earlier, with her hands on his face, his buried in her thick, honey-colored hair. That part had been easy, natural. The rest of it, though, was anything but.

Knowing it, and knowing he couldn't live with himself—whoever he was—if anything happened to her, he snagged the bedding he'd been lying on earlier, and cobbled together a makeshift pallet near the front door. It wasn't particularly comfortable, he found as he lay down and felt his bruises howl, his stitches tug. But that had been his plan—the discomfort would keep him from sleeping too deeply despite his injuries, meaning he'd have a better chance of hearing an intruder and re-sponding in time. He hoped.

He lay facing the door for maybe five minutes before he gave in to the temptation and levered himself pain-fully to his other side, so he could watch Sara sleep. She'd left on the same kitchen night-light as before, and the dim illumination cast soft shadows on her hands, which were tucked beneath her cheek. The pose might have been angelic, but even in repose her face lacked the pure sweetness generally associated with cherubs and angels. No, she exuded an earthy sensuality in the tilt of her high, elegant brows and the purse of her full lips. And there was an energy about her, a sense that she was never quite still, even in sleep, never quite at peace with herself, or maybe with what was going on around her.

Can you blame her? he thought sardonically, because of course he couldn't blame her one bit. But he could, and would, do his best to see that she didn't suffer because she'd helped him.

Forcing himself to turn away, he once again faced the doorway, and shifted the handgun to beneath his pillow, where he could grab it easily if he heard a suspicious noise. Then, knowing he'd better doze and give his body the time and resources to heal, he closed his eyes and put himself into a light, restorative trance he didn't know he knew how to do until after he'd done it.

In the trance he saw sounds as colors, a rainbow of soft nighttime noises, none of which alarmed him. Sinking a level deeper into the self-hypnosis, he heard the same whisper that had been nagging at him since he'd regained consciousness out in the woods. *The mission. Must complete the mission.*

Now, though, that wasn't the only thing he had to do. The mission—whatever the hell it was—might be his priority, but alongside it was another need, one very close to his heart. He had to make sure that Sara didn't suffer for his sins.

Chapter Five

The next morning Sara awoke stiff and sore, and for a moment didn't know where she was. Her living room came clear around her first, reassuring in its familiarity, and she had a half second of thinking she'd fallen asleep in front of the TV, which although rare, was something she did from time to time.

Then she saw the silhouette of a man standing at one of the front windows, peering between the drawn curtains. Heat shimmered through her alongside dread, though it seemed odd that the two could coexist. "See anything?" she asked softly.

His shoulders tensed, but he kept up his surveillance for a moment longer before he turned to her. "An unmarked sedan has been by a couple of times, no doubt thanks to your friend. I haven't seen anything I would consider suspicious."

Sara frowned and sat up on the sofa, rubbing her face to clear the sleep from her system. "How long have you been standing there? You're supposed to be resting that shoulder."

"I can rest when I'm dead for real." He paused. "I borrowed your gun. If that's a problem for you, just say the word and I'll hand it over."

She couldn't see his expression or read his mood, could only see the outline of his body against the light coming through the curtained window. Oddly, though, she wasn't bothered by the thought that he was armed. He'd been a cop when they met, so she was used to him wearing a gun. "Keep it. I'm not the world's best shot." She rose and crossed to him, putting herself between him and the window so she could see his face. "How are you feeling? And don't lie."

"Sore," he admitted. "But alive, thanks to you."

His face was drawn and tired, more gaunt than she remembered, and covered with a day's worth of stubble. She'd never seen him looking so rough before…and she'd never had a stronger impulse to throw herself against him and sob into his chest. Or kiss him. Or pound her fists against him.

Emotions jammed her throat, forcing her to swallow around a huge lump of tears, anger and elation.

His expression changed, going from guarded wariness to concern. "Hey." He reached out to her. "It's okay."

She jolted away, batting at his hands. "It is *not* okay." Part of her wondered if it would ever be okay again. She'd thought she'd gotten used to him being out of her life, first as an ex, then as a dead man. But now, having him standing in front of her…she didn't know how to cope, didn't know if she could.

She'd come to Bear Claw hoping for a calm, orderly

life, one where she could do good work for the ME's office and the young, progressive mayor. She'd found a home and friends she loved, and for a while, a man, as well. Even when her and Romo's relationship had ended, she'd managed to keep things on a relatively even keel, at least outwardly. She'd functioned. She'd dealt. She'd mourned his death. And time had gone on. Except that now, more than a year later, the city was under a terrible threat of violence, her job was on the brink, Romo was back and things were rapidly spinning out of her control.

"We should sit," Romo said. "We need to talk." He took her arm and urged her away from the window, in the direction of the kitchen. "Come on, I'll make us some coffee."

Near-hysterical laughter bubbled up in her chest. "My coffeemaker's busted. I broke it yesterday morning, back when my biggest problems were my wonky windshield wipers, my sticky office door and the acting mayor's vendetta against my staff." But she let him guide her to one of the stools at the breakfast bar. When he started boiling water for tea, finding the bags in the third cabinet he tried, she scrubbed her hands over her face again, and sighed. "God. I hate feeling so out of control."

"Finally. Something we have in common besides what I have to believe was some really great sex."

His offhand comment was so dry, delivered so perfectly, that she laughed in spite of herself. Then again, he'd always had a knack for turning her knee-jerks back on themselves, making her see them for the old patterns they were. That was why she'd agreed to go out with him in the first place, after resisting for nearly a month—he'd convinced her that despite his reputation, he was no playboy. He'd claimed that while he'd dated around when he'd first arrived in Bear Claw, he'd been a serial monogamist, and that a handsome, charismatic devil like himself was no more likely to cheat than any other man, comparisons to her father notwithstanding.

And he'd been right. For a while, anyway.

The memory didn't sour her mood so much as it reminded her of what she'd begun to process the night before, as she'd slid toward sleep—namely that the fact of Romo being alive didn't rewind the months prior to his death. If his funeral hadn't taken away the sins of his life, then neither did his resurrection.

"Here." He deposited a steaming mug of tea on the breakfast bar, took one for himself and made a vague gesture. "You want milk or sugar? Lemon?"

The question was a poignant reminder of how much he'd lost. The old Romo had kept a running file of her likes and dislikes in his head, which she'd taken as evidence that he'd paid attention, that he'd cared. And maybe he'd done both of those things. But he'd also played her.

She shook her head. "This is fine. I take it that means you didn't wake up with all your memories back?"

"I wish." He took the other bar stool, spinning it to face her and covering the wince when the move jarred his injured shoulder.

"You shouldn't be out of bed," she said automatically, though he looked far stronger than she would've expected, given what he'd been through the previous day, and far better than he ought to, wearing her sweats and tee.

"I shouldn't be here," he countered, seeming to search her eyes for a response she wasn't sure she could give.

"If we assume you were working against the terrorists—and, having known you as well as I did, I'm sticking with that assumption until given reason to doubt it—then I'm probably safer if you stay," she said bluntly. "They'll be looking for you, and eventually they'll look here, based on our past relationship if nothing else. I'd rather not be alone when that happens."

His face darkened. "You should go into protective custody."

"And tell them what?" she countered. "I can lean on Tucker for some extra drive-bys without too much of an explanation, but I'd need more than that to get myself locked down. I'd have to tell them about you, and without knowing who you were working for—and therefore who I could trust—I wouldn't be able to control the information flow within the task force. You'd have the cops and al-Jihad after you, doubling the complications you're going to have while you try to remember what you were doing, and for who." She paused and said dryly, "Not to mention that while you're putting on a good show right now, ten bucks says you're fast asleep within the next half hour."

Now that they were in the brightly lit kitchen and the caffeine was kicking in, she could clearly see the grayish cast to his haggard skin, the pain lines beside his mouth and the tired way he favored his injured shoulder and neck.

He grimaced. "Sounds like you've been doing some thinking."

"Hard not to."

"Yeah." He sat for a moment, pensive. "I hate that I've put you in this position. I wish…I don't know. I wish I'd gone any place but here."

"If you had, you'd probably be dead by now," she said with little conceit. "If you'd wound up in the medical system, they would've reported the gunshot injury and whoever is looking for you would've found you. If you holed up somewhere without treatment, you would've died from the shock and blood loss. And although there've been days I would've said I hated you, I'd still much rather have you in this world than not."

That earned her a sharp look, but he said only, "I saw the bag in the gun safe."

At first she winced, thinking he'd take that as a sign of disloyalty. Then she decided that she didn't care if he did. She said, "If you can't remember anything, maybe the evidence can help tell us."

He nodded, expression guarded. "My thoughts exactly. Did you keep the bullet?"

"Yep. I couldn't tell you what caliber it was, though. It fragmented, and is fairly deformed. I'd like to give it to Cassie, along with the clothes." When he stiffened, she said, "Cassie's the top forensic analyst in the BCCPD, and she's a good friend. I trust her with my life."

Do you trust her with mine? Romo's sardonic expression seemed to say. But aloud he said only, "Can you give her the evidence without telling her where it came from?"

"If I told her what was going on, she'd keep it to herself."

He must've seen something in her eyes, though, because he said, "You're not sure of that. You don't trust her."

"I do," she knee-jerked, but then clarified, "It's her husband, Seth. He's one of the top forensic analysts for the FBI, and I can't swear she wouldn't tell him."

"And you don't trust him."

"I trust him to do what he thinks is right, but that's not always what the person in question has asked him to do," she said, remembering a couple of times over the past year that Seth had gone against his word in making his own judgment call. Granted, those instances had worked out for the best, but she wasn't sure she dared run the risk.

Romo shifted in his seat, and was less able to hide the wince this time. "Then either you can't use Cassie for this, or you have to lie to her about where the samples came from. Can you do that?"

The answer should've been a categorical "no." But Sara found herself hesitating. "How about talking to Fax? He was undercover. If anyone knows who you'd be likely to report to, it'd be him."

"That's still assuming I was undercover," Romo said. "What if I wasn't?"

"Then I should definitely turn you in to Fax." She

paused, a little skitter of nerves dancing down her spine. "You're not saying…"

"I don't know what the hell I'm saying anymore. I don't think I'm a bad guy, but how do I know for sure? And if I *was* doing something wrong, then I need to make it right somehow, which means staying free long enough to figure it out." He reached out with his good arm and took one of her hands in his. "I hate that I've put you in this position."

"I'm not too thrilled about it, either." But the strange thing was, she wasn't entirely unhappy about how things were turning out. Surprising them both, she said, "I'll take the samples to Cassie and tell her they came from an informant." It wouldn't exactly be a lie that way.

He looked at her with wary hope. "You'd be willing to do that? Willing to get involved that way?"

She hesitated for a moment before she said, "Normally, the answer would be no. I'm not a risk taker, I like my life simple and this is pretty much the definition of risky and complicated. If I get caught, the acting mayor will fire me in a heartbeat, my friends will know I lied to them and I'll probably face some major charges. Not to mention what might happen to you. But the thing is, Bear Claw is my home, and it's under siege. If I can do something to help fix that, then I guess I have to, don't I?" Those were only some of the conclusions she'd come to as she'd dozed off, decisions that had been cemented in her mind as she'd slept.

Hiding from the police reports and task force bulletins because she'd felt she couldn't do anything to help was one thing. Refusing to do something that actually *might* help was another. And besides, regardless of how things had ended between her and Romo, the history was there. She couldn't turn him in until she was sure of his guilt. She just couldn't.

He squeezed her hand. "You're a brave woman."

"I never was before," she answered. "Maybe now is the time to start."

By midmorning, though, she wasn't feeling at all brave. She just felt like a total sneak.

She had falsified official documentation and basically lied her ass off to get Cassie to fast-track the processing of blood samples from two small pieces cut from Romo's shirt, and the analysis of the bullet fragments he'd had in his back.

Cassie, of course, didn't know that was where they'd come from. Sara had sent them over as "don't ask, don't tell" samples, which in task-force speak pretty much meant what it said. With so much of the suspicion falling within the law enforcement agencies themselves, there were undercover stings running within undercover stings. At least Sara got the feeling there were—she wasn't in the middle of the information flow. Which, she hoped, wouldn't trip Cassie's suspicions too badly, making her wonder why the heck don't-tell materials were coming through the ME's office.

Once the samples were sent off, Sara plowed through three routine cases while Stephen worked on the two dead agents. True to his word, the other ME had come in to work the cases, even though it was Saturday. On one level, Sara was beyond grateful that she didn't have to deal with those particular bodies, especially given her near certainty that Romo had been among the targets of the federal manhunt. On another level, though, she found herself wanting to be alone in the autopsy theater, wished she could turn off the relentlessly cheerful dance music Stephen liked to play while he worked.

As soon as she finished with the third case, she stripped out of her protective gear, cleaned up and escaped to the peace and quiet of her office, not even bothering to be piqued when the door stuck. She had way bigger problems than that. Like a lover returned from the dead, and the very real possibility that the terrorists, or the cops, or both, were looking for him.

Romo had insisted she carry the .22 when she went in to work. She'd agreed because she'd done the necessary paperwork to carry concealed, and was able to get the weapon through the heightened security measures that now surrounded the buildings that housed the BCCPD and ME's office. And maybe it made her feel slightly safer, knowing she had a means of defense. But still, she hated the necessity, and couldn't bear to imagine actually using the weapon on anything but gun range targets.

Hopefully, I won't have to, she thought morosely, then sighed, dug her fingers into her hair and muttered, "I hate this."

"Trouble?" a voice said from the doorway.

Sara looked up quickly, gasping a little at the jolt of surprise. Cassie stood in the doorway, holding an official-looking folder. Tall and blond, with legs that went a mile and pinup-type curves, Cassie was a bombshell who cared little for her own looks, and wore a don't-mess-with-me attitude that, according to Alyssa, anyway, had mellowed a fair bit in the years since her marriage to Seth.

As far as Sara was concerned, if this was Cassie in mellow mode, she must've been a holy terror before. Sara loved Cassie as a friend, but was a little intimidated by her at the same time. Especially now, under the circumstances.

"Hey!" Sara said, her voice cracking a little with the effort of trying to sound normal. Knowing the BCCPD's top forensic evidence analyst missed little, she nodded to the folder, which was of the sort usually used to transmit results from one division of the task force to another. "I didn't expect you to hand-deliver."

"A priority is a priority, especially these days," Cassie said matter-of-factly. Her words were friendly enough, but behind them was a hard edge that was pure business. The members of the task force—and ancillary members like Sara herself—had all lost acquaintances in the attacks, most had lost friends. They were committed to doing whatever it took to break al-Jihad's hold on the region and bring down his terror cells, including those potentially rooted within the BCCPD and FBI.

Swallowing against a knot of guilt at deceiving a friend, Sara asked, "Did you find anything interesting?" She tensed with hope, because "interesting" could mean the DNA from the blood spatter was a match to someone other than the dead agents, or that the bullet traced to a non–PD weapon. "Interesting" could suggest Romo hadn't killed either of the agents, that she wasn't being an enormous idiot by keeping his secret.

"Maybe," Cassie said, her eyes narrowing slightly. "And the hand delivery was because your message made it sound urgent. Which leaves me wondering about the source of DNA samples that didn't come from either of the bodies you're not autopsying." Her telling look went to the autopsy theater, where Stephen was hard at work on the dead agents, who hadn't been wearing clothing the same type as the ones Sara had sent over. Cassie looked back at her. "What have you gotten yourself into, Sara?"

Heart thudding as her panic level rose, Sara faked a grimace, and said, "I'm doing a favor for a friend who wants to keep a very low profile, that's all." It wasn't a lie. But it didn't feel good, either.

So turn him in, the logical part of her brain whispered. *Tell Cassie right now. Say, "Romo Sampson showed up at my place yesterday, wounded and covered in blood, alive, with no clue where he's been for the past bunch of months, what he's been doing, or who he's been working for."* Yeah, that was what she should say, she knew.

But she didn't.

Cassie gave her a long look, then shook her head. "I hope you know what you're doing."

Me, too, Sara thought wildly, hoping she wasn't in the process of making the biggest mistake of her life. "Did you get a hit on the DNA?"

Frustration glinted briefly in the analyst's eyes. "No, damn it. No matches in any of the databases. Not even a partial hit off a relative. You've got one male donor, and the DNA is useless until you've got another sample to compare it to."

"Isn't that the story of our lives?" Sara said, and she wasn't faking the regret. Although CODIS grew by leaps and bounds each year, the federal DNA database still only held a fraction of the available samples, and then primarily those belonging to major violent criminals, such as murderers and rapists. Although the repository of DNA profiles held millions of samples, matching an unknown was still a long shot. Cautiously she asked, "Did you check the samples against the PD and military databases?"

Romo would be in them, she knew, and the knowledge strung her tight. She'd been betting the blood contributions from the spatter would overwhelm any sweat contributions from his body, and she'd only given Cassie clothing fragments that hadn't been stained by the blood loss from his shoulder wound, but still, it had been a calculated risk.

Cassie lifted a shoulder. "Military, police. The works. No match."

Sara tried not to let her relief show. "Anything on the bullet or spatter pattern?"

"It's all in here." Cassie lifted the sealed folder.

Sara stopped herself from demanding a summary, reminding herself she was supposed to be nothing more than an educated drop point for some mythical undercover operative. There was no reason for her to want the nitty-gritty, beyond curiosity, and up to this point, she'd made a point of not wanting to know too much about the case, just as she'd tried to avoid the news bulletins the day before.

She'd done her work and helped where she could,

but—especially after Romo's death—had distanced herself from the details. Reversing that now would only draw a level of attention she couldn't afford. Technically, Cassie shouldn't even have done the work she'd asked. But friends trusted friends, which made Sara feel even worse.

"Thanks, I'll pass it along," she said. "Did you want to grab some coffee?" She would've rather kept sulking in her office, but she had a feeling the moment she and Cassie parted company, the astute cop's brain was going to circle back on dangerous questions, and Sara couldn't afford to let that happen. *Romo* couldn't afford for her to let it happen.

Cassie checked the time on her cell, and made a rueful face. "Rain check? I've got a meeting in twenty."

"Absolutely, rain check it is," Sara said, trying to keep the relief out of her voice. "Thanks for doing this." She held out her hand for the folder, hating the lies. The deeper she got into this, the worse it seemed. For several moments she was sorely tempted to come clean to Cassie, bring her friends in on the situation and let Romo be furious with her. Was that really such a bad idea?

But when Cassie sketched a wave and headed for the door, Sara didn't call her back.

Instead, she closed and locked her sticky office door, and broke the seal on the folder. A quick scan confirmed the negative results on the DNA profiling, and added two critical pieces of information, one good, one bad. On the good side, the bullet hadn't come from an official weapon and it didn't match any of the personal sidearms belonging to task force officers, which suggested Romo hadn't been shot by one of the good guys. On the bad side, the spatter pattern—what Cassie had been able to get off the small pieces of black T-shirt, anyway—was consistent with close-range arterial spray from a severed throat, and the shirt's wearer had most likely wielded the knife.

Sara had taken a good look at the patterns on the shirt, and though she was no expert, she'd been certain that the blood from Romo's injury had soaked in atop the edges of the spatter, giving the incidents a time frame. Adding the information together, she could come up with a hypothesis of sorts, namely that sometime the prior day, just before—or during—the op that led to the manhunt, Romo had cut a man's throat and then been shot in the back by someone other than a cop.

Sara blew out a breath. Between the blood and bullet evidence, it seemed reasonable to conclude that Romo had been the unidentified man who had escaped alone from the manhunt. She tried to tell herself that didn't necessarily mean he was one of the good guys, but on some level it felt that way. He'd turned on the terrorists, or they'd turned on him. Either way, didn't it stand to reason that the enemy of Bear Claw's enemies was on their side, more or less?

The logic wasn't perfect, she knew, but she thought it might be enough to help her convince Romo to give himself up to Fax or Tucker, both of whom she trusted implicitly.

Her friends might not have liked him much after the breakup, but they were all task force members, and at this point would take whatever help they could get when it came to getting al-Jihad, Lee Mawadi, Jane Doe and the others into custody. They would help…assuming she could talk Romo into turning himself in. Problem was, he could be seriously stubborn, and Sara had never once been able to make him do something he didn't want to.

"You'd better start now," she told herself. "Lives might depend on it." Hers. His. Those of the citizens of Bear Claw.

Thinking fast, she turned to her computer, logged on to one of the larger international databases of medical literature and started keying in queries on retrograde amnesia, and techniques for retrieving blocked memories. She pulled together a basic information kit that gave her a few ideas on how she might be able to help Romo, and then started shutting down for the day. Stephen waved on his way out, having completed the agents' autopsies and filed the necessary reports. Once she was alone in the ME's office, Sara told herself she was okay, that there was no reason for her to feel exposed. This was her space, her place in the world.

For now, anyway. She'd just that morning received yet another of Proudfoot's aggrieved memos, warning that she needed to minimize her department's overtime. Which she'd be able to do if he let her hire another examiner, damn it.

That added stress dragged at her, worried her and had her jumping at shadows as she headed to her car. Although it was Saturday, the lot between the PD and ME's office was nearly full, mute evidence of the double and triple shifts being pulled by the members of the task force. She didn't see anyone else headed out, but felt a strange prickling between her shoulder blades, as though someone was watching her.

She took a look around as she unlocked her hybrid, checking out the windows of the buildings nearby, but didn't see anyone there, either. Under other circumstances, she would've brushed it off as her imagination, fueled by the manhunt and the pall of fear that hung citywide. Given what was going on in her life—and the fact that she'd promised Romo she would get an escort home—she dug out her cell phone and called Tucker's cell.

There was silence for a moment before he said, "Are you ready to tell me what's going on yet?"

Sara winced. "Cassie blabbed."

"We're worried. This isn't like you. If you're…" The tough homicide detective, who'd been only slightly domesticated by his marriage to forensic reconstruction specialist Alyssa Wyatt, paused as if feeling his way through delicate territory. "If you're trying to atone for something you think you should've done before, please don't. Leave the cloak-and-dagger stuff for the professionals. Okay?"

Sara's throat closed a little on the show of friendship and trust—he knew she was up to something, but wouldn't interfere directly. He just wanted her to know that he was there, that they all were, to help her. That was how it had been with Chelsea and Fax, she knew. The friends hadn't agreed with all of Chelsea's choices, but they'd been there when she'd needed them. Now they would do the same for Sara, the moment she asked. "Okay," she said, her voice a bare whisper. "I'll…okay."

"I'll follow you home myself. Just give me a couple of minutes." He hung up before she could respond to that, but he didn't mean anything by the hang-up. That was just Tucker's way.

Five minutes later, he was in his unmarked sedan, following her home, making her feel safe—for the moment, at least.

ROMO WOKE groggily at the sound of a key in the front door lock, found himself facedown on Sara's couch, and cursed himself for the weakness that had come from his injuries. He'd hated lying low, hoping to hell she was okay. But he'd had no choice. His body needed to heal, so he'd been forced to trust her not to turn him in, and not to take unnecessary risks.

He didn't need all of his memory back to know that trust wasn't something that came easily to him.

Cautiously, he levered himself upright on the sofa and then to his feet. He thought of meeting her at the door, but then he stopped himself. She'd promised to have one of her cop friends get her a police escort home. Logic said that—assuming her protection was any good—the cop would want to come inside and look around, making sure the house was clear. Hell, for all he knew, she'd had too long to think about the situation, and had made the logical decision to turn him in. In a way, he wouldn't blame her if she had.

Okay, that was a lie. He'd blame her, and he'd feel betrayed. But he'd get over it. He'd somehow gotten over her, hadn't he?

Hearing a low, masculine voice outside, he stiffened,

then ghosted down the hallway, toward the rear exit he'd scouted earlier. Granted, he could be in trouble if the house was surrounded. He had a feeling, though, that he could take care of a rear guard or two.

Sara might've been hoping that the spatter analysis would suggest he'd been standing next to the blood donor when the blow was struck, but in his gut he knew he'd been the one to make the fatal cut. He didn't know how he knew that, or how he knew it'd been a knife rather than a close-range gunshot. But he knew, damn it. Just as he knew Sara would be better off if he left now, if he just walked out the door and disappeared. Her friends would help keep her safe.

But who would help him?

The question had him pausing with his hand on the doorknob. Not because he was afraid of going off on his own—he had a feeling he was used to that. No, what had him hesitating was the knowledge that if Sara's most optimistic hypothesis was the right one, and he'd been undercover somehow, working for al-Jihad, then him disappearing was exactly the wrong move to make. If he'd been undercover, they needed to figure out his mission, who he'd been reporting to, and find a way to get back into the loop. He could have important information inside his skull, maybe even something that would blow the whole case wide open.

You're reaching, his inner cynic whispered. *The story sounds good, except for one thing. If you were undercover, why aren't you getting any memory flashes of that? All you're getting are the bad guys.*

He should go, he knew. But he'd hesitated too long.

"Leaving?" Sara's quiet voice said from the other end of the hallway leading to the back door.

She stood silhouetted in the light from the main room. The illumination picked out golden highlights in her shoulder-length hair and emphasized the long, lean length of her body in its smart power suit. She wore a long raincoat of mossy green against the damp, late-summer day, and the belted waist emphasized the narrowness of her waist, the femininity of the curves beneath. She looked expensive and put-together, and probably should have made him feel underdressed, in his borrowed sweatpants, T-shirt and bare feet. Instead, he was buffeted by an unfamiliar sense of rightness, a surge of "oh, there you are!" that made him want to cross to her, kiss her and welcome her home for the night.

And he so wasn't going there. Didn't dare. So instead of approaching her, he held his ground. "I wasn't taking off. I was preparing in case your cop came in with you and I needed to do a fast fade."

She made a quiet humming noise that didn't quite call him a liar, but said only, "Tucker offered to come in and take a look around, but I declined, and he took me at my word." She paused. "If you were going to vanish, you could've done it hours ago."

He thought about denying it, but figured there was little more than patchy honesty between them at this point, and he didn't have the heart to take that away from either of them. "I would have, but I passed out and only just now came around."

"Maybe that's your subconscious telling you to stay put."

"Maybe."

They stood squared off opposite each other for a long moment. Romo couldn't see her eyes, could only see the dark outline of her in the low, golden light, but he knew she was studying him, trying to figure him out. He wanted to tell her to let him know what she came up with, and he wouldn't have been kidding. He had a feeling she'd understood him better than he'd understood himself, even before the amnesia. But if that were the case, why had he cheated? He didn't feel like a cheat, didn't think it was his normal M.O. It didn't make any sense. None of it did.

"Well, it's your call. As usual." The last was said with a faint bite as she took a step back into the main room, ceding the hallway. The move brought her out of the shadows and into the light, showing him her lovely face, which was wearing an expression that was simultaneously both composed and worried. Her tone, though, was even as she said, "If it helps, neither the blood nor the bullet came from one of the officers or agents on the manhunt."

It did help, but he latched on to what she *hadn't* said. "The spatter was consistent with me cutting the victim's throat."

She swallowed. "Yes. How did you know?"

"I don't remember what happened," he said, answering the unspoken question. "It was just a feeling."

Unfortunately, feelings were all he had to go on just then, and they included his growing attraction for Sara, which was starting to mess with his ability to assess and analyze all the other things going on around them. He suspected the pull he felt toward her was a combination of unremembered history, the situation, and the simple fact that he'd been attracted to her once before, and nothing had changed about his basic taste. The things that had drawn them together before were still in place. And he suspected he wasn't the only one feeling the pull. He didn't know exactly what had happened during their breakup, or why, but he thought part of Sara might be seeing the situation as an opportunity for a do-over. Or maybe he was the one thinking that. Either way, asleep or awake, he was filled with thoughts of her, of how she had tasted when he'd kissed her, how she had felt against him.

Aware that they'd both been silent too long, he said, "I should go."

"Where?" The single word was both a question and a challenge, making him feel as though she'd just called him a coward.

"Away from you," he said bluntly, expecting her to take it personally, in a way wanting her to, because he didn't know how to deal with his almost obsessive need to be near her. It was a selfish, destructive urge, one he needed to fight. And in doing so, he attacked.

Instead of taking offense, she tilted her head and asked softly, "Does the idea of trusting someone frighten you that badly?"

Instincts had him wanting to snap at her that he wasn't afraid, but that would've been a lie. He *was* afraid, not so much for himself, but for her, for what he'd brought into her life. But he didn't snap. Instead, he moved away from the door and down the short hallway, crossing the distance between them and stopping just short of the light. "What do you suggest I do?"

"Let me set up a meeting," she said immediately. "You, me, Fax and Tucker. All the evidence points to you being undercover for the good guys, Romo. Let them help us figure out who you're working for."

"Your so-called evidence is pretty damned thin from where I'm standing," he said dryly. "All we really know for certain is that the clues we've got don't conclusively indicate that I killed those agents. Everything else is conjecture."

"I know you," she said staunchly. "You wouldn't have faked your own death to join al-Jihad. You're a good man."

"I cheated on you."

Her eyes flashed. "You're trying to make me kick you out. I won't do it."

"You should." He stepped into the light, into her space. He stopped opposite her, with a few feet separating them. He had the sensation of drowning as he looked down into her caramel-colored eyes. "Tell me to leave."

"Stay," she said instead. "Let me call Fax and Tucker."

He touched a finger beneath her chin and tipped her face up to his. "You believe in me that much," he murmured, "because of what we were to each other."

He knew touching her was a mistake the moment his fingertip connected with her soft skin. First, because of the warmth that spread up his arm and lodged in his chest, threatening to undo all his best intentions. And second, because her eyes snapped dark with what he thought was fury, but was wiped away before he could be sure, to be replaced by cool, studied indifference. She eased away. "Despite the impression you might have gotten from my kissing you last night, I'm all too aware of our history. Trusting you got me a broken heart before. This time it could very well get me killed."

He let his hand fall, held his palms up in apology. "Sorry. I misread."

"Yes. You did."

"Then why are you pushing me to stay and meet with your friends?"

"Because Bear Claw is my home," she said simply. "I won't let al-Jihad destroy it. I've hidden behind my job for too long, and it's time I stopped doing that. Which means that if there's something I can do to help the task force break the case, then by damn, I'm going to do it." She fixed him with a look that held more challenge than entreaty. "Will you?"

She was asking for the impossible. She wasn't just asking him to trust her, she was asking him to trust her friends, people he hadn't met in this incarnation of himself.

He nodded slowly. "Okay."

Surprise flared in her eyes. "You'll meet with Fax and Tucker?"

"Yeah. I'll meet with them." But even as he said the words, something inside him warned he was making a huge mistake.

Chapter Six

The next morning, Sara left the house early wearing a light suede jacket and casually elegant pants with a tailored shirt a couple of shades darker than her hair. Her boots were low-heeled and rubber-soled, and her purse, which she wore slung over her shoulder, was heavier than usual, containing the loaded .22, along with extra bullets. She'd tried to press the weapon on Romo, but he'd insisted that she be the one to carry the protection. Some small, soft part of her had wanted to believe his worry was personal, intimate.

They'd both slept in the living room the night before, for a second night in a row, she on the couch, he on his makeshift pallet near the door, keeping watch. Sometime during the night, though, he'd moved closer to her, and she'd awakened to find her fingertips dangling over the side of the couch just brushing his shoulder. It hadn't quite been his old habit of wanting some part of him touching some part of her, but it had been enough to make her heart shudder a little in her chest. Enough to make her yearn, damn him.

Focus! she told herself, forcing her attention on the meeting at hand as she marched to her hybrid and climbed inside.

The skin between her shoulder blades prickled with the sensation of watching eyes, but she told herself to ignore it. If al-Jihad's people had figured out where Romo was hiding, they wouldn't be sitting around, watching. They would've done something already. The thought brought a serious shiver, but it did make a fatalistic sort of sense. Which meant that if she was being watched, it wasn't by one of the terrorists. More than likely, she knew, it was Tucker. Or, since Tucker was due at their meeting point, he might have deputized Alyssa to keep watch in his stead. The married couple made a formidable team.

Sara had called Tucker first, then Fax, and had told them only that she needed to meet with them in the utmost secrecy. She hadn't dared reveal more than that, for fear that the information might leak to one of the conspirators believed to still be within the task force. Not that Fax or Tucker would talk, but still…thanks to Jane Doe's defection, al-Jihad's people had access to the latest spy-ware technology and strategy. As Fax had once said, the task force members had to assume that the terrorists had all of the toys and know-how the good guys did, and then some.

"Which is so *not* an encouraging thought," Sara muttered to herself as she fired up the hybrid's engine and pulled out of her driveway. After taking a few turns through her neighborhood and deciding she wasn't being followed, she drove down a street two blocks

Internal Affairs

over from her house, and pulled up next to a thick stand of landscaped trees.

Romo slipped from concealment—she hadn't even seen him hiding there, though she'd been looking for him—and climbed into the hybrid, folding himself into the backseat and keeping his head down so it looked as though she were still alone. "See anything?" he asked as she pulled away from the bushes.

"Nope. But I'm not a professional, either."

"You do fine."

His calm assurance steadied her more than it probably should have. But then again, that was Romo. He'd always made her feel like more than she really was, as though together they made something that was better than each of them alone. She'd thought he'd felt the same way, until he'd proven otherwise. But although his betrayal was never far from the surface of her thoughts, she was startled to realize that the pain was beginning to fade, in a way it hadn't done during the months after they'd broken up, or after that, when she'd believed him dead. And that was a problem, she knew. Thanks to her mother, she was genetically and environmentally predisposed to forgive the man she loved, even when he patently didn't deserve forgiveness.

She could potentially get past Romo's disappearing act, presuming that he proved to have been undercover. They hadn't been together when he'd faked his death; he hadn't owed her an explanation or a warning, a sign that he was really alive. Or so she kept telling herself, and the logic worked even if the emotions lagged a little. What didn't work was knowing she was just as ready to forgive him for what had happened before then, when they *had* been together. All he'd had to do was send her some of his long, slow looks and a single hot, toe-curling kiss, and a large part of her was more than ready to forgive and forget, and give their relationship a second chance. Not that he'd even indicated that he wanted a second chance with her, she reminded herself. The weakness was inside her. It always had been.

"Problem?" he asked.

She glanced in the rearview mirror, saw him looking at her in it from his cramped position in the back. "Why would there be a problem?" she inquired with a faint bite in her tone as she returned her attention to the road. "My cheating ex comes back from the dead, bleeds all over my living room, forces me to lie to a friend and runs a strong risk of getting me killed. No problem there that I can see."

"All true, but none of it is news at this point. Which means there's something else going on in that head of yours that had you frowning." He paused. "You want to talk about it?"

"Not even remotely," she snapped.

"I'll listen. Venting might help."

She cut her eyes back to his in the mirror. "And that's the sort of thing that leaves no question you've got a head injury and amnesia. The old Romo Sampson never would've put himself in the line of fire for an emotional outburst." He'd avoided negative emotions, claiming he got enough of them at work; he didn't need to go looking for drama on his off hours.

"I'm starting to think I might not have entirely liked the old me," Romo said mildly.

"Join the club." But the absurdity of it tugged a reluctant smile from her as she turned onto the highway and then off it again.

She made a quick stop at one of the big box stores that dotted the region, and went inside to buy jeans, a white oxford and a black blazer for Romo, so he didn't have to wear her sweatpants to the meeting. He'd kept hold of his own boots, so she filled in the gaps with a package of socks and a pair of boxers. The clothes weren't the more expensive brands he'd preferred, but once he'd changed in the car—covering the winces as best he could, though obviously still in pain—he looked much more like the man he'd once been, albeit a version of himself wearing a layer of stubble and a hunted, haunted look in the back of his eyes.

Haggard or not, Romo's dark, sharp good looks had always drawn female attention wherever he went. And, damn it, his looks hadn't changed with the time away. If anything, his features had gotten even sharper with the loss of a few pounds, as though any softness that had once been inside him had been burned away by whatever he'd seen and done. *And it's that "whatever he's seen or done" that you need to focus on,* she reminded herself, forcing her eyes away from the mirror and gluing them back on the road.

She hadn't thought he'd noticed her glance. But moments later, he said softly, "I'm sorry I've made things so difficult for you, Sara."

He saw through her, damn it, saw into her. He knew

what she was thinking and feeling, and the knowledge made her feel stripped raw inside. But when she glanced into the mirror and away, she saw only compassion in his gorgeous green eyes with their ridiculously long, sexy lashes. "Just don't kiss me again," she said, voice going ragged before she could force it steady.

She expected easy assent. Instead, he said, "I can't promise that."

The quiet statement sent a bolt of electricity through her midsection as she rolled to a stop at a red light. She wanted to turn and look at him directly, but didn't dare, so she met his eyes once again in the mirror, and saw heat there. Desire. "Don't," she said, the single word coming out in a dry-mouthed whisper.

"I'm not the guy who cheated on you, Sara." His eyes were steady on hers.

"Yes, you are." But she knew that was a lie. The old Romo had been a charming rogue who'd committed himself fiercely to the chase once she'd let him know that she was attracted to him but made it a point not to date men who went through girlfriends with depressing regularity. She'd eventually given in and gone out with him, then had fallen for him, but he'd only let himself fall so far. There had been a distance between them, a barrier she'd been unable to breach.

With this man, though, there was no barrier that she could see. Stripped of his practiced game, he remained as fiercely protective of her as he'd been before, but he let her see it in him. His eyes showed his thoughts and feelings, and when he reached up between the front seats to touch her elbow in a brief caress that lit her body as though it had been so much more, there was an honesty in his touch that she didn't remember from before. It was as though, in losing himself, Romo Sampson had found a new, different man. A better one.

"Sara," he began.

"We're here," she interrupted, unable to deal with whatever he was about to say, knowing she wanted to hear it far too much. She turned into the small parking lot of the state park trailhead that Fax had chosen as a meeting place and saw two other cars already there, a dark green truck and a standard-issue sedan. "Those are Fax and Tucker's rides."

As she rolled the hybrid to a stop, Fax emerged from his truck. A couple of inches under six feet, he was tough and compact, with dark hair, piercing blue eyes and a thin scar running through one eyebrow. He looked healthier than he had when Sara had first met him, fresh out of his own undercover hell. He hadn't mellowed over the ten months, though, despite his engagement to Chelsea. If anything, Fax had grown even more intense as she had progressed through her FBI training, as though he was bound and determined to end al-Jihad's reign of terror before the woman he loved wound up any deeper in the danger. Even now, he practically vibrated with deadly tension as he rounded his truck to join Tucker, who leaned back against his car, arms folded over his broad chest.

Tucker was a couple of inches taller than Fax, with wavy dark hair, brown eyes and a swarthy tan and an air of unconstrained wildness that made him look more like a park ranger than a senior homicide detective.

Both men wore bulletproof vests marked with their

affiliations, and had guns on their hips. When Sara parked the hybrid and just sat there for a second, dithering, her friends moved to stand shoulder to shoulder, presenting a strong, united front. She told herself she should feel reassured by the sight. Instead, nerves skittered to life beneath her skin.

"They're going to kill me when they hear what I've done," she said, mostly to herself.

"They're not going to touch you," Romo said succinctly from the backseat, where he was still hunkered down, avoiding detection. "And for the record, the you-and-me conversation isn't over."

Her throat went dry even as her blood revved in her veins. "What if I want it to be over?"

"I can't let it be over," he said, and in his eyes she saw a raw honesty she'd never seen in his face before. "I don't know what the old me did, exactly, and I sure as hell don't understand why he did what he did, but I'm not that man anymore, Sara. And the man I am now wants his chance with you."

Her heart thudded unevenly in her chest. "I don't do second chances."

"It wouldn't be a second chance. It'd be a first one for the guy I am now."

A bubble of near-hysterical laughter rose within her. "For how long? As far as I know, you're thirty seconds from being dragged back undercover. And even if that doesn't happen, how long will it be until it all comes back, until the real Romo Sampson returns?"

"Trust me," he said. "I won't let you down this time. I promise."

But how could she trust him when she didn't really know who he was anymore? Before she could respond— before she could even figure out how she wanted to respond, as warmth and wishes swirled in her chest— he straightened up and slipped from the vehicle, leaving the door ajar as he headed toward where Fax and Tucker both went stiff and on point at the sight of him.

"Sampson!" Tucker bit off. "Son of a—"

Heart drumming, Sara hurried to catch up with Romo. They were maybe three or four car lengths from the men, and Sara could already feel the tension coming off them in waves. Figuring she should make a rearguard effort to smooth things over, she called, "Hey, you two. Thanks for meet—"

A whistling shriek cut her off, followed quickly by Romo's shout of alarm. Then he was slamming into her, driving her to the ground.

Half a heartbeat later, the world exploded.

They'd been ambushed! Sara's heart constricted in her chest as Romo covered her body with his own. "No!" she cried. "Tucker! Fax!" She tried to struggle out from beneath Romo, but he wouldn't budge, just hung on to her tightly, covering her ears with his big, strong hands.

A terrible noise blasted over them, coming from where Fax's truck had been. Waves of concussion battered Sara, even though she was protected by Romo's weight pressing her down into the hard surface of the parking area.

Her ears rang and went dull as panic gripped her, took her over, paralyzing in its intensity. She thought someone was screaming, realized a moment later it was her, and shut up. Heat flared in the air, bringing terrible, choking smoke.

Slitting her eyes, she looked toward the conflagration. Fax's truck was burning. Tucker's car was marked with blast char, its front quarter panel mangled. The two men lay twenty or so feet away from the vehicles, close to each other. Neither was moving.

"Fax! Tucker!" Hacking against the burning ash, Sara struggled to get up, to get to her friends. Then Romo rolled off her, dragged her up and pulled her into a shambling run. Only he was going in the wrong direction. He was headed away from the other men.

"No!" Sara dug in her heels and tried to twist away. "No, we've got to go back for them!"

"We can't." His grip was inexorable, his jaw set and his face colder than she'd ever seen it, even before the amnesia, when he'd been a far harder man.

"Romo, stop. We can't leave them." Tears stung her eyes, a combination of smoke and emotion.

"We don't have a choice. Move!" He shoved her into the back of the hybrid, shut the door and climbed in the driver's seat. He had the little vehicle moving before she even scrambled to grab the door handle with some mad intent of flinging herself out and running to Fax's and Tucker's aid.

She froze as a second missile whistled through the air and impacted the spot where the hybrid had been. The parking area cratered in an instant, and the little car rocked with the waves of concussion, but the tires held and the hybrid leaped away, engine racing as

Romo gunned it out of the parking lot. Sara clung to the door handle as the little vehicle flew away from the attack.

"Call it in," he snapped, attention divided between the road ahead and that behind them. "Tell them to get to Tucker and Fax ASAP, but don't say anything about us."

Mind blank with fear, Sara scrabbled for her pocket, pulling out her cell. She stabbed the familiar number and reported the attack in a voice that cracked with tears. When the dispatcher asked her name, she started to say, "This is Sara—"

"Give me that." Romo grabbed her cell and tossed it out the driver's-side window.

"What the hell?" she demanded angrily.

"You made your call. They'll get to Fax and Tucker in time, thanks to you. But we can't let them track the phone."

"Who, the cops?" Incredulity had her voice cracking, but inside her, sluggish fear stirred. "Romo, at this point we *want* the cops to find us. Don't you get it? Al-Jihad's people just tried to kill us to keep us from talking to Fax and Tucker." Her throat closed as the sight of their motionless bodies flashed in her head. "And now they're…"

"Stunned," he filled in when she faltered. "They'll be okay."

"We left them there!" she snapped, anger rising quickly. "What if the shooters go after them, to finish them off?"

"They won't." His voice rang with calm assurance.

"How do you know?"

"Because that's them behind us." He nodded into the rearview mirror.

That was when she realized he didn't have the engine redlined anymore; he'd eased up on the gas, though he kept steady progress up onto the highway, weaving through the sparse Sunday morning traffic.

Maybe a half mile back, there was another car making similar moves.

Sara's blood iced in her veins. "You're letting them *catch* us?"

He slid her a sardonic glance. "If they'd wanted to catch us, they would've by now. This putt-putt car of yours isn't exactly a hot rod."

She craned her neck. "Then what are they doing?"

"That's what I'm trying to figure out." He grimaced as he drove. "They aimed for the cops' vehicles, not the cops, and they didn't take a second shot at us, which they damn well had the time to do. Which means they were trying to break up the meeting without killing us—or more likely without killing me, no offense."

"None taken," she said grimly, as her mind moved ahead to the next logical conclusion. "You have something they want. Or at least they think you do. And they don't want the cops to have it."

"What's more, nobody followed us from your place," he pointed out, voice all but expressionless as he pulled off the highway at a random exit somewhere south of Bear Claw. "Which means that either the guys with the RPG were working with your friends—"

"They're not."

"—or," he continued as though she hadn't interrupted, "they found out about the meeting through your friends."

"Neither Fax nor Tucker would've said anything," she maintained.

"For all we know, they're being monitored. Or else someone on the inside recognized the samples you gave to the forensic analyst and put her and her contacts under surveillance."

That made sense, Sara realized. "But if that were the case, wouldn't they have been watching me?"

"Maybe they hadn't gotten there yet," he said, grimly navigating the hybrid through a set of back roads she didn't recognize. "You might not have been first on the list of people I'd go to, given that you're not a cop."

"But we had a relationship," she pointed out. "They would've looked at me eventually."

"True." He paused. "Maybe they did follow us from your place, after all. But if they knew where I'd been, why didn't they move in on me sooner? What the hell are they waiting for?"

"Maybe for you to complete your mission, whatever it was," Sara said cautiously.

"Damn it," he said, which she took as his way of saying she was right. But when he let up on the gas, she realized that wasn't the only thing bothering him.

"What's wrong?"

He turned haunted eyes toward her. "Two things. One, when we turned off, the chase car kept going on the highway. And two, I recognize this neighborhood."

Her stomach clenched into a hard, hurting knot. She looked around them and saw nothing familiar; she'd never been there with him, didn't know of any reason why he would recognize the area. They were maybe a half hour south of Bear Claw, in a typical suburban area that had little to distinguish it aside from its lack of distinguishing characteristics. This close to the highway, there were fast food and coffee shop drive-throughs on just about every corner, liquor and convenience stores, and a variety of more specialized shops. As they moved farther away from the highway, the commercial strip gave way to modest houses and multifamily dwellings, some in decent shape, others tending toward shabby.

It wasn't the sort of place the Romo she'd known would have hung out. But the man he'd become drove with quiet self-assurance, clearly knowing the way to his destination. Whatever that was.

Swallowing hard, she said, "You're starting to remember what happened to you?"

"Not remembering, precisely. But I know the way." He let the hybrid roll to a stop and pointed up and across a couple of blocks. "See that one up there, with the falling-down awning over the window? I'm pretty sure I lived there."

"Not while I knew you," she said immediately.

"No. Not then. After." His eyes were hard and remote, his jaw locked, his body language somehow more aggressive even though he was simply sitting in the driver's seat.

He looked like a dangerous stranger. The realization warned Sara that for the first time since the day before, she wasn't so sure of Romo's innocence. Their attackers had let him live, gunning down Fax and Tucker instead. But why?

"Either they need something from me, or they still think I'm on their side," he said, as though she'd asked aloud. Then again, it stood to reason that the question would be at the forefront of both of their minds.

Sara blew out a breath. "Were those men chasing you, or herding you, making sure you went where they wanted?"

"Damned if I know."

An icy chill shivered through her. "Which means they could be waiting for you in that house."

"I know." Parking the hybrid where they sat, he unhooked his seat belt. "Stay here. I'm going to check it out." He glanced at her. "I have to know."

She opened her mouth to argue, but could tell from his expression there was nothing she could say to change his mind. Reaching into her coat pocket, she pulled out the revolver and held it out to him. "Take this."

He stilled and looked at her, eyes dark. "You're sure?"

"Positive." It was a gesture of faith in the absence of evidence. She thought they both needed it.

He took the weapon, his fingers grazing hers. "Thanks."

"Be careful."

He left the engine running and she stayed put as he climbed out and sauntered along the sidewalk, past the house he'd indicated and then around the back. He re-appeared a few minutes later at the front door, did something with the lock—she didn't think she wanted to know what he'd done or where he'd learned to do it—and let himself in.

There was no sign of anyone waiting for him, at least not that she could see as the door swung shut at his back, leaving her staring once again at the house. She told herself to stay put, told herself to do as he'd ordered. He was the professional; he knew what he was talking about. She'd be safer in the hybrid, and he'd be safer in the house if he didn't have to think about protecting her.

It was all very logical, all very reasonable. And the arguments were still spooling through her head as she killed the engine, pocketed the key, locked the doors and headed across the street.

ROMO HELD HIMSELF TENSE and wary as he moved into the house, somewhat disappointed to find it empty. He'd been looking forward to pounding on someone who had the answers he sought. Since there wasn't anyone to "question," he was left with the house itself. Unfortunately, it'd been stripped of whatever personal touches it had once possessed. The single sad and lonely piece of décor was a heavily framed picture in the kitchen, showing an insipid child holding a sunflower.

He'd lived there, no question about it. He'd known how to jimmy the lock without effort, had known where to push on the dead bolt to pop it loose. He knew that the short entryway hall opened into a TV room with stained wall-to-wall carpeting and mismatched second-hand furniture, with a dingy kitchen beyond. He knew that the two doors off the main room led to a bedroom on the right, a bathroom on the left. But beyond those location-based memories, he didn't know jack.

The rooms held little more than basic furniture. There was no sign of how long he'd stayed there, whether alone or with company, and what he—or they—had done there.

"Come on, come on," he chivvied his brain, trying to remember something, anything. He had a feeling that all he needed to do was pull up one viable memory on command, and the rest would cascade from there. But recall remained stubbornly out of reach, leaving him frustrated and adrift.

He was acutely conscious of time passing, the weight of the gun in his pocket and the knowledge that Sara was sitting outside in her silly little car, unprotected. He had to get back to her, and make sure the guys in the chase car were really gone. Before the explosion he would've seriously considered heading out the back and disappearing. His shoulder was sore but usable, his head clear. Even Sara had admitted he was strong enough to go off on his own. But there was no way he could leave her now. Their attackers had seen her, had probably known all along that Romo had gone to her for help. They'd just been biding their time. Question was, how much longer would that last? He feared the answer would be "not long."

"What is the damned mission?" he muttered, crossing the room and sticking his head in the bathroom, then the bedroom. "Why did they want me here?" At first when the car had peeled off the chase, he'd assumed there would be someone waiting for him at his destination, some sort of information, or a threat. But the utter emptiness of the place didn't make any sense.

Unless there's a message, he thought out of nowhere.

He wasn't sure whether a memory clicked in his brain, or if it was just the one thing that jarred in the whole place, but he moved back into the main room, crossed to the kitchen and stood staring at the hideous print of the smirking child holding the half-wilted sunflower. He felt around the edge of the picture frame, thinking it might conceal a safe. It turned out to be nothing more than a frame hanging on a bent nail, but his fingers found a flat button on one edge.

Just as he pressed the button, the doorknob turned and the front door swung inward.

Swearing, he palmed the revolver and had it trained on the doorway as a lean, elegant figure stepped through, hands raised.

"It's just me," Sara said, shutting the door at her back. "I couldn't sit there any longer. Find anything?"

Before he could curse her for startling him, for walking into a situation she wasn't trained to deal with or for just generally making him crazy, a new voice interjected, coming from the kitschy, message-recording picture frame.

"You have something we need, Sampson." The voice was cool and sharply enunciated, and came with a sense of cold, reptilian violence. Without knowing how he knew, Romo was certain it was al-Jihad. The recording continued. *"We've left you free this long because we're giving you a chance to do the right thing. Deliver the stolen information to me within forty-eight hours of this message. If you do not, the people you once cared for will be killed, one at a time, until you do...starting with*

Dr. Whitney. Agent Fairfax and Detective McDermott were a warning. We can get to anyone, any time we want. Remember that when you try to figure out whose side you're really on."

Romo cursed bitterly, helplessly, as the recording ended. Not looking at Sara, he punched the button again, but somehow it had been jimmied to be a one-time-only message. Not that he really needed or wanted to hear it again. The words, and the threats, were burned into his cortex.

"Did you…" Sara began, then trailed off. Swallowing audibly, she tried again. "Who was that? Do you know what he's talking about?"

"It was al-Jihad," he grated, turning on her. "And he wants information. But what information? And where the hell am I supposed to deliver it?"

"We need to figure that out pronto," she said pragmatically. Her eyes were hollow with fear and her lower lip trembled faintly, but she didn't weep or wail. It might've been easier if she did, because then maybe he could've packed her off into protective custody in defiance of the terrorist's claim that he could get to anyone, anywhere. Surely she'd be safer with her own people than with him? But that was just it, he knew. They didn't have a clue yet who was safe and who wasn't. More, he was rapidly losing confidence that he could keep Sara safe, at the same time that her safety was becoming paramount to him.

She shamed him. She humbled him. And damned if he didn't think he was falling for her all over again.

Chapter Seven

Desperate for a status report on Fax and Tucker, Sara directed Romo to one of the area's ubiquitous convenience stores and bought a cheap disposable cell phone.

As Romo pulled them away from the curb and headed the hybrid back toward the city, Sara dialed Chelsea's number, her throat closing when Chelsea answered on the third ring. Chelsea had been Sara's employee and friend. And Sara had nearly gotten her fiancé killed.

"Hello?" Chelsea repeated.

"Chels," Sara said softly. *Do you know that it was my fault?* she thought, but didn't say.

There was a moment of stunned silence, then a long, shuddering exhale. "Sara." There was a wealth of relief and grief in the word.

"How are they? Are they going to be okay?" Sara's voice broke as grief, guilt and tears clogged her throat.

"I'm on my way to the hospital now—" Chelsea broke off, clearing her throat. "They're both going to be okay. Fax was stunned and knocked around, and cracked a couple of ribs. They're watching him for internal bleeding, but the outlook is good."

Sara's lungs had locked on the recitation, as the list of Fax's injuries brought home just what a terrible situation they were in. She'd wanted to hear "he's fine, just got the wind knocked out of him." It was what she'd expected for a man who'd always seemed a little larger than life, even back when she'd first met him and none of them—except Chelsea, of course—had been certain he was the deep-cover agent he claimed, instead of the fugitive the law considered him. For a man like Fax to be laid low…it was almost inconceivable.

"What about Tucker?" she whispered, tears blurring her vision.

"He's in surgery."

Sara's heart constricted and she stifled a sob. "I'm so sorry."

"It's not your fault," Chelsea said. "They were following up on something for the task force and wound up ambushed."

She didn't know, Sara realized. Fax hadn't told her that she'd been the one to set up the meeting. Then again, it stood to reason. She'd demanded the utmost secrecy from both Fax and Tucker. They hadn't even told their wives.

For a moment, Sara was tempted to confess everything. But then she thought of the recorded message and its overt threat. She had put Fax and Tucker in the terrorists' crosshairs by setting up the meeting. She wasn't going to repeat that mistake and endanger any more of her friends.

"I'm almost to the hospital," Chelsea said. "Are you on your way?"

"No," Sara said softly. "I'm not. But believe me, I want to be there."

There was a moment of silence before Chelsea's voice changed and she said, "Sara, what's wrong?"

"I've got to go." Sara gripped the phone tightly, wishing there was another way but not seeing it. "Tell Cassie…when you see her, tell Cassie to check those fabric samples again for a sebaceous donor. She'll understand."

"That's good, because I don't," Chelsea said, her voice gaining a note of pique. "If you're in some sort of trouble—"

"I'll be fine," Sara interrupted with a lie. "Just tell her. And tell Fax and Tucker I'm praying for them." She hung up before she lost her nerve entirely, glancing at Romo. "Fax is okay. Tucker's in surgery."

He didn't say anything, just reached across the space separating them and gripped her hand briefly in support. The gesture served only to remind her that they were, from that point forward, on their own.

"We can't go to anyone else for help," she said dully. The need and necessity of avoiding the people she cared about clutched at her, digging in claws of concern. "It's too dangerous." She glanced at him. "Cassie will find your DNA in whatever sweat deposits were left on that shirt. It'll take a couple of days, though, because they'll be focusing on the scene of the blast. By then it might not matter, because as soon as Fax and Tucker wake up, they'll remember seeing you."

"We hope," Romo said with a vague gesture to his own skull.

"I've been thinking about that," Sara began.

He cut a look at her. "Go on. What are you thinking, hypnosis?"

"Close, but not quite," she said, forcing her mind back on the practicalities when fear and grief threatened to swamp her. "I don't see you as being all that susceptible. I was thinking more along the lines of sodium thiopental."

That got his attention. "Is that anything like sodium pentothal?"

She nodded. "Same thing, different name."

"Where were you planning on finding truth serum?"

"The hospital." At his sharp look, she elaborated, "It's only a truth serum on TV and in the movies, really. Us medical types prefer to think of it as the first step in general anesthesia." She paused, and when he didn't say anything, continued. "There's no guarantee it'll do anything but really relax you, making you more likely to talk. But if the memories are close to coming through, what could it hurt?"

His mouth twisted in a wry grimace. "What, indeed?" He sent her a long, slow look. "You sure you want to hear my stream of consciousness?"

Aware that his mood had gone suddenly dark, more so even than before, she frowned. "What are you afraid you'll say?"

"I don't know," he said grimly. "But I don't want you to…despise me."

I won't, she started to say, but didn't because she

wasn't sure that was something she could promise. What would she do if he described himself murdering someone in cold blood? She wasn't sure she could handle that, whether or not the victim was one of the terrorists. So instead of going with the quick, too-easy lie, she went with the truth. "We'll deal with whatever happens, Romo. It's not like you're trying to impress me, right?"

He shot her an unreadable look. "What if I am?"

"Then trust me enough to let me load you up with truth serum." She'd intended for it to sound flip, but somehow it didn't. It came out more like a challenge. A test.

After a moment, he nodded. "Okay."

"Okay?" It wasn't until that moment she realized she hadn't really expected him to go along with the idea. New man or not, Romo wasn't the sort of guy who'd willingly strip himself bare…at least not mentally.

Despite everything, though, it was the passing thought of him stripping himself physically that stuck in her head as he drove them to the second of two area hospitals where she had staff privileges as a pathologist. She knew it was probably transference, her brain's efforts to distract her from thinking about less pleasant topics. And, as they went over the simple plan and Romo parked the hybrid in the hospital's guest lot, she decided to go with the delicious mental image. She was doing what needed to be done, damn it. She deserved a nice moment.

Thinking that, and thinking she could very well be

down to forty-six or so hours of safety based on the timeline in al-Jihad's threat, she leaned across the small car and touched her lips to Romo's. The kiss was brief, though suffered nothing in the way of warmth or zing. And when she pulled away, she saw the same knowledge in his eyes.

"For luck," she said.

"For luck," he echoed, and pressed the revolver into her hand.

She recoiled a little and would've insisted that he keep the weapon, but knew he had a point. Al-Jihad had given Romo two days to find and deliver the stolen information—whatever the hell it was—but that didn't mean he wouldn't take Sara beforehand, as added pressure. Not to mention that the task force was going to figure out her involvement sooner or later.

She forced her lips into a smile. "Lucky for me this particular hospital doesn't have a metal detector on the way in."

"Even more reason for you to take the gun," he said grimly. "You've got ten minutes." His expression made it clear that he hated the plan, even though they'd been unable to come up with one that would keep them together while she snuck into the hospital and filched the necessary supplies. "If you're not back out here by then, I'm coming in after you."

"Don't come in," she said, because they'd been over the idea already. "You won't be able to get past the front desk without ID, which you don't have because you're dead. I, on the other hand, have all the right identification. I'll be fine." She hoped.

Leaving him to stew in the car, she headed to the staff entrance of the medical center. She couldn't go to the larger city hospital, because that was where Fax and Tucker had been taken. It was sure to be swarming with task force members who would wonder why she wasn't with her friends, waiting for word on the injured men. So the medical center it was. She'd spent far less time there than at the hospital, but she was there every week or so, helping with on-site pathology when the occasion called for it. She knew her way around well enough. As an added benefit, the center was weekend busy, with more walk-in cases than doctors to handle them.

The resulting semicontrolled chaos meant she was able to slip in, find an unattended anesthesia station and relieve it of enough sodium thiopental to do the job, along with a handful of syringes and needles in their sterile packages. She felt bad knowing that the anesthesiologist in charge of the station was going to have to account for the missing items, but this wasn't the time for niceties. She'd lied to her friends; it seemed a short leap to outright theft from strangers.

It's for a good cause, she told herself as she ghosted back out of the medical center well within her ten-minute time window. *Everyone in Bear Claw—everyone who isn't a conspirator, anyway—wants to get al-Jihad back behind bars.* But as she crossed the parking lot to where Romo was waiting for her, she couldn't help wondering whether she was making excuses, looking for reasons to forgive him, excuses to reconcile what he'd done with the fact that despite it all, she was still desperately attracted to him. It would certainly fit her personal pattern.

"All set?" he said the moment she opened the door.

"Got it." Deciding she'd deal with all the doubts later, she slipped into the driver's seat. "Let's get out of here."

"Where to?"

"Someplace safe." She didn't care where they went, she realized as he pulled out of the parking lot. She leaned back in the seat and closed her eyes for a second. When she did that, she could see the explosion all over again, could hear it ringing in her ears. Fax had suffered broken ribs, Tucker more than that. Her fault, she knew. All hers. And the terrorists', of course, but if she'd called for help the moment she'd walked into her home and seen a man bleeding to death on her living room carpet, none of this would have happened.

"Hey." Romo touched her hand. "You okay?"

"Just torturing myself with a little game of 'what if?'"

"Like 'what if you'd gone into surgery like your mother wanted?'"

She smiled, her eyes still closed. "Yeah. Something like that." Then she stilled, and opened her eyes. Looked at him. "I didn't tell you my mother wanted me to be a surgeon."

He glanced away from the road and met her eyes, frowning. "Yes, you did. You—" He broke off, shaking his head. "It's gone now."

The suspicions she'd mostly managed to set aside crept back around the edges of her consciousness. "You're remembering more and more. Are you sure you want to go through with this?"

He cut her a sharp look. "Are you asking whether I'm

faking the amnesia? Seems like a moot point, given what you're about to inject me with. In about a half hour, you'll be able to ask me whatever you want and be certain of getting a real answer."

"According to some studies, the pentothal only works as well as it does is because subjects believe it'll compel them to tell the truth, so they do. Really, all it does is lower your inhibitions. It doesn't make you any less likely to lie."

"Are you saying you think I've been playing you all along?" Romo's voice was a low growl.

Sara's chest went tight, but she held her ground. "Fax and Tucker are in the hospital right now because of me. Cut me some slack, will you?"

He drove in silence for a few minutes, then exhaled a long breath before he said, "You've got an odd habit of straddling the line. I wonder if that wasn't what had me looking so hard at your office in my previous life."

She stiffened, stung. "What exactly do you mean by that?"

"I think you know, but let me give you a couple of examples…like how you've hidden me but dropped a raft of hints to your friends. Or how you've gotten involved with the task force, but not really. How you practice medicine, but not really. It seems to me that you do a whole lot of things in your life halfway. Then when they don't work out, you can content yourself with knowing you didn't try your hardest, so you didn't really fail, while at the same time, you failed, which means you were justified in not trying your hardest." He wasn't looking at her now, was concentrating on the road as he said, "I can't help wondering whether that wasn't part of what happened between the two of us. I might've screwed up, but how hard did you fight to keep us together, really?"

Her blood had chilled in her veins as he'd been talking, turning icy with anger, and betrayal. "How *dare* you?" she snapped. "Over the past two days, I've patched you up, I've hidden you, I've helped you above and beyond the call of whatever might've been between us in the past. If you don't call that me giving my all, then nuts to you. I don't need you, and I don't need your grief." Her voice roughened on angry tears. "And for your information, I didn't fight worth a damn to keep us together, because do you know what? I spent my childhood watching my otherwise intelligent mother take my cheating father back time after time. I heard all the excuses she made to herself, and to me. So forgive me if I don't do excuses anymore, and I don't beat my head against walls, or however you define giving something my all. If that means that I've been giving up on things by your definition, then fine, I give up. But only on goals and people that haven't given me any reason to fight for them." *Like you.*

She didn't say the last two words aloud, but they hung in the air between them as he turned off the highway and headed them into one of the long-term parking lots at the airport. They didn't speak again as he collected his ticket from the automated machine, and found an out-of-the-way space for the little hybrid. Once he'd killed the engine, they sat in silence for a moment, in the dim illumination of the badly lit garage.

"I'm nervous," he said finally.

It was the last thing she would've expected him to be feeling, never mind admitting it, that she just sat there a moment longer. "You're afraid of what you're going to remember? What you might've done?"

He nodded, jaw clenching and unclenching before his expression firmed once again. "Well, putting it off isn't going to change the past, is it?"

She shook her head. "Not in my experience, no."

"Then let's go." They locked up the hybrid, abandoning it for the time being in the long-term lot, knowing that sooner or later the task force was going to start looking for her, and they needed just under two days of space to do what they needed to do. They took a shuttle to the terminal, another to a nearby hotel, where they caught a cab to another airport hotel. There, figuring they'd muddied their trail sufficiently, they rented connecting rooms using the cash she'd pulled from an ATM when she'd bought the disposable phone.

By unspoken consent, they both went straight into his room. It was a supremely generic midscale hotel room, complete with mirrored closet doors, a generous marble-and-chrome bathroom, and a main room done in greens and browns, with a big king-size bed and bank of wide windows overlooking the parking lot.

Romo flicked on the lights, then crossed to the window and closed the curtains. He turned to her, seeming larger somehow than he had only moments before, his presence commanding her attention, her imagination. "Did we ever travel together?" he asked, his voice low and rough, almost wistful.

She shook her head. "No. We stayed close to home."

He grimaced. "Pity. I would've liked to be the sort of guy who took his girl down to Cancun for the weekend, just because."

You could be, she almost said, but the words wound up stuck in her throat because she wasn't sure that was the truth. If the pentothal worked and he regained his memory, he'd go back to being the man she'd almost loved, the one who hadn't loved her back. It didn't seem realistic to hope that he'd retain the more open, giving personality he'd shown her over the past few days. That wasn't Romo. It was…a fantasy, she supposed. A nice wish. The man who could've loved her back. The man, she thought, she would've fought for.

He smiled sadly, as though she'd said the words aloud. "Yeah. No second chances, right?"

"Right." She waved him to the single king-size bed. "Get comfortable."

He tried to send her a suggestive leer, but it fell flat. So instead he took a deep breath, toed off his shoes, shrugged out of his blazer and lay facedown on the bed, close to the edge of the mattress. She killed the room lights, leaving the small space lit only by the dim, indirect illumination coming from the bathroom. Then she pulled the desk chair up close to him, loaded a syringe, bared the crook of his elbow and injected the liquid into his vein with little ceremony.

As she did so, she hoped to hell she'd gotten the dosage right. Pentothal was a barbiturate, which meant if she dosed him too heavily, he'd fall asleep instead of remembering. So she went very light on the dose, thinking she could add if she needed to.

She thought she'd come close to getting it right, though. Within a few minutes, his eyes started going unfocused. His eyelids drooped and he looked at her with fuzzy good humor. "Am I remembering anything?" he said, voice blurry.

"You tell me," she said.

He smiled goofily. "Tell you what?"

The silly, too-open expression on his normally grim-edged face made her heart turn over in her chest, made her soul whisper, *Oh, Romo.* But she knew she couldn't let that show, couldn't let him know how close she was to falling all over again, for a man who didn't really exist.

ROMO WAS FLOATING on something warm and soft, surrounded by golden light, with an angel hovering over him. On one level, he knew he was in an airport hotel, that the angel was Sara and he was stoned on barbiturates. On another level, though, he was someone else, someone he didn't recognize. That man was closed and unhappy, angry with himself, untrusting of the world. He hoped that wasn't the real him. If it was, he didn't think he was going to like the guy very much.

The thought brought a pang of unease, a slash of grief, because now he better understood Sara's reluctance to give him a second chance. He couldn't blame her if this was the guy she'd dated, the guy who'd broken her heart. Romo would've fought the bastard if he knew how. He didn't, though, which meant that all he could do was howl in silent anguish as that dark, angry part of him overtook the man he'd been for the past few days.

The world darkened around him, grew dim and unhappy.

As if from far away, he heard Sara ask, "Do you remember the prison riot?"

Yes, he remembered. And he wished to hell he didn't, because the moment the floodgates cracked, the memories started spilling back. Shock rattled through him, tempered with excitement at the thought that finally— finally!—they were getting somewhere.

He could picture his contact, the man who'd recruited him as a code cracker, tempting him with promises of money and all the computer power he could want. The guy had said there wouldn't be any killing except for Romo's faked death and the subsequent body switch, which would be covered up by conspirators within the various organizations. The man had lied, though. Several guards and prisoners had died, along with the prison warden himself.

But then something seriously weird happened—the moment those images flashed in his reconnecting brain, they morphed to another scene entirely, one of rainy darkness and a blood-drenched alleyway. And a woman lying sprawled inelegantly on the street, her throat cut, her eyes staring up at him in accusation.

Where were you? her eyes demanded. *Why didn't you save me?*

Nausea and horror twisted through him as the rest of it came back. And he wished to hell he'd left it buried.

Chapter Eight

One second Romo was lying quietly, and the next, he arched back on the bed, his hands fisting in the covers and his face etching with horror.

"Alicia!" he cried. The word seemed torn from his throat, a single word of anguish, of despair.

Sara froze. "Romo?" she whispered. "What's wrong? What are you seeing?"

Ugly suspicions took root, bringing a flare of jealousy. Had he started a relationship under his postfuneral identity, whatever it had been? What had happened to the woman? From the sound of his voice and the pain on his face, it hadn't been good. Trying to calm the rapid gallop of her heart, telling herself it might be important, no matter how much it hurt to hear that he'd found someone after her, Sara made herself ask, "Who is Alicia?"

"Detective Alicia Frey." His eyes were closed, his face carved with terrible pain. "She was my partner back in Vegas, before I came to Bear Claw."

Surprise rattled through Sara, along with a good dose

of unease. He'd never talked about his years in Vegas, or why he'd left and come to Bear Claw, going straight into the internal affairs department, which was an unusual choice for a transferring cop.

That's old history, she told herself. *It's not important right now.* It meant the drug was working, though. She knew she should steer away from the subject, which wasn't related to the case at hand. But the weak, needy part of herself, the part that had wept for him long after he was gone, needed to know.

"What happened?" she asked softly, figuring that was a general enough question that it didn't entirely violate the trust he'd placed in her when he'd agreed to the pentothal. It came very close, though.

"We were working a series of casino robberies, armored cars being hit on a specific schedule. It was obvious that there were cops involved—payoffs and information being dropped, that sort of thing. We got too close and made the wrong people nervous. A call came in, we answered…it was an ambush. I made it out. She didn't."

The staccato recitation might have robbed the story of its horror if it hadn't been for the grief slashed across his face, the hollowness of his voice.

"Let's focus on—" she started to say, but he wasn't done.

"I didn't realize I loved her until she was gone," he said in a quiet tone that was laced through with self-recrimination. "We never dated, never even kissed. We both knew we couldn't have a relationship like that and stay partners. But eventually we stopped dating other people, too. We joked about our surrogate relationship, not realizing until too late that it was the real thing, at least for me. When she was gone…I lost it. I went after the men who'd set us up, nearly killed two of them, came close to getting myself chucked out of the force for good. But the powers that be were embarrassed by what had been going on under their noses, and let me transfer the hell out of Vegas instead. I couldn't stay there. Not after what had happened. But I couldn't let it go, either."

"So you came to Bear Claw," she said, losing track of the proprieties as things started lining up in her head.

His face smoothed some, though it remained etched with the echoes of grief. "The first week I was in town, I saw you walking from one building to another, wearing a long yellow coat and a wool hat. Pretty, pretty Sara. But I knew you weren't for me. After what happened with Alicia, I didn't want something serious, and you had serious written all over you. Still do."

She knew she should say something, knew she should redirect him to the months after his supposed death, but at the same time she was riveted by what he was telling her. She had a feeling this explained much of what had happened between them, but knew she was still missing pieces of the puzzle. Her moral core said she should stop him, that he'd never given her permission to grill him about his past. But the ex-girlfriend inside her, the one that had always wanted to understand what went wrong between them—that piece of her said to keep going.

Knowing she was better than that, and she owed both

of them more, she said, "The day of the prison riot, you were going there to meet with an informant. Did he have actual information for you, or was that part of the setup for faking your death?"

He frowned. "I don't know. I can't…I can't remember. I remember Alicia, and I remember you. It was that night in the alley, you know. That was the night I ruined everything."

It took her a moment. "You mean when those punk kids hassled us?" She'd all but forgotten about the incident, given what had happened later, when Romo had left the house, supposedly on a call, and had wound up in a bar, going home with another woman. Earlier that night, though, there had been an incident, she remembered now. It had just been another one of those city annoyances to her, but had apparently been more than that to him.

Casting back, she remembered that the night had been dark and rainy, the air heavy with the ominous tingle that presaged thunder and wind. She and Romo had been living together for a few months at that point, and things had been going great—or so she'd thought. They'd been out to dinner with Tucker and Alyssa, Cassie and Seth, and Chelsea and one of the few and fleeting boyfriends she'd had prior to meeting Fax. Sara and Romo had spent the entire meal playing footsie and exchanging caresses under the table, all an unstated warm-up for things to come when they got home. Blood pumping, feeling giddy and foolish with lust and—in her case, at least—love, they'd headed to his car wrapped in each other, oblivious to anything but the prospect of getting naked.

As they'd passed by the mouth of a dark alleyway, shadows had detached themselves from the darkness, two in front, two behind, punks wearing slung-forward hoodies and sneers. Under other circumstances it might've been a really bad situation, but Romo had flashed his badge and gun, and the punks had taken off. She'd been a little surprised that he hadn't detained them while she called for backup, especially knowing that four other cops had just left the restaurant and were close at hand. But that small oddity had soon been lost amid far bigger things, at least to her mind, in the days that followed. Things like infidelity. Like heartbreak. Like the fact that they hadn't gone home and made love; instead, he'd dropped her off and pretended to answer a damned call from his superior at IAD.

"I went back there later," Romo said, pulling her out of her memories and into the moment. "Back to that alley."

He'd opened his eyes and was looking straight at her. Aside from a slight dilation of his pupils, he looked pretty normal. Had the injection worn off so quickly? She didn't know the answer to that any more than she knew why he was suddenly determined to rehash their breakup. But by the same token, she could no more bring herself to stop him now than she'd been able to forgive him back then.

"Why?" she asked softly, beginning to realize there had been far more to that night than she'd ever begun to imagine.

"Because I was furious," he said, his voice all but inflectionless. "Because for a moment, when they were standing around you, making their sleazy threats, I flashed back on what it'd felt like to lose Alicia, and I froze."

Sara frowned. "You didn't freeze. You chased them off by showing them your badge and your gun."

His eyes went cold, reminding her all too strongly of the man he'd been back then. There was zero warmth in his tone when he said, "I didn't go for the gun intending to wave it at them."

"Oh." Blood rushed through her ears, sounding like the ocean. "But—"

"I went back later," he repeated, "because I wanted to teach those guys a lesson. I found two of them, and beat the crap out of them, nearly killed them. I was…I was completely outside myself. Didn't recognize the thing I'd become—all that rage, all that guilt. Until then, I'd been holding it together as our relationship developed. I'd told myself that it was okay, that I could deal with the things I felt for you, because you weren't a cop, weren't likely to find yourself on the wrong end of a gun. But then you did, and I froze. If those punks had been more committed, that night could've ended very, very badly for you."

"That night *did* end very badly for me," she snapped. "Or have you conveniently blocked out the part where you—I'm guessing here, so correct me if I'm wrong—finished your revenge and went straight to the nearest bar, where you bought yourself a couple of shots and a waitress."

He winced and said, "I was all messed up inside my head at that point." It wasn't much of an explanation, but was still more than he'd given her previously regarding the incident. "I'd never told Alicia how I felt—she died not knowing I loved her, with us not ever giving it a chance."

Something went very still inside her. "I'm not Alicia, and you and I were giving our relationship a chance. At least I was. In retrospect, I wonder whether you ever really did." *You never said the words,* she wanted to say, but didn't because that was too weak, too female. She hadn't needed the words—though they would've been nice. What she had needed was fidelity.

"I tried," Romo grated, which wasn't the same as saying that he'd loved her. "But I was starting to struggle even before that night."

She shook her head, baffled. "Struggle with what? I thought we were great together!"

"We were, and that was the problem. The harder I fell, the more terrified I was of losing you. I had nightmares, reliving Alicia's death over and over again, only it wasn't Alicia, it was you."

A half-remembered conversation suddenly clicked into place. "That was why you wanted me to go full-time over at the hospital in the pathology department, rather than sticking with the ME's office."

"I hated that you were anywhere near police work. I wanted to keep you safe, but I knew I couldn't follow you every moment of every day. It wouldn't have been healthy."

"A great deal of this sounds unhealthy," she observed. Leaning forward, she checked his eyes, which looked almost normal. "Is this you or the pentothal talking?" It had to be the drug, she knew. It wasn't as if the real Romo would've voluntarily given up so much of himself, offering her more insight into his inner workings than she'd ever had back when they'd been a couple.

"A combination of the two, I suspect." He rolled his head on his neck, wincing slightly, no doubt when his stitches twinged a protest. "The room's stopped spinning, and I don't feel stoned anymore, but the memories have stuck with me." He paused. "I think I remember everything up to the prison break and the events surrounding it. I've got my parents and my childhood back, which is a huge relief. I've got Vegas and Alicia back, which is far less of a relief, except that it gives me a much better understanding of why, even though we'd broken up, you remained the one person I trusted with my life when I needed help."

"Because you didn't love me as much as you loved Alicia," she said bitterly, finally seeing it after all this time. It wasn't that he'd been fatally flawed as a human being, unable to stay faithful. It had been far worse than that. He had, whether consciously or unconsciously, done the one thing he knew she'd be unable to forgive. He'd wanted out of their relationship, but hadn't had the guts to dump her. Instead, he'd forced her to dump him.

Bastard.

Crossing her arms over her abdomen, where a sharp ache had taken root, she turned partly away from him, wishing she could go to her room and lie down for a few hours. But she'd been the one to drug him. She'd see it through, no matter how badly it hurt.

"You've got it wrong," he said, his voice rough with emotion. "In fact, you've got it entirely backward."

"How's that?" she asked without looking back at him. She didn't want to see the emotion in his face, didn't want to be reminded of the man she'd gotten to know over the past few days, the one who'd accepted his own feelings—and hers—far more readily than the old Romo ever had. He had his memories back; he knew who he was, knew almost everything that mattered. The new Romo was gone, subsumed in the old one, or maybe by the man he'd become over the months he'd been undercover.

But the man he was now—whoever that was—wouldn't let her avoid his eyes. He reached out, pried one of her hands loose from their defensive clench, and clasped her fingers in his. "I sabotaged our relationship because I panicked, pure and simple. I'd started to realize that what I felt for you was ten times stronger than what I'd felt for Alicia. Which meant that the fear of losing you, the terror of having something happen to you, of having to live through that again, was ten times worse, too, if not more." He grimaced and shook his head. "I couldn't…I couldn't be with you, fearing every time you left that you might not come back."

His words tugged at something wistful deep inside her, but she scowled. "So your solution was to sleep with someone else, knowing I'd dump you?"

"It wasn't a solution. It was panic. Only it didn't really fix anything, because even after we broke up I couldn't stop thinking about you, worrying about you. I knew almost immediately that I'd made a huge mistake, but I also knew that it would be a long time— if ever—before you could learn to trust me again. I started seeing a shrink, started trying to fix myself before I tried to fix things with you. Then there was the prison break and the task force, and things went downhill fast."

"You sure picked a strange way to show your affection," she snapped. "Your investigation almost gave Proudfoot the excuse to shut down my office." She tried not to acknowledge that the events of the past few days could very well have sealed that deal for the acting mayor. By now he might know she'd set up the meeting that had nearly killed Fax and Tucker, might even know she was harboring the target of Friday's manhunt. Even if he didn't know those things, there was no way she could show up at work on Monday. She'd be too much of a target.

"My official investigation moved away from the ME's office within the first few days after al-Jihad's prison break," Romo said, his eyes intent on hers, losing the last of their blurriness as she watched.

"Like hell it did. You were breathing down my neck for months after that."

"It was the simplest way to stay close to you and make sure you kept out of the case." His fingers tightened on hers. "When you and the others went off the radar to help Chelsea and Fax that first week after the prison break, I almost lost my mind trying to find you. It…well, let's just say it wasn't pretty." He paused. "I've made mistakes with you, I know that. But I never set out to hurt you. Please believe that, if you believe nothing else about me."

Sara stared at their joined hands for a moment, not sure what she was supposed to say, how she was supposed to feel. One part of her was wearily grateful to finally understand what had gone wrong. Another part wanted to tear at him for pushing her away instead of letting her in on what he was thinking and feeling. And still another part of her—the weak, wanting part—was whispering at the back of her brain, saying that he'd changed, that they might have a chance, after all.

Yeah, rationality said, *just so long as he spends the rest of his life on a low dose of sodium pentothal.* Which so wasn't an option. It was too bad that was what it seemed to take to make him a functional human being.

"My father was a smooth talker," she said slowly, wanting to get the words right and give him the same level of honesty he'd finally given her, drugged or not. "Good apologies aren't enough, though. What I'm looking for— what I deserve—is someone who's willing to be honest within each moment, not after the fact." Forcibly recalling herself to the task at hand, she let go of his hand and reached for the pentothal and another syringe. "Lie back. I'm going to hit you with another dose, see if we can't get you to remember the important stuff."

He sat up, caught the hand that she'd reached toward the drug and once again twined his fingers around hers, hanging on as though he never intended to let go, ever again. "No, don't. I don't think it's a good idea to try again until morning. Besides," he continued before she could argue the point, "I need to tell you something."

She told herself to pull away from him, but couldn't. Instead she looked at him, found herself trapped in his eyes as she whispered, "What?"

The moment the word left her lips she damned herself because she knew—even if he didn't—that she'd just given him permission to break her heart all over again. She hadn't shut him down when she knew she should. Instead, she opened the door a crack.

"I'm not the same man I was," he said, his words ringing with quiet conviction. "I may not know what I've done over the past few months—and trust me, that scares the hell out of me—but I'm sure it involved lots of time alone, probably in that crummy apartment we visited today. Logic says I was cracking code and hacking whatever al-Jihad and the others told me to, but I know from experience that jobs like that involve lots of sitting and thinking."

She told herself she didn't care, that this was just more smooth talk, but couldn't keep from asking, "Thinking about what?"

"Death," he said, which wasn't what she'd expected him to say, and had her jerking her eyes to his in surprise. He smiled grimly, and continued. "And life. I don't remember what I was doing or why, but I guarantee I was thinking how sometimes someone dying is just crappy bad luck, and it doesn't mean the people left behind should stop living."

Emotion balled hard and hot in Sara's throat, but she forced it down, swallowing before she said, "It sounds like being dead was good for you."

He gave a bark of surprised laughter and swung to sit on the edge of the mattress facing her, his knees bumping hers, his face too close, his eyes too intent. "I think it was. The guy you met as he was bleeding all over your living room the other day? That's the man I want to be with you, once all this is over. If you'll give me the chance."

What was she supposed to say to that? She didn't have a clue, knew only that her body was telling her one thing, her head another. And her heart? Well, it had long proven unreliable when it came to Romo, so she didn't figure it should get a vote.

Experience and logic told her that the smart answer was to tell him no, they wouldn't be together ever again. But she couldn't help thinking that he really wasn't the same man she'd known before; she'd recognized it even before he'd made the claim. Whatever he'd done over the past months, whoever he'd become, it had changed him, making him simultaneously more open and more complex, as though his experiences had forced him to accept the part of him that had mourned his dead partner and nearly killed her killers, and later had sent him after the street punks who'd menaced him and Sara in a similar alley.

It was that violence she sensed inside him now, a wildness he hadn't harbored before, or had buried so deeply she hadn't seen it. Somehow in bringing that part of himself to the surface, he'd found the rest of himself, too. She couldn't regret that. But she also wasn't sure she could trust it.

"Please," he said. "Let me make up for everything I did wrong."

Something quivered deep inside her, as she wondered whether he was seeing her as a means to atone for more than just the mistakes he'd made in their relationship. Because of that, because of so many things, she couldn't say yes. She didn't know if she dared try again with him, didn't know if she could trust him going forward. But at the same time she was viscerally aware of the hours passing, of the countdown al-Jihad had imposed on them. It seemed pointless to worry about things that might or might not happen in the future, when she wasn't entirely sure there was going to *be* a future. Yes, she believed that Romo would never willingly allow al-Jihad to harm her—she'd known that even before he'd told her about Alicia, and knowing about his guilt over his dead partner only added another layer of determination. Romo would protect her or die trying. But that was the problem—so far, the terrorist leader had proven untraceable and indefatigable; if he promised to target her, then he would. And he would most likely succeed, unless they somehow managed to outwit his plan. But how were they supposed to do that?

Romo didn't remember what he'd done or who he'd worked for, and he was probably right that she shouldn't repeat the pentothal dosing so soon after the first injection. If she were a trained anesthesiologist, maybe, but she was a pathologist. Keeping her cases alive had never been an option before, much less a priority. She didn't dare take the risk. Which left them—where? They were out of plans, out of ideas. She couldn't contact her friends for fear of endangering their lives more than she already had. Romo couldn't contact his superiors until and unless he remembered who they were, who he could trust.

Despair rose up inside her, threatened to overwhelm her. How was she supposed to think about anything but the danger?

Except that she wasn't thinking entirely about the

danger, was she? Maybe because the situation was so dire, her mind locked on to Romo's plea, his offer. Could there be a future for them? Did it really count as giving him a second chance when he'd changed so thoroughly?

Men don't change; they just say they have, said her inner cynic, who'd learned that lesson early in childhood.

But even though she knew that was true, Sara found that she couldn't bring herself to care about the future just then, didn't really believe she had one. As far as she knew, she had another day or two at the most, and—assuming that they didn't figure out what Romo's mission had been, and use it to bring down al-Jihad—then she'd be headed into protective custody and WitSec relocation at best, a body bag at worst. Most of those options didn't involve her being in Bear Claw beyond the thirty-some hours they had left on their clock, one way or the other.

Given that, logic said they should be focusing on other ways of coming up with Romo's mission and figuring out what information he was supposed to be delivering. Or better, who—if anyone—he could trust within law enforcement, and how he could use that to trap the master terrorist within his own plot. But logic also said they'd tried all the avenues they could for now, that they both needed to rest and recharge. They were as safe as they could make themselves. They needed a break.

And she was rationalizing, she knew. Because, deep down inside, she'd already made her decision.

"No," she said, voice soft because his face was still

very close to her own. "I can't promise to give you another chance once all this is over." She leaned in, closing the distance between them so her words were a breath across his skin as she said, "I will, however, agree to give you the next six hours or so to make your case."

His dark green eyes widened a moment in surprise, then blurred dark, almost black with passion as he closed the final inches between them. His lips brushed against her cheek when he whispered, "Are you sure this is a good idea?"

"Probably not." She reached up and cupped his stubbled jaw in her palms in a gesture that twisted her heart with its awful familiarity, and the brutal heat and longing it brought. "But at this point I don't really care anymore." She blinked hard, and was faintly surprised to feel tears well. "I missed you so damn much," she whispered, her voice breaking.

And even though she knew she was giving in to the weakness and the heat, she couldn't bring herself to care as his lips crushed down on hers in a kiss that washed away indecision and brought with it only heat. Only desire.

Only him.

Chapter Nine

It had been more than a year since the last time Sara and Romo had been together, but those months telescoped to a bad dream at the first touch of his lips, the first soft caress of his tongue against hers. His taste filled her, buoying her with impossible joy that was only slightly tempered by the knowledge that the heat was born of desperation and danger rather than the love and respect she'd once thought they shared. Then even that moment of regret was gone, swept away on a rising tide of need as his lips slanted across hers and his tongue slid along hers in a move that brought a sharp stab of desire deep within her.

The dim light coming from the bathroom lent an air of romance to a room that was anything but romantic. Or maybe the romance was in the moment, in the impossibility that she was once again twining her arms around Romo's neck, that his hands were once again sliding down her body on either side, then up again, cleverly working beneath her shirt to touch skin on skin.

She'd wept at his grave. She'd left flowers, more for

herself than him. It was impossible that she could be touching him again, but his taste was achingly familiar, sharp and edgy, and potently male, like the man himself—Romo the crusader, the warrior. An island unto himself.

Pushing that last thought aside, along with the small, weak part of her that wanted to argue that he really had changed, that he was an entirely different man now, she lost herself in the moment, in the press of his hard, masculine body against hers. She rose against him, twined around him and they eased down to the mattress together.

In deference to the healing wound on his shoulder, they lay on their sides, face-to-face, kissing and touching. Sara's blood spun through her, warm and effervescent as her body shaped against his. She worked her hands beneath his shirt, relearning the warm, yielding flesh she'd touched three days earlier when she'd tended his wounds and marveled at the heat of him.

He groaned, his breath coming fast. Hers was, too, and as they met for another kiss, she felt his excitement as her own. It had been a long time since she'd been with anyone—after a couple of attempts to reenter the dating scene after she and Romo had broken up, she'd turned her attention to her work out of necessity. She didn't ask whether he'd been with anyone in the interim, didn't want to know. And in a way it didn't really matter, because this was the first time for this new—and apparently improved—version of him.

She sensed the differences in him even on the most basic of levels, as he drew his hands along her spine, across her hips and up again to her breasts, where he shaped her most sensitive flesh with gentle, inciting caresses. Pleasure spun through her. She arched against him, rubbed her body along his, wanting to share the powerful sensations. Always before he'd been a thorough, demanding lover. Now, though, he let the moment linger, let the sensations turn soft for a moment before bringing her back to flashpoint with a kiss and a whisper.

She clung to him, shuddering with the enormity of emotions that went way too far within her. All she'd wanted—all she'd been prepared for—was to reconnect with the man she'd loved, and who now claimed he'd cared for her but hadn't known what to do with the feelings, or the fear brought by those emotions. She wasn't ready to open herself to him. Not yet. Maybe not ever again.

Buffering herself against the poignant connection, she turned her face to his and kissed him openmouthed, hard and hot, demanding that he respond in kind. Heat leaped between them, flaring to lust between one heart-beat and the next. He caught her in his arms and held her close, so their bodies shaped one into the other with no gaps, no distance. She could've wept with the mad joy of holding him, and wanted nothing more than to hang on forever, never letting him go.

He's not yours to keep, her inner cynic reminded her, though even that part of her sounded vaguely sad about it.

He paused midkiss and pulled away to look at her with eyes gone dark and serious. He cupped her face in his hands. "Sweet Sara," he said, voice husky with emotion. "I was such a fool."

And there, she realized, was what she'd needed from

him back then. Not the apology, but the owning of what he'd done, what he'd forced her to do in response. And with that acknowledgment, somehow, it was finally, really and truly okay.

Her lips curved and the tears receded, giving way to true pleasure and a sense that she was, for the first time in a long while, exactly where she wanted and needed to be. Yes, terrible danger waited for them beyond the anonymous safety of their hotel room, and there seemed little certainty of success in what they needed to do. But at the same time, somehow, they'd found each other again, had found the connection they'd lost along the way.

Her smile widened. "Hey, Detective," she said, as she'd called him before. "Welcome back."

The creases beside his beautiful eyes deepened and his voice was husky when he said, "It's good to be back."

They left the rest unspoken, because for the moment, just being back was enough for both of them.

After that, she stopped comparing the Romo she was with now with the one she'd loved before. She stopped thinking or planning, stopped analyzing and let herself simply feel. A quick dip into her badly battered handbag yielded the two condoms she carried as much from habit as optimism. She returned to the bed and sank back into Romo, into a kiss that quickly morphed into a hurried race to shed clothing, albeit with some care for his bandages.

His body was lean and tough, roped with capable muscles that slid effortlessly beneath a layer of slick skin and textured with masculine hair. She touched him with her hands, with her mouth, and was surprised to find that they didn't fall back into any sort of rhythm from before. It truly was as though they were coming together for the first time, though with the benefit of some familiarity. She found a new scar along his ribs, another at his hairline, and told herself not to think of where they'd come from, or what he might've done to his attacker. But that fear added poignancy to their next kiss, and brought a sharp edge to the pleasure as he touched her with clever, inciting fingers, bringing her to a point hovering at the edge of madness and keeping her there as they twined together, bound by need and remembered loneliness.

In that moment there was no past or future, there was only sensation. The world coalesced to the feel of skin on skin, the taste of him on her lips and tongue, the sound of his harsh groans, his voice whispering praise and pleasure. Foil ripped and he dealt with the condom, then returned to her, touching her once again, bringing her up until need coiled hard and hot and joining with him was as necessary as her next breath.

"Romo," she said in invitation, in demand. It wasn't a plea, though. She was done asking.

She arched against him, heard him catch his breath as he shifted, rose above her and paused a moment, poised to join his hard length to her body.

"Sara," he said, and stayed motionless until she opened her eyes. She found herself trapped in the openness of his expression, the intensity and unexpected tenderness when he said, "If you remember nothing else about me, re-member this—you've been in my heart all along, even when I was too stubborn, too scared to admit it."

Tears skimmed along the surface of her soul, adding an aching sweetness to the moment when he shifted and slipped inside her. There was a pang of resistance, a stiffness of muscles long unused; then there was nothing but the feeling of him, of the two of them together. He filled her, surrounded her. Completed her, though she'd always hated the word, and the concept. She was fully complete on her own. But she was more than that when she was with him, she knew, and damned herself for the knowledge.

Twining her arms around his shoulders and turning her face into his neck as he thrust home, she told herself that it was just for tonight, no future or past, no expectations. If she expected nothing, she couldn't get hurt again, right? Then her body started moving in time with his, in a rhythm as ancient, natural and life-giving as the act of breathing, and she wasn't thinking anymore. She was feeling.

They surged together and apart, together and apart, loving each other without calling it love. The tempo increased from a slow wave to a slap of flesh on flesh, a building burn of intensity. Sara closed her eyes and pressed her cheek to his, giving herself over to the moment, to the man. Heat spiraled within her, took her over. She burrowed into him, clung to him, shuddered with him as they chased each other over the edge into madness.

The orgasm gripped her in a wave of sharp-edged pleasure, stealing her breath and her thoughts. She bowed back, crying his name as he cut loose within her and came, shuddering in her arms.

Pleasure suffused her, took her over, held her motionless for an eternal moment that ended far too soon. Because once it ended, once the madness dimmed and reality returned, she found herself wrapped around Romo, clinging to him as though he were the only solid object in the universe they'd found themselves in. She might as well cling to quicksilver, she knew, because he wouldn't stay put, wouldn't be tamed, no matter what he said about being a new, improved version of himself.

But even as she thought that, she couldn't help the wistful wondering of *what if?* What if he'd truly changed? What if they made it through the next few days somehow? What if there actually could be a future for the two of them, a second chance that wasn't really a second chance?

"Hush," he said, kissing her brow.

She frowned up at him. "I didn't say anything."

His lips quirked upward in a smile. "You're thinking very loudly."

That startled a laugh out of her. "Sorry to disturb you."

"No problem. But do me a favor and don't overthink it quite yet, okay? Tomorrow will be here soon enough." There was a trace of sadness in his words, as though he, too, recognized that they were out of options and plans, that there didn't seem to be a next strategy to try.

He shifted to his side, and slid from the bed to use the bathroom. When he returned, he slipped in beside her and gathered her close, fitting them together back to front. Looping an arm around her, he linked their fingers over her heart and simply held her as the hotel quieted around them and night took hold.

They dozed for a bit, ordered room service near midnight, made love again and then slept, exhausted. Sara dreamed of him as she hadn't done since the funeral, which had put a final end—or so she'd thought—to any prospect of them being together ever again. She woke early, just as the sun was starting to lighten the world beyond the window. The dim light showed her his stern profile, gone soft at the edges in postcoital sleep.

He slept sprawled on his stomach, with his face smashed into the soft hotel pillow and one of his hands loosely holding one of her wrists, touching her in sleep as though he feared she might disappear on him.

How many times had she watched him like this, and wondered what he was dreaming? Always before, she'd known he had secrets that drove him, corralled him. Now, knowing about what had happened to him in Vegas, she thought she understood better why he'd had a hard time accepting that he'd fallen for her, and that their relationship should follow the more or less natural progression from dating to lovemaking, to nights spent at each other's places, to living together.

In retrospect, she was almost surprised they'd gotten that far. Him moving into her house had been his idea, one that had seemed more than reasonable given that they spent most nights there together anyway. It had, again, seemed more than reasonable for him to keep his own apartment for six months or so, in case it didn't work out, or it turned out they needed more space than offered by her little house. At the time it had all seemed perfectly logical. Now she realized it had been more of a test than she'd realized at the time. He'd been challenging himself, experimenting to see whether he could live with her and still hold a piece of himself apart.

It'd be different for us this time, she thought, though the words rang hollow inside her own skull. That hollowness weighed on her, prompting her to lean in and touch her lips to his, waking him with a kiss.

His lips curved under hers and he kissed her back thoroughly, wonderfully. Humming her pleasure, she moved into him, but he didn't take it further, instead easing away to look at her, his green eyes serious and searching. "Morning," he said, but what she thought he meant was, *Do you regret last night?*

"Morning," she returned, and let the warmth in her soul turn her lips up in a smile that she hoped answered his questions.

Instead of easing, his expression grew darker. He sat up, pulling the sheet with him to pool in his lap. "Sara, we need to talk, and you're not going to like what I have to tell you."

Something froze inside her. Fear flared. *Oh, God. What now?* Whatever it was, she could see from his face that it was serious, and very bad.

Feeling suddenly too naked and vulnerable, she slipped from the bed, taking the comforter with her as a shield. "Let me get dressed." She grabbed her clothes and escaped to the bathroom, where she glared at herself in the mirror. "Don't," she said harshly, "be an idiot." That was the only pep talk she could come up with, because she didn't know what was coming next. It might be some sort of dangerous plan she wouldn't like—at this point she almost hoped it was, because the alternative was something along the lines of "it's not you, it's me."

Grimly determined not to lose her cool, she washed her face and brushed her teeth with the toiletries they'd had sent up with their room service meal. She heard Romo's voice out in the other room, and assumed he was ordering breakfast, or at the very least, coffee. Neither of them was at their best before caffeine in the morning. By the time she returned to the main room, he was dressed once again, and had pulled the bed to rights, albeit without the comforter she'd dragged into the bathroom.

Trying not to feel as though he'd tried to erase the evidence of their lovemaking from the hotel room, she returned the comforter to the bed and sat cross-legged at the foot of the mattress, facing him. "Did I hear you calling down for breakfast?"

"Among other things," he said cryptically. "Coffee and bagels will be up in a few minutes."

"And after that?" she said, figuring there was nothing to be gained by delaying.

"I don't need more pentothal," he said simply.

It took a moment for the words to penetrate, another for her to grasp their meaning. "You remember the rest of it now?" Maybe sleep had helped his brain sort out the flashes. She had the sinking feeling that wasn't what he was saying, though.

He shook his head, grimacing. "Not just now. I remembered it all right away." He paused, and then said harshly, "I lied when I told you I didn't remember anything past the prison break. I had all of it, right up here." He tapped his temple, as though daring her to respond.

She would have, but she didn't know how. "What…" She trailed off, brain spinning, and was saved from continuing to flounder when a knock at the door announced the arrival of their coffee and bagels.

Her appetite was gone, but she went for the coffee while Romo tipped the hotel staffer for the delivery. Loaded with cream and sugar, the coffee warmed her where she'd gone cold, steadied her where she'd gone unsteady. Her body vibrated with confusion and the hollow hurt of betrayal, but over all that was a stinging sense of self-disgust that she'd left herself open for his apparent lies and betrayal by doing exactly what she'd promised herself time and again that she *wouldn't* do.

Yes, Romo had lied to her; yes, he'd betrayed her. But she'd given him the opportunity and power by letting him back into her heart when she knew better, damn it.

When they were alone again, she returned to her seat on the bed and wrapped her chilled fingers around her mug of coffee. Romo took his own coffee and leaned against the bureau. His eyes never left hers as he lifted his mug and sipped, waiting for her response, braced for the fight, for the recriminations and the blast of her fury.

"I'm not going to yell at you, or get hysterical, or cry and accuse you of being all the things you already know you are," she said finally, feeling a wave of weariness that cut through her to her bones, chasing away the warmth she'd so recently felt in his arms. "Why bother? It didn't seem to make an impact one way or the other the last time, and this time is no different."

Something flashed in his eyes, and he moved as if to set the coffee aside and cross to her, but stopped himself and stayed put. His voice, though, grated with raw intensity when he said, "This time is entirely different. *I'm* different."

"Not from where I sit," she said. When he would've argued, she raised a hand to stop him. "Please. Let's not do this. There are more important things to deal with than who said what, or who did or didn't do the right thing." She paused, waiting for his shallow, tight-lipped nod before she said, "Tell me everything." Which, she suspected, wouldn't actually be everything. Instead, it would be what he chose to share with her. As usual.

"You were right from the very beginning," he said, as though that should matter to her at this point. "I can't tell you all of it, for both our sakes, but suffice it to say that when I was contacted by what I thought could be an arm of al-Jihad's network, looking for a programmer with federal database experience and an expensive lifestyle, I played along while contacting someone we both trust higher up in the task force. He put me in touch with the right people, and we cobbled together a plan to put me undercover. Al-Jihad's people faked my death and set me up in that crummy apartment, with a fat offshore account and all the computer power I could want. I hacked into the accounts they told me to, cracked the codes they needed, always just seeing little pieces of the puzzle, never the whole." He paused and fixed her with a look. "And like I said, I had lots of time alone to think about where I'd gone wrong in my life."

Sara shook her head. "I can't care about that anymore." She knew she should feel vindicated to learn that she'd been right about him, knew she should probably be proud of him for sacrificing his life and his freedom in an effort to bring peace back to Bear Claw. All she could find inside her was emptiness, though. "What was the mission?"

"My federal contact wanted me to find a missing USB key that Lee Mawadi had hidden in a ceramic statue belonging to his wife, Mariah. She had divorced him while he was in prison, but the statue was her mother's, and had enough sentimental value that he figured she'd keep it with her. Shortly before the prison riot, the task force became aware of the existence of this flash drive, and that the statue had been returned to Mariah's mother. The FBI almost retrieved it in time, but Mawadi got to one of the drivers, nearly got to Mariah, too. She survived, thanks to her FBI protector, Grayson, but al-Jihad's people had the flash drive. That was right about when I was first contacted, so the thought—the hope—was that they'd called me in to work on whatever information was contained on the drive. We figured my first few assignments were more tests than anything, so I played them straight, trying to work my way into the terrorists' confidence."

Sara's stomach soured on the image of Romo sitting alone in that depressing apartment, working for the terrorists. He would've been in fear for his life every moment of every day. Technically he'd already been dead, at least as far as the rest of the world had been concerned. One misstep, one mistake, and the terrorists could have killed him and hidden his body, and only a few people would've known anything had gone wrong. From what little she'd learned of Fax's undercover experiences—and she had to assume Fax was the "mutual friend" Romo had gone to for his undercover contact— the covert agency he'd worked for was quick to cut its losses, and was as compartmentalized as the terrorist networks it targeted, meaning that help and trust were often rare commodities.

She thought about how he must have lived, and instinctively knew it'd been worse than she could probably imagine. "What happened in the end?" she asked dully.

"I earned the trust I needed, and got called to meet a couple of guys on one of the state forest access roads. They brought me to a cabin, handed me a laptop and ordered me to break the encryption on a group of files that dated back to when Mawadi hid the flash drive. I cracked the code, waited until they weren't paying attention and copied the files to my own flash. I erased the hell out of my tracks, but somehow I tripped up and they figured out I was working for the other side." He grimaced. "Either that, or my work was done and they had decided I was expendable. Regardless, it became clear real quick that they didn't intend to bring me back to my truck." He lifted a hand to his healing shoulder. "I fought them off, killed one and went after the other. I'd warned my contact where I was going, so when I got the Mayday out, he had a team after me almost immediately. Unfortunately—and this is where it's still a little fuzzy—I took the bullet and the blow to the head, and lost track of who I could trust." The look he sent her said, *Except I knew I could trust you.*

She couldn't let that matter, though. Not anymore. "Where's the flash drive?"

"Hidden in my shoe." His lips twitched. "An oldie but goodie."

She glanced at the battered boots he'd retrieved from her gun cabinet that first night, and sighed. "So what now?" She knew she should be relieved to know they weren't on their own anymore, that he knew who he could call for help, that maybe they would be able to deal with al-Jihad's threat, after all. But the realization did little to improve the hollow, empty feeling that came from knowing that Romo hadn't changed at all. He'd lied to her. Again, and for the last time.

"I called in already." Romo glanced out the window. "There are cars on the way, one to bring me in, the other carrying a couple of guys who'll take you someplace safe while we get this taken care of."

He might've couched it all in very vague terms, but she got the gist that she was to be locked away under protective custody while the covert group, using the information encrypted on Romo's flash drive, tried to bring down the terrorist mastermind once and for all.

A week ago, she would've jumped at the chance to disappear from the dangerous situation. She was a pathologist, not a cop, an agent or a spy. She had liked her life simple and even-keeled, and had wanted more than anything for al-Jihad to be recaptured and life in Bear Claw to return to normal, including plans for the special election that would—she devoutly hoped—replace Percy Proudfoot with a somewhat more forward-thinking mayor.

Now, though, she found herself resisting the idea of passivity. She wanted to go with Romo, wanted to understand how he could walk away from his life with no guarantee of safety or success.

He'd said he'd lusted after her from afar, that he'd gone into counseling, hoping that they could start over. But how did that mesh with his decision to go under-cover? How did a man who wanted a future throw his present away and let the woman he supposedly loved think he was dead?

He'd been watching her process all the new informa-tion, and must have seen something of that confusion on her face, because he crossed to her and touched her cheek. "This terrorist thing is bigger than the two of us, Sara. It's bigger even than Bear Claw. I didn't have a choice. Al-Jihad doesn't make many mistakes, but he did with me. I had to take advantage of that. I hope you can understand that, and forgive me."

His words and the fleeting caress left sparks behind, making her want to snap at him because of the way he could make her body respond, despite every-thing that kept happening between them. But because her body's response was her problem, not his, and because he was right about the terror threat being more important than individual lives at this point, she held in her frustration.

Just because she understood, though, didn't mean she had to forget. She lifted her chin and looked him in the eye. "I can forgive you for dying on me. But I can't see that there's any excuse for you not telling me all of this until just now. You should've told me last night."

He looked away. "I wanted to tell you how I felt without the other stuff overshadowing what I needed to say."

"Baloney," she said, sick at heart because she saw the lie for what it was. "You wanted to get laid."

His eyes went very hard, and it was entirely the old Romo who said, "That's ugly."

"Truth hurts."

"Especially when it's your version of the truth." His voice was as cold as his expression, though she thought she saw a layer of hurt beneath.

"There's no such thing as different versions of the truth," she retorted. "It's either true or it isn't."

He gritted his teeth, looking furious, but his voice was somehow soft and sad when he said, "I was miserable without you, Sara, and crazy with it. I was just starting to get less crazy when this undercover thing came up, but instead of making me more crazy, somehow it simplified things for me. I want to be with you," he said, while emotion froze her in place and stole the voice from her throat. He continued. "But I'm not perfect. I want you, and when this garbage is over I want to try to make a life with you. But I can't tiptoe on eggshells, trying not to make mistakes and trigger your no-second-chances button. You're going to have to learn to accept an apology and move on, or this can't go anywhere."

The sense of hope that had tried to flare died beneath a wash of cool reality. She rose from the bed, moving past him. "I assume your reinforcements are waiting for us downstairs?"

His eyes blanked. "They should be."

"And you're sure you can trust the men in this group?"

"Fax does," he said, as if he instinctively understood that she'd take her friend's word over his own at this point.

She nodded. "Let's go."

But he blocked her at the doorway, the chill in his expression losing way to cold fury and hot, spiky frustration. "That's it? That's all I get from you?"

"You want more?" She drilled a finger into his chest, forced herself not to let the touch linger. "Fine, here goes. Fundamentally, people don't change. I've always known that, and I've always applied the knowledge to choosing the people I care for. But you know what? It applies the other way around, too. You're asking me to accept that you are who you are. I can respect that, but I don't think I can do it, because you're asking me to change something that's fundamental to me. You don't like my take on no second chances? Well then, tell me where it stops."

She gestured around the room, encompassing the two of them, and their shared history. "I'm supposed to forgive you for cheating on me, because you were scared, and because you were dealing with some baggage that you've gotten some counseling for. Okay, so say I forgive you for that one. But after that you practically stalked me in my office, endangering my job just because you wanted an excuse to be near me." She ticked off the points on her fingers. "Then you fake your own death and disappear on me for half a year. After that, you come to me, endanger my life, put my friends' lives at risk, tear me away from my work and my home…and when you finally have an opportunity to come clean, you don't. You tell me just enough to make me want to be with you again, saving the rest for the morning after." She broke off, breathing hard, as though she'd been running for her life instead of listing off his sins. "So you tell me. Where does the flexibility stop and the truth begin?"

Romo's eyes had gone hooded during her recitation, his face set in stone. At her question, he dipped his head so they were eye level when he said, "It begins with faith. And you have none."

Without another word he turned and yanked open the door, and all but hauled her downstairs. He handed her off to her new guards—two stone-faced men in gray suits who could've been bookends for each other— and slammed into the second car without looking back.

Sara climbed into the dark SUV her guards had arrived in, and held herself stiff and still as they pulled away from the hotel, headed for a safe house.

For the first few miles, she saw nothing but Romo's face, heard nothing but his voice. After a while, though, she put that aside, realizing none of it had an answer. Looking around herself, she saw that she was separated from the driver and his buddy by a layer of dark, tinted glass. There were no lock releases on the doors, no button to buzz down the partition, suggesting she was riding in what might normally serve for prisoner transport. The realization brought a flash of unease, quickly swept away when she remembered what Romo had said about Fax trusting the people she was with. That was good enough for her. It was going to have to be.

"See? I have faith," she said to the lingering memory of Romo's accusations.

Numbly, she watched the scenery pass her windows, as the suburbs went to forest and the road began to climb. It wasn't until the vehicle turned onto an access road and stopped beside a low-slung sedan that her nerves started to flare. She reached to fumble for her purse, only then realizing that one of the guards had taken her bag when he'd helped her into the SUV. He must have the purse—and the .22—in the front.

Panic threatened. However, when a tall, elegant, professionally dressed woman emerged from the sedan, Sara relaxed and blew out a breath, telling herself not to freak out. They were just picking up another agent, this one a woman. Her sex shouldn't have mattered, but Sara thought she'd rather not be surrounded entirely by men for a while. They were getting on her nerves.

The woman opened the far door of the SUV and climbed into the compartment where Sara sat. The driver stood behind her, glowering, all but daring Sara to try to make a break for it. But he probably looked at all his protectees that way, she reassured herself as the woman slid in beside her and nodded for the driver to lock them in.

"Are you another of my guards?" Sara asked as the SUV got under way again, heading deeper into the woods.

The woman nodded, her lips tipping up slightly. "You could say that."

"I'm Sara."

The other woman hesitated, then held out a hand.

"It's a pleasure to finally meet you, Dr. Whitney. You can call me Jane Doe."

Sara's relief morphed to panic in an instant as she recognized the name of Fax's former boss, the one who'd put him undercover in the ARX Supermax Prison and later proved to be working on collusion with al-Jihad himself. Terror spiked adrenaline into Sara's bloodstream and she reacted instantly, hurling herself at the window beside her. It gave slightly but didn't crack. She was trapped!

She didn't scream because nobody there would care that she was afraid. Instead, gritting her teeth, she lunged up on the seat and kicked at the window, cursing and spitting.

"Relax," Jane said, and Sara felt a prick on her right butt cheek. An injection!

Now she did scream, and she lashed out a kick at the double agent. But the kick didn't land. Instead, her legs went to water and she slumped down as the drug Jane had injected her with took hold and the world went gray.

"Help me," Sara slurred as she collapsed and unconsciousness closed in, leaving her last few words to echo only in her skull. *Romo, damn it. Where are you when I need you?*

But the answer was obvious, wasn't it? He was gone, because she'd told him to go. There were no second chances in her world.

Chapter Ten

When the dark SUV pulled up to the curb midcity, Romo recognized the building in the heart of Bear Claw, though he'd only been there once before. The average passerby never would've guessed the space had been taken over by a covert ops group so secret it didn't even really have a name. The building was squat and rectangular, stuck amid several similar buildings, with nothing much to recommend it aside from its relative anonymity.

But M. K. O'Reilly and the other members of the Cell preferred it that way. Anonymous was effective, in their line of work.

Flanked on either side by his driver and another agent, both fully armed and silent, Romo headed for the boss's office, aware that his escorts would shoot him without a qualm if it looked for a second as if he posed a threat. Mission or no mission, nobody trusted an undercover agent fresh in from the field.

Well, that was fine with him; he didn't intend to pose a threat to anyone except al-Jihad and his people. He wanted to get this over with, so he could... Hell, he thought, frustration and anger combining inside him, forming a hard knot in his gut, he didn't know what he was going to do next, but he knew he damn well didn't want to do it in Bear Claw. He was done with the city, done with trying to make things work for him there.

He'd left Vegas for Colorado to forget Alicia and the mistakes he'd made with her. He had a feeling he was going to have to go farther than a state or two away before he started to forget Sara.

Damn it, he wasn't blameless in their issues, it was true. But he couldn't do all the work, either. She was going to have to meet him partway. Or rather, she would have to meet him if she had any desire to make it work. She'd said she loved him, back then. But he was starting to think she'd loved him only when it hadn't been complicated for her, when it hadn't challenged some of the rules she'd set for herself long ago.

"In here." One of Romo's heretofore silent escorts waved him through an office door, interrupting his inner frustration with Sara's intransigence, and his own inability to just walk the hell away from her.

The name on the door was M. K. O'Reilly, with no rank or position listed. But then again, nobody who got this far inside the building needed O'Reilly's status spelled out. He was, quite simply, the boss. The fixer.

O'Reilly was a no-nonsense career agent in his midfifties with thirty years on the job and an unimpeachable record. He'd taken over the nameless covert ops group formerly headed by Jane Doe, and had immediately set about bringing them partway into the light.

Where before the group had been off the books, funded through a shell within a shell, out of discretionary funds leeched off several other groups within the CIA and FBI, now it was an official covert ops group called the Cell. The Cell was still organized as it had been under Jane Doe's leadership, with the main operatives working independently of one another, often tasked with specific projects without knowledge of the larger whole, much as al-Jihad's dispersed network was arranged. However, under O'Reilly's leadership, the operatives each interfaced with two senior agents in addition to the boss, so as to avoid—in theory, anyway—the isolation that had led to Fax being put deep undercover, unknowingly working on behalf of the terrorists when Jane Doe had turned traitor.

The reorganization, however, didn't mean the Cell was warm and fuzzy, by any means. The building—dubbed the Cell Block, both as a nod to the group's new name and because of its austere nondécor—was a spartan setup intended more for function than comfort. O'Reilly's office was a plain room decorated with basic furniture, a high-powered laptop, and drifts of papers, photos and printouts. Much like the office, O'Reilly himself was spare and functional looking, and a little disheveled in a dark suit and striped tie. His salt-and-pepper hair was neatly trimmed, but stood on end as though he'd run his hands through it in frustration one too many times. His careworn face was set in dour folds that lightened fractionally when Romo strode through the door.

"Damn good to see you alive, Detective."

"Technically, I'm not," Romo said dryly, but shook

hands with his erstwhile boss. "Sorry I got delayed." He'd sketched out the situation when he'd phoned in, hitting the high points while glossing over a few details—such as how he'd finally regained his memory, and what he'd done in the aftermath of the pentothal dosing. At the time, making love to Sara had seemed like an excellent idea. Now, fully sober, he had to admit it hadn't been one of his better moves.

Undoubtedly taking Romo's grimace as pertaining to his bout with amnesia, O'Reilly said, "Understood, but you're here now. Let's see what you've brought us." He waved Romo to the desk, with its powerful laptop. "Did you get a look at the file's contents when you were decrypting the flash?"

"Just a glance," Romo answered as he snagged O'Reilly's chair, slipped off one of his battered boots and retrieved the flash from the deceptively simple hiding spot he'd hollowed out, hidden beneath the sweat-stained lining and Odor-Eaters he'd installed to dissuade casual searchers from groping around in the boots. Fitting the flash into the USB port on the side of O'Reilly's computer, he said, "It looked like a detailed schematic of the ARX Supermax Prison, which stands to reason given that al-Jihad, Mawadi and Feyd all broke out. They would've had to explore a bunch of options before deciding on using Jane Doe to put Fax in place with instructions to help them escape. Except for one thing." Romo flicked a glance at O'Reilly.

The senior agent muttered a curse, seeing the problem. "Mawadi hid the flash drive before he was arrested for the Santa Bombings."

"Which would suggest they expected—or had planned—to be incarcerated in the ARX Supermax," Romo said as he pulled up the files and started the decryption chain he'd worked out right before al-Jihad's thugs had attacked him in the forest cabin, trying—and failing—to tie up the loose ends. *Well,* he thought, *if I have anything to say about it, this loose end is going to be the key to unraveling this whole mess.* Which was an optimistic thought, granted, but he figured he could use some damned optimism right about then.

For a moment, the thought of personally helping to bring down al-Jihad sent a thrill of anticipated victory through Romo's bloodstream, muting his frustration with how other things were going in his life. Or the life he meant to reclaim as soon as all this was over. Still, though, there was a small kernel of sadness at the back of his brain, one that said he might not come out the winner in all things. In the end, he might not win Sara, despite having done the best he'd known how, under the circumstances.

Yes, he hadn't been fully honest with her, but his secrets had been on the level of national security. Surely she could see the difference there? He shook his head, telling himself she was being unreasonable, telling himself to ignore the buzzing suspicion that she hadn't been wrong about all of it, that he was still missing something.

"If they were researching the prison even before the bombing, then this entire thing has been part of one overarching plan." O'Reilly leaned over Romo's shoulder. "Yeah, that looks like the ARX, all right. But if that's the case, then his message to you doesn't make any sense. He's already out, and he's got his own copy of the plans. Why would he care about having you return this one?"

"There's another file." Romo pulled it up, showed his boss a second set of schematics. "It's a tunnel system of some sort—maybe mine shafts? I don't know where they start or end, though."

There was dead silence from O'Reilly.

Romo looked over his shoulder, and decided he didn't like the look on the senior agent's face one bit. "What is it? You recognize the second map?"

"I sure do," O'Reilly growled. "Except there's a tunnel that shouldn't be there." He pointed to a long, straight line that started at the very edge of the clustered shafts, and headed due west.

A cold chill shimmered down Romo's spine. "Don't tell me. This mess is east of the prison."

"Okay. I won't tell you."

Romo ignored that and paused, frowning. "But why the hell would they want to get themselves tossed in the jail, go to the trouble of escaping, but then, what? Try to break back in?"

"They must've needed to set up something on the inside," O'Reilly muttered. "Something al-Jihad himself had to oversee."

Romo sent him a sardonic look. "This can't be the first time the possibility has come up."

The senior agent's expression went shuttered. "There are a million theories, any hundred of which could fit the evidence, depending on the details."

In other words, O'Reilly wasn't sure how far he trusted Romo, who was a newcomer to the Cell, lacked federal training and had been undercover for most of the time he'd been affiliated with the group. Rather than taking offense, Romo nodded. "Understood."

O'Reilly's expression flattened and the men stared at each other for a long moment before the senior agent sighed heavily. "Oh, what the hell. We're at a standstill here. Maybe you'll see something we've missed." He nudged Romo aside and called up a trio of files onto the computer screen. "These are encoded—maybe encrypted?—transmissions we've intercepted over the past week. The chatter says something big is coming down the pipeline, and thanks to the intel you just brought, we can guess where it's going to happen, but we need more than that before we can move. We're pretty sure al-Jihad is planning a massive jailbreak, partly as an outright terror attack on the region, partly as a means to release a number of key operatives from other major terror groups. Some of the rumors suggest that he's looking to centralize all the major anti-American groups, with the aim of striking a fatal blow against the country as a whole. If he gets the political prisoners free, earning their loyalty—or at least putting them in his debt—well, what happens next will make the Santa Bombings look like a warm-up act." The senior agent sighed heavily, the prospect cutting deep grooves in the tired lines of his face. "We need a timeline, and details. Al-Jihad is smart. Too smart. There's no way he doesn't have backup plans within backup plans. Take a look at the transmissions, will you? Maybe you'll see something we missed."

Romo swallowed heavily, appalled by the picture O'Reilly had painted. "I'll see what I can do." He glanced up at the senior agent. "You want me out of your office?"

"No. Stay. That computer is a closed system, not networked to anything. It's as safe as you're going to get."

"Gotcha." But the mention of safety brought up the specter that hovered far too near Romo's conscious mind at all times these days—the safety of the people in Bear Claw who had become so important to him. "How are Fairfax and McDermott doing?" he asked, guilt stabbing as he realized he hadn't yet asked, when he'd been at least practically responsible for their injuries. Amnesia or not, he should've been smarter about setting up the meeting, more careful about the peripherals.

"McDermott is on the mend. Fax was discharged yesterday, though he'll be on restricted duty until those ribs heal." A faint smile touched O'Reilly's lips. "I gather his fiancée is sticking him with the remainder of the wedding planning while she finishes her training."

Romo snorted appreciatively at the image that brought, of petite, dynamo Chelsea turning into a superagent, while Fax—who already was a superagent—ordered flowers and sorted RSVPs. In the craziness of the situation, Romo was only just beginning to realize how much more than just himself he'd regained when he'd gotten his memory back.

"Any word from Sara's detail?" he asked next, knowing they both knew she was really the one he wanted to know about.

He couldn't get past the look she'd had on her face as he'd told her the truth about his memory. He'd made a judgment call in not telling her right away that he'd regained all of his memory, and even after the fallout, he still thought he'd done the right thing. True, if he'd copped to the other memories right away, he could've returned to the Cell a few hours earlier. But he'd wanted—needed—that time for himself, damn it. He'd needed it for them, as a chance to tell her all the things he'd wanted to tell her months earlier, but had instinctively known she wasn't ready to hear. He hoped to hell when all this was over she could forgive him for it, that she could find a way to understand and be flexible.

Unfortunately, that thought bumped up against the fear that she wouldn't be able to find that flexibility, or that he'd damaged their relationship so deeply she wouldn't want to try.

"The agents with her checked in on schedule," O'Reilly said, voice faintly dismissive, as though protective custody of a single medical examiner was the least of his worries. Which it probably was. For Romo, though, it was a primary concern.

Making love to her the night before had been incredible. It had been healing. Cleansing. A homecoming. But at the same time, his timing had been off. If he'd been fully in control of himself, he probably would have waited. Then again, he acknowledged inwardly, maybe not, because there was no guarantee that there would be a tomorrow for either of them. Not unless he and the others made some major breakthroughs, fast.

"I'll get to work on this," he said, nodding to the information on the computer screen.

"I'll lock you in," O'Reilly said on his way out, and suited action to words.

Months ago Romo would've taken offense at the show of caution, becoming angry that he'd walked away from his life, sacrificing himself in the name of justice without gaining the trust that sacrifice should imply. Months ago, he'd been an idiot, he admitted inwardly as his fingers flew over the keyboard in familiar patterns, beginning the decryption process. Or if not a complete idiot, at least far too caught up in his own wants and needs, his own bruised ego and what he perceived himself as being owed. Being dead had taught him a few things, not the least of which was that there were times and places where the individual didn't—couldn't—matter.

When he'd been a kid, watching his family nearly fall apart under the strain of the false accusations against his father, he'd been dimly aware of the larger scope of things, and how the ripple effect of the embezzlement had hurt families beyond his own. But his parents, their lawyers and the cops who'd eventually cracked the case and arrested his father's partner instead...they had all focused on the small stuff, the little details. They'd had to—that had been the nature of the case.

That had been true for most of the cases Romo had investigated throughout his career, too. He and Alicia had worked at the local level, albeit on the high-dollar scale intrinsic to Vegas. Even the corruption they'd stumbled on had been very personal—a handful of dirty cops and two very powerful moneymen. After her death, he'd run from his grief—he was willing to admit now that he'd run rather than dealing, rather than healing. He'd wound up in Bear Claw working internal affairs, which had suited his need for justice while staying on the small, familiar scale. Then al-Jihad had escaped from the ARX Supermax, and that small, familiar scale had widened abruptly.

At the time he'd thought he'd been doing everything right, bearing down on the hints of local-level corruption and conspiracy because that was what he knew how to do, and because it freed the federal agents to do the bigger-picture stuff. But over time he'd realized this wasn't the sort of case that could be deconstructed to the smaller scale, not really. In leading a witch hunt in his own PD, he'd taken attention away from where it needed to be—higher up the food chain.

Which, he realized as he came up against a dead end in his decryption, backed up and tried a different route, wasn't unlike what he'd done with Sara. He'd accused her of being intransigent, and dared her to give him another chance. As with making love to her under only partial honesty, the challenge had seemed like a good idea at the time, but as he worked on the encrypted transmissions, he started to wonder whether that hadn't been another misstep on his part. He had, whether he'd intended to or not, asked her to give him a pure pass on one of her most fundamental beliefs—that of fidelity.

Yes, he'd apologized for what he'd done, and he'd explained the situation, at least partly. But he'd never really admitted he'd been wrong to do it. And he'd never promised not to do it again. Without those assurances, how was it fair to put the fault back on her?

"Damn," he muttered under his breath. "I *am* an idiot." However, on the plus side, it'd only taken him a few hours to realize it this time, rather than the weeks or months he'd gone previously. Surely that was evidence against her belief that people couldn't change?

He should call the safe house and—

His fingers paused as his eyes locked on a piece of code. One part of him had been hard at work while his heart thought of Sara, and damned if he didn't think he'd found what the other analysts had missed. Maybe he'd seen it because he'd looked at so many other of the terrorists' files, maybe because he hadn't been trained in the FBI program, who knew? What mattered was that he was pretty sure he could break the damn thing.

Focusing, setting aside his other thoughts and worries, he got down to the serious business of decrypting. When O'Reilly checked on him fifteen minutes later, he was halfway there. The senior agent left the door unlocked when he ducked back out, and coffee appeared at Romo's elbow a few minutes later.

Something unknotted inside him—a tightness he'd been carrying for so long now, he hadn't really been aware of it until it was gone, banished by the feeling of finally having come in from the cold, finally being a part of something larger than his small, angry world.

Just under an hour from when he'd entered O'Reilly's office, Romo pushed away from the computer with a sound of satisfaction. "Gotcha, you bastards." His satisfaction, though, was badly tainted with dismay, because the information he'd uncovered meant that they didn't have much time to counter al-Jihad's nefarious plan.

O'Reilly appeared in the doorway, though Romo hadn't been aware of the senior agent hovering. More than likely, he'd tasked an underling to keep an eye on Romo's progress and signal him when it looked as though things were getting ready to break free. "Tell me something good," O'Reilly demanded.

"I can tell you something, all right."

"But not good."

"Not so much." Romo waved the senior agent forward, so they were both looking at the screen. After a quick rundown of the methods he'd used to crack the encryption, he summarized, "It's a set of instructions to Weberly."

"Damn it." A muscle pulsed alongside O'Reilly's square jaw at the news. Weberly was the new head warden of the ARX Supermax, having been promoted into the position following his predecessor's death during the prison riot. "The riot wasn't just designed to cover your death," O'Reilly growled.

Romo shook his head. "I think that was a side benefit. The main goal was clearing the way for Weberly. Hell, for all we know, that was why al-Jihad, Feyd and Mawadi orchestrated their arrest and incarceration, as a means to develop the most useful contacts inside the prison." He grimaced. "It houses the worst of the worst, which is why the terrorists targeted it. Al-Jihad and the others wanted to do some internal recon."

"But why al-Jihad himself?" O'Reilly wondered

aloud, then shook his head. "Never mind. What else did you find?"

"A timetable of sorts." Romo brought up the message on-screen. "Even decrypted, it's couched in double-speak. You'll probably want to have the pros go over it, see if they're seeing what I am." He pointed out a couple of key phrases he thought referred to the planned jail-break, along with what he thought was a schedule. "Which means that if I'm right," he continued, "and if they're still on this same schedule, we're less than a day away from the jailbreak."

O'Reilly cursed under his breath. "You got any idea how it's going to go down?"

"No details," Romo said with ill-concealed regret. "There are a couple of references I can't place. Maybe your agents will be able to provide some insight."

"I'll get it right over to them." O'Reilly stuck his head out into the hallway and barked some orders. Moments later, the laptop was whisked away by two heavily armed, grim-faced men. O'Reilly himself, though, stayed behind in the office. "We're getting somewhere, at least."

The senior agent's body thrummed with barely re-strained eagerness, and some of the lines in his face had eased. That, more than anything, proved to Romo that O'Reilly was the right man for the job at hand. Although a few years older than the average field operative, the senior agent was clearly chafing at the Cell's recent lack of action, and the knowledge gaps that had ren-dered the task force unable to respond to the growing terror threat. That was why Romo had agreed to fake his own death and go undercover, he remembered now. Not just because it had been the right thing to do, but because he'd believed in his backup.

Hoping he wouldn't find out that his belief had been misplaced, Romo said, "Al-Jihad gave me forty-eight hours to return the flash drive to him. I don't know why he wants the thing back, or why he gave me so long to retrieve it, but if—and that's a big assumption, granted— he truly wants the thing back, we might be able to use it as bait."

O'Reilly regarded him steadily. "What did you have in mind?"

Romo lifted a shoulder. "We're running out of time to figure out what else is on the drive that he's so anxious to recover—frankly I don't see it, period, which makes me think the countdown was intended to get me focused on the wrong things."

"Misdirection." O'Reilly nodded. "It's consistent with al-Jihad's overall actions over the past eighteen months. Hell, the FBI didn't catch the significance of the hidden flash drive until it was almost too late. They were so busy trying to protect Mawadi's ex-wife, they let him get away with the drive."

Romo remembered that part of the investigation, and knew there had also been some infighting within the federal arm of the task force, and an affair between Mariah and her FBI protector, Grayson, which had further complicated things. But again, that had been the nature of al-Jihad's plans all along: sleight of hand and, as O'Reilly had said, misdirection.

"So what if we do some misdirection of our own?" Romo suggested.

O'Reilly's eyes narrowed with interest. "What do you have in mind?"

"I'm not sure yet." Romo thought for a moment, frowning. "Al-Jihad's men tried to kill me, to keep me from escaping from them in the woods. I get that. What I don't get is why they didn't move in on me while I was at Sara's, but instead went after Fax and McDermott before I could make contact in person. Then, instead of chasing me down, they herded me to the old apartment, where they'd planted a message that gave me enough clues to break the amnesia." He glossed over Sara's involvement in that aspect, hoping to keep her out of trouble. "Which suggests they knew about the amnesia somehow and wanted me to get my memory back. But why? The first thing I did was bring you guys the flash drive." He stalled, sucking in a breath. "Which might mean…"

"He wanted us to learn about the tunnels, but feel clever about it," O'Reilly said, then cursed viciously under his breath. "So we have to go on the assumption that either it's another misdirection, or it's a hell of an ambush."

"Or both," Romo muttered.

Before O'Reilly could say anything else, the office door swung open to reveal one of the heavily armed men, looking even grimmer than before. His eyes flicked to Romo and away.

"What's wrong?" Romo asked, surging up from the desk chair as every warning bell he possessed started clamoring all at once. "What happened?"

The agent looked at O'Reilly, who said, "I'll be right

there." The younger agent nodded and hurried from the room without looking at Romo, making him wonder whether the emergency had something to do with him, or whether he simply wasn't in the circle of trust.

"Come on," O'Reilly ordered, gesturing for Romo to join him and the other agent as they headed for what proved to be a conference room with a podium at one end and a long table. There were already a number of other Cell members seated at the table, a disparate half-dozen men who were very different in their outward appearances, ranging from a slick business type to a big guy who borderlined on thug territory. Romo was surprised to see Fairfax at the far end, looking paler than his usual tough-guy routine, and sporting a line of stitches along his scalp, but seeming otherwise okay. Romo sketched a small wave, got an even smaller, cool-eyed nod in return and figured he'd have to be satisfied with that.

If Sara's friends had been inclined to be angry with him for dumping her, he could only imagine how they felt about him now. But at the same time, he wasn't planning on letting that stop him from going after what he wanted. Not this time. He wanted all this to be over so he could go to her, sit her down and clear the air. Yes, he needed her to be flexible, but he needed to give her a better reason to take that chance. Simply demanding it wasn't enough, he'd realized.

He only hoped he hadn't realized it too late.

After O'Reilly closed and locked the door, and turned on some sort of scrambler apparatus that sat in the center of the long table, the meeting began. There were no introductions made, no real explanations before the slick-looking guy got up at the front of the room, pushed a couple of buttons and brought up a schematic that made Romo freeze in place. He was admittedly no expert, but the picture looked an awful lot like a large air-to-ground missile.

Slick said, "Based on our heuristic analysis of the transmissions Detective Sampson was able to decrypt, we believe the terrorists have acquired an incendiary bomb, and have placed it in the tunnel system very near the prison."

O'Reilly cursed bitterly. "Why are we just now hearing about this?" Then he shook his head. "Never mind. The how and why isn't important right now, not on this tight a timeline. Tell me what we know, and what we're going to do about it."

Over the next fifteen minutes, Slick—who Romo learned was actually named Wilson—went over the sparse details the Cell had managed to amass, which summed up to a very grim picture. The device, if it was what they thought it was, would crater the hell out of the tunnel system and the prison, killing everyone within either location. Al-Jihad had apparently named his successor within his terror organization, and a trans-mission intercepted only minutes earlier suggested that, in the event that the jailbreak failed, al-Jihad intended to martyr himself while making the explosion look as if it had been part of an FBI attack on the tunnel system and the prison itself, thereby inflaming the passions of terror leaders worldwide, and achieving his desired end of uniting America's enemies against her.

The concept was all the more chilling because none of the gathered agents was willing to say it wouldn't work.

Soon, the meeting moved into a response planning phase, and it became clear why O'Reilly had wanted Romo sitting in. He asked about numbers and thought processes, and about the men Romo had met personally during his months stuck in the crummy little apartment. If the senior agent had asked him going in whether he'd be able to help or not, Romo would've said no. But it turned out that he knew more than he thought, and the small details the Cell agents managed to pull from him helped shape the beginnings of a planned attack on the tunnel system. Other groups—including the FBI and BCCPD—would be brought in when the time came, of course, but for the moment, O'Reilly made it very clear that the plans stayed within that one room, period.

At the hour mark, once things had gone well beyond his areas of expertise, Romo held up a hand. When O'Reilly acknowledged him, he said, "No offense, but I don't think you guys need me here for this. I'd like to take another crack at the files on the flash drive, see if I couldn't find something we're all missing, some reason why al-Jihad would want to ensure that he got the copies back before launching the attack."

"Of course. The laptop is back in my office." O'Reilly tossed the key card to his office and waved him from the room, calling an absent thanks as the Cell members returned to their strategizing.

Romo found his way back to O'Reilly's office, used the key card to let himself in and sat back down at the computer. But he'd be damned if he could see what he was missing. There had to be some reason al-Jihad let him live as long as he had.

Staring intently at the files he'd pulled from the terrorist leader's computer, he muttered, "What if—"

A digital burble sounded, interrupting his half-formed thought. It took him a moment to remember the disposable phone he and Sara had been using. He pressed the button to answer, remembering that they'd only used it to call Sara's friends, and O'Reilly himself. The phone lacked caller ID, but since O'Reilly was just down the hall, Romo had to assume it was Fax's fiancée, whom Sara had called on the phone the day before. "Hello?" he said into the small unit. "Chelsea?"

There was a long pause before a soft voice said, "Romo, I'm in trouble. I need you to listen carefully and not freak out. Okay?"

It was Sara. And her tone left no doubt that there was something very badly wrong.

Adrenaline surged through Romo, jolting him to fight mode in an instant. There would be no "flight" this time. He only had "fight" left in him when it came to her. But, mindful of what she'd said, he marshaled his immediate response, "I'm listening. Go ahead."

His heart drummed against his ribs in the seemingly endless silence that followed his words. Then, finally, she said, "The men who were supposed to be taking me to the safe house were loyal to Jane Doe. Do you understand?"

He closed his eyes on a spear of panic so acute it was like pain. "I understand." She'd been taken. She'd trusted his word that she'd be safe, and she'd been kid-napped instead. Damn them.

"You need to come to the tunnel entrance. If you're not here in an hour, I'm dead."

The bald pronouncement speared through him, though of course that was the terrorists' modus ope-randi. "I'll be there," he promised, knowing damn well the location was closer to two hours away driving the legal limit. "What do they want me to bring?" he asked, still thinking he'd misconstrued al-Jihad's reference to wanting information from him.

"Nothing. Just yourself." Her voice was fading and strengthening, wavering, though he didn't know whether it was because she was injured or because someone was holding the phone to her mouth at an in-consistent distance. "Don't tell anyone where you're going or why. No messages, no clues. Just get up and walk out now. You're being watched."

A chill raced through him alongside confusion, but he didn't dare ask for clarification. Her voice and his own gut instinct told him they didn't have much time left on the call. "I'll be there, sweetheart."

He practically choked on the last word. Maybe it was a bad move calling her that, as it would clue any listeners in to their relationship. But he needed her to hear it, needed her to believe in him, in them. And besides, al-Jihad had been a step or two ahead of law enforcement all along. He had to know she was im-portant to Romo.

Forget "important," he thought angrily, realizing he was once again minimizing his feelings for the sake of his own emotional safety. The terrorists already knew he'd do anything to protect her. She was the one who needed to hear it from him. "I love you, Sara," he said finally, his voice catching on the words. "Do you hear me? I. Love. You."

There was no answer. The phone had gone dead.

Chapter Eleven

Silent tears tracked down Sara's cheeks as Jane snapped the phone shut and tucked it into the pocket of her suit, which was navy, fitted and totally at odds with the tan fatigues worn by the three heavily armed men who had escorted them to the tunnel mouth for the phone call.

The day was sunny and cool, the sky a deep, cloudless blue. Sara stared up as a hawk passed overhead, and panic lumped in her throat at the sudden certainty that once she went back down into the tunnels, she wouldn't ever be coming back out.

"Come on." Jane headed back down into the tunnel, trusting the armed guards to bring Sara and not caring whether she came willingly or had to be dragged kicking and screaming. The former covert operative had already made it very clear to Sara that she didn't care what it took as long as the job got done. In this case, the job consisted of getting Romo out to the tunnels, though Sara wasn't clear on why that was so necessary. From what she'd seen inside the tunnel system in the hour or so since she'd awakened from her drugged stupor, the terrorists were horrifyingly well organized, well funded and well stocked for the planned attack on the ARX Supermax. What did they need Romo for?

When the guards closed in on Sara, she raised her hands in surrender. "I'm going." She'd tried resisting when they'd come to bring her to the surface for the phone call, and one of the men, without changing his expression an iota, had slammed his rifle butt into her stomach. While she'd been doubled over, retching, he'd grabbed her arm and force-marched her along the tunnel. Having no desire to waste her strength repeating that futile effort at rebellion, Sara followed Jane along the corridor-like tunnel that had been bored into the earth itself. The tunnel was lit by fluorescent lights bolted to the rock ceiling at regular intervals, and conduits and wires ran along one side, bundled together and branching off into each intersecting tunnel they passed.

Sara was following orders, but she was also waiting for her chance to run. She might be nothing more than a doctor who—as Romo had unkindly but accurately pointed out—hadn't even had the guts to treat living patients, but she damn well wasn't going to sit by and let the terrorists destroy her home. Not if there was anything she could do to prevent it.

Her mother had eventually come to grips with her sham of a marriage and the wounds it was inflicting on Sara. She'd gotten a divorce, and met and married a sturdy, good-hearted man who would give her the world if he could. Sara had been grateful for her stepfather, and had maintained a relationship of sorts with her father, who hadn't remarried, but instead floated from affair to affair. Her parents had found their places eventually.

Maybe she had, too.

The problem was, she didn't have a clue what to do, or how. She needed help. She needed Romo, she thought, on a mix of fear and wistful hope that he could somehow manage to slip a rescue past Jane and the agent who was supposedly still acting within the antiterror group Jane had once led, feeding her information on Romo's progress and movements. But there was little hope of that, Sara knew. And if he tried some sort of heroics, Jane had said, Sara was dead. The ex-agent turned traitor was an elegant woman in her early forties, made up and well put together. But she was icy cold, and all but radiated purposeful evil. Sara didn't doubt her word for one second. If it came down to it, Jane would kill her without hesitation.

The knowledge was a hard knot in Sara's stomach, but she forced herself to hold it together, trying to keep track of the tunnel's turns they made on the way down from the surface. Just in case.

Men—and a few women, but only a few—moved through the tunnels with quick, purposeful strides. Some wore tan fatigues, others street clothes. Most were armed. None met Sara's eyes.

The realization brought a renewed chill.

Focus, she told herself. *Look for things you can use, things that might be important.* She had to keep thinking about her escape, keep planning for it, because if she didn't, she thought she would break down.

She counted hallways, saw hollowed-out chambers containing piles of equipment, one filled with a strange piece of machinery that looked like something out of a science fiction movie. Before she could fully register the apparatus, Jane continued onward, but waved for the guards to peel off. They prodded Sara into the same chamber she'd awakened in. The vaguely rectangular room seemed to have been part of an offshoot tunnel at some point, but now was capped off at either end with huge steel plating that extended from floor to ceiling and was set into grooves on either side. There was a door in one of the slabs; after pushing her through, the guards stepped out and locked her in, leaving her alone.

She stumbled to the far side of the room, where there was a single folding chair and a half-full bottle of water that had been that way when she'd awakened. At the time, she'd been disgusted by the thought of drinking a stranger's backwash. Now she downed the liquid gratefully, replenishing the hydration lost to the drugs, and the weakness of tears.

Those tears were done with now, she told herself. She needed to pull it together and figure out her best course of action. She hated that Jane was using her to bring Romo to the tunnels, where God only knew what would happen to him. But she had an hour, maybe less, before he arrived. What if she could get free before then, meet him at the entrance with information on the tunnels, manpower and equipment?

It might be an unlikely scenario, but it was one that gave her a buzz of hope. She needed to believe that she would see him again, that they would have a chance to talk about what had happened back at the hotel. Not just the lovemaking—though she had a few things to say to him on that score—but what he'd said about her needing to want him enough to find a way to forgive him. Maybe that wasn't exactly what he'd said, but that was what she'd taken away from the fight, and that was what she'd thought about after she'd regained consciousness, while she'd huddled in the chill, sparsely furnished room accompanied only by her thoughts.

She'd thought about Romo. And she'd realized he'd been right. Not about all of it, certainly. But he'd been right about enough of it that she'd been forced to admit he hadn't single-handedly destroyed their relationship. She'd played a part in its deconstruction, too. And in the end, if fidelity had been a test for him, then commitment had been a challenge for her. She'd held part of herself away from him, as though she'd been waiting all along for him to make the mistake he eventually had. Yes, he'd deliberately chosen to do something he knew she wouldn't be able to forgive…but she'd let him know in so many little ways that she was waiting for it to happen. In the end, while that didn't make his actions right, it did make her fears something of a self-fulfilling prophecy.

Neither of them had been blameless, by a long shot. And in reality, maybe that was the take-home of their former relationship. Maybe they hadn't been ready for what they'd found together. She might've thought she was at the time, but she hadn't been, not really.

She was now, though. In losing him she'd found a part of herself that had been missing before—the part that now told her she had to fight for him, no matter what it took. Which also meant fighting for Bear Claw, because there was no way the two of them could move forward unless Jane Doe, al-Jihad and the others were brought to justice, once and for all.

"Which sounds great in theory, but is going to be hard as hell to pull off in practice," she said aloud. Nonetheless, she had to do something.

Gritting her teeth, she lunged to her feet, grabbed the folding chair and slammed it into the wall. She screamed as she swung, not caring who heard her, not caring what they thought. The impact reverberated up her arm and stung her hands as the chair crumpled and dented. She ignored the discomfort and swung again. And again.

On the fourth swing, one leg started to tear free, leaving a jaggedly pointed end. On the sixth smashing blow it came free, and she had herself a pry bar. And a weapon.

Heart pounding, she set to work, hoping to hell that she and Romo wouldn't miss each other again. Their timing had been off before. She didn't intend to let it be off again, because this time, getting it wrong could get both of them—and many innocents—very dead.

A few months ago, that knowledge would've sent her into hiding. Now it just made her work faster.

ROMO SLIPPED FROM THE BUILDING where the Cell was headquartered, took a cab to the lot where he'd left his truck days earlier and considered himself lucky to find the vehicle still waiting for him, keys hidden where he'd left them. Inwardly, he was on the brink of panic. Outwardly, he forced himself calm, made himself do what needed to be done. He paid the cabdriver, got in the truck and navigated out of the city, moving fast but keeping it close enough to legal that he didn't find himself pulled over.

Sweat prickled across his shoulder blades, itching along the stitches. His mind raced as he tried to figure out al-Jihad's plan. The terrorists didn't care about the flash drive anymore, that much was plain. But why did they want him? Was there yet more vital information locked behind an amnesiac block? He didn't think so— he felt as though he'd gotten it all back, remembering what he'd needed and wanted to remember. Was it a case of simple revenge? Al-Jihad might be seeking to maintain face at having been taken in by an undercover operative who not only wasn't trained for undercover work, he wasn't even a true operative, merely an internal affairs detective who'd gotten an offer he'd told himself he couldn't refuse.

That scenario played, he supposed. But it didn't offer much hope for his or Sara's safety.

Romo cursed under his breath as he cleared the city limits and hit the gas, spiking the odometer well past eighty miles per hour, edging toward ninety as he headed hell-bent for the tunnel entrance. *What do they want?* he kept asking himself. More, how was he going to get Sara to safety without hinting to the terrorists that the Cell and other agencies were strategizing an attack?

He didn't know, and the lack of a plan had him beyond worried. He'd done his best to alert O'Reilly that there was a serious problem, leaving the senior agent's office in disarray on his way out. He hadn't dared leave a note, because he had to believe that there were still more conspirators within the Cell. Which meant there really wasn't anyone he *could* trust at this point, didn't it?

Sara trusted Fax, he remembered. O'Reilly also trusted him. And, if he was really honest with himself, Romo realized that on some level he trusted the big, brooding agent, too. Even injured, he was more backup than Romo'd had in many months.

As he blasted along the highway, Romo waged an inner war. The instructions Sara had relayed, coming from Jane Doe and the terrorists, had been explicit—tell no one. But he couldn't do this alone. He needed help, not just to get Sara to safety, but to avert al-Jihad's terrible plan.

Cursing bitterly, Romo yanked out his phone, re-called the last number dialed off the disposable phone and hit Send. When a woman's voice answered, he said, "I need Fax's cell number, right now."

"Who is this?" Chelsea responded, immediately suspicious.

He hesitated the briefest instant before he said, clearly and calmly, "This is Romo. My death was faked. I've been undercover the whole time with al-Jihad's people, except for the past week, when I've been living with Sara, trying to keep us both alive. I messed up, though, big-time. Jane Doe has Sara in a set of mining tunnels north of the prison. I'm meeting them there, I need help and I don't know who else I can trust." He paused, and when there was no response, he tossed his damned pride out the window and said, "I know you don't have any reason to trust or believe me at this point, not after the funeral, and after what happened between me and Sara. But please, for her sake, help me. Give me Fax's damn number."

This time there was barely a pause before she said, "I'll do better than that. Tell me exactly where this tunnel is."

It was a test, he knew. A challenge. His trust for hers. Before, he would've hung up. Now he took a deep breath, and told her, finishing with, "Tell Fax there's someone inside the Cell funneling reports to Jane Doe. So he's got to be absolutely sure of anyone he talks to."

"Understood," Chelsea said briskly, all business now. "Promise me that you'll wait for us?"

"I—" He broke off, went with the truth. "I'd promise you, but it'd be a lie. I'm going to get there and see what the situation looks like. If I need to go in to keep Sara alive, that's what I'm going to do, and I'll be keeping my fingers crossed that you guys get there in time to haul us out if things go bad."

He reached the highway exit leading into the back-country. Letting up on the gas only slightly, he sent the truck roaring in the direction he needed to go. The cheap cell started to hiss and spit as Chelsea said, "You always did go your own way, Detective."

"You'll help?"

"Of course. See you there." Chelsea cut the call, leaving Romo hoping he hadn't just made the most costly mistake of his—and Sara's—life. But if he'd demanded that she learn to be more flexible, he had to give the same in return, which meant asking for help when he needed it. Like now. He'd told her to have faith in him, but it wasn't fair to ask for something he wasn't willing to give.

Working off the map that had been on the flash drive, the details of which were seared into his brain thanks to his near-perfect recall of math, computer and engineering stuff, Romo turned onto a narrow dirt track leading into the scrubby woodlands that made up the outlying tracts of the Bear Claw Creek State Forest. The undeveloped land was state-owned but not part of the park itself, which meant it wasn't ranger-patrolled and didn't get much attention. Although the land around the prison was secured for several miles in each direction, the tunnel system began outside that range, which was undoubtedly why al-Jihad's plan had gone undetected for so long. That, along with some help from the new prison warden, Weberly.

It was simultaneously an intricate plan and a damnably simple one, Romo thought, still unable to figure out why the terrorists wanted him there. Vengeance was certainly a possibility, but it seemed a risky conceit at this point in al-Jihad's plan. Regardless, Romo kept the gas pinned to the floor, sending the truck hurtling up the dirt road because there wasn't another option as far as he was concerned. He'd left Sara twice before, once when he'd betrayed her with another woman, and again when he'd faked his own death. He wouldn't do it a third time. He was done running away.

By the time he was within sight of the tunnel mouth,

he was a good twenty minutes over the time he'd been given. Short of hijacking a helicopter, there hadn't been any way to get there sooner, though. He hoped to hell the terrorists recognized that, and had given him the deadline to ensure that he left the Cell building in a hurry.

The tunnel mouth was empty, though. There didn't seem to be anyone waiting for him. Had they decided he wasn't coming? Had they—

"No," he said aloud. "Don't even go there." Palming the cheap phone, he tried to return Sara's call, but couldn't get a signal. No doubt the phone she'd called out on had been a slicker model with a stronger signal— a satellite phone or the like.

Muttering a curse, he jammed the disposable phone in his pocket and parked the truck. After hiding the key, he strode toward the tunnel, hoping to hell nothing had gone badly wrong in the nearly hour and a half it'd taken him to reach the meeting point.

"Hello?" he called when he reached the tunnel, which proved to be a rocky conduit liberally braced with timeworn timbers that had been reinforced with new-looking metal, presumably when al-Jihad took over the tunnel system. When there was no answer but the echo of Romo's own voice, he moved into the tunnel. "Sara?" he called softly. "I'm here, sweetheart."

A rustle of motion from behind him had him spinning and raising his fists in defense. He found himself staring down the barrel of an autopistol held by a stone-faced man in tan fatigues.

He nearly leaped at the guy, as his blood drummed with the need to get to Sara, to make sure she was okay.

But he controlled the impulse and forced himself to hold out his hands, showing that he was unarmed. "I'm just trying to get to my meeting, understand? I'm not looking to make trouble. I just want my woman back." It was partly a lie, partly the truth. He most definitely did intend to make trouble, but he intended to get Sara to safety before he did. "Take me to Jane Doe. Please."

A hard blow caught Romo from behind, driving him to his knees. He bellowed in pain, tried to spin and meet the new attack, but lost his equilibrium and fell instead. The next few seconds were a blur of kicks and punches, with Romo taking far more of them than he managed to dish out. He cursed and scrabbled, fighting dirty, but the two guards subdued him, binding his hands behind him and securing the knot to a tight nylon rope that ran around his throat, biting into his windpipe. It was a simple system, but all too effective. If he didn't keep his bound hands high up between his shoulder blades, the rope dug in and he started choking. Add in the pain from his healing wound, and he was unable to do much more than curse as the guards searched him roughly, pocketed his phone, then dragged him into the tunnel system. As the artificial light of the fluorescent tube–lit tunnel closed in around him and the view of blue skies and freedom disappeared, Romo found himself hoping to hell that Chelsea was as good as her word, because he had a feeling he was going to need backup badly, and soon.

After a forced march of five minutes, maybe longer, during which he tried to keep track of his location relative to the schematic in his head, the guards yanked him to a halt just outside a steel-paneled doorway. One held a gun on him while the other unlatched the door and swung it open.

A blur erupted from the other side of the doorway, screaming and swinging something in a lethal arc. There was a sick thud and the guard nearest the door went down.

Part of Romo froze in shock and fear when he realized the blur was Sara, that she'd just ambushed one of al-Jihad's guards with what looked like a leg off a damned folding chair. Fortunately, though, the instincts that had brought him through months of treacherous undercover work were still close to the surface, and had him head-butting the second guard even as the first one went down. He caught his guard in the split second of shocked distraction when Sara attacked. The guy's gun went flying. A second head butt sent him folding to the ground, though Romo nearly choked himself to death in the process.

He folded, gagging.

"Romo!" Sara was at his side in a second, quickly untying his bonds.

"Thanks," he said, his voice rough with a whole lot of emotions that had no place just then, as he and Sara grabbed the guards and dragged them into the cell where she'd been held. "Nice job."

"Thanks," she said, breathless. "Are they—"

"They'll live." At least until al-Jihad or Jane Doe learned of their mistake. Then all bets were off. He didn't say that, though. Instead he said, "Help me get their uniforms off." She frowned but didn't argue, and they quickly pulled the tan fatigue shirts on over their own.

"Pants, too?" she asked.

He shook his head. "Shirts only, in case we need to lose them quickly." As in, he didn't want to be mistaken for the wrong side if—no, when—backup arrived, whether it was Fax and the others, or the entire Cell-backed response, traitors and all.

Once they had their disguises in place, Romo guided Sara back out into the hallway and shut and locked the door on the unconscious guards. Then he turned to her and gave himself a second to stare, memorizing the sight of her and beginning to believe he'd made it this far, at the very least. "You're okay?"

"Scared and furious, but generally unharmed." Her words were flip, but she was staring at him with an intensity equal to his own. "You came alone?"

He was tempted to tell her that backup was theoretically on the way, but he didn't dare tip his hand if there was surveillance. And besides, that wasn't what he wanted to tell her in the scant seconds before they had to be on the move. So he said simply, "I came for you."

"Oh," she said on a quick inhale. A wash of color touched her pale face, and she lifted the broken chair leg, which was wickedly pointed at one end. "I was coming out to help you."

"I think that makes us even." Knowing it wasn't the time or place for deeper revelations, he dropped a quick kiss on her lips, scooped up the men's guns and handed her one. "Come on. Let's get out of here."

They moved through the tunnels without incident, with Romo leading the way. They were less than half-way out when sirens erupted and all hell broke loose.

The tramp of booted feet rang out nearby, along with men's shouts of alarm, with a cool, commanding female voice rapping out orders over the din, then snapping, "I don't care. *Find them!*"

Sara grabbed Romo, dragging at him. "That's Jane! She must've realized we escaped."

He nodded, heart and mind racing. Sara's safety was his priority, but what if their escape had just created a larger problem? What if al-Jihad decided the risk was too great, and triggered the bomb outright? If that happened, there wouldn't be any place safe within a dozen miles of the tunnels.

"We're going to have to run for it," he said, hefting the autopistol and hoping to hell he didn't have to kill anyone on the way out. He didn't want her to see that side of him, had hoped to never have to use it again.

She tightened her fingers on his. "I'm right behind you."

He moved out, and didn't look back.

They hurried along a long hallway that paralleled the one the guards had brought him down. Romo heard the shouts and footsteps of search parties, and the rumble of what sounded a great deal like heavy equipment, which made him wonder if the terrorists still had digging to do, or if they had moved up the prison break for some reason. Thinking of O'Reilly's timetable, he cursed under his breath. If Fax didn't come through—

No, he couldn't worry about that now. He had to concentrate on getting him and Sara the hell out of the tunnels.

When they reached a crossway, Romo hesitated, then turned away from the loudest noises of search and pursuit, even knowing it tacked them away from the surface. His mind raced as he went over the map in his head, trying to figure out where they were, where they could go. If they were where he thought, then there should be another cross tunnel—there! Moving fast, he tugged Sara toward what ought to be a shortcut to the surface.

He rounded the corner, leading with the autopistol. Seeing nothing in the dim tunnel ahead, he moved into the smaller shaft, ducking to clear the single string of bare bulbs that lit the space. "Come on," he whispered almost soundlessly. "This should lead out."

The sounds of pursuit faded. Hope started to stir in his chest, hastening his steps. He kept his weapon up, though, stayed alert for problems as they sped along the tunnel.

Moving too fast, he passed a cross-tunnel that shouldn't have been there, at least according to the map. Motion blurred in his peripheral vision and his instincts shrilled a warning, but it was already too late. A shadowy figure lunged out of the tunnel as he spun. The tan-clad guard slammed into him, grabbed his wrist and bashed his gun hand against the rock wall of the tunnel, sending the weapon skittering away.

Growling near-feral denial that their escape had been foiled so close to success, keeping his voice low so they wouldn't attract attention from the other searchers, Romo grappled with the guard and hissed, "Go, Sara. Run!"

But he heard her shriek, heard another struggle nearby and realized she'd been grabbed, too. Knowing there was nothing to be gained from silence now, Romo howled and fought his attacker, shouting rage and fury at the top of his lungs, in the hopes that Fax and the others would hear.

But there was no response, no backup. The guard slammed a stiff-armed punch into Romo's temple, leaving him dazed. His head spun and the world lurched as the guards dragged him to his feet and he was once again force-marched back into the warren of tunnels, this time with Sara right behind him. He cursed bitterly in his soul, hoping to hell he could figure a way out of this mess, fearing he might not be able to.

That fear intensified to near certainty when the guards shoved him through a doorway into a larger, well-lit room that held two men—al-Jihad and Lee Mawadi—one woman—Jane Doe—and one seriously nasty-looking piece of machinery…the incendiary bomb.

Chapter Twelve

Sara's head spun and her stomach pitched at the sight confronting her and Romo. If she'd been free to move, she would've grabbed his arm and clung, not out of terror, though she was thoroughly terrified, but to prevent him from breaking away from the man who held him, and flinging himself at the assembled group in some sort of mad suicide rush. He didn't, though. He stood fast and glared at the man in the center of the room.

Al-Jihad was square-shouldered and dark-eyed, and carried an aura of command like a second skin. Jane Doe stood on one side of the terrorist mastermind. On his other side was a blond, good-looking man who wore tan fatigues along with an air of deadly menace. Sara was pretty sure he was the last of the escapees, terrorist Lee Mawadi, whom Fax had described as being somewhat lacking in initiative, but not in killer instincts. More, since Mawadi's ex-wife, Mariah Shore, had been put well out of his reach under the watchful eyes of her new lover, FBI task force agent Michael Grayson, Mawadi had been increasingly associated with the most deadly of the smaller incidents in and around Bear Claw. Sara had heard Fax say that Mawadi was on a downward spiral. She could easily believe that, based on the mad glee in the man's eyes and his possessive stance near the huge missile-like contraption that took up half the room and could only be, even to her disbelieving, untrained eyes, a bomb.

Sara clamped her lips against a whimper that came from both fear and discomfort as the man holding her twisted her arm a little higher behind her back.

Not looking at her, Romo faced al-Jihad, his jaw set. "I came like you told me to. Let the woman go."

It was Jane who answered coolly, "That wasn't the deal."

Romo flicked a glance at her. "Then what *was* the deal?"

"O'Reilly is planning an attack," she said. "I want the details, and I want them now."

"You've got someone inside the Cell already. Why not ask them?"

"Your girlfriend's guards were the last two upper-level operatives loyal to me, and I needed them to bring me my leverage." Jane nodded in Sara's direction. "Even at their level, O'Reilly wasn't bringing them in on the really hot stuff—he kept that to him, Fairfax and a few others. My one remaining asset inside is way out of the loop—she told me there were meetings, maybe a plan, but couldn't get anything more. That's why you're here. We needed someone inside the circle of trust."

"You…" Romo trailed off, expression firming. "Son of a—this was what you were planning all along, wasn't it?"

Al-Jihad said, "This was one of the eventualities, yes. We projected that once you escaped, you would eventually return to O'Reilly, and that he would bring you into his confidence once we added the pressure of the flash drive. We didn't care about the maps. We wanted you back inside the Cell Block, and that was the simplest way to get you there." His eyes flicked to Sara. "And we knew you were vulnerable. Since Fairfax put his woman out of our reach, you were the next best option."

"Plans within plans," Romo muttered. "We knew that much, but didn't see where they were headed."

"The same place they've been going all along," Mawadi said with a sneer on his face and in his voice. "Toward victory. In less than an hour, we will have breached the ARX. With the help of our men on the inside, we're going to unleash hell on your earth." His lips turned up in a smile of pure joy that looked so very wrong on a man who had grown up in a middle-class family and gone to an Ivy League school, where he'd found a series of anti-American groups that had provided an outlet for his anger and sociopathic tendencies.

Sara shuddered involuntarily. She'd been afraid before, when Jane had forced her to make the phone call. Now, though, she knew they were at the end of things, and she was terrified. The immediate future of Bear Claw and many of the people she loved rested on what she and Romo did in the next few minutes.

"Don't tell them anything," she blurted. "Don't."

After a glance back at the man who held him with an autopistol stuck in his side, Romo turned to her. His eyes were cool and steady, though she saw a layer of anguish beneath. "I won't let them hurt you. I love you."

At times in the past, she would've given anything to hear those words, under any circumstance. Now, though, she found herself flaring. Anger spiked. "Don't you *dare!*" she blazed, taking a step toward him. The guard holding her must've been surprised—or amused—by her response, because he let her go, though kept his gun trained on her. Sara continued, her volume increasing. "Don't even think you can make this be about you and me. I'm not asking you to tell them anything. Hell, I forbid it. You say you love me? Well, that's too little too late, given that you've spent the past couple of years proving otherwise. So prove it now. Don't tell them a damn thing."

"Sara, listen—"

"Stop it!" Heart thudding sickly in her chest, she rounded on him, moving in and getting in his face, keeping the attention centered on their fight, knowing they didn't have much more time before the guards broke it up. Almost screaming now, hoping the flare in his eyes meant that he'd caught on, she railed, "And don't you dare say you love me now."

He took a step back, face blanking as he jostled against his guard. "Look, sweetheart, I didn't mean— *get down!*" Breaking off, he spun on his guard and went for the autopistol.

Sara flung herself flat and scrambled behind the big machine as shouts rang out and men grappled. Only then did it occur to her that she'd taken shelter behind a really big bomb. She didn't know what would trigger it, hoped it wasn't twitchy.

"Don't shoot!" Jane snapped, apparently thinking the same thing. "Not in here."

The guards piled on Romo, punching and kicking, while Jane and Lee Mawadi broke for the door. Al-Jihad, though, headed straight for Sara. Or rather, straight for the bomb.

She saw the mad fury in his eyes, along with a calm fatality that scared her far more than almost anything else she'd seen or experienced in her life. Once before, when she'd been unable to avoid hearing her friends talking about the case, Fax had said, "There's nothing more dangerous than a true believer." She hadn't gotten it at the time. Now she understood.

Al-Jihad was not only willing to kill thousands of Americans on behalf of his cause. He was willing to die for it himself, and thought he was doing what was right and just.

His eyes met hers as he reached for a keypad inset into the side of the device. She saw in his expression, disconcertingly, a profound and gentle sadness. He tapped a couple of keys, and a subsonic whine began.

He was going to kill them all.

"No!" Sara lunged out from behind the machine and slammed into al-Jihad, sending him staggering a few steps back.

Taller and bigger than she by far, the terrorist leader bellowed and grabbed her, tossing her aside. She hit the wall hard and slid down it. Dazed, she heard gunshots out in the hallway, and a commotion.

Romo roared her name and fought his way toward her. Dragging her up, he gripped her tight for a moment, his skin hot against hers. Then he pushed her at someone else. "Take her. Get her out of here. Get *everyone* out of here!"

Her head cleared as someone grabbed her and started hustling her away. She saw the guards motionless on the ground, one bleeding, saw Lee Mawadi hissing and spitting, struggling as a tall, gray-eyed man in a suit and Kevlar cuffed him roughly, his face etched with hatred. Jane Doe, unconscious and handcuffed, was being hauled out over the shoulder of a big man in SWAT gear.

The cavalry had arrived, Sara realized, and they were in mop-up-and-retreat mode. Which meant they thought the bomb was going to go off.

Yet Romo was staying behind.

"No!" She struggled and fought, trying to get back to Romo as he lunged for al-Jihad, who had returned to the keypad.

Then she was being dragged through the door and out into the hallway and someone was shouting her name. It took a moment for that to penetrate, another for her to focus and recognize the man who held her.

"Fax!" She gripped his forearms, saw him wince. "What are you doing here?"

"Your boyfriend finally wised up and called in a favor." Fax looked to where the others were hustling Jane Doe and Mawadi out of the tunnel system under a six-man guard. Gunfire barked intermittently in the distance, and she heard shouts and screams. "We got here just ahead of O'Reilly, and made a few adjustments to his plan."

"The bomb!" Sara said in horror, as the door to the bomb room swung shut and locked. *"Romo!"*

"Go!" Fax shoved her after the others. "Get out of here. I'll help him."

She wavered, knowing she couldn't help, but needing to be there, wanting, crazily, to be with him if the worst happened. "I don't—"

"Trust me," Fax said stolidly. His eyes darkened. "If you can't do that, then trust him. If anything happens to you that could've been prevented, dead or alive he'll never forgive himself."

She looked at Fax. "I thought you didn't like him."

"I don't have to like him. You're the one he's in love with."

Romo had said the words only moments earlier, and she'd tucked them next to her heart. Now, hearing it again, even from an outside source, the words expanded into a burgeoning warmth that suffused her, flowing through her on a burst of belief. "Yes," she said, a smile touching her lips. "I am." She sucked in a deep breath, pulled herself together and nodded. "I'm going. You help him."

She took off, and she didn't look back. She had to trust Romo, trust Fax, to bring down the terror leader who had kept Bear Claw locked in a state of suspended panic for nearly a year.

As she fled the tunnels, she passed other operatives coming in. One made a grab for her, no doubt because she was wearing the tan uniform shirt, but a woman's voice called, "Don't, she's with us!" Then Chelsea was there, short and curvy as ever, but these days wearing Kevlar and a tense, businesslike expression. Sara's former assistant waded toward her, grabbed her and pulled her outside, into the light of day, where the sun still shone down from a perfect blue sky, despite the danger down below.

"Romo's still in there." Sara gripped her friend's arms. "Fax is with him! We have to—"

"We have to let them do their jobs," Chelsea said, but her eyes were full of fear and anguish.

A gray-haired man Sara guessed was O'Reilly stood just outside the tunnel mouth, shouting orders. Vehicles were headed away from the site, undoubtedly racing to get outside the blast radius. Sara and Chelsea, though, looked at each other and stayed put, Chelsea shaking her head in a firm negative when O'Reilly sent a glare in their direction.

They were waiting for the men they loved, Sara thought, realizing that the word really, truly applied to her for the first time. She loved Romo. She didn't want to live without him. Been there, done that. More importantly, she believed in him, and in Fax. She believed, maybe for the first time, in love.

Fax and Chelsea had met because of al-Jihad. Sara and Romo had been separated because of him. She couldn't—wouldn't—believe it would end because of the terrorist leader.

Please, she thought in a prayerful moment, tightening her fingers on Chelsea's as the minutes ticked down and the activity at the tunnel mouth stilled. Nearby, terse reports filtered to O'Reilly's radio, noting that the new warden and his henchmen had been taken into custody, and the digging party poised to break through into the prison confines had been stopped and subdued. Helicopters lifted off on the other side of the low mountain, bearing the agents and terrorists wounded in the skirmish.

Then there was a flurry of activity at the tunnel mouth. Sara's heart leaped at the sight of two bedraggled men, one wearing Kevlar, the other a tan uniform shirt, emerge from the tunnel, dragging the limp form of al-Jihad between them.

"Romo!" she cried, with Chelsea only seconds behind her, shouting Fax's name. The women broke and ran to their men as a cheer went up at the sight of al-Jihad, recaptured at long last.

Bodies jammed the tunnel entrance as O'Reilly's trusted agents took control of al-Jihad, escorting him to a nearby vehicle under heavy guard. Sara was dimly aware that two other vehicles held Jane Doe and Lee Mawadi, while knots of tan-clad men, with a sprinkling of women, were being held within rings of armed agents, each overseen by a key member of the task force.

Those were peripheral inputs, though, far secondary to Sara's focus on the tall, dark-haired man who had moved to the edge of the scrum, gladly relinquishing control of his prisoner. He wasn't at the edge of the crowd because he didn't belong, though. Not anymore. No, he'd worked his way free because he was anxiously scanning, looking for someone. Looking, Sara knew, for her.

She called his name, but her words were lost in the din. Chelsea dove into the crowd, headed for Fax, and Sara angled to the edge, toward Romo.

He saw her and went still, his eyes locked on her.

She hesitated fractionally, unable to read his expression, which was somehow simultaneously fierce and gentle, angry and elated. As he moved to close the distance between them, anxiety rose from deep within her—old fears, old insecurities. Not about his commitment to her—she was finally past that, finally believed that he wouldn't just stay faithful to her, he wouldn't just die for her, he'd live for her, too. But about her own ability to make a long-term relationship work.

Then he reached her and they finally stood opposite each other, close enough to touch, as the chaos of the official response ebbed and flowed around them, somehow yielding an island of calm in the middle of the craziness.

"It's over," he said. "Thank God it's finally over."

"I trust you're referring to al-Jihad's reign of terror in Bear Claw, and not us," she said, her stomach knotted on the utter certainty that it was now or never for them.

Heat flared in the depths of Romo's eyes and he moved closer, seemed to grow larger, until he blocked out everything else around them with his presence, and with the certainty in his expression. "We are most definitely not over," he said, then paused with a quirk of one eyebrow, as though daring her to argue.

She said quickly, "I didn't mean most of what I said down there, you know. I was picking a fight to draw their attention."

His lips twitched. "Yeah, I got that. But I also know there was a bit of truth to all of it." When she would've protested, he held up a hand. "The other day, I demanded that you get over yourself and learn to be flexible, but I never really gave you any assurance that it'd be worth the change." He paused, his eyes going smoky. "I cheated. It wasn't because of you, or her, or anything but me and being all messed up in my own head, but that doesn't excuse the fact that I cheated. If anything, it makes it worse, because on some level I think I must've done it deliberately, as you said, to force you to dump me. I'm not proud of it. I'd take it back if I could. But I can't, so the best I can do is own it. I did it, and I swear on my soul that I will never cheat, ever again."

Sara had thought she'd gotten past their tumultuous history, had thought she was over the waitress. But she found, when her throat closed and tears filmed her eyes, that she hadn't been completely past it. She'd needed his promise, and hadn't even known it. But by the same token, she had something she owed back to him. "You were right about me, though. I was so used to thinking of relationships as being either perfect or complete failures, I didn't fight hard enough to work things out when the going got tough between us." She paused, then went with the rest of the honesty. "I think…I think I wasn't ready for you, didn't know how to deal with what I felt for you. I wanted everything to be calm and easy, and that's not real life."

Something uncoiled in his expression, in his body. The immediate bustle had died down, the prisoners had been driven away. Sara was aware of Fax and Chelsea standing nearby, twined together, completing each other. For a moment, Sara was reminded of sitting in her office—had it really been less than a week ago?—trying not to resent Chelsea's happiness. Now, Sara knew she was on the verge of claiming that same sort of happiness, if she could be strong enough to reach for it, and to make it work even when the rough patches came.

The tough stuff wasn't over, either. Bear Claw and the BCCPD were going to be headed into some serious mopping up, as the task force rooted out the last of the conspirators and the city headed for a special election that would—God willing—put in place a mayor she could actually work with, and who would work with her. But that didn't mean she should wait around until all that settled down to take what she wanted, did it?

Love wasn't about everything being perfect, she was starting to realize. It was about caring enough to make the imperfect moments work.

Romo's expression eased; a faint, hopeful smile touched his lips. He held out a hand to her. "Can I come home now?"

And then, finally, it was easy for Sara to take his hand, to smile up at him and say, "God, yes. I've missed you."

He drew her close, touched his lips to hers. "I love you."

Before, she'd yearned for the words. Now they were nothing more than a part of the whole. Still, though, they brought a warm, soft glow to her heart as she leaned into the kiss, and whispered, "I love you, too."

They kissed again, long and soft, and full of promises for tomorrow and the day after, on into the future. They didn't break apart until an officious throat clearing sounded, demanding attention.

It was Fax, grinning sardonically. "You two willing

to take it somewhere else?" He gestured to the growing crowd that now eddied around them, as a second wave of responders arrived and moved in on the crime scene.

Sara flushed, but smiled at her friends, then up at Romo. "Do you need to do anything more with O'Reilly?"

He shrugged. "I'm sure he'll track me down if and when he needs me. I have a feeling he's done with me for the time being, though."

The four friends turned away from the tunnels and the ARX Supermax, linked arm in arm as they headed back to Bear Claw. They, and the city itself, would start a new chapter now that the terror threat was ended.

Who knew what the future would hold? Sara thought, a bubble of exhilaration rising in her chest. Whatever the outcome, she knew, she and Romo would face it. Together.

* * * * *

"Kerry, we have to be sensible about this. I'm not going to dangle you out there like a Judas goat."

"But that's what I am. Or I should be." She leaned back against the cushions, closing her eyes. "I'm not afraid of dying."

"No," Adrian said. "Has it occurred to you that I might be afraid of losing you?"

"Adrian…" She couldn't bring herself to open her eyes. Her heart seemed to stop midbeat, and the breath sailed out of her.

"Just don't argue with me, Kerry. Just don't argue. I know you're bait. But none of us, me most especially, is willing to risk you recklessly. You've got to understand that."

At that she opened her eyes and looked at him, reading the urgency in his face, the deep concern, even the flicker of fear. She understood that it would kill him to lose someone he was protecting again. Almost as if to reinforce his message, he swept her up off the couch and carried her back to her bedroom.

PROTECTOR
OF ONE

BY
RACHEL LEE

All the characters in this book have no existence outside the imagination of the author, and have no relation whatsoever to anyone bearing the same name or names. They are not even distantly inspired by any individual known or unknown to the author, and all the incidents are pure invention.

First published in Great Britain 2010
Harlequin Mills & Boon Limited,
Eton House, 18-24 Paradise Road, Richmond, Surrey TW9 1SR

© Susan Civil-Brown 2009

ISBN: 978 0 263 88264 3

46-1010

Harlequin Mills & Boon policy is to use papers that are natural, renewable and recyclable products and made from wood grown in sustainable forests. The logging and manufacturing processes conform to the legal environmental regulations of the country of origin.

Printed and bound in Spain
by Litografia Rosés S.A., Barcelona

Rachel Lee was hooked on writing by the age of twelve, and practiced her craft as she moved from place to place all over the United States. This *New York Times* bestselling author now resides in Florida and has the joy of writing full-time.

Her bestselling CONARD COUNTY series has won the hearts of readers worldwide, and it's no wonder, given her own approach to life and love. As she says, "Life is the biggest romantic adventure of all—and if you're open and aware, the most marvelous things are just waiting to be discovered."

For all my readers, each and every one,
who help me keep Conard County alive.
Hugs to you all!

Prologue

It was a dark and stormy night. The most clichéd opening line in literature should have been the start of the story, Kerry Tomlinson would later think. As an English teacher she had used the line often to instruct.

In reality, it was a bright and sunny autumn morning, redolent of coffee, sizzling bacon and the nutty aroma of grits and cheese. In the background, the radio played some lively but pleasant music. She sat at her table with the *Conard County Courier* open in front of her, waiting for the strip of bacon she intended to crumble into the steaming bowl of grits beside the stove.

She heard the newsbreak start, the report of two

bodies being found on the edge of the state forest in Conard County, two hikers...

Then her world turned upside down.

Chapter 1

Adrian Goddard sat in Conard County Sheriff Gage Dalton's Office, about as unhappy as a man could be short of death or major injury. He'd left law enforcement two years ago and he wasn't happy to be dragged back in. But a double homicide had caused Gage to call on him, and his sense of duty wouldn't let him refuse.

A lean, rangy man with a face marked by weather and strain, his gray eyes pierced whatever he looked at and nearly matched the early gray at his temples. He looked as if he might have been chiseled out of the granite of the Wyoming mountains. He had one of those faces that made guessing his age nearly impossible, yet few would have believed he was only thirty-five.

He'd spent the day at the crime scene, gathering the kind of information a photograph or a report might overlook: angles of attack, best vantage points, surrounding cover. The little and big things that could answer the question: why did this happen here and not elsewhere? Given the relative isolation of the wooded murder scene, that question had gained a lot of importance.

Gage returned to the office, looking as tired as any man who'd spent the day looking at two partially decomposed bodies while marching up and down rocky ground looking for footprints and cartridge casings. Maybe worse than tired, because Gage lived his life in constant pain, the only outward signs of which were his limp and the burn scar on his cheek and neck.

"Nate's going to come in tomorrow," Gage said.

"Good," Adrian answered. Nate Tate was the former sheriff of Conard County. He'd retired a couple of years ago to be succeeded by Gage Dalton, a man still referred to as "the new sheriff." But Adrian had worked more often with Nate over the years than he had with Gage, so he knew the man's mettle and doubted anyone on the planet knew this county better. If anybody in Conard County had a screw loose, Nate would know who it was and would probably even have the guy's phone number memorized. A good starting place in a case like this.

Gage settled in his chair, a pillow behind his back, reflexive pain showing only in a minute tightening around his dark eyes. "Okay," he said, "we're getting nowhere fast. We should probably call it a night."

"Probably." Oddly, however, Adrian felt reluctant to return to the peace of his ranch. The place he had chosen to be his hermitage. His fortress.

"I don't get it," he said. "Was it a hate killing? It looks like it. The way these guys were arranged...."

Gage winced again, this time at the thought. "I don't want a Matthew Shepard thing in this county."

"Who does? But it doesn't feel right anyway. You saw them. Something about it keeps nagging at me. Misdirection. That's what I'm thinking."

Gage nodded, pulling a couple of the crime scene photos toward him. "I guess we won't know for sure until we find out who they are."

Any identifiable items had been removed. Adrian stared at a photo, thinking. "If it was a hate crime, wouldn't they want us to know who the vics are?"

"You're talking about a rational mind, Adrian."

"Even neo-Nazis can be rational. They're just *wrong*."

At that a faint smile flickered over Gage's face. "Maybe."

"Well, the statement gets kind of overlooked if it takes us weeks to find out who these guys are. By then the news will have moved on."

"Don't mention the news. The major media are going to crawl all over us tomorrow." Gage heaved a resigned sigh.

"Too bad," Adrian said, "that these guys couldn't have been on state forest land."

"Yeah. Then we could have called in your old buddies."

Adrian had retired on disability from the Wyoming

Department of Criminal Investigation. He would have loved to turn all of this over to them.

Or maybe not. Despite himself, his interest was piqued.

"Too bad," Gage said, "it didn't happen in Denver. Anywhere but my county."

"Gage?"

At the soft voice both men looked up to see Emma Dalton, Gage's wife, standing in the doorway. The years had dissolved none of her beauty, and to Gage she still appeared to be the redheaded, green-eyed goddess he'd fallen in love with in the darkest time of both their lives. "Have you got time to listen to a witness?"

"Witness to what?"

"The murders. Kerry Tomlinson. You remember her. She had a vision about it."

The two men looked at each other, neither of them knowing what to make of this announcement. It was almost as if they had just ridden over the hump in a roller coaster, the word *witness* starting to fill them with excitement just as the word *vision* sent them plunging. But there was Emma, a paragon if ever there was one, asking them to listen.

Gage cleared his throat. "I didn't know Kerry was a psychic."

"She's not." Emma stepped into the room and closed the door behind her. She smelled like rose water and the library, and a touch of cold autumn air. "But she's very scared and very frightened, and she can't shake the images out of her mind. So you are going to listen to her and reassure her. If she's got information you can use, good. If not you can at least put her mind to rest about whether she's really seeing the murder victims."

Gage and Adrian exchanged looks again. To Adrian it seemed both of them felt the same reluctance.

"Okay," Gage answered after a moment. "But we're not shrinks. Let me just put all this stuff out of sight."

Emma glanced down and her lips tightened. "Please do," she said. "I don't need to look at that, either. Let me get her."

Emma hovered over her like a guardian angel, Kerry thought as they walked down the hall to the sheriff's office. The sense of having an ally in this craziness reassured her almost as much as the sense of an unseen presence just behind her shoulder disturbed her. Emma might spread her metaphoric wings, but those wings seemed unable to hold back the push from the invisible presence.

This is insane.

But insane or not, she had the strong feeling that if she didn't spit out these images, they were going to plague her forever.

She entered Gage's office tentatively, giving him a small, weak smile. Then she saw the other man. Tall, rugged-looking, dark hair with a dash of gray at the temples. Adrian Goddard. What was he doing here?

At that instant she almost turned and ran. Being crazy was one thing. Announcing it to a whole bunch of people, one of them almost a stranger, was entirely another. His gray eyes flicked over her, as full of doubt as any atheist's when inside a church.

"I can't do this!" The words burst from her and she started to turn, but Emma gently caught her arm.

"You can," Emma said firmly. "None of us know what happened to you this morning. Nobody can say whether it was something random occurring because of the news you heard, or whether you really saw something. But one thing I *do* know, Kerry. You're not crazy, and if there's even a slender hope that you might have picked up on something useful, you owe it to the victims to tell Gage."

Kerry closed her eyes a moment, felt again the pressure pushing her forward, thought she almost heard a whisper in her ear. "Okay," she said, squaring her shoulders. "Maybe if I tell you all, I can forget about it, which would be a blessing."

She took one of the two chairs facing the desk, refusing to look at Adrian Goddard. Right now she needed his apparent dubiousness as much as she needed another vision. Gage merely looked inquiring. And kind.

"It's okay, Kerry," he said. "Before this week is out we'll have had a handful of people claim to have committed these murders even though they had nothing to do with them, and a thousand useless tips. And we have no leads at this point. So a vision of any kind is welcome, okay?"

Kerry nodded slowly, trying to find the persona that could control a classroom full of rowdy teens, and leave behind the disturbed woman she had become today.

"Okay," she said. "Okay." But it was going to be one of the hardest things she'd ever done.

Adrian leaned back in his chair, folding his hands on his flat stomach, trying to appear impassive. His gaze bored into Kerry Tomlinson, though. A schoolteacher with visions. He'd noticed her around, of course. You couldn't live in Conard County for long without noticing just about everyone.

She was tiny, almost frail-looking, with long dark hair caught in a clip at the nape of her neck. Her dark eyes were large in her face, her cheekbones high and her unpainted lips invitingly shaped. Pretty, but able to pass unnoticed if she chose. A quiet prettiness, the kind that for the right person could easily turn into brilliant beauty. A man would have to approach carefully, slowly, and gently, to bring that out, but once he did...

Catching himself, Adrian almost shook his head to bring his attention back to what she was saying.

"It's hard to explain," she said, looking at Gage. "I was just sitting there waiting for my breakfast to finish cooking..." She trailed off and looked down at her knotted hands.

"Start wherever you want," Gage said gently. "You don't have to get right to the vision."

That seemed to reassure her. Her head lifted, and Adrian now saw the woman who taught for a living, the woman who could handle rooms full of teenagers.

"All right," she said, her voice taking on a somewhat stronger timbre. "When I was in my senior year in college, we were driving back to school after the holidays when the car skidded on ice and went over a cliff. My two friends died. Probably the only reason I'm still here is that I was in the backseat, and an EMT saw us go off the road."

Gage nodded, didn't ask her how this was related. Just let her tell her story her own way, which was often the best way.

"Anyway," Kerry continued, "I died twice."

In spite of himself, Adrian sat up a little straighter. Gage leaned forward and repeated, *"Twice?"*

Kerry nodded. "That's what they tell me. I was clinically dead twice before they managed to stabilize me. I'm lucky not to have suffered major brain damage."

"I would say so!" Gage agreed heartily.

A faint smile flickered over Kerry's face. "I'll spare you the tale about going into the light. My near-death experience was pretty much the same as everyone's you hear about. *I* know it was real. I don't need to convince anyone else."

Gage nodded. Adrian sat frozen. He would have liked to demand the details for himself, but held on to his desire. Another time. A better time.

"Anyway," Kerry said, "I recovered, I finished school, I came back here to teach. You all know the rest. I've been teaching here for eight years now," she added to Adrian, as if he might not know. "But I changed after the accident."

"Most people do," Emma said comfortingly. She would know. A senseless, brutal crime had once torn her life apart.

Kerry looked at her and nodded gratefully. "Anyway," she continued, returning her attention to Gage, "everything checked out, not even any brain damage that they could find. I was lucky. I was blessed."

Gage murmured agreement. Adrian could tell that Kerry didn't really feel blessed and suspected some survivor guilt. She'd be less than human if she didn't feel it.

Kerry drew a deep breath, clearly ready to plunge in to the hard part. "I sometimes get these feelings. I call them my quirks. But sometimes I know things that are going to happen. Or I know things that happen elsewhere that I only hear about later. I usually shake them off. Coincidence. Probably the result of some minor brain damage."

Gage nodded. "Possibly."

"But this morning..." Kerry hesitated. Finally she closed her eyes, as if to pretend she were alone, and said, "I heard the news announcement and then everything just shifted. In an instant I was somewhere else and the things I saw were all jumbled."

Gage leaned forward now, picking up a pen and holding it over a legal pad. "Can you organize it in any way?"

Kerry compressed her lips before speaking. "It was like a rush of things, disjointed, some not clear, others almost too clear. Sounds. I heard men laughing. I heard them opening cans, and could smell the beer. I smelled cordite. I saw...I saw... I saw two men lying on the ground. They were facing each other, and each had an arm over the other's body. And blood. There was blood every-where... They were shot. Twice each. Once in the chest, once in the head. But they weren't lying like that when they were shot. They were dragged there. Positioned."

Her eyes snapped open. "It's supposed to look like a message, but it's not."

That was the moment Adrian felt the hairs on the back of his neck stand on end.

Kerry waited, but she hardly saw Gage and Adrian now. She had returned to this morning, that bright beautiful morning that had been suddenly and inexplicably blighted by evil. At some level she smelled the bacon burning on the stove, but her mind had attached itself far away from the kitchen.

"Kerry?" Gage's voice recalled her.

"Yes?"

"Can you wring any more details out of what you sensed?"

She met his gaze and saw something there, something that suggested she hadn't just flipped a brain circuit. "You mean what I saw was real?"

Emma squeezed her arm again. Gage hesitated. "I'm not supposed to discuss the investigation. So can we just say that you hit on something that no one outside the department should know?"

"Oh, God." Kerry lowered her head, her stomach sinking at the same time. "I don't need this. I don't want this...this whatever it is."

"I don't blame you," Emma said quietly. "But for whatever reason, it happened."

Kerry nodded, fighting for equilibrium and battering down the fright. "Okay. Okay. Let's just say that somehow, some way, I saw something that was real. At least in part. You want me to try to wring more information out of what I saw?"

"If you can."

"It was all so jumbled, and I've been trying not to think about it all day." Her fingers twisted together. "Let me think. Focus on it. But at this point I'm not sure I wouldn't just confabulate stuff."

"Wouldn't it feel different?" Adrian asked, speaking for the first time.

Kerry looked at him, her jaw dropping a little. "Yes," she said finally. "It would. There was something about what happened this morning that was so...real. Almost hyper-real."

He nodded. "Then don't worry about making things up. Just focus on what feels like that."

"Good idea," Gage remarked.

Kerry decided that would make a good guideline. Somewhere through her distress a flicker of humor emerged. "I'm not a pro at this. No practice to guide me."

At that even the stern-faced Adrian smiled. "I've never consulted a psychic before so I don't have any hints for you."

"I'm not a psychic. I just—" She broke off suddenly. "Sorry. It doesn't matter what I am or am not. Whatever this was, it happened. So I just need to make sure I tell you everything."

Gage nodded encouragingly. "That's the stuff. Then maybe you can go home and forget it."

"That would be a relief. All right." She closed her eyes again, this time not trying to skip quickly through the images that had imprinted themselves earlier that day, but instead to look hard at them.

"The victims were friends. One of them—there's a woman starting to worry about him. A young woman. She wants to report him missing."

"That'll help," Adrian said.

Kerry ignored him, reaching out into whatever it was that had happened this morning, unsure but driven to find something, anything that would get this off her back and help the police if she could.

"They'd been on a long hike," she said. "Getting near the end. Several days, maybe a week. I see a camera. A camera was important to one of them. And a funny-looking hammer. They both had these hammers on their belts before they were killed. The murderer took them, and some other things."

Where was all this coming from? But the words kept tumbling from her lips, sometimes fast, sometimes hesitant. "There's more than one murderer," she announced suddenly. "I get the feeling of competition. This won't be the last killing."

Then it was as if a bubble burst. Everything drained from her mind, leaving her relaxed. Whatever she had needed to do was done now. Finished.

She opened her eyes again, looking at the two men. "That's it. It's gone."

"Gone?" Gage asked.

"Gone. The vividness is gone. It's just like any memory now."

Emma spoke. "That's good. Now you're free of it."

Kerry poked around inside her own head as if she were using her tongue to find a sore tooth. "Yes," she said presently. "It's gone." And with it all the pressure that had been working on her all day. Gone, too, was the sense of a presence. All of it, gone, and for the first time since the news had come on that morning, she felt like her old self.

"Thank God," she said. A long sigh escaped her and she started to smile. "All right, that's it. I told you. I hope it helps, but I'm done with it now."

Gage rose and reached to shake her hand. "Thanks, Kerry. I appreciate it. You *did* help."

Chapter 2

Fifteen minutes later, Kerry closed the front door of her house behind her and locked it. Home surrounded her with welcoming familiarity. The smell of burned bacon still clouded the air, however, and she immediately headed for the kitchen to clean up the mess she'd left behind. The congealed grits still sat beside the stove, now in a condition to be used for glue. The blackened strip of bacon looked like a desiccated finger. All of it went into the garbage disposal, and the dishes to soak in hot soapy water.

She used a can of air freshener throughout the house, spraying it freely, because the smell of burned bacon kept trying to carry her back to that morning. She had to get rid of it. Soon a lemony scent had erased the reminder.

From the freezer she chose a prepackaged dinner because she didn't feel like cooking today. Ordinarily she made herself do it because it was healthier, but cooking for one was rarely fun, and tonight she just couldn't face it.

Something in her had changed today, she realized as she carried her microwaved dinner into the living room and reached for the TV remote. Ordinarily she didn't notice the silence of her house, but she was feeling it now, oppressively. Usually she picked up a book, not the TV remote, and only if she didn't have papers to grade.

She had a stack of essays waiting for her, plenty of books nearby, but she needed the companionship of sound, even the manufactured sounds of television. She chose a nature program about birds—the sound of their songs felt cheerful—and tried to focus on the narrator's voice only to discover a gloomy description of the decreasing number of birds in the U.S.

Maybe she'd assign an essay on conservation or the environment next week. Or maybe not. Reaching for the remote, she began flipping through channels seeking anything that would shake the cloud of murk that seemed to have descended.

In the end, though, she quit trying to distract herself. The vision may have loosened its grip, but the fact that it had occurred remained a problem. Instead of looking at this morning's experience directly, though, she chose instead to move back in time, to the moment when she had, as they said, "touched the light."

She'd read all the explanations of the experience,

from both the scientific and religious sides. But none of it could erase or in any way diminish her experience. As much as she had loved in her life, she had never known a love like *that*. Just remembering it still had the power to leave her feeling homesick, the only word she could think of that even approached the yearning she felt for that moment out of time.

Nor could anyone or anything convince her that that love wasn't waiting for her when she died the final time.

She had managed to fit that life-altering experience into herself and her being, and used it as a touchstone, a constant reminder of what she owed her fellow humans, the world as a whole.

But now this. What the hell had happened this morning? Now that she was free of its stranglehold, she needed to explain it somehow. Deal with it. Find a way to slip it into the defined realm of possibilities in her life. Most people weren't comfortable with loose ends and she certainly wasn't.

Apparently, from the reaction she had received—unless Gage and Adrian had been indulging her—she had said something that got their attention. But what did it *mean*?

The sound of the front doorbell replaced silence with cheerful promise. She and her friends observed an "open-door" policy. Nobody needed an invitation or to make a phone call before dropping in.

But when she opened the door, she found not one of her friends, but instead Adrian Goddard. The sight so startled her that she didn't greet him immediately.

"Sorry to drop by like this," he said. "Do you have a minute to talk?"

"Sure," she said after a moment's hesitation. Stepping back, she allowed him to come inside, along with a gust of cold air.

"Winter's not far away," he remarked with a smile that didn't reach his eyes.

"No, but this is my favorite time of year. Autumn is special. Would you like coffee or something?"

"No thanks. I don't want to impose. Just a brief chat."

She nodded and led him to the living room, wincing as she saw her solitary, hardly touched meal still sitting on the coffee table. Talk about revealing!

He settled on one end of the couch at her invitation, and she took the rocking chair that faced him kitty-corner. She reached for the remote and then shut off the TV.

"This isn't official or anything," he told her. In fact, she thought he looked awkward. "I was thinking as I was getting ready to drive home. How hard this must have been for you. What you saw, and having to tell us, then our reaction to it. I just wanted to make sure you're all right."

"All right?" She looked at the table with the microwave tray on it, at the glass of milk beside it, at the TV remote she had reached for because tonight she needed some kind of companionship. She could have called a friend, but that would have meant discussing this morning, the last thing she felt like doing. Then the conversation she wanted to avoid had walked through her door anyway. "I guess."

"You guess? That doesn't sound good."

She shook her head. "No, that's not what I meant. I just found myself wondering what *all right* is. I mean... I've been coming home to this house for eight years, every night. I make myself a dinner, something usually better than this. Friends drop by. Sometimes I cook for all of us or go over to their places. But tonight nothing feels the same. I'm not sure anything is all right anymore."

He nodded slowly. "Life does things like that. Without warning, everything's off-center. It's like you have to reinvent yourself."

"That's a good description." She looked at him, taking in his attractive features. A little flutter reminded her she was a woman. "Tonight I feel like a stranger to myself."

"I know that feeling. That's why I stopped by. I could tell earlier you were having as much trouble with having *had* the vision as you were with what was in it."

She nodded, leaning back. "I sure wouldn't tell anyone else about it."

"That's what I wanted to suggest. Keep it quiet."

She didn't know if she liked that. Frowning, she asked, "Why? Because everyone will think I'm crazy? Because *you* think I'm crazy?"

He shook his head quickly, leaning forward. "I don't think you're crazy at all. Which is not to say I believe in psychics, but I've got an open mind and you obviously picked up on something. But you're certainly not crazy."

"Then why?"

"Because, if word gets around, it might put you in jeopardy with the killers."

Gut-punched. She couldn't even breathe. Stunned, she tried to absorb his words. Wings of panic started fluttering around the dark edges of her mind. Finally she said, "But I didn't identify anyone! I couldn't!"

"Do they know that?"

That was the question, wasn't it? "Are you trying to scare me?"

"I'm trying to protect you."

She couldn't doubt his sincerity. She'd heard that he'd been with the Department of Criminal Investigation before coming here to ranch. Gage apparently trusted him enough to ask for his help in the murder case. But even without that, something in his gaze seemed to reach out reassuringly. "I wasn't planning to tell anyone. Not even my friends. I keep these things to myself when they happen. Although it's usually nothing like this. Usually it's just a quick glimpse of something right before it happens."

He nodded and appeared to relax.

"I only told Emma because I couldn't hold it in anymore, and I trust her. She never gossips. Ever. But I couldn't bring myself to come in alone and tell Gage."

"Yet you felt you should."

She nodded. "It was like a pressure. Like something was pushing me, and it wouldn't leave me alone. Almost like someone was right at my shoulder, refusing to go away until I told you." She shuddered even now at the memory of that psychic push.

That caught his attention. "I take it you believe in the afterlife?"

Where did that come from? she wondered. "Most people do."

"I'm more of an agnostic. I don't know. But...you experienced it?"

She hesitated. Unlike some people, she didn't tell the story often, but rather hugged it to herself. "I don't know," she said honestly. "How could I? It's called a near-death experience, or NDE for short, because those of us who have it come back. The debate is about whether we experienced death at all, or just oxygen deprivation. There are widely separated camps on this."

"I would imagine so. But you must have made your own decision."

She bit her lower lip, searching his face, deciding she saw only genuine interest there. "Whatever I experienced, I have no doubt it was real, maybe more real than this chair I'm sitting in right now. I have no doubt that I had a glimpse of something so beautiful that there's no way I could describe it to you. It changed me. It certainly rid me of any fear of death."

He nodded, absorbing what she said, not immediately leaping forward with questions or conversation. She liked his thoughtful manner. She liked that he gave things time to settle as he took them in.

"I'm not so sure that's a good thing," he said presently.

"What?"

"Not being afraid of death."

At that she couldn't repress a smile. "I'm not jumping from airplanes without a parachute, if that's what you mean. I take reasonable precautions like everyone else. I'm just not afraid of the inevitable outcome of *every* life."

A smile creased his face in return. "Good point."

"We all get there sooner or later. The problem comes when we spend too much of our time and efforts trying to avoid it. I pity people who are obsessively afraid of dying."

"Anything can take over your life," he agreed. "That's a common obsession. Others of us have different ones."

She nodded, wondering if he was taking this conversation somewhere. At the same time, she didn't want him to leave. Earlier the house had felt empty and oppressive. Now it felt as home should. Normal sounds, warmth, friendliness. And she was feeling a kind of attraction she hadn't felt in quite a while. Was he married?

"Let me get you a coffee," she said. "And a slice of cheesecake. I imagine you spent most of the day outside." She paused, filled with the need to know. "Unless you need to get home to your family?"

This time he didn't decline. "No family," he said. "And coffee sounds really good now. It's getting cold out there."

So no family. That pleased her more than it probably should have. As she rose from the rocker, she took her congealing dinner tray to the kitchen, deciding she might as well have some cheesecake, too. Sometimes she needed comfort food, and tonight was a good night for it.

The wind blew some dead leaves against the kitchen window, rattling them as they passed. She stared out into the darkness, but saw only her own reflection in the glass. A lingering whiff of burned bacon wafted past her nose, barely detectable, and soon disappeared in the aromas of fresh coffee and chocolate-caramel cheesecake.

She placed everything on a serving tray, and returned to the living room, setting it down on the coffee table.

"Wow," he said appreciatively as he eyed the cheese-cake. "Did you make this?"

"I get cravings for things like this sometimes. Besides, it's always good to have something like this on hand for visitors."

He smiled as she passed him a plate. "I need to drop by more often."

She laughed, inordinately pleased by the idea. "Just let me know if you mean that. I'll make sure not to run out of desserts."

He dug in with relish and complimented her generously. She sat back in her rocker, nibbling at her own slice, enjoying herself for the first time that day. The shadows that had haunted her had dispelled as if Adrian had brought light with him.

Life went on, she thought. Even when terrible things happened, people had to continue living. It was a hard-learned lesson, after her friends died in the accident. Sometimes she still felt guilty, very guilty, despite her experience of the light and her absolute conviction that her friends had gone to a far, far better place.

"Life has its charms," she said, before she realized she was going to speak out loud.

He looked at her with an arched brow. "It does," he agreed.

But she detected some kind of hesitancy in the way

he said it, a hesitation that convinced her he carried his share of ghosts, too. Maybe that's why he had gently steered her to talk about her near-death experience. Maybe he needed some kind of reassurance.

He rose suddenly, placing his plate and mug on the tray. "Can I carry this out to the kitchen for you?"

"No, no thanks. It's not a problem."

"It's time for me to be getting home," he said. "Tomorrow's going to be another long day."

"Yes." She nodded and stood, wondering why his mood had changed so abruptly.

He started toward the front door, then paused and looked back, his gray eyes serious. "Let us know if you sense anything else. Please."

The request surprised her, but what it hinted at made her shiver. "I hope I never sense another thing."

"I can sure understand why." He nodded, opened the door and disappeared into the dark evening as the door closed firmly behind him.

Kerry remained standing, ignoring an urge to get a sweater, thinking over his visit. It had been odd, she realized, about something other than what she had reported earlier.

But whatever had brought him, she was glad he had stopped by.

She heard the heat kick on, and as she carried the tray back to the kitchen, felt the first musty stirrings of hot air.

Time to put it all behind her, she decided. Today needed to be put on the shelf along with the other mysteries of her life, such as why she had survived an accident that had killed her two best friends.

Some questions just couldn't be answered.

Hours later, after a long, aimless drive, Adrian climbed out of his car in front of the small clapboard house he now called home. Around him spread the small ranch he had bought with his savings just before he retired with disability from the DCI.

The night, undisturbed by city lights, boasted a sky so strewn with stars that it looked like a black sea into which someone had tossed millions of diamonds. The swath of the Milky Way could be seen clearly, and its misty glow provided the answer to why the ancients had often believed it to be a heavenly river.

He loved it out here. The scent of sage and grass outperformed any aromatherapy. The minute he smelled the cool fragrant air, he always felt at peace.

He tried to soak up that feeling now, before entering his house, hoping to banish the day's images of mayhem. Trying to think of something pleasant.

Cheesecake. Yeah, that was pleasant. Good coffee, a cute schoolteacher...

But as soon as he tried to summon the images, reality called him back. Change that to unnerved and unnerving schoolteacher, pretty or not. For the first time he considered the possibility that being psychic could be real and, worse, it could be awful.

He'd had so-called psychics try to provide information before on his cases. On the rare occasions when they were right, no one knew until they'd developed the information through ordinary means anyway. As a result, he hadn't given the idea much thought over the years.

All that had changed in a few heart-stopping moments this evening when Kerry Tomlinson had described several unique aspects of the crime scene, aspects that couldn't have been known to her. Then she had said the bodies had been positioned to send a misleading message.

That statement drew him up short, because it was exactly what he had been thinking about the carefully posed bodies. Something he couldn't prove without a confession, something that on the face of it was a stretch.

Yet she had spoken his own impression aloud, an impression that he had shared only with Gage.

Impossible.

Except that when he looked up at the night sky, he sensed a universe that brimmed with possibilities that no one had yet imagined. Standing with his head tipped back, looking up at billions of suns, millions of which might have planets, hundreds of thousands of which might have life, he couldn't deny any possibility.

Certainly not after today.

Of course, he'd given up on the whole idea of anything being impossible when he'd discovered his own partner at DCI had turned on him. The last person on earth he would have ever expected to betray him. If that could happen, anything could.

Then, on the still night air, he heard two pops from far away. He froze, listening intently, wondering if they had been gunshots.

There could be so many reasons for someone to shoot at this time of night. This was ranch country. An injured or sick animal might need putting down. A coyote might have been preying on someone's sheep or chickens. So many legitimate reasons.

But something made him turn around and get back in his truck anyway.

Kerry turned in the damp sheets, eyes flittering to and fro beneath closed eyelids, her muscles rigid as if fighting to wake her....

"I'm starting to get really worried," Leah said to Georgia. "The guys should have joined us by now."

Georgia leaned closer to the campfire, seeking its warmth. "I didn't think it was going to get so cold so quickly."

"Georgia!"

Georgia looked up, smiling. "Cut it out, Leah. You're driving me crazy. The minute you put Hank and Bill into the woods, they turn into Lewis and Clark. We don't have to get back until Sunday, and neither of them is going to quit until they explore a cave or something. You know that."

Leah rubbed her jersey-clad arms. Her down vest ordinarily proved sufficient, but not tonight for some reason. "Something's wrong. I know it."

Georgia reached for a stick and poked at the fire, stirring up sparks, causing flames to leap higher. "Well, we can't leave the camp. They won't know where to look for us. So you're just going to have to relax until Sunday."

Leah finally quit pacing and came to sit on one of the dead logs they used as benches by the fire. "They always do this," she remarked.

"Exactly." Georgia smiled at her friend. "Every damn time. They say they'll be back by Friday so we can spend the weekend together, and they never make it. So relax. It just gives us more time for girl talk."

Leah managed a tight smile. "How many years have we been doing these trips?"

"Well, I know this is our eighth trip, and we always go twice a year so..." Georgia shook her head. "You know exactly how long we've been doing this. What are you trying to say?"

"I don't know."

Leah hunched toward the fire, wondering why she felt so on edge. This always happened. The guys went off by themselves to take some more rugged hikes while the girls stayed close to camp. The two men always returned late, usually because they'd found something exciting—it invariably surprised Leah what could excite a geologist—and when they marched into camp eventually, they always bubbled over about some find. Meanwhile Leah and Georgia were merely glad to enjoy the break from their jobs and spend a week in the woods with nothing to do but read good novels and relax.

Hugging herself, waiting for the warmth of the fire to penetrate, Leah looked up at the shadowy trees looming over them. "I've always loved the woods at night," she remarked.

"It's primal," Georgia said. She had a tendency to explain everything in life in terms of archetypes, genes and human psychology. That one simply had feelings never contented her. There always had to be a *reason*.

Leah shook her head. "How about I just *like* it?"

"But don't you want to understand yourself?"

"Not to the point that I atomize and pigeonhole everything."

This was an old disagreement, so old that it had become comfortable, and hence provided a good distraction.

Georgia sighed, a sound almost lost in the crackle of the fire. "You have no spirit of adventure."

"Adventure? Analyzing my every thought against some template is an adventure?"

Georgia grinned. "Then what do you think is an adventure?"

"Sitting in the woods at night around a campfire, listening to an owl hoot, and wondering where the hell the guys have gone."

"You *are* single-minded."

"No, just realistic." A twig snapped behind her in the woods and she looked around. "Did you hear that?"

"Yeah. Probably a raccoon."

"Or a wolf."

"Don't tell me you're afraid of wolves. Believe me, they're more scared of us."

"Then bears."

By this point both women were grinning at each

other, building a story from the crack of a branch. "Yeah, bears," Georgia agreed. "A mother and two cubs. Hungry. Annoyed because we're between them and the bacon grease I dumped up the hill this morning...."

"Ooooh," said Leah appreciatively, "that's it."

"Yeah. Are we supposed to run uphill or downhill?"

"I can't remember."

"Some adventurer you are..."

Just then a doe poked her head into the circle of light cast by the fire. Her eyes reflected red at them, and she froze.

"How beautiful," Georgia whispered.

"You're feeling a purely instinctual prey urge," Leah started to tease her in a whisper. "No appreciation of the beau—"

The word never fully left her mouth. Before her very eyes, Georgia's face transformed into a twisted mask as something sprayed from the side of her head. A split second later, a loud crack rent the night and echoed off the cliffside.

Leah froze like the deer had moments before, but the doe chose a different course, darting off into the woods.

Another crack and Leah felt a searing burn in her arm. She looked at it and saw a glistening wetness start to spread.

In the firelight, the wetness looked black.

Before she consciously comprehended what was happening, she turned away from the noise and fled into the night, running faster than she ever had in her life. Faster even than when she had been a sprinter in college.

Her body understood the situation even if her brain didn't...or wouldn't.

She had become the prey.

Kerry, who felt as if she had barely dropped off to sleep, woke up screaming from the nightmare. Even in her own ears the terrified sound seemed to echo. She sat up abruptly, feeling breathless, searching her room for a reason, a cause for the horrifying dream. Everything looked as it always did.

Just a dream, she told herself.

But then she switched on a light, climbed out of bed and began to dress. The compulsion could not be ignored.

Chapter 3

There were a lot of ways to make a living, Gage Dalton thought, that didn't involve climbing out of a warm bed in the wee hours, leaving behind the soft heat of a beautiful wife. His mouth twisted with grim humor at the thought, because all his adult life, with a break for recovery after a car bomb that had killed his first wife and family, he'd been doing exactly this. DEA, Conard County Sheriff's Office, all the same, just a difference in degrees.

The call from Kerry Tomlinson had sounded nearly panicky, and she insisted there was no time to waste. He was halfway down the stairs, headed for the front door when his cell rang. This time it was Adrian Goddard.

"I heard two gunshots," Adrian said. "I wish I could tell you for certain where they came from, but it *seemed* like the same general direction of the vics we found yesterday."

"I'm on my way to the office. Kerry just called me. Something's wrong but she could hardly talk and she said she had to get out of her house."

"I'm already on my way. Another ten minutes."

"See you there."

On impulse, as Gage clipped the phone to his belt, he turned around and headed back upstairs. He went to their son's room, the little boy they had agreed to adopt a couple of years ago. The three-year-old Jeremy at once filled Gage with blazing love and desperate terror. He knew what it was to lose a child. Bringing Jeremy into his life had been an act of faith more difficult than anything he'd ever done.

Peeking in, he saw that the restless child, as usual, dangled one leg over the edge of the bed, and barely had any covers over him at all. Moonlight, thin and weak, barely touched him.

Again on impulse, Gage scooped the sleeping child up. The boy barely stirred. He carried him in to the master bedroom and slipped him under the blankets with Emma.

Emma stirred, murmuring quietly, and with a mother's native instinct rolled over until she was wrapped around their child.

Gage adjusted the blankets a bit, then left as quietly as he could, sending up a prayer for their protection.

He thought he knew evil. He'd sure as hell seen enough horror. But tonight, somehow, he felt there was something even darker stalking this county.

* * *

Kerry waited, shaking, in her locked car outside the sheriff's office. What was taking Gage so damn long? She drummed her fingers nervously on the steering wheel, while the back of her neck prickled as if a predator watched her. No amount of telling herself it was just a dream could erase the urgency she felt. The terror she felt.

And this time she didn't care if anyone thought she was nuts.

At last headlights appeared, slicing through the darkness of the quiet main street. The moon, a mere sliver tonight, shed only the palest light, and the street lights, recently changed to stylish Victorian imitations, didn't seem to do much better. It was as if the darkness refused to give ground.

But at last the sheriff's SUV pulled into the reserved slot and she saw Gage's silhouette at the wheel. He climbed out quickly, after turning off his ignition, and came around to Kerry. She rolled her window down as he bent to look in.

"I think it'd be warmer inside, and I can make us some coffee or tea."

Clenching her teeth so they wouldn't chatter, she nodded, turned her own car off, and purse in hand followed him into the office.

The lighting was dim. The night dispatcher, a young deputy, half dozed at the console. He jumped when Gage and Kerry entered, but Gage waved him to relax. "Nothing?" he asked.

"Not a peep, just the regular check-ins."

"Start the coffee, would you? I think we're going to have a busy night."

At that the young deputy perked up. "I just made a pot. What's going on?"

"I'll know more after Adrian gets here. Just bring us the coffee, please. I need to get Kerry warmed up."

"Yeah, sure, Chief."

In his office, Gage turned on a portable electric heater to add its warmth to the air blowing through the vents in the floor. "Never gets warm enough back here," he remarked. "For myself I don't mind. That's what jackets and sweaters are for, but you look like you need to thaw out."

Kerry nodded gratefully. "I don't think I've ever felt this cold. Ever. And it's not that cold outside."

"Adrian's on his way," he said again as the young deputy entered and brought them coffee. Kerry suddenly remembered she'd had him in English class only two or three years ago. Calvin Henry, that was his name. "Thanks, Cal," she said.

He smiled. "Anytime, Ms. Tommy." The name the students called her. He looked at Gage. "Anything else?"

"Just send Adrian back here. I'll let you know when I know."

Cal nodded and walked out.

"Why is Adrian coming?"

Gage hesitated.

"Gage, please." She needed something, anything, to right her reeling world.

"He heard a couple of gun shots tonight. From the same general direction where we found our vics."

That was not what she needed. Not to set her world right. All it did was cause her to teeter more.

"Two women," she said. "One is dead. The other wounded and running." Her voice rose, almost to a keen. "Oh, God, Gage. We have to get out there! She's running and alone!"

The convoy built as Gage led the way out toward the place where the murders had happened. Deputies and state police pulled off their routes and out of bed created a steadily lengthening train behind him. Kerry, in the backseat, leaned forward and looked between Gage and Adrian toward the dark hulk of the mountains ahead of them.

"Keep watching to the right," she said suddenly. "The women had a campfire. You might catch a glimpse of it."

"How far right?" Adrian asked.

Kerry closed her eyes. "One or two o'clock," she said finally. "I'm not a hundred percent certain, but that's what I keep seeing."

"You got it."

"Tell me about the dream again," Gage said quietly.

"I already did."

"I might pick out an important detail that I missed before."

"All right." Cold to the bone, despite the blast from the car's heater, she forced herself to summon the images that had scared her awake.

"Two women," she said. "Friends. They camp a lot together. They were waiting for someone who was delayed."

"Any idea who?"

Kerry started to shake her head then. "My God! I think they were waiting for the men who were killed. One of them was worried, but the other wasn't. As if...as if these guys are often late getting back to camp."

Gage looked at Adrian. "That's a link we didn't have before."

Adrian nodded. "Anything else, Kerry?"

"Just the same thing as before. I saw the side of a woman's head explode. Then the other one was hit in the arm. She started running, away from the shots. She's cold and terrified, and I think...I think she's hiding. I think she found a place to hide."

"Is she still being hunted?"

Kerry squeezed her eyes shut, reaching even though she didn't want to, trying to pull more substance out of the nightmare that had torn her from sleep. "I don't know. I just don't know."

Gage pressed on the accelerator. "Then we'd better move even faster."

Radios crackled back and forth throughout the trip, ideas shared, plans for the search worked out. No one seemed very hopeful they could find anything before dawn. The night was too dark, and once they got into the woods, it would only become impenetrable.

But dawn was no longer far away.

* * *

Ten minutes later, just as it seemed they were about to enter the abyssal darkness of the woods, Adrian leaned forward in his seat. Then he spoke above the radio chatter. "I think I see a campfire. About two o'clock. I can only catch it out of my peripheral vision, though."

Kerry understood. Once you began operating on night vision, the clearest images were peripheral. She'd first noticed that when studying the sky at night as a girl. Some stars were so faint that you could only see them when you looked far enough to the side.

"There's a fence road up just ahead," Gage replied. "I'll take a right turn on it. Tell the rest of the crew."

The message passed by radio. Two minutes later Gage turned them onto a track that clearly served no other purpose than to allow a pickup to ride along a ranch fence.

"Chester McNair's place," Gage said, as if giving a travelogue.

"That's where the others were found."

"I know. I know. But you've seen Chester and his kids. The only way they could be involved in this is because they let hikers traverse the ranch where it abuts the state forest."

"Why does he do that anyway?"

"Because above that point the terrain gets really difficult to cross. Besides, Chester thinks it helps keep the wolves away from his place. He might be right. Those wolves are so damn shy it's hard to know how many of them we have up there."

Kerry spoke, trying to cling to normalcy even though her heart had begun to hammer. "I have a friend who works in the zoology department at the university. She says they just about despair of finding a number anywhere close to exact."

"They can range these mountains from Texas to Alaska, and beyond," Adrian agreed. "Good for them. We never should have hunted them in the first place."

Kerry decided this reserved ex-lawman could be likable as well as sexy. The thought shocked her, seeming as it did so out of place under the present circumstances. But there it was, as if her brain and body were trying to remind her that life was good, that life continued, that whatever lay up ahead, it didn't have to uproot her from her own reality.

A soft sigh escaped her, because she suddenly wished she could believe her life would ever be normal again.

"There it is," Adrian said, now pointing to the left. Somehow the road had turned them around.

Kerry looked, but wasn't certain she saw more than a dull orange glow up the mountainside a bit. Almost as soon as she looked at it, it vanished.

"I see," Gage said. He immediately pulled the SUV over beside the rusty fence and put on his flashers. Then he aimed his spotlight up toward the woods.

"Roof flashers," Adrian suggested. "In case the woman can see us. To reassure her."

Gage nodded and hit the switch. Instantly, swirling red and blue lights joined the spotlight glare. Behind them, more than a dozen other vehicles pulled to a stop and followed suit.

Gage turned on the seat and looked at the two of them. "I don't want to leave Kerry here alone, so you stay with her, Adrian."

"No," Kerry said, astonishing herself. "I have to come with you. Whatever's up there, I need to see it for myself." Because it would verify her vision? Or because she hoped to find out she was wrong and could stop worrying about visions altogether? She didn't know. "Besides, I may be able to help find the survivor."

Gage looked as if he'd swallowed cod liver oil, but after a couple of beats nodded. "Okay. Just stick close to the two of us, no matter what."

"I'm not crazy. But I have to see."

And she didn't feel as if she could fight what was happening any longer, not if a woman was out there hiding, wounded and terrified.

She'd left her house dressed warmly, and wearing jeans and hiking boots, as if at some level she'd known this would come. At this point she couldn't have said for certain whether her clothing choices had merely been practical in response to feeling cold, or whether something else had guided her.

For better or worse, something had taken over her life. She just hoped it was temporary because right now she felt as if she blindly climbed onto a roller coaster and now all she could do was endure the ride to the finish.

They used the bullhorns first, the amplifiers on the cars, announcing they were police, and they were coming into the woods. Some objected on the grounds that they might scare off the killer. Gage remained firm.

"We have reason to believe there's a wounded woman hiding out there. At this point she's my top priority."

Kerry gave thanks that no one asked how Gage had come by his information. Of course, she realized, word of her vision might already be spreading. Cops gossiped like anyone else.

Regardless, after announcing repeatedly to the dark woods that they were cops, they picked up flashlights and shotguns, spread out and began to climb in a carefully spaced line toward the dull glow of the dying campfire.

With their arrival, the forest had silenced itself, except for one annoyed owl that complained from a treetop up the slope. The distance to the fire's glow didn't seem that great, but the climb was taxing and slowed them down considerably. Not far in space, Kerry thought as her nerves stretched tighter and tighter, but endless in time. The owl continued to comment from the sidelines.

"We probably scared all the little critters into their holes," Adrian remarked to Kerry. "His dinner vanished."

"Most likely." She leaned forward and grabbed a rock for support as the ground turned even steeper for a short distance. The darkness thickened around them, and the flashlights seemed less and less able to penetrate it. Her sense of foreboding deepened with every step. Her heart, already accelerating with exertion, began to hammer.

The law officers, men and women, periodically called to one another, keeping themselves together when a flashlight would suddenly disappear from view behind a boulder or in a gully. They only quieted when they paused to listen for human sounds. A cry for help maybe. And sometimes, as if it appreciated what they were doing, the irritated owl fell silent with them.

But no human voice called out to them. The woods, fragrant with pine and spruce, might have been empty except for them and the owl.

Kerry's reluctance grew. The urge to turn and flee kept rising from the pit of her stomach even as something seemed to keep pulling her forward. She didn't want to be part of this. She wanted to be somewhere else, tucked safely away in sleep, unaware that such ugliness and horror shared the planet with her. Vain wish, she knew, but reading it in the papers was a far cry from this. Dread marched beside her in a way it never had before.

Finally the glow of the campfire came into clearer view. Steps quickened, and from along the whole line of searchers, people gasped for air as they hurried up the steep slope, Kerry among them. Each and every one of them was propelled by the hope of arriving in time to save a life. Any other thought faded into inconsequence.

At the last second, though, Adrian grabbed Kerry and turned her away from the fire, pressing her face into the shoulder of his nylon parka. "You don't want to see," he said.

A part of her wanted to agree with him, but that pressure inside her head was back, demanding, calling, urging. She could no more resist than she could have vanished from the spot.

She pulled her head back, reluctantly stepping out of the protective circle created by his arms. "I've already seen," she said unsteadily.

"Not in real life," he argued gently.

"I think I have."

Turning, she faced the glowing campfire and stepped forward. She sucked a shocked breath.

Not because of the scene, but because she had already seen it so accurately. It was *real*.

The world darkened, leaving only a pinpoint of light, then even that turned black.

Chapter 4

Adrian caught Kerry just as she started to topple. Holding her beneath her arms, he moved her away from the ugly crime scene, just a few feet, just enough to conceal it from her. Then he gently lowered her to the ground, sat with his back propped against a tree, and cradled her head on his lap. The warmth generated by the climb deserted him almost immediately. For the first time he realized just how cold it had become, but the fact barely registered in his concern for Kerry.

She returned to consciousness almost as soon as she reached horizontal.

"What happened?" she asked.

"You fainted."

"I don't faint."

"You just did, sorry to say." He couldn't stop himself from reaching out to stroke her hair soothingly, and was surprised by how silky it felt. Nor could he swallow the concern he was beginning to feel for her. "It's been a rough twenty-four hours," he continued. "I'm not surprised you couldn't take any more. And that was a shock."

"But I'd seen it in my dream. It looked exactly like my dream." A shiver passed through her. "I think that's what's so horrible. It was *exactly* like my dream."

That comment truly gave him pause. Ugly as the murder scene was, he had to admit it would be equally, if not more, shocking to realize you had seen it precisely in a dream. Unfamiliar uneasiness tickled the base of his skull as it struck him that he hadn't fully believed her before. That part of him had held back, not wanting to accept that she really *did* represent something beyond his ken.

Shivering again, she turned toward him and pressed her face against his hip. A sizzle of unwanted excitement passed through him, then submitted to his will. No room for that right now. He patted her shoulder, then rubbed it gently.

"The ground is cold," he said, conflicted by desires to protect and to get some distance. "You shouldn't lie on it longer than necessary."

She nodded. He felt the motion through the denim as he continued to rub her shoulder.

Already the crime scene tape was being strung, and they were within the circle. Flashlights were scouring the ground for evidence of any kind.

Kerry groaned and sat up. Adrian kept a steadying hand against her back. "I'm not done," she said. "There's more here...somewhere."

"What?"

She didn't answer, but struggled to regain her feet. He arose behind her, moving quickly, ready to catch her if she fainted again. But it was as if some kind of steel had stiffened her.

She walked toward the campfire. Gage stepped toward her, as if to stop her, but then halted. Everyone halted, watching Kerry. It was as if they knew something was about to happen.

She tilted her head back, eyes closed, avoiding the now-covered body on the ground. Then her arm lifted slowly and she pointed. "She's out that way. Hiding. She's weak. You have to hurry."

Perhaps even stranger than Kerry's announcement, Adrian thought, was the way not a soul questioned her. Gage gave the order and the searchers fanned out again in the direction she indicated. Gage went with them, after ordering Adrian, Kerry and two officers to remain at the scene.

The wind shifted without warning, probably driven by the warmth of approaching dawn, and the stench of death overcame the smell of the pines. Adrian drew Kerry away, to where the breeze freshened with life.

"Are you okay?" Adrian asked her.

"Yeah." She nodded slightly. "It's starting to let go."

"What do you mean?"

"The compulsion." She lifted her gaze to his. "I don't

know what's worse, the fact that I'm having these visions or the fact that I feel so compelled to act on them. It's like being pressed from behind and not allowed to gain your footing, if you know what I mean."

"Like being pushed by a crowd?"

"It feels something like that." She shook her head and wrapped her arms around herself. "I can't ignore it. And I'll be honest with you, if it saves that woman's life, it's worth it." But she would still have to live with it, and the idea soured her mouth.

"It certainly would be."

"I just hope this never happens again."

He put an arm around her shoulders, telling himself he wanted to help warm her, but in all honesty he couldn't have said which of them he wanted to warm. He had put his judgment about what was happening with Kerry on hold until later, when he could review in retrospect, but it remained he wasn't sure what was happening here, and if they found a wounded woman tonight, he knew he was going to dislike what he would have to believe.

Kerry leaned into him, still holding herself, seeming grateful for the support. The calls of the search team were steadily moving away, upslope. Adrian looked up at the sky, and thought he saw a faint grayness outlining the tops of the dark trees. Soon daylight would answer other questions.

All of a sudden he felt Kerry stiffen.

"What's wrong?" he asked.

She whispered, "He's out there. Watching."

Adrian lowered his voice. "Who's out there?"

"The killer."

Adrian felt the back of his neck prickle. "Where?"

She moved closer. "I'm not sure. I just feel him. He won't shoot now."

"How many?"

She shook her head. "I think only one, but it feels like someone else could be involved, too."

"Hell." He muttered the word and turned her so that she had a tree at her back and him at her front. "Remind me to get you a vest."

"Vest?"

"Armor."

The relative quiet of the scene began to give way to the sounds of people coming up the slope from below. Flashlights appeared, their beams darting around.

"The coroner and the crime scene unit," Adrian said. They came from a neighboring, more heavily populated county. "That was fast. Where do I tell them to start looking for the killer?"

"Don't tell them, Adrian." She shook her head. "Look, it was just a funny feeling. Whatever. I don't even know if he's watching. It came and went in an instant. I don't want to be the county freak show."

"I understand," he said. "So I'll have them secure the scene here. But you'll have to stay with them, and I mean right beside them, because no matter what you say, I have to go out and look for tracks, if there are any. So what direction do I look?"

Kerry tried to lock in on the feeling again, but it was

gone for good. She pointed vaguely. "That way, I think. But I can't be sure."

"Okay. You stay with the coroner till I get back."

Another shudder passed through Kerry as she nodded. "You know, you don't have to protect me. There are other cops around."

"Let me, it's good for my ego." Few things were anymore.

At that, even in the very dim light, he saw her smile.

"It's an awful night," she said.

"Among the worst."

"I don't want these visions and dreams anymore."

"I don't blame you."

"It's awful knowing something and being unable to stop it. Like standing in front of a train."

"I can only imagine." Which wasn't completely true. He'd had a glimpse of that particular nightmare, but only a glimpse, and it still haunted his life.

"But if we get that woman," she repeated without finishing the statement, more to herself than him. As if to remind herself once again that some good might come out of this.

"I guess that would go some way to making this experience a little easier to live with." If anything could. Old bitterness tasted like bile in his throat, but the last thing he wanted to tell her was that some things never grew easier. Ever.

She nodded again, then turned her head to watch the crime scene people arrive and scatter around. A portable generator roared to life. It wasn't long before flood lights and photo flashes punctured the night, and markers began to cover the ground.

Kerry waited with the coroner while Adrian briefly circled through the woods. He returned ten minutes later, shaking his head. He found her sitting against a rock, her face illuminated from the side by all the lights. When she said "Hello," her voice was almost lost in the roar of the portable generator. He couldn't connect with whatever she was feeling, except that it must be like the hunches that had once guided him. He decided that for now he had to trust her as he had always trusted his hunches. There didn't seem to be another choice.

"We'll search the perimeter again when we've got decent light," he said by way of reassurance. "But that guy isn't out there now."

"I know. There're too many people around now," she answered. She leaned her head back against the tree, and closed her eyes. "I don't know how I'm going to teach today."

"You're not. Call in sick. Tell 'em you're helping the cops. Whatever. But you're not going to work."

Her eyes snapped open, weary and red. "Why not? It's not your decision."

"Well, let me put it this way. You said the killers were watching."

"So?"

"So they know you were here. And maybe they know you're not a cop. Maybe these bastards know exactly who you are. No, Kerry, whether you go to work today or not, you're going to be under protection from here on out."

Her eyes widened, whether at the determination in his voice or his choice of epithet, but before she could respond there was a shout from up the mountain. They both tensed, listening, then another shout reached them.

"She's alive!"

The ambulance pulled away with the victim while the sky lightened to a pale blue. Color returned to the world, reminding Kerry that it could still be a beautiful place. The night's horrors seemed to be washed away.

"She's conscious," Gage told her and Adrian as he approached his car where they waited. "Suffering from exposure and blood loss, and pretty dazed, but still conscious."

"Thank God!" Kerry said. For an instant she actually felt blessed to have had that nightmare. But almost as soon as she felt that, she crashed again. She was exhausted, her hands had gotten scraped up during the climb, and all she wanted was for life to return to normal. As if it ever could.

Without another word, she climbed into the backseat of Gage's vehicle and closed her eyes. Fatigue instantly carried her to the borderland between sleep and waking, and distantly she felt the car start and begin to bump down the road. She could hear Gage and Adrian talking, but their voices were quiet and she had no energy to strain to hear them. Even ten minutes ago she would have believed she was too keyed up to sleep for hours, but as soon as the car hit the smoother surface of the county road, her head lolled back and she fell into a deep, dreamless place.

Escape. For a little while. She had absolutely no idea that the discussion in the front seat indirectly involved her.

"I can't do it," Adrian said. "And you know why."

"It's not the same situation," Gage replied. "Look, she's not a criminal informant like the one you worked with before. Giving her protection is a just a precaution, not a necessity."

"I can't do it. You know what happened. I don't trust myself."

"Why? Because your partner lied to you and killed your informant? That's a whole different kettle of fish."

"No, because I can't trust *myself.*"

Gage fell silent for a moment, then said, "Then it's time you learned how to again."

A car door slammed, waking her, then she heard Gage say, "I'll bring it over."

Wanting to groan, she opened her eyes to a bright autumn morning, just as Adrian opened the car door for her. Blinking, she stared at him, trying to place herself in time and space.

"We're at your house," Adrian said. "Gage is going to have someone bring your car back from the police station. Keys?"

Automatically her hand went to her jacket pocket and she pulled them out. "House key," she said, surprised by how dry her mouth felt.

"I'll unlock the door," Adrian reassured her. "The car keys are on this ring as well?"

"Yes."

As Adrian walked away, she rubbed her eyes and yawned.

"I'll call the school," Gage said. "They won't expect you before Monday at the earliest."

"Thanks." At this point she was past wondering what excuse he'd give, and what kind of gossip would begin to make the rounds. Not that it mattered. Gossip pulsed through the arteries of this community like blood, most of it simply newsy, not malicious. Right now all she cared about was a tall glass of water and her bed.

"There we go." Adrian's voice reached her as he came round the car to the driver's side and handed Gage the keys through the window.

"I know you'll take care of her," Gage said. There seemed to be some kind of undercurrent in his tone.

Take care of her? The words galvanized Kerry enough to slide off the seat and out of the car. Her legs felt stiff as she turned and faced her house. The door beckoned her, and beyond it the bed.

She probably should have said something to Gage, but the car door slammed and he drove away almost before the thought formed and reached awareness. Adrian's hand gripped her elbow gently.

"To bed with you," he said kindly.

"Water first."

"Water first," he agreed.

Inside everything looked normal, which for some reason surprised her. She filled a glass at the tap of the kitchen sink and downed it in one long draft before re-filling it and drinking again. God, she was thirsty!

"Thanks," she said to Adrian as she walked past him toward the hallway and her bedroom at the back of the house. "Please lock the door when you leave?"

"Sure," he said.

She couldn't imagine why he sounded so amused, nor at that moment did she care. She fell facedown on her bed without even removing her boots. Tension, it seemed, had taken an even greater toll than a nearly sleepless night.

She awoke during the early afternoon feeling cruddy, filthy and sore all over. Where ordinarily she might have taken a few minutes to savor waking up, she couldn't wait to push herself out of bed, strip off her dirty clothes and boots and climb into the shower. Under the hot, stinging spray, muscles began to ease and her mind began to work.

She was sorry when it did. Last night insisted on popping to the forefront of her thoughts, and she realized reluctantly that she needed to run it over and over until she could assimilate it. That was what she had needed to do after the accident, and the hospital psychologist had told her that was a perfectly normal coping mechanism. Only when it was interrupted did problems arise.

So she shouldn't interrupt it, but she'd like to put it off until after she'd eaten something.

Finally, dressed in fresh jeans and a baggy flannel shirt, with her hair wrapped in a towel, she emerged from her bedroom with one goal in mind: the kitchen.

She stopped in astonishment on the threshold as she encountered Adrian. He was still here. What was more, he was cooking bacon, from the aroma, and had a bowl of beaten eggs beside the stove.

And coffee. Oh, Lord, she needed the coffee.

"Take a seat," he said as if he invited her to her own table every day. "Coffee black, right?"

"Right."

He turned from the stove to grab a cup from the cupboard, and filled it with dark, steaming brew. Then he put it on the table. How did he know where she usually sat?

Somehow he did, and she rounded the table to take her seat.

"I heard you get in the shower," he said. "I figured you must be hungry."

"Starved." She reached for the mug and took a cautious sip. "Mmm, you make good coffee."

"Thanks. How crispy do you like your bacon?"

"Just a little."

"Rye toast?"

"Please."

Sip after sip, the caffeine reached her brain and with it a sense that right now everything was okay. It might not stay that way, but for now she enjoyed the illusion.

She looked at his back. "Heard any more about the survivor?"

"She's going to make it. And she didn't see anything at all except her friend getting shot. She said they were waiting for their husbands to come back from an extended hike. Apparently the men were geologists as well as hikers."

"Does she know yet...about...?" She couldn't bring herself to finish the question.

"Not sure yet," he said, turning with the frying pan to fork strips of bacon onto a plate covered with a paper towel. "She's not too coherent yet, and re-member, we found no ID on the male vics. Can't be absolutely certain."

She shook her head sadly. "Those were their husbands, you know."

"Likely, yeah."

"That poor woman."

"I've got a suggestion," he said as he drained the grease from the pan.

"Yes?"

"Let's think about something else. I found over the years that it's easy to let these things take over your life. You certainly don't need to do that."

"No, you're right," she agreed. "But it's like some-thing I can't shake."

He set the pan back on the stove and turned the flame to low. "Let's work on it. Normalcy must be maintained."

Something about the way he said it made her chuckle, a reluctant sound. Some part of her whispered that she ought to be crying, not laughing and living, and getting ready to eat. "Believe me, I'd be happy to have *every-thing* return to normal. Somehow I don't think it will."

"Eventually it'll feel normal again." He spoke with the certainty of experience, she thought, and took comfort from it. "There's a difference between normal and the same."

"You've got a point."

"Of course!" He flashed an attractive smile and poured the beaten eggs into the pan.

Kerry looked down into her coffee mug, trying to center herself in the here and now. Adrian's presence aided her because she wasn't at all used to having anyone else cook in her kitchen, and most certainly not a man. A good-looking man. A nice man. That's what she needed to focus on, not nightmares and visions.

Besides, she told herself stoutly, she was probably done with that whole mess now, and could resume her usual life. Whatever had connected her to those events was gone now, surely, especially since her connection had seemed to be with the victims, not the killers. Experience had long ago taught her that you couldn't just stop living because something awful had happened.

They ate together at the table. Adrian proved to be a master with eggs, perfectly cooked without a hint of brown to embitter them. The bacon was just right, too, chewy with just a hint of crunch.

"Do you enjoy teaching?" he asked her as he passed her the stack of toast.

"Nothing else could make me do it."

His eyes twinkled. "That bad?"

"No, it's not. I love it. It's just that it requires a lot of patience, a lot of planning, a lot of people skills and the pay isn't that great. If you don't love it, you won't last long. But I guess you can say that about a lot of jobs."

"I imagine so. People certainly don't go into teaching to get wealthy."

"Or ranching."

He chuckled. "Not these days. Like you said, a lot of hard work and the pay is lousy. Not that I'm deeply into it yet."

"What drew you to it?"

"Having a piece of wide-open space for myself."

That struck a chord with her. "That would be so nice."

"It is."

"Is someone taking care of your livestock?"

He tilted his head a little. "I have a hired hand, but I don't have a lot of livestock. I'm not sure how far down that road I want to go. I grew up on a ranch so I wouldn't be a complete tyro, but on the other hand, I left the ranch. Coming back doesn't necessarily mean I want to get involved in the business side. Right now I have a few saddle horses, and some mustangs I adopted and let range free. Beyond that, I haven't made any decisions."

"Sounds nice," she admitted. "A bit of freedom."

"For now. Like everyone else, though, I'll have to figure it all out sooner or later. A man needs to work at something."

"Why'd you leave the department?" As soon as she asked the question, she knew she'd gotten too personal. The man who had seemed relaxed just the instant before, stiffened.

He put his fork down, frowning in a way that deepened the lines on his face. "Some...bad stuff happened," he said finally. "I'm out on disability."

He wasn't telling her something, of that she was sure, but she didn't press any further on it. Hard to believe they had met for the first time only yesterday. Events had conspired to make her feel closer to him than she really was. She needed to keep that in mind.

They washed the dishes together then retired to the living room. The first thing Kerry noticed was the bullet-proof vest lying on an ottoman. "That's not for me," she said, denying it.

"Yes, it is. I had Gage send it over."

She shook her head. "No, I don't think so. I don't need it."

He touched her shoulder with his fingertips until she looked from the vest to him. "Think about it, Kerry. You said the killers were up there watching last night. If they figure out who you are, that you're not a cop, that you're the one feeding us information, do you really think you'll be safe?"

"There's no reason to think they know anything about my visions!"

He shook his head. "Get real. Do you really think *all* those cops are going to manage to keep their mouths shut? Even with the best intentions, if one tells his wife and she tells a friend, it gets all over the county. Or if one tells her husband."

"Adrian!"

"No, think about it. One loose mouth and that's it. And husbands and wives tend to trust each other with stuff even when it's supposed to be confidential. Or one guy trusts a friend. You were up there with us last night.

You pointed out the direction the woman had fled. Everyone was listening to you. Some of the guys may not know why we were listening to you. They may think you're an informant. Either way, if the killers identify you, they'll know you know something about them. And these guys clearly don't care who they shoot."

She didn't want to accept his argument, but with a sinking sensation she knew he was right. If these killers thought anyone might be able to finger them for any reason, that person might well wind up in their crosshairs. Adrian certainly believed so.

And for some reason, she trusted both him and his judgment. Right now, she wasn't sure she trusted her own at all. And while dying didn't frighten her anymore, she was hardly in a rush to do it again. Life still offered opportunities she wanted to enjoy, like eventually marrying and having children, or the look on a student's face when a connection finally happened. Lots of things worth living for.

She dropped gracelessly onto the sofa. "Okay," she said grimly. "Okay. But not in the house." Life may have put her on a roller coaster again, leaving her feeling exhausted and depressed, but her native stubbornness refused to cede every inch of her existence to the horror these killers were creating. If stubbornness was all she had to prop her up through this, then stubbornness it would be.

"And I'm going to stay here," he announced flatly. "You're not going to be alone again until these guys are caught."

At that her head jerked up. "What if I'm not comfortable having you around all the time? What if I like my privacy?"

"You gave that up when you came to us with these visions." There was a fire in his eyes now, a fire that warned her they were getting near to something that made him dangerous. Whatever it was, this wasn't the time. She could see that in every line of him. She smothered an uncharacteristic urge to swear at the impossible situation.

Finally she nodded. "So I'm a prisoner?"

"No. You're under protection."

She grabbed a throw pillow and hugged it. "Then why does it feel the same?"

"Only because you haven't been imprisoned. You can't imagine how bad it really is."

"Cold comfort."

"Yeah, probably." He sat down beside her. "But I can't let anything happen to you."

The word *can't* caught her attention. Maybe because she was an English teacher and very aware of the word's proper use. Or maybe, she thought, because she sensed he *had* used the word properly.

What was going on here? And how long was it going to last?

She might as well have been cast adrift on a stormy ocean, with no land in sight and no compass to guide her. Once again, as after the accident, she felt everything had flown out of her control.

She *hated* that feeling.

Chapter 5

Casino-quality poker chips clattered steadily as the two men sat beneath an overhead light. They liked to play with their chips, riffling them as they considered their next move. Across the table from them sat a woman, filling in as dealer. She was the younger man's wife, but the older man was in control of everything. She had no idea what they were playing for, nor did she care. When they played they weren't giving *her* a hard time.

She was glad to see the older man was heading toward a win. He hadn't been happy the other day when he lost.

A baby wailed from the next room, and she looked at her husband. He nodded his permission, so she jumped up and went to take care of their son.

The two men at the table exchanged looks.

"What was the schoolteacher doing there?" the older man asked the younger.

"I told you, I don't know. But they were all listening to her. I couldn't figure it out."

"You must have screwed something up." The older man stood, shoving his huge stack of chips to the side. "Did you talk to anyone?"

"Do you really think I'm that stupid?"

"See if Cal knows anything. He used to be your friend."

"He still is. I'll sound him out."

"But be careful." The older man pointed to the chips. "I get to choose this time. Make sure I don't choose you."

The younger man froze, then nodded. "Look, man, it's just a game. That's what you said."

"Yeah. Unless we get caught. You already messed it up by not getting both of them."

"She didn't see me. No way. Damn it, she was next to the fire and it was dark. She couldn't have seen anything even if I'd been close, but I was so far away that she wouldn't have been able to see me in broad daylight."

"That's what you say." The older man shook his head. "I told you, it's more exciting than stalking deer. But it's also more dangerous, 'cause these deer can talk. Remember that, and don't miss your next shot."

"I won't."

Finally the older man smiled and returned to the table. Picking up a stack of chips, he began to riffle them. "It's better than going all-in at Vegas, isn't it?"

The young guy grinned. "You bet."

"The ultimate gamble."

"The ultimate thrill."

The two men were still laughing when the woman returned to the room with the child in her arms.

Adrian sat in the easy chair in Kerry's living room, reading a history of the Napoleonic Wars. The floor lamp over his shoulder cast the only light in the room. He'd drawn the insulated drapes over the sheers on Kerry's front windows, ensuring that no one could see into the room from outside.

Kerry herself, apparently able to relax for the first time since all this had begun, had fallen asleep again, this time on the couch. A crocheted afghan covered her, and a paperback book still dangled from one hand. He had thought about removing it, but was afraid he would wake her.

Instead he sat watching her, thinking what a beautiful woman she was. She had the quiet kind of beauty that he had always liked. He also wondered why the hell he'd allowed himself to be pressured into protecting her. He should have learned his lesson on that one. He had no business accepting this kind of trust.

Yet, oddly, he didn't trust anyone else to do it. Or maybe not so oddly, given what had happened with his partner.

At times, the urge to walk out of here before he garnered another nightmare nearly overwhelmed him. Twice he considered calling Gage and telling him to put a deputy on this.

But he couldn't do it. He couldn't turn this woman over to anyone else's protection. If he did that and something went wrong, it would be the nightmare all over again anyway. Any way he looked at it, it was a lose-lose situation unless he brought Kerry safely through this.

But he hardly felt adequate.

Rising, he walked through her small house, once again checking doors and windows, making sure that every possible curtain was drawn. Even with the heavy curtains in most of the rooms, the night's chill crept in through invisible crannies in the old house, stirring up icy drafts. He expected there'd be frost by morning. The first frost.

Just as he was about to walk out of the kitchen, the phone rang. He leaped for the wall set, hoping to catch it before it woke Kerry.

He grabbed it just as the second ring began. He expected to hear Gage's voice.

"Hello?"

Silence. Then a *click,* followed by the drone of an empty line.

He returned the phone to its cradle, frowning. Wrong number? Or something else? His hand hovered over the receiver, but after a moment he decided it wasn't enough to call Gage about. People dialed wrong numbers all the time, and an amazing number of them weren't even polite enough to say, "Sorry, wrong number." He tried *69, but received a message, "Number not available." Okay, then, probably an automated sales call. There sure were enough of those during any given evening.

As he returned to the living room, Kerry was sitting up. "Who was on the phone?"

"Wrong number," he answered with more certainty than he felt.

She nodded and hid a yawn behind her hand. "Sorry, I don't know why I'm so sleepy."

"No need to apologize." He settled into the easy chair. "You've had a stressful time. Stress takes it out of you faster than lack of sleep."

"I guess!" She rubbed her eyes gently with her fingertips. "You're going to go crazy sitting around here with nothing to do except watch me."

He picked up the book he'd been reading and showed it to her. "You have a pretty good selection for an English teacher."

At that she smiled, filling him with pleasure. "I'm a bit of a dilettante when it comes to books. My students may think I only read Shakespeare, Sophocles and Dickens, but the best thing I can say about living here is that we don't have a book store big enough for me to go broke in."

At that he laughed. "But you can order online."

"And I do. But it's harder to just browse there. When I go to the mall my bank account takes a nuclear hit."

"Have you read all those books in the next room?"

"Almost all."

"Wow. I love to read, too, but I've never had a library anything like yours."

She curled her legs beneath her, still smiling, and tugged the afghan around her shoulders. "I go beyond loving to read. I love the books themselves. The way they feel in my hands, the smell of them, the weight of them. I'll probably always be a Luddite when it comes to books. I can't imagine getting the same pleasure from reading an electronic version."

"The younger generation probably will."

"Maybe. But they still use books in classes."

He raised a teasing eyebrow. "And that's supposed to be a recommendation?"

She laughed. "You might have a point there. My sophomores are currently complaining about having to read *Antigone*. I should put it on as a play, so they'd get the impact as it was written, but I don't have the actors."

"Maybe you should appeal to the community. Or the local theater group. I know they usually only manage to produce a couple of plays a year, but maybe some of them would enjoy doing something like that."

She nodded. "That's a great idea. I'd hoped to get students to do it. I'd like to crack a few more nuts than I do now. Literature is important, of course, but reading and writing are equally so, and there are connections there that a lot of kids don't seem to get. It's as if they don't understand how fundamentally important communication is, apart from talking to each other. And texting! That's killing writing."

He gave a quiet chuckle. "Tell you what. Why don't we arrange to bring some of your classes out to my ranch? I've got some great rock paintings out there. Maybe it'll impress them that thousands of years ago the native peoples were leaving messages for each other."

She brightened at that. "I never thought about that."

"It's basically the same thing, in a different medium. Think how critical that kind of communication must have been for them, that they'd go to all the trouble to paint or carve symbols on rocks to pass something along."

She was nodding, clearly liking the idea. "Yeah. It all began with the need to pass information, and it kept growing."

"What's more, it's always been an art form."

Just then the phone rang. It was on the end table beside her, so before he could reach it, she had lifted the cradle to her ear.

"Hello?"

He watched her face drain white, and her hand start to shake. A second later she slammed the receiver down.

"What?" he demanded. "What was that?"

"A man." Her voice cracked. "He said I'm next."

Gage arrived twenty minutes later, accompanied by the former sheriff, Nate Tate. Nate's decision to retire didn't mean that anyone had stopped treating him as if he were still in the job he'd held for more than thirty years.

Nate himself looked hale, his permanently sunburned face lined with weather and the responsibilities he'd held for so long. But he also emitted a warmth that made most people trust and like him.

"So what the hell is going on?" Nate demanded as they all settled in the living room, Adrian on the sofa beside Kerry. "How would anyone know that Kerry has been having visions?"

"The killer watched us at the crime scene," Adrian said. "Or at least that's what Kerry felt."

Nate and Gage zeroed in on her. "You felt him there?" Gage asked. "When?"

"After everyone moved on to look for the woman. I just felt it for a moment. It didn't last long."

"Why didn't you say anything?" Gage asked.

Adrian stepped in. "She told me. But what were we gonna do? Call off the search for the wounded woman so we could hunt in the dark for a killer who didn't want to be found? I made a quick sweep of the area where she thought he might have been, but I didn't find anything. What was left to do, except search more closely at daylight, which you all did."

Nate seemed to agree with this, but he kept silent, deferring to Gage's official authority.

"Yeah," Gage said finally. "Yeah. You're right."

Adrian shook his head. "No, I was wrong. It was your decision to make, not mine. I'm a nobody in this. No authority."

Nate's attention shifted to Gage.

"This isn't about authority," Gage said flatly. "I invited you in on this, and as far as I'm concerned you have as much authority as anyone, just like Nate here. I agree we wouldn't have changed the search, so your decision was right. What wasn't right was that I never heard about it."

"It was just a feeling," Kerry said, feeling a need to defend Adrian, which surprised her. He seemed perfectly capable of defending himself. "And it only lasted a second or so. I wasn't even really sure of it."

"We've been running a lot on your feelings," he reminded her, "and they've turned out to be unbelievably accurate. So just don't keep them to yourself, okay?"

She nodded. "I hope to God I don't have another one."

Gage gave her a half smile. "I would have agreed with you until Adrian called. I was hoping this would be it, and we could settle down to finding our killer. Apparently there's going to be no time to settle down. Not with you in the crosshairs."

"How did she get in the crosshairs?" Nate asked.

"Because she was out at the scene," Gage began, then he paused. "I see what you mean."

"So do I," Adrian said.

Kerry spoke, tightening her hold on the afghan around her shoulders. "Will someone please enlighten *me*?"

Adrian spoke. "There'd be no reason to single you out unless someone fingered you as an informant."

Gage continued. "Exactly. Which means these guys are local, they're afraid someone else knows what they're up to."

"Unless," Nate observed, "someone has already put it out that you're psychic."

"But nobody except us knows that," Gage said. "I think we've been *very* careful with that."

"Except for one thing," Kerry said. "I stood at the scene and pointed out the direction the victim had fled. It was a fresh crime scene. We found no blood trail. No time for the killers to have talked to anyone. So how else could I know where she went, if not for my visions?"

"It's possible, I suppose," Gage agreed reluctantly. "But it's a big leap. It's not like we've ever relied on a psychic before."

"I'm not a psychic."

"At the moment," Adrian argued, "you seem to have been."

"Well, I hope that's the end of it." But did she really? After that call, shouldn't she be hoping she'd sense it if the killers came close to her? Dread, that damned presence, was beginning to sit on her shoulder again. Her heart sped up, uncomfortably so.

"We need to discuss the phone call," Gage said. "Did anything about it catch your attention? Accent? Voice? Background noise?"

Kerry shook her head. "Not really. The voice sounded fake. Like he was trying not to sound like himself. And he only said two words, so it wasn't like I had a lot of time." But the memory of those words sent a chill racing down her spine.

"It could also mean almost anything," Nate remarked. "They'd have to be fools to go after her now. She's been threatened and you're going to put a watch on her, right?"

"It's already been ordered," Gage said. "And Adrian's going to be with her every minute."

"Well, as a rule I've found criminals to be more stupid than they are smart. But this call was really stupid if he meant it. Anybody with two brain cells to rub together would know Kerry's going to have heavy protection after that."

"You'd think," Adrian agreed.

"So maybe," Gage suggested, "he just wants to scare her away from passing any more information." He looked at Adrian. "We'll have the autopsy and CSU prelims by noon tomorrow. Let me know whether you want to come by the office to see them, or have them brought over here. As for tracing the calls, the phone company doesn't keep records of local calls. All they can do is add a tap to your line to keep the numbers of future callers."

Nate and Gage departed a short time later. They didn't have a lot of facts about the case to discuss yet, and no one really felt like indulging in polite chitchat.

That left Kerry and Adrian sitting almost like mannequins in the living room, silent and unmoving.

"You must need some sleep," Kerry remarked when the silence grew too oppressive.

"I've been catnapping all day. I'm fine." He smiled but the expression didn't reach his eyes. "Don't answer your phone again," he suggested. "Let me get it for you."

"No!" The word burst out of her. She didn't even know where it came from, but it was as if a huge bubble of anger and resentment had been lying below the surface and suddenly found a way out.

"No," she repeated, throwing off the afghan and pacing the rug in her socks. "This is insane. I didn't ask for these visions or dreams or whatever they are. They just happened. But in two days, they've taken over my life. I can't go to school, I can't go out, I've got a live-in bodyguard and now I can't answer my phone? I don't think so!"

"Kerry..."

"Did I do anything wrong? Not that I can remember. I didn't commit a crime. In fact, I may have helped save a woman's life."

"There's no doubt about that," he said quietly.

"So why should I have to be locked up in my own house, cut off from even answering my own telephone?" She faced him, spreading her arms. "If you want to tap my telephone, fine. But I'm going to answer it when it rings, damn it. It's still my house and my phone!"

He was nodding. He didn't even smile, which might have led her to believe she was being ridiculous. In fact, he looked as if he understood completely.

Which rather took the wind out of her sails. You can't fight when no one fights back.

She continued pacing, circling the room, working off a burst of unpleasant energy. Cripes, she couldn't even go jogging now.

"How long is this going to last?" she asked the air. She didn't get an answer, nor did she expect one. There *was* no answer. As long as it takes, that was the answer.

Finally running down, she returned to the couch, tucking her legs beneath her and folding her arms across her breasts.

Adrian finally spoke. "It stinks," he agreed.

"Yeah, it does. But I'm acting like an idiot."

"No, you're not."

She glared at him. "Yes. I am. Things happen to people all the time, things they don't want. Like I have more to complain about than the woman in the hospital who was shot? Not likely."

"Feelings don't always give way to logic." He reached out and clasped her fisted hand. His hand was big and warm, even a bit callused, and she enjoyed its comforting touch. After a moment she opened her hand and turned it so that their fingers could clasp. He squeezed back.

"My girlfriends were supposed to come over for dinner tomorrow," she said presently. "I guess I'll have to call it off."

"Why?"

"Because I haven't done the shopping yet. Looks like I can't do it now. Besides, I'm not sure I'd want them to come over here. I'd feel like I might be drawing that madman's attention to them."

She could feel him hesitate. Big, strong and warm beside her on the couch, his grasp on her hand protective, he was still the kind of man who would actually think about how to enable some silly girls' get-together dinner. All the more impressive when he could just agree with her and tell her it was impossible.

Instead he said, "Let me think about. Maybe I can figure out how to make it happen."

She shook her head. "Thanks, Adrian, but I think it would be wiser to cancel it. Maybe we can do it next week."

"It's only temporary," he agreed.

She didn't think either of them believed it at that moment, though. They knew so little and the threat was so big. Who the hell would run around killing people for a *game*? She couldn't begin to imagine the mind-set, yet everything she had sensed so far had given her that impression of these men.

Needing something more stable than the strange

world she'd been inhabiting since yesterday morning, she turned a little and looked at Adrian.

He was already looking at her. She couldn't read his face. It seemed to be carved in stone, as if he were tightly holding something in check. But as their gazes met and held, something changed. The air seemed to lighten and sparkle.

Then, without a word, a question or a warning, he bent his head and kissed her.

Firm lips against soft lips. Just a gentle kiss, nothing more. Not even a hint of passion. Just...something kinder and even warmer.

When he slowly pulled back, his eyes were still fixed on her. The air seemed charged with expectation.

As Kerry continued to stare into his eyes, she felt little sparkles of excitement skipping around her nerve endings as if they wanted to wake her from the nightmare of the last two days. The sensation was delightful, more than she could ever have imagined from a mere touching of lips, but it was also powerful enough to focus every cell in her brain right here, right now, aware only of herself and Adrian a few inches away.

Her world, which had tipped too far into oppressive darkness, seemed to spring back a little, reminding her again that life was good.

She smiled and leaned back on the couch, choosing to rest her head on his shoulder. That didn't seem too forward after the kiss. A kiss that neither of them appeared to want to discuss. The touch had said everything for now.

"You asked about my accident yesterday," she said. "I didn't really answer."

"Well, you did. As much as anyone would want to tell a stranger, I suppose."

"After what you've seen in the last day or so, I don't feel like we're strangers anymore. You've had a clear look inside my warped psyche."

He stirred. "Who said it was warped?"

"Well, most people don't have visions like that."

"How would we know? Most people could have them and never tell anyone because they're afraid of being laughed at."

"I never thought of that possibility."

"Sometimes," he said, "you just know things. I know I do. Me, I call it hunches. Psychologists would say it's a combination of experience and fresh input, causing snap judgments that I don't have to think through. But sometimes it's a bit odder than that. I think it must be for everyone. But it's so easy to call it coincidence."

Kerry nodded, her cheek rubbing against his shoulder. "Yeah. That's what I always called it before. Mainly because it was nothing as big as this. Usually it was little stuff."

"Exactly. So who's to say this isn't just a normal thing blown larger than life?"

"You're so reassuring."

At that he gave a deep rumble of laughter. "Yeah, sure."

She smiled again, even though he couldn't see it, and tried to focus on the past, if for no other reason than to escape today for a little while.

"So what happened?" he prodded.

"Well, it was the end of winter break. A bunch of us had left our families a couple of days after Christmas to go skiing, and from there we were heading back to college. It was on the way back to school that it happened."

She closed her eyes, this part of it etched so vividly on her memory. "The roads weren't bad. The sun was out, it hadn't snowed in a couple of days. But we were busy chatting and laughing, and I guess my friend wasn't paying as close attention as she should have, because the snowmelt was running across the pavement, keeping large patches of it wet. Safe enough until she rounded a tight curve into the shadow of a mountain where the sun hadn't hit the road that morning. She should've seen it, would've seen it if the rest of us hadn't been carrying on like fools."

"That happens."

"So we hit that shaded spot and it hadn't thawed yet. Black ice covered the whole section of road, they told me later. All I remember is that suddenly we had no traction and were sliding across the road. We hit the guard rail and flipped and...I don't remember a thing after that. Apparently the car tumbled down a cliff about two hundred feet. Anyway, an EMT was behind us and saw it all happen. Unfortunately my girlfriends didn't make it. Both of them died at the scene."

"I take it you weren't much better?"

"Apparently not. I had a lot of injuries. Broken bones, cracked skull, a couple of fractured vertebrae. That's why they tell me I died twice before I reached the emergency room."

"Why did they tell you that?"

She moved her head, although not even she was sure if she meant it in denial or something else. "My parents told me. They'd been scared to death and it all just came bubbling out. But I already knew anyway."

"You *knew?*"

She sighed. "I knew. You see—" she gave a little laugh "—this is the point where a lot of people start to back away. Except for the ones who already believe and want to make me into something exceptional. I think the only evenhanded person I talked to about it was the hospital psychologist. She told me the experience was a common one, and until she had it herself, she wasn't going to judge it. She just said to take it for what it was, and if it changed me into a better person, as such experiences often did, then she certainly wasn't going to tell me I imagined it."

"Sounds like a smart lady."

"Very. She helped me through a lot, I can tell you. Right when I needed validation most, she was there."

She felt rather than saw his nod. "Anyway," she continued, "while I was supposedly dead, I was awake. That was the strangest part of it. My body was dead and I was outside it, watching. Detached. I even had the thought that that must be how a butterfly felt about its chrysalis."

"That's really something."

"Yeah. Anyway, I heard them say my heart had stopped, I watched them defib me, try to get me breathing, all of it. I knew it was me they were working on, and I didn't especially care. Because there was something else. Something more important."

"And that was?"

"This feeling," she said. "This incredible feeling I can't even begin to describe. Love, so much love. I felt as if I were floating in a sea of it. And when I turned away from my body, I saw this brilliant light. A light so pure and crystalline I could almost touch it. And then I was moving toward it faster and faster, and I saw people, mostly silhouettes, but I knew them all. I even saw my two friends who were in the car when we crashed. That's when I knew they hadn't survived. I knew it, and I raced toward them, wanting to hug them.

"But then I stopped. I couldn't fly forward anymore. And Ginny, the girl who'd been driving, said, 'Kerry, it's not time for you yet. You have to go back.'"

"I'm getting chills here," he said quietly.

"I do, too, at this part. I said I didn't want to go back. But she said I had to, that I wasn't finished. But she wouldn't tell me what I still had to do. The next thing I knew, I was waking up in the emergency room, hurting like hell, hearing people barking orders to one another. Then, for an instant when I opened my eyes, it was as if they all grew still. As if they didn't believe what they were seeing. Next thing I remember, my gurney was being rushed down a hallway. I guess that's when I went to surgery."

"That is some story," he said quietly.

"Yeah." She sighed, closing her eyes again, reaching back to the aftermath. "I felt so guilty that I was still alive when my friends had died, but at the same time I felt so envious because I knew where they'd gone. It took me a while to work through all that."

"I would think so. Losing friends causes a lot of conflicting feelings."

"Exactly. In the end I was just glad I hadn't been driving. I think if I had been I never would have been able to handle it. But while I was feeling so guilty for surviving, the feeling of the light stayed with me. At first I was resentful that I'd been told to come back. Then I realized Ginny was right. For some reason I needed to stay here. And instead of being resentful, I started to carry a piece of that light inside me. A memory maybe, but a kind of guidepost, too."

"How do you mean?"

She tilted her head up and looked at him. "You can never forget being touched by that kind of love. And when you have been, you know what you need to give back to the world. There's no question after that."

His face had settled into a deeply thoughtful expression, as if he was internalizing what she had told him. She liked the way he responded, seriously, neither dismissing her nor lauding her. It was, after all, just an experience. It certainly didn't give her an edge, and it certainly didn't make her crazy. If anything, it had ratcheted up her conscience in unexpected ways.

Then of course, she had lost her fear of death, which made her a pretty odd bird in most circles. That didn't mean she would recklessly risk herself, but she honestly didn't spend a lot of time trying to avoid the inevitable.

She wasn't afraid, for example, to eat a strip of bacon or an egg when she felt like it, any more than she felt virtuous for eating a salad for dinner. Preoccupation with those things, so much a popular concern, seemed like a waste of time. Everything in moderation was her rule, and then forget about it.

The feeling extended throughout her life, focusing her attention on those matters she believed to be far more important, like the development of her students.

As she had once joked to a friend, God had thrown her back in the pond. Apparently she wasn't ready yet.

"You know," she said a couple of minutes later, "it's weird."

"What is?"

"These feelings I have that I have something I need to do before I die."

"I think a lot of people feel that way."

"Really?"

"Really. The need for purpose is a common human trait."

"Maybe so. But it takes on a little more meaning after you've been tossed back."

At that he chuckled. "I guess it would."

She gave a little laugh, too. "I don't mean to sound self-important. Because I really believe *everyone* has a purpose."

"I wasn't taking it that way."

"Good. But maybe what I'm trying to say is that I'm a little more fatalistic? Like, when my number is up it's up?"

"I can understand why you would feel that way."

"Yeah, I guess a lot of people do from what the psychologist said. But at the same time, it makes me more grateful. I'm not saying I'm perfect by any means. I still take things for granted. But it has certainly refocused me."

He touched her chin with his forefinger, gently lifting her face until they could look at each other. "You don't need to explain. I've got a pretty good idea what you're talking about. Part of the reason I retired was that I couldn't spend another day dealing with the underside. I needed to get into the fresh air and sunshine and remember that the world is a good place. Getting wounded was a good excuse."

"How badly were you hurt?"

"I've recovered." He withdrew his finger from her chin, making it clear he wasn't prepared to venture into that territory.

"You stay here for a few minutes," he said, rising. "And don't answer the phone."

"Where are you going?"

"I'm going to walk around outside and make sure everything's in place. Then I can doze off in a chair for a little while."

The door had shut, she realized. Whatever chasm they'd been crossing, the drawbridge had just closed with a loud bang.

Chapter 6

"That was a stupid move," the younger man said, his voice rising nearly an octave. His eyes had a wild look.

"Shut up and listen!"

"But that phone call warned them. They'll have cops all over her now."

"That was the point."

The younger man's jaw dropped. "You're crazy."

"I've been right so far, haven't I?"

The younger one nodded reluctantly. A kind of misery had framed his face, but there was something else there, too. Something excited.

"Listen," the older man said. "Hunting is great when the animal doesn't know you're there. But it's a helluva lot better when the quarry is on guard. Ready for you.

Ready to run. It's a bigger challenge and it makes it so much sweeter. Trust me, I know."

The younger man hesitated. His friend had been right about everything so far. And he had to admit he liked the power he'd felt when that woman's head had exploded. His only disappointment had been that it was too dark to chase the other one successfully.

"Okay," he said finally. "Okay. But you better have an idea how to do this."

"I have lots of ideas. One thing I know for sure is we can't go after anyone else until we get her out of the way. Not if what your friend told you is right."

"I'm not sure he knows what he's talking about. It sounds so crazy. Besides, even he thought it was a pile of crap."

"Except that she was there. You saw her. And they listened to her."

The young guy shrugged. "Yeah, I guess."

"So she's next. And we'll do it together."

At that the younger one seemed to brighten. It didn't sound so impossible now.

In the morning after breakfast, Kerry called her friends to postpone the weekly dinner. All of them were understanding but Joyce and Marybeth wanted to come over anyway.

"Please don't," Kerry begged. "I don't want you to get into the middle of this."

"In the middle of what, for heaven's sake?" Joyce

said. She was always the most assertive of the group, ever since they'd met in kindergarten.

"I can't tell you," Kerry said firmly. "I can't. All I know is that you'll be in danger."

Joyce fell silent for several long seconds. Finally, "Kerry, are you in trouble?"

"Not in any way you can help. Honestly. The sheriff is taking care of everything. I just don't want you all involved in any way."

"That's not how our gang works, Kerry."

"It has to this time. It *has* to. If you come over here, things might get worse."

That was the argument that silenced Joyce at last. "All right. But when this is all over I expect every single detail."

"I promise."

When she replaced the receiver in the cradle once again, she turned to find Adrian standing in the doorway, arms folded as he leaned against the frame. "You have some very loyal friends."

"I'm very lucky. We've been friends since we were little kids."

He arched a brow. "Always?"

Kerry had to smile. "Oh, there were times we went our separate ways. Plenty of them. College was the longest. But we always get back together again. It's like gravity. You're eventually going to come back to earth."

"That's pretty special."

"Yes, it is."

"How are you doing?"

Her smile faded about two degrees. "Well, there are lots of ways I could answer. I'm well. I hate being locked up like this. I'm worried that I may not be able to get back to work on Monday. I'm disappointed I can't have my friends over, and I think I already have a touch of cabin fever."

"That's pretty encompassing." He smiled broadly.

"So which 'doing' did you want to know about?"

At that he laughed. "Okay. I got my answer."

She joined his laughter. "Sorry, I was being a pain. I'm always telling my students to be as specific as possible in their writing. Not to leave room for doubts or confusion. And since I spend all my professional time hammering that, I'm probably too sensitive to ordinary courtesy questions."

"I wasn't just being courteous. I really wanted to know. On the other hand, I wasn't expecting a verbal joust."

She laughed again. "Good luck. You can take the teacher out of the school but you can't take the school out of the teacher."

His shoulders shook with amusement. "I imagine you can't stand the question 'How are you?'"

"Now there's an open-ended one. Do you take it as a question about the general state of your life or only your existence at that particular moment? Either way, nobody wants a real answer."

"Yeah, just the 'I'm fine, and you?'"

"Exactly. So when some of my students argue those things against me when I demand specificity, I tell them there's a whole lot of difference between a courtesy that helps grease the cogs of society, and writing a paper or trying to make a point."

"Good point, teacher."

She gave a mock bow. "Thank you."

The wind chose that moment to gust against the side of the house. Old wood creaked an aged protest, and in places the curtains stirred as air snaked through hidden cracks. Just as the house stopped creaking, the sunny day darkened. A cloud had moved overhead.

"This is one of the things I love most about autumn," Kerry confided. "The way the weather can be so changeable. One minute bright sun, the next a cloud darkens things."

"Does that fireplace in the living room work?"

"Actually, yes. I had the chimney cleaned a couple of months ago, too."

"Wood?"

"There's a stack by the back door."

"Then what do you say we light a fire? The weather forecast is for cold and rain."

"That does sound cozy. Should I make hot choco-late or soup?"

"Maybe later. Let me get the fire going first. Then we can watch a movie or play cards."

He was trying to entertain her, she thought. Then she realized she wasn't the only one trapped in this house for the duration. They both needed a break.

Deciding it might be time for some B movie with lots of monsters and plenty of unintended laughs, she went to search her DVD collection. There could, she reasoned, be some good points to being locked up in her house with an attractive man.

It was certainly something she hadn't tried in a long time.

Rain fell steadily, heavily. Thunder rumbled in the distance but never seemed to draw closer. Inside, with a nice fire and *Tremors* on the TV screen, life seemed pretty good.

It seemed even better to be holding hands, and Kerry wished she had the nerve to press the issue further, like turning into him and kissing him. Instead she kept her gaze trained on the screen and tried not to notice how good he smelled, and how beckoning his body heat seemed.

She could, she thought, develop a real crush on this man. Unfortunately, that would be unwise until she found out what was behind that door he had slammed shut.

Not that her hormones cared. Heck no. They'd have been happy with a rough and ready tumble in the hay. Right now, they kept her in a state just below true arousal, somewhere around a tentative range that would take only one spark to set off the blaze. Every now and then she had to recross her legs to try to minimize the subtle ache at her center.

He was so attractive, she thought dreamily, forgetting everything else for now. So attractive. The aromas of man and soap combined into a heady mixture, and the feeling of calm strength he exuded called to her.

Only when you've been on your own for a long time, she realized, could you truly appreciate what it felt like to not be alone. Or could you truly realize how nice it could be to let someone else take charge for a bit.

She didn't feel weak or anything. But she liked being able to let go of the burdens for a bit. Liked forgetting every damn thing, knowing the man beside her was there to protect her from disaster. A brief break on the road of her life, to be sure, but one she welcomed.

It was, she thought with an inner laugh, almost like abandoning adulthood for a while.

But no, that definitely wasn't her, and besides, what she was feeling right now classified as adult. Definitely adult. R-rated. Potentially X-rated.

She stole a glance at him from the corner of her eye. He certainly seemed to be involved in the movie. That was fine, but at the moment she wished she'd picked something else. Something a little more suggestive. Something that fit her tingling nerve endings better.

A gust of wind rattled the windows again, another rumble of thunder in the distance. If there was any lightning, it failed to penetrate the heavy curtains.

"I love this movie," Adrian remarked with a laugh as it neared its climax. "I never get tired of it."

And something rattled at the windows.

At once Adrian stood up, movie forgotten. "Stay right here," he said. "I'm going to check things out."

She realized he was hyper-alert, more than she would have expected, actually. Yes, she'd had a threatening phone call, but Gage had put deputies on watch, and surely Adrian or she would hear if anyone tried to get inside.

So why was he so edgy?

Something rattled against the front window again, and she thought it sounded like sleet. She wanted to look but restrained herself. And at that instant she realized this situation would become intolerable before long. Not able to look out her window to check the weather? Not able to pop out to the store when she felt like it? Watched every minute?

But she'd already had her little temper tantrum. Having another would be beyond childish. Besides, all she had to do was remember what she had seen in her visions and in the woods to know there was no room right now for irresponsibility or childishness.

But that didn't mean she had to like it.

The petulant thought leavened her mood a bit, and while the rattling against her window intensified, and the wind decided to imitate a banshee, she listened to Adrian's footsteps as he moved through her house.

When he returned she raised a brow. "So, did anything unlock itself?"

For an instant he appeared taken aback, then he gave a laugh. "No, of course not. I was just being extra cautious. It's sleeting. Maybe we should check the weather."

She flipped to the weather station with its familiar faces and they waited for the local forecast. Winter was moving in almost before autumn had begun. Snow was on tap for the night.

She looked at Adrian. "That's good, isn't it?"

"I think so. We've already warned people to stay out of the woods, but the snow should deter even the diehards."

Kerry nodded agreement. "I think we can take a

breath and relax." Rising, she announced she was hungry. "I'm going to go make us something. Any preferences?"

"Whatever you feel like."

In the kitchen, by herself at least for a minute or two, she opened the refrigerator door and tried to decide what she could make easily and quickly that wasn't a frozen dinner. At the moment, she was low on supplies, as it was just about time for her to do her weekly shopping.

Finally she settled for heating a couple of cans of chili—always good on a cold night—and dressing it up with some cheese and tortilla chips. Sleet battered the windows periodically, sounding like the rattle of claws.

All of a sudden she felt uncomfortable. It was as if something dark had moved into her kitchen, something just beyond the reach of her five senses. Ordinarily this was about the coziest room in the house, but right now it didn't feel cozy at all.

She grabbed a tray and carried the supper out to the living room where she set up wooden TV tables for each of them. With the fire burning cheerfully, the uneasiness that had found her in the kitchen drew away. The chili was warm and satisfying in a way only a few things could be on a cold stormy night. Like a warm blanket, but on the inside.

The weather still filled the TV screen, but the muted audio got lost in the sounds of the crackling fire and the wind outside.

Kerry spoke. "It must have been something, working for the department."

"Why do you say that?"

"Well, it's sort of like the state FBI, right?"

"In some ways. But this is Wyoming, remember?"

At that she laughed. "But we have our own share of crime. Admit it."

"That's true. Just on a smaller scale usually."

"Well, we wouldn't need them if local police could handle everything."

He looked amused. "What do you want to know?"

"Oh, I don't know. What the work was generally like."

"We helped local law enforcement a lot in counties where they couldn't afford all the bells and whistles. We joined investigations that crossed county lines. And occasionally we had some really big stuff, like rustling."

She nodded. "I think you're minimizing your role."

"I think I'm not blowing it out of proportion."

She laughed. "Okay, okay."

"A lot of it was pretty humdrum, Kerry. Most investigations are. If you followed the average investigator for a month, you wouldn't get half the excitement you can get on a TV show. In fact, you might mistake us for clerks."

"Oh, come on..."

"I kid you not. You talk to a lot of people, you take a lot of notes, you spend hours on the phone and you try to put puzzle pieces together. That's most of it. Once in a great while you get something much bigger. Like the time a few years back when we learned that cocaine was being shipped in cattle trucks, buried under the manure."

"Oh! I think I remember that!"

"It was interesting enough to make the news," he agreed. "You know how bad a cattle truck smells."

"Oh, yeah. I was picnicking at a rest stop one afternoon on my way to Helena to visit a friend. Just as I started eating my sandwich, a cattle truck pulled in."

He laughed. "I feel oodles of sympathy."

"You should. My God, the stench. The place was basically just a roadside turnout with a couple of tables. I still don't know why that trucker had to stop *there*. But he did and I couldn't even swallow. So I left and waited until I got to Helena to eat."

"It's certainly a rich aroma. But that was basically the idea. Haul the cows and the coke across the Canadian border, and cover any possible scent the K-9's might detect with that wonderful, unforgettable...aroma."

"Did it work?"

"Nobody even thought of it until we got a tip. That's when the fun began. We had to find a cattle truck that was actually transporting the stuff."

"Oh, Lord."

"Exactly. It was definitely a...crappy job."

She laughed. "So how'd you solve it?"

He gave a quiet chuckle. "Out tipster got us information on a specific shipment. Thank God. I thought I was never going to get the smell of those trucks out of my nose."

She joined his laughter. "But what a clever idea!"

"It was. It most definitely was. But after we stopped that one truck we found out something fascinating."

"Which was?"

"The dogs could still smell the cocaine. Despite all that overriding odor. Most amazing thing I ever saw."

"Dogs are incredible."

"I couldn't agree more. I got to thinking it was like a partnership. The dogs made up for our lacks. We see better, but they smell so much better."

"Sometimes, too, I think we get misled by our eyes."

"Yeah, we do. But it's not easy to mislead a dog with odors."

The wind whistled with renewed strength and they paused, listening.

"I'm glad I don't have to go out tonight," Kerry said. "It sounds unfriendly out there."

"Decidedly so."

That's when she realized that dark feeling was coming back, the one she'd had in the kitchen. What was going on? She'd always been perfectly comfortable in this house. Even all alone, everything seemed welcoming.

But tonight... Tentatively she looked at Adrian. "I'm feeling something," she told him hesitantly.

He cocked a brow. "Feeling something?"

"Something...dark. It's making me uneasy, silly as it sounds."

"After the last two days, nothing you feel sounds silly to me. Can you figure out what it is?"

"No. I don't like it. I felt it in the kitchen while I was heating the chili, but when I came in here it was gone. Now it's coming back."

He moved his table to one side, meal half eaten. "I'm

going to check outside. Lock the door after me, and resist any urge to look out, okay?"

"Adrian..."

"It'll be okay. Trust me. Just do what I said."

Chapter 7

Not that he trusted himself all that much, he thought as he pulled on his jacket and shoved his feet into his boots. But he also couldn't trust anyone else. He'd learned that lesson the hard way. When you couldn't even trust your own partner, who could you trust?

He stepped out the front door into the early autumn night and the gale, waiting until he heard the lock turn behind him. Sleet stung his cheeks, and an unusual icy rime was beginning to build on tree branches. Not normal weather at all for this part of the world. Usually it was too dry here for this, and dryer than ever when it grew cold.

Street lights danced off the building ice, giving the world a glittery look. The wind had ripped most of the leaves off the deciduous trees in just the last couple of hours, leaving bony, icy fingers behind, and only a few hangers-on.

The deputy's car was still parked two houses down, in a puddle of darkness between two street lights. He doubted the guy was even getting out of his car to walk around now. This was a night for all living things to find shelter. Still, he'd have to say something.

He stepped off the porch and began to walk around the outside of the house. It was darker, of course, once he left the front, but he was glad to see that little light emerged from the house in cracks around the heavy curtains. It wouldn't be easy to guess where Kerry was by the lights. And it would be impossible to look in.

The browning grass, icy now, crunched beneath his boots. Silent approach had become impossible. He paused frequently to listen, but little could be heard over the wind. Another spray of sleet stung his cheek and caused him to close one eye.

It only took him ten minutes to walk around the house slowly, checking every shadowed spot. Nobody had been out here since the sleet had started though. His own footprints were as clear as neon signs right now.

No one was out here. No one. He headed down the street to the patrol car, bent on asking the deputy why he hadn't taken a walk around like he was supposed to. He could understand not wanting to get out of a warm car in this weather, but the man still had an assignment to perform.

His long strides carried him past the front porch of

Kerry's house just as she flung it open and called his name. He whirled at once.

"I thought I told you to stay inside."

"Something's wrong, Adrian. Terribly wrong. I can feel it growing."

Words seemed to fail her at that point. He looked at her figure, silhouetted against the bright doorway, the sleet catching fire as the light struck it.

"Get inside and close the door," he ordered her. "No arguments. I'm on it."

To his vast relief, she obeyed him, closing the door with a thud. He thought he heard the snick of the lock.

No one appeared to be out in this miserable weather. From end to end, the street seemed empty except for parked cars. Even the shadows had lost some of their depth and darkness as the sleet splintered and spread the light around.

Shouldn't the deputy have at least gotten out of his vehicle to see what Adrian was doing prowling in the yard?

Dread, no stranger to a cop, returned to its familiar perch at the edges of his mind. When he reached the driver's side of the car, he couldn't see anything inside. The windows were steaming up, including the windshield. What the hell? Why didn't the guy have the defroster on?

He pounded on the window, feeling the stirrings of an anger he hadn't felt for a couple of years now. Not since that night in Gillette... He brushed the thought away and pounded on the window again.

"Deputy!"

Finally the window started to roll down and he found himself looking into a young, drowsy face.

"Have you been sleeping?"

A shame-faced look answered him. "I didn't mean to. The last thing I knew I was awake...."

Adrian stifled a frustrated sound and bent down to look straight in at the guy. "If you can't stay awake, call for a replacement. If somebody goes for the teacher tonight and you're asleep, they might take you out, too."

At that the young man completely woke up. His eyes were suddenly wide and clear.

"Now get out of the car, lock it and come for a walk around with me. It'll get your blood stirring. Then call for relief and stay awake until it gets here. Got me?"

The man nodded. He rolled up the window, then climbed out of the car and locked it.

"Let's go," Adrian said. "Something's wrong, and I'm not sure it was just you sleeping."

"I'm sorry," the younger man said. "I can't believe I did that."

"It's easy with the car heater on," Adrian said a bit more amiably. "Stakeouts are hard at the best of times." He looked at the deputy as they walked toward the yard. "Cal, isn't it?"

"Yes, sir."

"We'll pretend this didn't happen."

"Thanks. I appreciate it."

"Okay," Adrian said, stopping them at the driveway.

"The only footprints in the yard around the house should be mine. I followed a pretty straight path, so they won't be scattered around. If you notice anything else, sound out."

"I will."

At that moment, a dog down the street started barking, penetrating the otherwise quiet night.

Adrian stiffened, and felt Cal do the same.

"Cat?" asked Cal.

"I don't know. Let's keep together and make a quick tour around." He was rewriting the plan in his mind quickly. "Then we're going to go inside together. You can call for backup from there."

Cal paused midstride and looked at him. "You think something's wrong."

"Didn't I say so? Call it a hunch. Something's not right."

Another dog took up the frenzied barking of the first, this one closer. That did it. Adrian decided to skip circling the house again. Instead he motioned Cal to the porch and knocked. "Kerry? It's me."

An instant later the door opened and she peered out. "What's going on?" she asked as she saw Cal.

"I don't know." He looked at the deputy. "Get inside. Kerry, put on that vest. Cal, show her how. I'm going to look around some more."

"But..." Kerry didn't look as if she liked this.

Adrian shook his head. "You said something was wrong. I feel it, too. Now just do what I asked, would you?"

As soon as she nodded, he closed the door on both of them. "Lock it," he said. He heard the bolt snap into place.

Then, reaching under his jacket, he felt for the snub-nosed .38 he carried everywhere, because once you'd been a lawman, there was always someone who wanted to get you. It was usually invisible under jackets and sweatshirts, except at the height of a summer day. Most people probably never even guessed he went everywhere armed.

Revolver in hand, he started once again to circle the house, listening to the dogs, trying to discern their message. When another one started barking, he froze in his steps, sleet stinging his face, listening intently. On a night like this, dogs should be inside. Some people had apparently forgotten that.

But were they just stirring each other up? Or were they reporting a prowler? More than once in his life he had wished dogs could talk. They perceived a different world, and much more acutely than any human could.

By the time he had circled the house again, the barking had begun to abate. Either owners were rescuing their animals from the cold, or the disturbance had passed.

He still didn't like it.

Returning to the front of the house, he climbed onto the porch and stood scanning the neighborhood. Sleet sparkled in the air like falling diamonds, but nothing in the shadows moved. Finally he turned and knocked. Cal let him in.

Kerry sat on the sofa, wearing the vest, looking half disgruntled and half frightened.

"Nothing out there that I could see," he said.

"Can I take this thing off now?"

He cocked his head to one side, rising on his toes to try to restore circulation to them, and half smiling at her. "You said something was wrong. Do you still feel that way?"

She hesitated, then shook her head. "I don't feel anything anymore."

"Good. 'Cause I don't feel anything in my feet, either. It's cold out there."

That evoked a smile from her. He looked at Cal. "Did you call for relief?"

He nodded. "Should be here in fifteen minutes or so."

"Good. Go ahead and relax until he gets here."

"I can't figure why I dozed off like that," Cal said. "I'm usually a night owl. That's why I volunteer for night shifts all the time."

Kerry spoke kindly, even as she was trying to undo the Velcro tapes holding the vest in place. "We're all a little wired and tired after the last couple of days, Cal. Darn, this thing is heavy."

"But warm," Adrian observed.

She scowled at him, but then a little laugh emerged. "True. I'm certainly not cold."

He bent over and helped her yank the tapes. Armor was something you had to don and doff a couple of times before you got used to the method, even though it was basically simple. Then he helped lift it over her head and put it on the couch beside her.

"I can't imagine having to work in one of those!"

Both men answered at the same time. "You get used to it."

"I guess."

Adrian saw her try to smile, but the brief moments of humor had fled. He could certainly understand why. The lurking horror didn't leave room for much else.

A knock on the door summoned him, and he opened it to find Deputy Virgil Beauregard waiting. Beau, as he was called by friends, had been on the force long enough to considerably relieve Adrian's concerns.

"I'm here to take over," Beau said in his easy drawl. He looked past Adrian. "You go on home, Cal. The roads are getting really dangerous."

"Thanks, Beau," Cal said as he slipped past the two men. "It's an awful night."

"Worse than awful," Beau remarked. He pulled the fur collar of his heavy jacket up tighter around his neck. As soon as Cal got into his car, he returned his attention to Adrian.

"I don't know if that boy has what it takes. It's not that damn late."

"I know. But he's still young."

"Young enough to get his butt killed." Beau shook his head. "I walked around the house. Two sets of footprints. Yours?"

"Mine."

"Okay. I'll be in the car if you need me."

Kerry had come up beside Adrian. "Do you need any coffee or food?"

Beau smiled at that. "Ma'am, my wife sent me out with enough coffee and food to get me through a week." He touched the brim of his hat. "Have a good night." He turned to go back to his car.

Adrian waited until he saw the deputy get safely inside his vehicle, and only then closed and locked the door.

"I feel better about that," he remarked.

"He's a good deputy," Kerry agreed. "He's always been great about coming to the school and talking about law as a career field. The students really like him."

"I don't know him all that well, but from what I've seen he seems to be capable and levelheaded."

"I agree with that."

The conversation tapered off, though. There seemed to be little to say, possibly because there was little enough they could think about except the killings and the threat against her.

But it was all she could think about, her brain running like a hamster on a wheel.

She shook her head, clearly not really meaning anything by it, perhaps responding to the entire situation. "I don't get it."

"Get what?"

"Why this happened. Why *I* had those visions. What good did they really do?"

"How can you ask that? Without you, we'd never have found that woman in time. She would have died out there one way or another. We've already discussed this."

Her head jerked a little. "You're right. I'm being selfish."

"I can sure understand why. Nothing wrong with it. I get selfish, too."

She looked at him, one corner of her mouth lifted, though it was a poor attempt at a smile. He felt something in his chest tighten, and he wished he could wave his hand and erase her worry. "Nooo," she said sarcastically.

"Yesss," he repeated in the same tone, then shrugged. "I didn't want to be responsible for your safety."

She started to stiffen, and he was certain she would tell him to leave then, but he squeezed her hand. "Not because of *you*," he said quickly. "Because it scared me."

She turned a little to see him better, but left her hand in his as if she took comfort from it. "Really?"

"Really." He hesitated., wondering why he felt compelled to bring this up now. All he knew was that he needed for her to understand him better. At the moment, with the words hovering on his lips, he didn't want to think about what that might mean. It was enough that at some level he needed her to know. Needed to make a connection with her that he had long refused to make with anyone else. The words nearly erupted from that need.

He said, "I don't tell many people about what happened, but it wasn't just a wound that made me take early retirement."

"No?" Her expression grew intent, caring.

"No. There was something else." He shook his head. "Sorry, I still find it hard to talk about, although I'm not sure why. Basically what happened was that I had an informant. He called me in a panic, telling me they were after him, that I had to pull him in before they killed him.

So I headed over to his place, and had a flat tire on the way. I'll never forget how impatient I got. It wasn't like I was somewhere I could just call a cab. We were out in ranch country. Anyway, I changed the damn tire as fast as I could, cursing all the while, then floored the car to get to his house."

"You were too late." She squeezed his hand and held on tight.

"Worse than that. I was barely too late. And because of that I found out my partner was in league with the bad guys. He had just killed my informant when I walked in. After that...well, it's a blur, but my partner's dead and I was wounded pretty badly. I just managed to call for help."

She nodded slowly, holding his gaze. "So he betrayed you, and you failed your informant."

"Basically, yeah."

But the description, accurate as it was, failed to convey the emotional reality of it. "I was a mess for a while, and not just from the bullet. My *partner*, for the love of heaven. My partner. The informant trusted me, and all the while the guy I trusted with my life was a traitor. So my informant, hardly more than a kid really, maybe twenty-two, was dead because he trusted me."

"You can't blame yourself for that."

"Logically, no. Emotionally is a very different thing."

She nodded slowly and laid her other hand on his knee. "I can understand that."

"Can you?" A harsh, bitter laugh escaped him. "I'm not sure I do. Anyway, when Gage asked me to stay with you I couldn't quite...feel comfortable about it."

"You're afraid you'll fail me, too."

"Of course I am. And now we're looking at a situation where someone may have said something they shouldn't have, which put you at risk."

"The nightmare all over again."

His chest had squeezed tight, but he refused to give in to the welter of emotions that wanted to overcome him. Her voice and face conveyed such sympathy for him that he almost felt embarrassed.

"I don't want to be a baby about it," he said after a few beats.

"I don't think you're anywhere near being a baby about it. Once burned is twice shy, cliché or not. And you got a double burn. There'd be something wrong with you if you weren't uncomfortable having to protect me in this situation."

"Maybe so." He still felt as low as chicken droppings, though.

"No maybe about it. To this day I avoid driving on mountain roads in the winter. I'm so scared of black ice even thinking about it makes my heart race. We're getting to the time of year when I become a homebody. No, I'm not afraid of dying. But I *am* afraid of having another accident. Does that make sense?"

"It does to me." Without giving it a thought, he leaned back on the couch and slipped his arm around her. It felt good when she leaned into him and put her head on his shoulder. How long had it been since he had held a woman like this? A long time. Too long. Had he been avoiding women to punish himself?

The question caught him unawares, and for an instant he had that odd feeling of standing outside himself, seeing himself from a different point of view—a perspective so different that it approached a complete personality shift.

"Adrian?"

He looked at her.

"Are you okay?"

He realized that his momentary start must have conveyed itself to her. "Just reevaluating something about myself."

She nodded and snuggled her head against his shoulder, leaving him with his thoughts.

How many women in his life had been willing to do that? he wondered. Not many, if any. Just as men wanted a solution to every problem, women seemed to want an emotional therapy session that picked over every detail as if that would make it better.

Not this one. She seemed to understand that when he was ready he would speak...or not.

Oddly comforted by the simple offer of quiet companionship, he lowered his head to one side until it rested against her silky dark hair. She smelled so good. With that thought, he closed his eyes and gave himself up to the moment.

There were times, he thought, when it felt sufficient just to be alive.

Kerry would have thought it impossible, after sleeping so late, and with so much tension, to doze off. But somehow with Adrian's arm around her, she did just that.

Dreams came, pleasant ones and silly ones, fleeting and never to be remembered. But then something else started creeping in at the edges. Even in her sleep she tried to batter the darkness back.

But it would not go away, and as it grew denser and began to take over, she became restless.

Finally a voice plucked her out of the morass.

"Kerry." It was Adrian. "Kerry, wake up. You're having a bad dream."

Her eyes popped open, taking in the warmly lit living room, the fire in the fireplace, the familiar surroundings. Instead of comforting her, they disturbed her. As if they were a mirage behind which evil dwelled.

"God!" she said, shaking her head to free herself from the lingering tendrils of her nightmare. "Oh, God."

"What?"

"It's there again. I hate this."

"What?"

"The feeling in my dream. Something's going to happen. And I don't want to know about it!"

His other arm closed around her and held her tight. She burrowed into the comfort his warm strength offered, and tried not to let the darkness in.

Outside the storm howled. Sleet still rattled against the windows, portending an ice storm of record severity. No one, she thought, no one could get around in this. Not even the killers. For tonight everyone should be safe.

But it didn't feel that way to her.

Words escaped her before she even knew what they would be. "Is that woman we found under police protection in the hospital?"

"I don't know." Adrian grew tense against her. Then he dropped one arm from her and fished in his pocket, pulling out a cell phone.

The county had repeaters everywhere these days, but apparently the reception was poor tonight. Very poor. At last he gave up and used the land line.

"Gage?"

Kerry listened as she wrapped her arms around herself, as if her own embrace could block out the ugliness.

"Is that woman we found in the woods under protection? Kerry's worried about her."

Silence except for the rattling of ice.

"Okay, thanks."

He replaced the handset in the cradle and returned to her side. "He said he pulled the deputy who was watching her because there've been a pile of accidents on the state highway, and they asked the hospital staff to be alert to anyone approaching her room. But he's sending someone now."

She nodded, feeling like her neck had stiffened and the movement was too much to ask. She tried to tell herself that the stiffness came from the position she had slept in, but instead of lessening, it seemed to be growing.

"I want this to stop." It was unclear even to her whether she spoke to Adrian, or to the universe at large. "It *has* to stop."

"I agree. All of it. The murders, your visions... You can't keep up this way."

She looked at him then, a sinking feeling in the pit of her stomach. "But maybe I have to. Maybe that's what it's all about."

"What's all about?"

"My near-death experience. The strange premonitions I've had for so long. My quirks, as I called them. Maybe it all was to make this happen."

"But why?"

"That's asking too much," she sighed. "Do we really have to know the *why*? Sometimes I think *that* part is way beyond our comprehension."

"Well, it probably is."

She nodded, then leaned back against the cushion. "It's one of those things where we just have to trust."

Trust. That was a word that nearly made him shudder. Some betrayals were so huge that you couldn't trust ever again. Certainly not without a fight.

Being a cop required a certain natural level of suspicion, but he'd gone way past that since Barry's betrayal. Way past. He ought to be able to get over it. People got over things like that all the time. Divorced people, for example. Was his situation so much worse?

Somebody had died because of it.

Could that and that alone be enough? Or was he simply refusing to let go of the wound, instead choosing to hide behind a high emotional wall so that it could never happen again?

Probably the latter, he thought grimly. Nor was that necessarily foolish on his part.

Yet look at him now, thrust into a similar position with this woman, thanks to Gage, who knew exactly what he was asking of Adrian. Well-meaning friends and all that.

Hell.

But after finding Cal napping instead of keeping watch, he knew he couldn't walk away from this. He didn't trust anyone but himself. A sorry situation, one just confirmed by Cal's slip.

What an irony.

Needing to move, to expend some tension, he rose and went to peek out the front window, moving the curtain only marginally. The night outside had gone far past the glitter of falling diamonds. He could see now that ice rimed the bare tree branches in thick layers.

"This could be really bad," he remarked.

"What?"

"This storm. The ice is building on the branches of the trees. Most likely on power lines, too. We'd better gather up candles and figure out how to stay warm."

"I've got plenty of wood out back."

"Then I'll bring some in while you put together candles and flashlights. Then I think we need to make a bed for you right in front of the fire. On the couch."

"Maybe I should get out the air mattress."

He turned in time to see her rising from the couch, and again felt that odd squeezing in his chest as he noted her innate grace, noted once again how pretty she was. No matter how broken he might be, he was still a man, and the sight of her awakened his appetites.

Bad timing, he told himself. Bad, bad timing. "Yeah," he said. "That would be good."

Chapter 8

In the kitchen, Kerry hunted up every candle she had, and the two flashlights along with spare batteries. Power outages were usually a spring or summer thing around here, when severe thunderstorms and tornadoes blew through. The winters usually didn't get bad enough in terms of snow and ice to slow things down too much.

But that had been changing, she reminded herself. What had once been a fairly dry climate had grown increasingly wetter, and storms more severe. She understood you weren't supposed to generalize about the climate from short-term experience, but people who lived close to the earth and depended on the climate noted long-term changes more quickly than city dwellers.

Ranchers around here talked frequently about the changing climate, commenting on the increasing number of severe storms, on how it rained more often, how they'd been steadily adjusting their practices to the changes.

So now an ice storm unlike anything she'd seen in her entire thirty years in this county.

Maybe she'd assign a climate essay after all, asking students to write about their parents' and grandparents' perception of changes in the climate. That could be interesting for them and for her.

Adrian passed her several times with armloads of wood as she moved necessities to the living room. It would be cozy in there no matter what happened. A couple of oil lamps sat on her bedroom dresser, and she decided to bring them out, too. She seemed to remember having a bottle of lamp oil in the cabinet.

Every blanket she had, all the spare pillows... The living room soon looked more like a nest. Adrian inflated the air mattress with her blow-dryer, then together they made up beds. In the background, the TV still flickered, but with the sound off.

"Okay," she said when they were done. "All we need is popcorn."

"For what?"

"For the pajama party."

He chuckled. "I've never been to one."

"Now that's a pity! I'll have to introduce you."

He pretended to frown. He was kneeling on the floor beside the air mattress while she sat on the edge of the couch. "This isn't supposed to be fun," he said mock-sternly.

"Well, I don't see any point in being miserable on principle."

At that his frown quivered, trying to turn into a smile. "You're a hedonist."

"No such thing."

"You could fool me." He surprised her by holding out his hand. She didn't even hesitate, but took it. He squeezed, then astonished her by tugging her forward onto the air mattress. A second later he was lying beside her, propped on an elbow to look down at her.

"So," he said, his voice a trace husky, "tell me about this pajama-party thing. What did you girls do?"

"We giggled a lot." She felt as if she couldn't quite catch her breath, and the feeling grew stronger when he rested his hand on her midriff. The warm, light pressure felt *so* good.

"About what?"

"About everything." Closing her eyes, she cast her mind back in time. "About boys, about each other, about silly games we played. There wasn't much that didn't make us giggle. We'd get excited just being together."

"Sounds like I missed a great thing."

"Poor man." She opened her eyes and smiled at him. "It would have driven you crazy at that age. All those girls being silly over stupid things."

"Like guys weren't being silly over stupid things at the same age."

"Different things, though."

He shook his head, smiling. "Actually, it was probably about the same kind of stuff, except that we took ourselves oh-so seriously."

"I sort of remember that part."

"I certainly do."

His face seemed to have come closer, and Kerry held her breath, forgetting everything except a sudden, intense hope that he would kiss her. The power of the need swamped her, even as some corner of her heart wondered how she could feel something so innately fragile at a time like this...because all such things were fragile in the end. The powerful urge today could easily be gone tomorrow.

But she didn't care. As he lowered his head, she closed her eyes and waited for the touch of his lips, feeling as if every cell within her strained to reach him.

Then she felt the warm touch on her mouth, a gentle touch, asking, not demanding.

Almost without being aware of it, she raised her arms and placed her hands on his shoulders, opening herself completely to the moment. *Yesss!*

He took the invitation, his lips deepening the kiss, one arm slipping beneath her back to draw her closer.

That's what she wanted, she thought, to feel him all along the length of her body. To feel the warmth, the heat of desire, and through it the wonder of being alive. She needed that desperately right now. Needed *him* desperately right now.

The savagery of the need astonished her even as it swept her away. Elemental.

His tongue found hers in a dance of promise. It drove heat through her to her very center, until she felt herself throb inside in time to his thrusts. No one in her life had ever taken her so far so fast.

She felt him harden against her, a sensation that filled her with fierce pleasure. He felt it, too.

Then his hand slipped to her breast, a touch so light through the fabric that she shivered as much in anticipation as response. Ah, it was so good to be alive!

The crackle of the fire blended into the sounds of the ice storm without, creating a cocoon of sound around them, punctured only by sighs, and soon soft moans.

When her shirt started to ride up, and his hand moved with it, warm against the skin of her midriff, coming closer and closer to her breasts, she caught her breath, hoping against hope that he would not stop.

But he teased her for a little while, changing his kisses to gentle sips, like a bee tasting nectar, while his hand made slow circles on her skin. Then he dropped kisses across her cheek until he placed one on the tender spot behind her ear. At the same moment his warm breath puffed in her ear, and a shiver of delight shook her from head to foot.

A quiet, satisfied chuckle escaped him as he read her response as encouragement to continue.

Which it was. Her mind had gone hazy, able to think of only one thing... if that was even thinking. A groan rose deep from within her as she pulled him even closer, feeling that if she could fuse them into one it still wouldn't be enough.

A thrill ripped through her as her front-clasp bra gave way, allowing her to spill free. Then his hand found and cupped one breast. Warm. Hot. Hot as flame, shooting burning desire throughout her body.

When his thumb brushed her hardening nipple she arched against him and tightened her hold on his shoulders desperately.

Let it never end. Never.

His mouth replaced his thumb, sucking deeply, until moans escaped her helplessly again and again. Eager for more, she tried to find the buttons of his shirt, and when she couldn't she tugged at his collar, trying to push it out of the way.

He obliged her, sitting up quickly to shed it, then coming back so that bare skin touched bare skin in the most exquisite way.

"Ooh," she sighed contentedly, a contentment that didn't endure long as other, deeper needs clamored for attention. She writhed against him, trying to get closer, running her hands over the warm, smooth skin of his back.

"No hurry," he mumbled, to both of them it seemed to her, a reminder to enjoy every moment of this most wonderful of life's offerings.

But then her fingers felt something and she froze. A deep, puckered hole in his lower back. Awareness shoved her back to hard, cold reality. "What's this?" she asked in a tremulous whisper.

He stilled, and she knew the magic of the moment had snapped for him, too.

After a few beats, he rolled onto his side, carrying her

with him so that she was still securely tucked against him, her bare torso protected. Shielded. As if he sensed embarrassment might intrude.

"I was shot," he finally said.

Her hand found the scar again. "It was bad."

"Every gunshot is bad."

"No, I mean...there's a hole."

"That's the exit wound. They tend to be big and ugly, and take part of you with them."

"How bad is bad?"

"I lost a kidney."

"Oh, my God!"

"Hey," he said quietly. With one hand he began to tuck her shirt around her, covering her. Protecting her with her clothing as well as his body. Did he have any idea just how sensitive he was? How caring? She doubted it.

"Hey what?" she asked finally. "It's awful."

"I won't deny that. But I'm healthy. All I did was lose a spare. I'm lucky."

"Somehow I don't feel that way about it. How can you? Was that the only permanent damage?"

"I don't have a spleen anymore, either. But I'm still lucky. I should probably have died."

"Your partner did that?"

"Yeah."

She wrapped her arms around him as tightly as she could. As if she could squeeze away the pain and the memory. "And you had to kill him?" The true horror of it all finally dawned on her. His superficial explanation earlier hadn't really hit home. Now it did.

"Yeah." He shook his head, as if a fly were annoying him.

"Adrian. Adrian tell me."

"I did."

"No, I think you left things out. What exactly happened when you got to the house?"

"I told you, my partner was there. Talk about a shock. He was there, his gun was still in his hand, and he was standing over my informant. He'd just finished him off with a shot to the head. Why he didn't run when he heard me pulling up, I don't know. Maybe he thought I was someone else. Or maybe he honestly believed I'd just let him go."

"Let him go? Why? What do you mean?"

She felt his jaw clench, heard his teeth grind briefly.

"When he saw me, he sort of shrugged, as if it didn't matter. Then he said, 'Well, it had to be done. He's just scum. So we won't say anything about this, will we?'"

"Oh, God."

"Yeah, exactly. I guess he thought our partnership would mean more than the fact he'd killed a criminal. The thing was, it never meant more than that. It couldn't. And I knew immediately why he'd done it. He was dirty, covering his tracks by killing my informant. Did he really think that just because he was my partner I'd keep silent?"

"Maybe so," she said softly.

"All I know is, I told him to drop the gun, that he was under arrest. Instead he started walking toward the back door, away from me. He didn't think I'd stop him. So I pulled my weapon and fired at the wall beside him. That's when he turned and shot me. I was so full of adrenaline by then I hardly felt it."

He paused and she waited, knowing that he needed to gather himself. "Maybe he thought one shot would put me down and he'd be able to get away. Maybe he wanted to let me live. For damn sure that wasn't how we were trained to shoot. You fire three times. You make sure the perp is down and not getting back up. But he didn't."

"Odd."

"Yeah. But my training kicked in. I didn't shoot just once. I shot him three times, center mass."

She tried to squeeze him tighter, to let him know she was with him, because he seemed to have gone somewhere far away.

"He managed to stagger out the back door, but then he fell. By that time I knew I was in serious trouble, so I called for help. I don't know how I managed to remain conscious until they arrived, but I knew that I couldn't risk having him turn on me again, or that someone else would arrive and I'd be unprotected."

"I'm so, so sorry."

"Yeah. Me, too. Anyway, end of story. Help arrived before I passed out. I don't remember much after that. When I woke up again, I was out of surgery and they told me I'd recover. That I was lucky. I didn't feel lucky right then."

"No. I can understand that."

At last his gaze returned to hers. His eyes were dark with remembered pain. "He was my *partner*. For *five* years." As if that explained everything. And maybe it did.

Kerry tried to imagine that kind of betrayal, but all the times she'd felt betrayed paled by comparison. It wasn't like finding out a boyfriend was dating your best friend, too. This was far, far worse.

"I'm glad," she said, "that you're still alive."

"Sometimes I am, too." He sighed, and she loosened her hold on him just a bit. "That sounds ungrateful, doesn't it?"

"Well, I can see why you'd have a little trouble celebrating the whole thing."

He gave a short, mirthless laugh. "That's a fact. Anyway, when I recovered, and after some therapy, I realized I couldn't do the job anymore. I couldn't trust that way again, and that would make me a liability to a partner. I developed some paranoia."

"Understandably so."

"I also started doubting my own powers of observation. In retrospect, I sometimes think I should have caught on that something was going on with Barry before it came to that. Hindsight being twenty-twenty and all that. But the thing is, if I could miss that once, how could I be sure I wouldn't miss it again? So I'd never be able to work with a partner again. Or trust my judgment in quite the same way. I decided I'd be better off on my ranch, working with animals."

"Then you get dragged right back in."

"Well," he said with an evident attempt to lighten the

moment, "it didn't exactly happen right away. I've had two years to get over myself."

"Why do you think you need to get over yourself?"

His gaze grew quite serious. "Because people have to deal with even worse things than what happened to me."

"And that lessens what happened to you how?" Kerry shook her head. "I hate that attitude. Not that I think it does any good to drown in self-pity. Not that. But a trauma is a trauma, and comparing it to someone else's is as useful as comparing apples and airplanes. All each of us can do is handle our own life as best we can, and help those around us when we can. But it isn't helpful at all to belittle our own problems. You can't deal with a problem if you feel embarrassed about even having it."

"You might have a point there."

"Of course I do. I deal with teens all the time. Everything in their lives is magnified but it's wrong of an adult to minimize what they're experiencing. It's part of their growth curve, and if it seems like they're overdoing it, too bad. Because to *them* it's every bit as major as it feels. You can't help them at all if you dismiss what they're feeling, or if you try to minimize their problems. Perspective will come with experience, and *yours* will never work for *them*. They need to grow their own."

He nodded, one corner of his mouth curving upward.

"Anyway, don't dismiss your own experience and pain. Time may give you a different perspective, but you can't force it by comparing yourself to others."

"Thanks, Teach."

She looked at him suspiciously, but didn't see

anything in his face to suggest he was making fun of her. In the same moment, she became acutely aware of how they were lying, of how close they had come to a huge intimacy that she wasn't sure she was ready for.

She dropped her gaze, nearly closing her eyes. "I'm sorry," she said. "I can't."

"I know." He hugged her again, wanting to kiss her but not daring, holding her for several seconds before beginning to tug her shirt down again. "No apology needed, Kerry."

She nodded, grateful for his understanding, half-sorry she had ruined the moment by asking about his scar, and relieved that she had. Whether or not they ever made love, she sensed that it couldn't possibly be casual. There'd be a heavy risk for both of them, it wouldn't be something they could just walk away from as if nothing had ever happened.

She returned to her perch on the couch, unable to tear her gaze from the ripple of his muscles as he pulled on his shirt. She noticed he kept his back away from her, as if he didn't want her to actually see the scar she had touched.

He probably wanted to end that discussion, and she couldn't blame him for that. She had her own limits when it came to discussing the car accident and her near-death experience. One could easily cross the line between caring and prying.

"I'll make some hot chocolate," she said, the urge to do something overcoming her. Get back to normal. Get back to normal *now*. The only route to safety.

She rose and hurried from the room, seeking the

sanctuary of her favorite room in the house. As she pulled the mix from the cupboard, she heard Adrian step out the front door again to make his rounds. The instant she heard the door close behind him, it was as if the house emptied, leaving her alone and lonely. In that instant he took all sense of life and vibrancy with him.

The house felt as empty as a tomb.

Chapter 9

Lying on the couch with her head toward the fire and her feet toward the door, Kerry sought sleep and lost. Wide awake, she stared at the ceiling, watching the play of orange firelight and shadow on the ceiling.

She sensed that Adrian was awake, too, because he remained too still. Tossing on an air mattress could be noisy, but he didn't even roll over. If she paid attention, she could hear his measured breathing over the crackle of the fire. In fact, she could almost feel how intently he listened for any sound out of the normal.

But it wouldn't be a sound that warned them first. Somehow she knew that she would sense the approach of the killers before they tried to get in the house. If they came tonight.

That certainty surprised her, because her quirk or talent or whatever one wanted to call it could hardly be deemed reliable.

Yet there it was, that certainty. Comforting in a way, but discomforting at the same time.

Why had she even tuned in on this horror? It went so far beyond any past experience that all hope of understanding eluded her.

Unless...

The thought filled her veins with ice and she sat bolt upright.

"Kerry?" At once Adrian sat up, too, looking at her. "Did you hear something?"

"No. No. I just had a thought."

"What thought?"

"What if I know these guys?"

Everything seemed to hush, the fire and the wind both giving way in the face of some other dimension. Seconds stretched as nothing moved.

Then Adrian asked, "Why would you think that?"

"Because I've never experienced anything like this before." She turned her head on a stiff neck so that she could look at him directly. "I was wondering why I even picked up on this stuff. My past experiences with this...this ESP if you can call it that, were all about minor, inconsequential things that would affect me directly. This is a whole different scale. A whole different thing. And I didn't know the victims, so why would I pick up on it?"

He shook his head slightly, not in disagreement, but as if to say he had no answer.

"It just struck me that maybe I picked up on these crimes because I know the killers."

"I wish I could help you answer that."

"I can't answer it myself. Yet. But it would make sense. I mean, I'm not seeing other crimes, other murders. It's not that they haven't happened since the car crash, but I've never before gotten any information about them."

"So this stands out in more than one way."

"You could say that."

He scooted closer until he was sitting on the floor right beside the couch, facing her. "That's a really awful supposition."

"Tell me about it." She looked past him into the darkness beyond the range of the fire. "But it *feels* right if you know what I mean."

"Unfortunately, I do. The question is, how can we use the information?"

"But I don't know if it's accurate," she argued. "It was just an idea."

"For the sake of argument, let's assume you're correct. Does it tell us anything?"

She looked rueful. "It might if I didn't know most of the people in this county."

"True." He started to smile, but it never quite blossomed. "It's an interesting idea, though. One that might be worth pursuing."

"In what way?"

"Well, do you know anyone you suspect might be capable of something like this?"

"You know, that would be a funny question if this weren't so serious."

"I know. Ha ha."

"Exactly. What is it they always say? 'He was so quiet and kept to himself.'"

"Yeah, that's the line."

"Do you believe it?"

A small shake of his head. "I sometimes wonder. I mean, if you've got a guilty conscience or something to hide, yeah, you'd keep to yourself. But other people keep to themselves because they're introverts, or whatever. So it's hardly a diagnostic. Besides, all too often bad people don't see themselves as doing anything wrong. It's weird, but true. They always seem to have a good reason, at least from their perspective."

"Exactly." Sighing, she lay back against her pillow, resuming her contemplation of the dancing orange light on the ceiling. "I'm not going to sleep. But I doubt I'm going to get any answers. I could probably think about it all night and not come up with a likely suspect."

"So don't try to think about it. Sometimes things pop into our heads when we're not trying to get at them."

"Oh, *that'll* help," she said drily. "Don't think about it. Works every time."

He chuckled. "It's also possible you have no personal connection with any of this."

"I'd like to believe that." She frowned faintly, pondering. "That darkness is still out there."

He stiffened. "Getting closer?"

She shook her head. "It doesn't seem to be. But it's still there around the edges."

"Can you tell anything about it?"

"I'm not sure I want to. I'm thirty years old, Adrian, and I've been lucky enough never to have come face-to-face with real evil. I don't think I want that to change."

"But something has changed."

"Unfortunately." She closed her eyes, mentally feeling around. "Have you faced real evil? I don't mean just badness, but real *evil*."

"I know what you mean. I thought I had that day with Barry but you know, that wasn't evil, not the way you mean it. You mean it as something beyond ordinary human frailty, don't you?"

"Exactly." She rolled on her side so she could look at him. "I've always felt that evil resides within us, as part of our nature, that any of us is capable of terrible, terrible things. Sort of a feeling that who needs the devil when we've got us."

He nodded slowly. "I can see that. I've often felt that way. We can do truly great things, and then we can do truly terrible things."

"But..." She hesitated. "You ever see that picture of Charles Manson? The one where his eyes look so dark and empty? It was as if you see the abyss when you looked into them."

He nodded encouragingly.

"So when I go around making my blithe statements about evil, I have this niggling memory of Charles

Manson's eyes. There was something *in* there, and it wasn't Manson."

"You're talking about a different kind of evil."

"Exactly. An evil that's a force apart from us. That maybe takes us over and drives us to...something beyond ordinary human evil."

He nodded. "I know exactly what you mean."

"Have you ever encountered it?"

He hesitated. "Once. I interviewed a serial killer. Some of them are truly tormented people, but there are others who are so cold. Cold as the depths of hell."

She nodded. "And that's the feeling I'm getting, Adrian. Maybe that's why I sensed all this. There's something more to what's going on. Almost like possession."

She gave a nervous laugh. "I can't believe I'm talking like this."

"I won't tell, Teach," he said almost jokingly, but his expression remained deadly serious. "I know exactly what you're talking about. Don't dismiss it. I'd be the last person to claim I know the nature of true evil, but whatever its nature, it exists. And maybe that's what you're sensing."

"I think so. I don't even want to get close to it. It's hovering out there, and I feel like I want to pull the blankets up over my mind's eye so that it doesn't notice me. But it already has," she added, remembering the phone call. "So I guess playing ostrich would be stupid now, wouldn't it?" And as rationally as she was trying to discuss this, everything inside her seemed to be cringing away, seeking a bolt-hole to hide in.

"Well, it depends. Hiding physically could protect you. Hiding mentally could put you in danger."

"That's what I meant." She settled back against her pillow, and closed her eyes. "Always in the past I just got flashes of things. This is different. It's persistent."

"Maybe you need to stop fighting it then."

Her eyes snapped open. "I'm not fighting it."

"Are you sure? You don't want to know what it is. It scares you. I understand that, believe me. I was blind once, too, and I often think I refused to see what was right in front of me. Maybe this hovering darkness you sense is the same sort of thing. Something you'd prefer not to know because it could change everything."

She opened her mouth as if to argue, then closed it again. What if he was right? What if answers lay within her grasp but she was holding them at bay because she feared what she would learn? How could that serve anyone?

But by the same token, maybe whatever she was sensing was holding *itself* back, unwilling to be known.

That thought sent a shiver running down her spine; could she really attribute awareness to that darkness she sensed?

But she did, she realized. She had personified it, justifiably or not. Another shiver ran through her and she tugged the quilt up to her chin.

"What's wrong?" Adrian asked. "Do I need to throw another log on the fire?"

"I'm not cold. I'm scared."

He reached beneath the quilt and took her hand, giving it a reassuring squeeze. "You're not alone."

"I know." She squeezed his hand in reply, grateful for the warmth, grateful for the strength she felt there. "You really believe I'm sensing these things?"

He snorted. "I'd have to be an idiot not to. Think about it, Kerry. I wasn't a believer in psychic stuff before, but I am now. At least, I believe in *you*. I'm sorry you had to have these experiences, but you saved a life out there."

"And now you're having to sit up all night like a watchdog."

At that he winked. "Hey, sweetie, I'm better than any watchdog."

She nearly blushed, or maybe it was the heat from the fire. Handy excuse, anyway, for the warmth in her cheeks. And an equally handy moment of distraction. She would have bet he offered it deliberately. "You didn't just say that."

"Of course I did. And you know what? I can't be distracted by a hamburger thrown on the floor."

She couldn't help but laugh. "So you're a watchdog and I'm hamburger?"

He shook his head. "Oh no, Kerry. *You* distracted me."

"That does it." With her free hand, she pulled the covers over her head. A moment later he tugged them back down, smiling at her.

"No hiding from me. I'm your bodyguard, remember."

"That's what you call it?"

A full-throated laugh escaped him, then he leaned

closer, saying huskily, "Trust me, I'll guard your body even better when the time is right."

Any embarrassed impulse to laugh it off died as she looked into his eyes. Caught, she watched the firelight reflect there, but saw something even hotter behind the reflection. Every cell in her body turned instantly to warm honey, and she knew, just knew, that whatever her reservations, she needed to make love with this man.

Spending the rest of her life wondering would be the worst possible outcome, worse even than giving herself only to watch him walk away.

Never before had she felt this way about anyone. She almost pulled him toward her, determined to answer all her questions and needs right now.

But before the urge took over, she realized the timing couldn't be worse.

And in the instant it took to realize that, the darkness surged from the edges of her mind to front and center.

It enveloped her, smothering her, freezing her, holding her prisoner in her own mind. She heard a laugh, a voice she almost recognized, then a whisper, "You're next."

All of a sudden, so quickly it was terrifying, the darkness let go. She gasped for air, shuddering violently as if she had been buried in a snowbank, and vision returned.

"Oh, my God," she gasped. "Oh, my God!"

Adrian had her by the shoulders. "Kerry! Kerry, what happened? Are you okay?"

"No...no..."

He gathered her up then, pulling her into the warm shelter of his arms, tucking the comforter around her as if he could feel how cold she had become. Shivering violently, she pressed her face into his shoulder, seeking whatever heat she could find.

"What happened?" he asked again, working his fingers into her hair at the base of her skull, stroking soothingly.

"I don't know," she finally managed to whisper. "It was as if the darkness took over. I couldn't move, I was so, so cold, I couldn't even see. Oh, God, I felt invaded!" And soiled in some way. She wished crazily that she could toss her own mind into the washer.

He snuggled her even closer, sliding her from the couch to his lap as if he would surround her with himself. Little by little, feeling returned to her fingers and toes, making them sting as if she had been on the verge of frostbite.

Slowly she lifted her face to look at him. "It took all the heat from my body."

"It took the heat from the room right around you," he said grimly. "I felt it."

"God, what *is* it?"

"I don't know." His arms tightened even more. "I don't know what we're dealing with here anymore, Kerry. Honest to God, I don't. But I don't believe in possession. I don't believe disembodied spirits are hanging around the planet trying to do mischief. Do I believe in heaven? You bet I do. Do I believe that we survive after death? Absolutely. But I can't believe something disembodied took you over like that."

"Then what was it?" she demanded. "What happened to me? Damn it, Adrian, it wasn't natural!"

"I know that. I know that. But...but if you can psychically pick up on what these killers are doing, then why can't that same door work both ways?"

She bit her lip, trying to think. Even her brain seemed to have been laced with ice. "You mean like some kind of psychic telephone?"

"Maybe. Sort of. I guess what I'm saying is, if you can hear and see what they're hearing and seeing, maybe that's what just happened again. Only this time you picked up more strongly on their intentions, especially since they're directed at you, if that phone call wasn't just a prank. Maybe they're so focused on you that they broadcast those feelings."

"I'm not sure that makes me feel any better."

"It's better than positing a demon, don't you think?"

"Well, of course." The cold seeped away, and in its wake she felt utter exhaustion. Relaxing into his embrace, she stared into the fire and forced herself to think about what she had just experienced, much as she yearned to erase it completely. "I *did* hear a voice saying 'You're next.' And a laugh. And I felt there was something familiar about the laugh, but I can't place it."

"Well, don't worry about it. There are probably a lot of laughs that would sound familiar to you."

"I'm sure." A small sigh escaped her as she relaxed even more. "The mind-body connection is a strong one."

"Yes?" The single syllable encouraged her to talk as he began to rub her shoulder and stroke her arm.

"Well, yes. I'm sure you've heard how we can ramp up our immune systems merely by concentrating on it. Things like that."

"Some things, yes."

"Well, take just a small example. If you prick your finger with a pin, you feel it. But if you stimulate the same part of your brain, you'll feel that prick even though it hasn't happened. Or if we get scared, the body responds by pumping adrenaline. It's all of a piece. It's why, for example, curses can kill people who believe in them."

"Right." If he wondered where she was headed, he didn't press her to reach her destination quickly.

"So I was just thinking, the way I got cold and couldn't move or see, that may have been my brain's response to what I was sensing and it played out in my body."

"I see what you're getting at. That makes sense, actually."

"It makes more sense to me than that some kind of entity just walked into my mind and took over."

He nodded. "Me, too."

She sighed again, as if each sigh she managed to issue released more tension from her. "Whatever, I guess it doesn't matter. What I do know for sure now is that those killers are fully focused on getting at me."

"And that's when we'll get them."

She wished she could be as sure of that as he seemed.

Morning arrived covered in ice that coated every branch, every eave, every sidewalk and driveway. The grass sparkled as if it had been scattered with jewels and the ice in the trees acted like prisms, scattering light.

"A winter wonderland," Adrian remarked as he looked out the front window.

"It's amazing," Kerry agreed. "I don't think I've ever seen this before. Certainly not here."

With the sunrise came an easing of the night's tension, but Adrian thought the two of them looked like soldiers who'd been on watch all night in a battle zone. Or like hungover drunks after a binge. Red-eyed, rumpled and weary, neither of them looked fit to make it through the day.

Of similar minds, they'd already started perking a pot of strong coffee. Neither of them really had any energy for cooking, so Kerry pulled out some refrigerated cinnamon rolls and popped them in the oven.

"I'm not hungry," she remarked, "but maybe some calories will wake me up."

"Sleep will wake you up. After you eat, just go lie down and try to relax."

She gave him a wry smile. "Oh, sure. And you're going to stay awake?"

He couldn't resist her smile, and returned it. "Well, I wake easy. I know that for a fact."

"Yeah? How?"

"Hey, didn't I tell you about my experience with Uncle Sam's Misguided Children?"

"Who?"

"The marines. Four years, and I can sleep standing up with the best of them."

As he'd hoped, she laughed. "Why do I find that believable?"

"Because it's true. Ask any soldier. Being able to sleep anywhere, anytime, under any circumstances becomes a major talent. Pity those who can't learn."

She nodded. "You still look exhausted to me."

"I've been taking micronaps most of the night."

The oven timer dinged, and she pulled out the pan of rolls. The aroma alone made her mouth start watering. "So you were in the marines, and then you went into criminal investigations?"

"That's right. Can I put the frosting on those?"

"They need to cool for a little, first. Otherwise you'll need to eat the icing with a spoon from the bottom of the pan."

"That works, too."

She smiled again and he realized that somehow, some way, the entire atmosphere in this house had lightened again. As if the darkness had moved on. At least for now.

"You've done quite a bit in your life," she remarked.

"So have you."

"Well, I followed a pretty straight line."

He tilted his head to one side, studying her, thinking how beautiful she looked even after a sleepless night. "So did I. Macho meathead, that was me. Only I had to prove it. There were other ways I could pay for a college education, but I chose the manliest one I could find. The corps let me take correspondence courses, too, so when I got out, I had a lot of college under my belt already.

And my focus was always on criminal investigation. I always wanted to be a cop. Always."

She leaned against the counter and faced him. "And now? You're awfully young not to still have a dream."

He learned something about himself then. Something he thought he had lost was still there. "I'll find one," he said. And for the first time in two years, he believed it. "Maybe I'll just be the best damn gentleman rancher who never does a thing this county has seen."

She laughed again, the pretty, clear sound that made him think of small bells. "Somehow I don't think that will content you forever."

"Probably not," he admitted. "Now can I frost them?"

"Are you hungry or something?"

"I could eat a horse, if that didn't mean rustling one. Let me at them."

He shouldn't be feeling so good this morning, he thought as he drizzled the cream-cheese icing over the rolls. He should be uptight and worried and worn. Instead he had the craziest feeling that right now, just right now, everything was okay. That might change in an instant, but for these minutes, everything was fine. Better than fine.

Breakfast at the dinette in the kitchen turned into a good time. Coffee, rich rolls and good company. An unexpected reprieve in the series of bad days they'd been having. And so welcome after last night.

But Adrian couldn't fully lower his guard. A threat against Kerry lurked out there somewhere, and while part of him could take pleasure in their meal together, another part remained constantly watchful.

Nor did it soothe him to know the roads would probably remain impassible for several hours yet. The layer of ice out there was thick, and even if the day began to warm to more normal autumn temperatures, it would take time to thaw. Sand trucks had probably been out since before dawn, but the major roads, like the state highway, would be tended first.

Even as he had the thought, the ice claimed its due for the first time in town. The power flickered, then the house fell utterly silent. The heat had turned off, the light over the table blinked out. Even the hum of the refrigerator vanished.

"A tree must have fallen on the lines," he remarked. "Or at least I hope that's all it is."

Kerry nodded. "It may have, outside town."

"Keep the fire going," he said. "Use it to make us some coffee. I'm going to step outside and check around."

"Okay."

He pulled on his parka, checked his gun, then went out the back door, headed straight for where the power lines came into the house. Nothing there had been touched, which would indicate the problem lay elsewhere. A loud crack behind him startled him, and he whirled in time to see a branch tumble from a towering oak in front of the neighbor's house.

A lot of that had probably been happening around the town and county, of course. It was unlikely there was anything sinister going on. Still, edginess rode him like a goad. As if each passing minute only brought the threat to Kerry nearer.

A new deputy was parked out front, and he stopped by to chat with him. Except that him turned out to be her, Sara Ironheart. He had liked Sara from the first instant he clapped eyes on her, and she greeted him with a smile as she rolled down the window.

"I'm surprised you came into town," he said by way of greeting. "The roads must be hell."

"They are, but chains work well."

"How about Gideon and the kids?"

"They're fine without me. We lost power during the night, so they're camping in front of the wood stove and telling ghost stories. Oh, and drinking enough hot chocolate to sail a battleship."

Adrian laughed. "But there must have been someone closer to town to do shift."

Sara shook her head. "I've known Kerry most of my life, Adrian. I'm a lot older so we didn't hang out together or anything, but I know her. Like everyone around here, she's part of the extended family. I'll do my share, and I don't want any arguments about it."

"I'm not arguing. I'm actually glad to see you."

"I heard Cal was falling asleep last night."

Adrian winced. "I didn't want that to get around. He's young."

Sara smiled. "He confessed on his own. It's important to know the weaknesses of your fellow officers. You know that."

And boy, did he ever. He nodded, spoke with her a little longer, then returned to the house.

"Sara's on watch," he told Kerry.

"Good. I trust her."

"Me, too."

He found Kerry rinsing plates at the kitchen sink with cold water and stacking them. When she finished, she dried her hands on a towel. "I'm getting really cold," she remarked. "Back to the fireplace."

"You need a wood stove. Much more efficient."

"I know, but do you have any idea how expensive they are?"

"Actually, yes."

She looked rueful. "Every time I light a fire, I think about global warming. Some example I set for my students."

"Maybe you should build an igloo for the winter and wear sealskin."

"What, and kill all those seals just for clothes?"

He put his hands on his hips in mock irritation. "There's no satisfying you. You're ashamed not to be freezing to death because you're emitting carbon with your fireplace, but you won't kill a seal to make clothes."

"Think how much carbon I'd respire into the atmosphere with heavy breathing while I build the igloo."

"True."

"And I can't imagine how many months I'd have to chew the sealskin to make it soft enough to wear."

"You'd freeze by then."

"Most certainly. And wear my teeth to nubs. So I still need a fire, I guess."

"Damn, but it looks that way."

He knew he wore a cockeyed grin, but he was fairly certain it wasn't any more cockeyed than hers.

"So what's the solution?" she asked.

"We could follow the geese south."

"Only if we walk. Anything else will require planting a forest to balance the emissions."

"Hmmm. That's a long walk, and right now I don't think we'd get past the edge of town."

"So we're stuck for the winter."

"At least."

"Which means," she said, "that I'm heading for the living room to take advantage of the emissions I'm currently responsible for."

"Makes sense to me. I mean, if you're going to burn the wood, you might as well be warm."

Still smiling, she headed that way with him on her heels. The living room was pleasantly warm, not overheated as it would have been had she put on too much wood. They sat side by side on the couch, silent now. He supposed they were both remembering the waiting game they played.

For many years he had noted how the male deer would seem to fade away come hunting season. You'd still see the does, but the bucks, either with a biological rhythm born from years of being hunted, or alerted by the first gunshots of the season, seemed to vanish from the earth.

Hence the deer feeders so many hunters relied on now, something he thought utterly unsportsmanlike.

But thinking about how the bucks faded into the deepest woods when they were hunted made him wonder if they were making a big mistake by keeping Kerry at her house. Still, in a place like this where gossip could pass to the farthest end of the county between dawn and dusk, he wasn't sure anywhere else would be safe, either.

And there was another thing, an unspoken thing, something he suspected Kerry already knew.

She had become bait.

Chapter 10

The phone rang, startling them both. Kerry hadn't switched over to the cordless variety—the only reason she still had service. Paling slightly, she watched as Adrian answered it. A moment later she relaxed as she realized he was talking to Gage.

"Yeah," he said, "everything's okay here. Except for the power outage. How bad is it?" He listened. "Okay. No, we've got enough wood to get by and there seems to be enough food for a day or two. How about the victim in the hospital?"

When at last he hung up the phone, he turned to look at Kerry. "Well, the outage is bad, and we can probably expect not to have power in this part of town until early tomorrow, if then."

"And the woman in the hospital?"

"She's talking, but basically she didn't see a thing except her friend getting shot. As soon as she felt the bullet in her own arm, she took off away from the sound of the shot."

Kerry nodded. "All she could do."

"Yeah. Thank God she did. But apparently it was her husband and her friend's husband who were the first victims. The two guys were rock hounds who'd take trips two, maybe three, times a year looking for unusual specimens. Apparently one of them taught at the university in Laramie and the other taught high school science."

"That poor woman!"

He nodded grimly. "Right now I'm feeling like I'm on a shrinking ice floe."

The reference to their earlier joking held no humor. That was exactly what it felt like, Kerry thought. That or a tightening noose.

"I'm sorry," he said abruptly. "If I could, I'd take you as far away as I could get you."

"I know, Adrian." She believed he would. "But that's not going to happen."

"Not this morning at any rate."

"Not at all." She shook her head a little and looked down at her hands. "If they're stupid enough to come after me, it's the best chance you'll have to get them. I read enough to know that finding a killer who isn't connected in any way to a victim can be extremely difficult."

"Well, harder than if it's the husband."

The attempt at humor fell utterly flat in the too-quiet house.

She gave him a wan smile. "I could use a little ESP right now."

"Let me know if you get any. Because right now I'm willing to act on anything you pick up."

She nodded. "It seems to me that having a deputy parked right out front is more of a hindrance than a help."

He drew a sharp breath and she watched the frown crease his face. "Kerry, we have to be sensible about this. I'm not going to dangle you out there like a judas goat."

"But that's what I am. Or what I should be. We've got to stop these guys, Adrian. And at the moment I seem to be the only connection you have."

"No."

She leaned back against the cushions, letting her head loll and closing her eyes. "I'm not afraid of dying."

"Has it occurred to you that I might be afraid of losing you?"

She couldn't bring herself to open her eyes. Her heart seemed to stop mid-beat, and the breath sailed out of her. "Adrian..."

"Just don't argue with me, Kerry," he said urgently. "Just don't argue. I know you're bait. I know you have been since that phone call. But none of us, me most especially, is willing to risk you recklessly. You've got to understand that. You've got to."

At that she opened her eyes and looked at him, reading the urgency in his face, the deep concern, even the flicker of fear. She understood that it would kill him to lose someone he was protecting again. She also understood that if he was ever to trust again, she had to do what he said. Unfortunately for them both, there was a life in the balance, and it might not be hers.

"I won't do anything stupid." That was as far as she could promise.

"Did I say you would? But don't ask me to send the deputy away. There are two of them, you said. There's only one of me. That's not enough coverage."

Almost as if to reinforce his message, he swept her up off the couch and carried her back to her bedroom. Any objection she might have framed vanished in the wonder of his concern. In the strange security of being in the arms of a man who could carry her so easily. Why should that make her feel safe?

But it did, and more, it yanked her out of the frightening present to another place, a warm place where the sun could shine again and she could forget all this horror. Yes, she'd said she didn't want to make love. Yes, she'd meant it then. But not anymore.

Turning her face, she buried it in his shoulder. "Adrian...I...want you..."

"Shh," he said gently. "I want it, too. And God help me, I need you now."

He placed her on her bed, and she watched through heavily lidded eyes as he stripped away his clothes. God, he was beautiful, she thought hazily. So beautiful. And somehow she sensed that his willingness to toss away his clothes was a huge emotional step for him. That he was saying he had begun to trust her.

That thought added an emotional warmth to the physical heat that seemed to come out of nowhere and light every nerve ending with a flame.

Whatever he was trying to tell her, she was more than ready to listen.

Kneeling beside her on the bed, Adrian began to undress Kerry, taking his time to drop kisses on each newly exposed area. From her throat down, he worked his way slowly, trying to draw out this moment even as his own body throbbed insistently.

Somewhere in the mix of heady desire, he was aware of the risk he was taking, a risk for both of them. But he had to convince her not to take a foolish risk. He had to convince her how much it mattered to him that nothing harm her.

Issues of trust hardly seemed to matter when compared to the enormity of the threat she faced, and the worse threat she was prepared to face out of some crazy idealistic notion that she mattered less than stopping these killers.

He could think of no other way to persuade her that she mattered just as much as any other possible victim, not less just because she knew she was in the line of fire.

And this seemed to be the only way he could speak of his deep fears for her, of his need for her, of all the things that had become paramount for him over the last few days.

There weren't words for this, not even for a poet. What he felt was so deep and so elemental he wasn't sure he understood it himself.

But he could talk with his hands, and his body, could try to make her feel all that he was feeling.

And that's exactly what he did. He devoted himself to her pleasure. He wanted to give her an experience that would make her want to live, an experience that reminded her that even though death didn't scare her, there was something to *live* for.

He teased her nipples with his tongue, enjoying the way she began to moan softly, the way she began to move, at first gentle lifts of her hips. When her hands reached for him, he shifted away, denying her only because he wanted to draw this out, and because he wanted to drive her mad with longing.

Her skin was soft, smooth, living satin. As he teased her breasts with his mouth, his hand began to wander, finding every little place that could make her shiver. When he at last reached the pelt between her legs he found it soft, too, and a chuckle almost escaped him when she arched upward, seeking more than teasing touches from his hand.

Not yet. Not yet.

His own excitement kept him on the precipice, too, the throbbing of his body strengthening until he dimly realized that never, ever, had he felt desire this strong. And he was determined to make her feel the same.

Kerry's whole world settled between her legs. Every touch he gave her only added to the deep, pulsing ache she felt. Her entire body responded, lifting toward him, writhing in harmony to the heavy pulsing deep inside.

Each time she reached for him, he seemed to slip away, but never did he leave her.

She hardly knew the deep groans she heard were her own. Somehow the physical sensations in her body transcended the physical, became something more, something greater.

Hunger, yes. But a divine hunger, man for woman, lover for lover.

At last she could bear no more of his teasing and she turned herself toward him, seizing him, finding one of his nipples with her own mouth, nipping gently with her teeth until a groan rumbled upward from his depths.

There was a horrible moment when he stopped. "No condom."

"No!" She tried to grab her bedside drawer. There were a few there, kept for a dream that hadn't happened until this moment, probably way too old, but nothing was going to stop her now.

He helped her grab one, then she tore the packet with her teeth and rolled the latex onto his staff, watching the way he grimaced with pure pleasure at her touch.

Moments later he was over her, then sliding into her, into a place so long-empty she had forgotten how glorious it felt to be filled.

He whispered her name, then moved. His thrusts were deep, demanding. His body shook with the power of his need, and his need fed hers until she rose to a place where pleasure and pain became the same thing, a need so strong it actually hurt.

And then...and then...

She found a different kind of heaven. Moments later he shuddered and collapsed on her.

She never wanted to let go.

They cuddled together on the bed, covered by the quilt, entwined tightly. If either of them could speak, neither of them wanted to for a very long time. To hold and be held, to feel skin on skin. Did life offer anything better?

But eventually the sound of an icicle dropping from the eave outside her bedroom jolted them both back to reality.

He looked at her, cradled her face in his hands, and kissed her soundly. "We need to get dressed. This was dangerous."

She assumed he meant because someone wanted to kill her, but she also suspected there were other ways the hour just past could be dangerous to both of them. She didn't want to think about that now.

Rising, her entire body telling her that it wanted to remain in the warm bed with Adrian, she pulled on her clothes. By the time she finished, Adrian had already gone to prowl the house.

To escape her, she thought sadly. To pull back from an intimacy he didn't want. Could she blame him?

No, but she felt as if her heart were ripping open anyway.

She stepped into her flannel-lined moccasins and slowly followed him back to the real world. He was in the living room, reheating the coffee by the fire. "Want a cup?"

Between one second and the next, something in her shifted. A different connection snapped into place.

With deep certainty, she started speaking, though she couldn't have identified the source of the knowledge, only her certainty. "The killers are stalkers. They'll wait out the ice. They'll wait for an opportunity to get at me, Adrian. And they'll get one. But if we don't catch them soon, someone else is going to die first. The compulsion...won't let them stop."

"Compulsion?"

"It's a game. But it's more than a game. One of them is compelled like an addict. The other one is getting there. And someone else will die. A woman. A woman with a baby."

At that she gripped his forearm and leaned toward him. "A woman with a baby. We have to stop them, Adrian."

"Then tell me where they are. But for God's sake don't ask me to stake you out in the open and hope I can move quick enough from behind some blind."

But she had gone to another place, one farther away, slipping there without consciously realizing it. "They already have her," she said. "She lives with one of them. This weather...this weather is causing problems. He needs his fix, but he can't get out to hunt. The hunger grows in him, every time he looks at her. He's already thinking about how her eyes will look as her life fades...."

When she returned to self-awareness, Adrian was already on the phone, relaying the information to Gage. He looked at her. "How old is the baby?"

She felt strangely disconnected, and there seemed to be a fog or a mist in her mind, concealing things, making it hard to think. But then, "Just a few months."

Adrian relayed the information. She hardly heard him wind up the conversation, really noticing only when he drew her into his arms.

"They're going to look," he said, almost rocking her. "They're going to look. There aren't that many babies that young in this county."

"They've got to save her."

"If they can they will." There was no mistaking the steel in his voice. He'd made up his mind about something, but she didn't want to ask. All she wanted to do was let him hold her close and keep the demons at bay.

And yet the vision would not leave.

The woman took the baby. She felt the eyes of the older man fixing on her in a way that deeply frightened her. She didn't know for certain what her boyfriend and that man meant when they talked about their hunting, but she had a terrifying idea they weren't comparing elk to deer.

So while they played cards in the front room with the curtains pulled against the blinding brightness of the light that splintered off all the ice, she slipped into the baby's room and wrapped the infant in every piece of warm clothing and receiving blanket she could find. She stuffed the diaper bag with necessities and the little bit of money she had saved from her limited household budget.

Then, nearly tiptoeing, she eased into the mudroom, closing the door silently behind her. The baby slept, thank God, and remained sleeping as she hastily pulled on her own cold-weather clothes. Better clothes were available these days, but he wouldn't get them for her, so she made do with her father's insulated work pants and her mother's old wool coat, and a knitted wool scarf and mittens she had made herself.

Then, with only the merest creak of hinges, she stepped outside with her baby and closed the door tightly.

There was only one direction she could take that would not bring her in sight of the windows of the front room. Even though the curtains were drawn, she feared one of them might look out.

She headed straight back for the woods, knowing her trail would be plain to see unless the sun melted the ice swiftly.

But she knew in her bones that remaining here exposed her to even more danger. She knew those men were able trackers who could probably follow her to the ends of the earth.

But she also knew some secrets, secrets she had never shared with anyone. If she could make it to the creek, she could cover her tracks and make her way to a cave that was so well hidden she had found it only by falling into it as a child.

She could hide there.

The only question was how long she could survive in the cold.

Kerry snapped back to herself, shaking from a cold and a horror that penetrated to her very bones.

"Oh, God. There's such little time!"

Chapter 11

Around midday, the temperatures began a sharp rise, melting the ice swiftly. The county began to move again, and even from the vantage point of her house on a narrow side street, Kerry could tell that people had begun to hurry around to deal with their regular Saturday chores and errands.

It would have been nice to do the same, but she didn't even ask Adrian if they could. Much as cabin fever had begun to irritate her, some other sense kept her nailed indoors.

It was, she thought, as if she were waiting for something.

Her imagination, perhaps, ignited by the threatening phone call? Possibly.

But something was about to happen, of that she felt increasing certainty.

The phone rang, and once again Adrian took the call. "Okay," he said. "Good."

When he hung up, he turned to Kerry. "They've pretty much talked to all the new mothers."

"And?"

"There's one missing. Her husband's missing, too, and some guy who lived with them."

"That's them!" How she knew, she could not say. "Did you get a name?"

He shook his head. "So now we know who we're looking for, I guess. But whether the woman and her baby are still alive, no one knows."

Kerry closed her eyes, seeking a flash of perception, suddenly longing for the visions she had never wanted to begin with. Nothing answered her, not one damn wisp of intuition. "I don't know," she said finally.

"No reason you should." His voice suggested that he wanted to comfort her, but it also suggested something else.

Fear.

The killers were out of pocket, assuming the absent men were the right ones. They might even now be killing the woman with the baby. Or they might be coming for Kerry. She knew what he was thinking without asking.

Because she was thinking the same thing.

"I don't like this," he said finally. "Most of the deputies are out looking for these guys and the woman with a baby. Hardly anybody's here in town."

"I'm exposed."

"That's what I was getting at, yes."

"It's okay."

"No, it's not!" He snapped the words and she took a step backward, her eyes widening.

"Sorry," he said after a moment during which he visibly gathered himself. "But we've got a couple of killers running around the county, they've threatened you, and my backup is that kid in the car out there."

"Kid?"

"The one who fell asleep at the wheel last night. He replaced Sarah."

"Cal? He's an okay kid. I taught him."

"I don't trust him. He fell asleep on the job."

"It's daytime now."

"Yeah. Sure."

He started pacing, and she had the feeling of a huge wolf on the prowl. He was as tired of being locked up as she was. But was there an alternative?

That's when it struck her. "Let's go."

"Go?" He froze, staring at her with disbelief. "Go where?"

"Let's go looking for them."

"You're out of your mind."

"No, I'm not." She leaned forward earnestly. "Think about it, Adrian. They're out there somewhere and they know where I live. I'll be safer on the move than sitting in this house."

He shook his head sharply, but it wasn't exactly a

denial. After a moment he said, "Do you think you might get some sense...if we're out on the road?"

"I don't know," she admitted. "But sitting here is making me feel like a target in a carnival booth. And you're right. We have too little backup here, not with everyone out looking for a woman with a baby. It's worth a try. It has to be. I can't just sit here and do nothing."

He was thinking about it. She could see it in his eyes. He hesitated for at least a full minute. Then he wagged his finger at her. "You sit right here. I'm gonna go talk to Cal, then I'm gonna call Gage. After I talk to them, I'll decide just how harebrained this is."

"Of course it's harebrained. But it could work."

She could tell he didn't like the idea at all. But he didn't say any more. He simply left her in the kitchen and headed out front.

Sitting there by herself, she wondered if she'd lost her mind, or if this was as good an idea as she thought when she had formulated it.

Because there was no mistaking that she was offering to put herself in a noose.

Gage proved remarkably sanguine about the whole idea. He stopped by in answer to Adrian's call.

"Sure," he said. "It's a good idea."

Adrian frowned. "She's already a target, and I'm supposed to expose her all over the county?"

"Moving targets are harder to hit."

"My thinking exactly," Kerry said. Although in fact

she was beginning to doubt her own sanity. She was actually volunteering for this?

Now Adrian frowned at her. "You're not afraid of dying. Do you know how much that terrifies me?"

Gage ran his fingers through his hair, the gesture of a man who has just realized he may have put his foot in it. Before he could reconsider, Kerry spoke.

"Look Adrian, if it's any comfort, the idea scares me, too. I don't *want* to die, and I promise I won't behave rashly. But this has to *end*. Quickly. I can't stay in this house forever, and I certainly don't want to keep having visions of people being murdered. Do you know what kind of hell that is? Plus, I couldn't live with myself if someone else dies because I sat here and did nothing except hide. You should be the last person I need to explain that to."

Gage looked at Adrian, wisely keeping his mouth shut.

"I know. I know," Adrian said finally, repeating himself as if reassuring himself in some way. "It's just that..." He appeared unable to find the words he wanted.

Kerry had no idea what possessed her then, but she said something brutally true. "It's not me you don't trust. It's yourself."

If it were possible, Gage seemed to blend with the wall.

Adrian gave a sharp shake of his head. "You sure don't pull any punches, Kerry."

"Should I?"

Adrian looked away, seemed to stare at something beyond the walls that surrounded them. "You'll have to wear the armor," he said finally. "And promise me you won't do one damn thing without my permission."

"I'll try not to."

He glared. *"Promise."*

"I can't. I never make promises when I'm not sure what might happen."

"God!"

"I can send Cal with you," Gage offered. "It'll be some added protection."

"No," both Kerry and Adrian said at once, rounding on him.

"Cal is useless," Adrian said. "He'd probably just get in the way. He's too new, and I don't need to be looking out for anyone else."

Kerry added her own objection. "We're just going to be driving around. Didn't we agree a moving target is harder to hit? They won't know where to look for me. All I want is to get a fix on where *they* are."

Somehow, however, Gage seemed to think the matter was settled. "You've got your hands full, Adrian. I'll get you both fresh radios. They're in my car."

He departed through the front door, leaving Adrian and Kerry to stare at each other.

"I'm sorry, Adrian," she said quietly. "But I *have* to do this."

After a couple of seconds he nodded. "I get it," he said. "Believe me, I understand. But I don't like it."

"Neither do I, honestly."

The bubble of tension between them began to deflate,

and the space between them no longer felt like an emotional no-man's-land.

"It's that woman and baby," Kerry said quietly. "I can't ignore them."

"No. I can't, either. I just wish there was another way."

"Maybe there will be. Gage must have people searching all around that house."

"Of course he does. He told me as much. Which is why I'm having trouble with the idea that you have to get involved."

"Would you have found that wounded woman if I hadn't been there?"

"No, but that's not the point."

"Isn't it?"

"It's not like you can be a hundred percent sure you'll pick up anything."

"But I have to at least try."

Apparently he could understand that, because he loosed a sigh, shook his head and then turned to get her body armor. Gage returned then with two radios. "They haven't found a thing out at that ranch where the woman and baby live. But they're still looking. If either of you gets any other ideas, let me know."

Despite the possibility that he might be driving Kerry into the lion's den, Adrian headed straight for the ranch where the searchers were already looking. It seemed like the best place to start.

Between them on the seat was a thermos of coffee.

Behind him on the gun rack were his two favorite shotguns.

"You ever use a shotgun?" he asked Kerry.

"Of course. I live in Wyoming."

"You take one, then, if we get out of the truck."

"Are they loaded?"

"Not at the moment. Ammo is in the glove box."

"Okay. Which one do you prefer?"

He glanced at her. "You take the Mossberg," he said finally. "It auto loads six rounds."

She nodded. "I've used one."

He took what solace he could from that and the fact that you didn't have to be a sharpshooter to hit your target with a shotgun. Whether she could actually bring herself to use it against a human target remained to be seen.

"I've got low-recoil mag rounds for it," he went on, wanting her to have any little bit of info that might prepare her. "But you've got to be ready to use it, Kerry. Otherwise you might as well carry a club."

"I hope I don't have to find out if I can."

"Me, too." To his everlasting sorrow, he *knew* he could fire at a human being. He'd have vastly preferred to never learn that about himself. He hoped like hell Kerry could escape that discovery.

They were still on the county road, climbing steadily toward the mountains, within five miles of the ranch they sought when Kerry said, "Pull over."

He didn't bother to question, just edged over onto the muddy shoulder, keeping two wheels on pavement.

When they stopped, he quietly waited for her to speak again while keeping an eye out.

Trees dotted the landscape here, and they clustered as if outlining a stream bed that ran toward the mountains. Out here a lot of the ice still remained in patches of shadow.

After a couple of minutes, Kerry shook her head. "Nothing," she said. "Let's keep going."

He shifted into drive and pulled them back onto the road with only a brief wheel spin in the mud. "Did you get something?"

"I thought maybe. But it was just a fleeting thing."

"Maybe you shouldn't try. I mean, everything else you've gotten has been pretty much when you weren't expecting it."

"True." She settled a little more comfortably in the seat. "Have you ever noticed how uncomfortable these vests are?"

"Every time I wear one. They've gotten a little better over the years, but not a whole lot."

"I guess that's basically irrelevant when you think about *why* you're wearing one."

"Unless it gets really hot, yeah."

"Don't turn off at the ranch."

The command was abrupt, and Adrian glanced her way. Her face seemed to have frozen. Questions weighted the tip of his tongue, but he swallowed them, not wanting to disturb whatever sense she was getting.

Just a few weeks ago, he would have believed he was on a wild-goose chase. No more. At this point he was willing to credit her instincts as much as his own. After all, who was to say where a hunch came from?

Sure, the argument said they were based on experience, some idea or feeling arising from the subconscious assemblage of knowledge gleaned over time, but when he watched Kerry do this thing of hers, he wasn't at all sure that was the whole story.

How many times had he acted on a hunch he couldn't explain even to himself? Plenty. Maybe the only difference between him and Kerry was that he could point to his experience as a police officer to justify his hunches, while she had nothing to point to except the feeling itself.

Wherever they came from, her intuitions had made a believer out of him.

A sheriff's car with flashers on was parked at the entrance to the ranch. The Crooked M. Kerry struggled to remember who owned the place. The deputy motioned them to stop, so Adrian braked. Almost at once he was recognized.

"Hey, Adrian," said Fred Wehrung. "Do you need to go up to the house? I'll need to call ahead."

"No," Adrian said. "We're on our own goose chase."

Fred half smiled. "Hope you do better than us."

"Is there any indication these folks left the ranch?"

"Other than them being gone, you mean?" Fred shook his head. "All vehicles registered to them are still there. It's got us all wondering if they might be vics, too."

"No," said Kerry. "The men are the perps. The woman is a victim. Or will be soon if we don't find her."

Fred hesitated, looking at her, but apparently he'd heard about her visions, too, because he nodded. "You be careful then. Do you want any help?"

"Not yet," Adrian said, feeling reluctance all the way to his bones. A posse would have been a nice thing right now. But it might also interfere with the very thing he and Kerry were out here trying to do.

"Stay out of trouble," Fred said, waving them on.

Adrian hit the accelerator, and the mountains came a little closer. "Stay out of trouble?" he repeated. "If we were going to stay out of trouble, we'd be on our way to Laramie. Or Gillette, or Casper, or Denver, or..."

Kerry gave a little laugh that didn't sound as if she really meant it. "Maybe we can do that later."

"Yeah. Keep saying things like that and I might hold you to them."

She glanced at him. "Do you think I wouldn't want you to?"

He turned and met her gaze as a deep pothole shook them. "Ask me that again when this is over."

Kerry sank back into her seat and wondered how to take that. Yes, she'd realized when they made love that might be as far as he would ever go, but then to say he might hold her to her offer to take her away, and back off just as quickly...

Oh, what did it matter? she asked herself irritably. Her whole life had turned on its head since her first vision—gee, was that only a couple of days ago? It seemed like an eternity now. Which was probably a measure of just how much had happened and how much it had changed her. A lifetime, it seemed, had compressed itself into a handful of days.

Nothing looked the same anymore, not the countryside around her, or the looming mountains, or even her self-image. Did she even know herself anymore?

The last time she had felt so shaken in her world had been after the accident. Now here she was again, shedding an old self the way a snake shed its skin. Growing pains? Or something else.

She didn't know.

All she could be certain of right now was that something was pulling at her, tugging her forward, making her do things she wouldn't have done even one short week ago. And part of that tug came directly from the man beside her.

She hated to think that Adrian would most likely return to his own life after this was over, and put her as firmly in his past as he had put other things. As everyone had to put things.

Because life seemed to move only in one direction, and right now they were hurtling blindly along some road, carried on a stream of forces that felt beyond their control.

In fact, if she allowed herself to really think about it, she should tell him she was nuts, that he was nuts to listen to her, that her ESP must be evidence of insanity and following her in this proved *his* insanity and...

This whole line of thought seemed to spring more from a sudden panic than from reason, she realized. Although reason had little to do with the visions she'd had, reason demanded she not ignore what had already proved itself.

"Stop!"

The command erupted from her lips before it reached her brain. Adrian jammed on the brakes, throwing them both hard against their seat belts.

"What the—"

"Just stop," she said, her voice suddenly reedy. "Just stop. I don't know..."

Her voice trailed off and she began to look around, feeling frightened, yet knowing at the same time that it was not her own fear she felt.

"Someone's scared," she said. "Terrified."

"Nearby?"

"I don't know. Just wait. Please. Wait."

He fell silent.

She looked around, her gaze bouncing from tree to bush to fence post and back as if she couldn't find exactly what she sought. Finally she reached for the doorhandle and started to open it.

Adrian grabbed her arm, his grip viselike. "Don't," he said.

"I have to get out. I have to."

"Then just wait a minute. Let me check around first."

The compulsion that gripped her at that instant didn't want to yield to caution or reason, but she forced herself to nod. Her hand never loosened its grip on the door handle, though.

Adrian set the parking brake, then climbed out. She watched impatiently as he walked around the truck, taking stock of their surroundings. It took him entirely too long, and impatience built in her, growing as rapidly as the fear she sensed. Apparently nothing worried him because he finally came to her door and opened it.

"Okay," he said.

She accepted his help as she stepped down. As soon as her feet his the ground, however, the feeling dissipated.

"Damn it!"

"What?"

She looked up at him, feeling as if her entire face had grown pinched. "It's gone. Just like that it's gone!"

He exhaled heavily. "Okay. Okay. Look, let's just stay right here for a few minutes, have a little of that coffee we brought along. If it comes back, it comes back. If not, we'll drive a little farther."

His plan made as much sense as any at that point. He helped her back into the truck and poured them both a steaming cup of coffee in the mugs they'd brought along. Kerry cradled hers in both hands, as if to stave off a chill, but the chill she felt lodged deeper inside, in a place no coffee could reach.

"I hope they didn't find her," she said.

"God!" He didn't have to say any more.

"But I don't think it's that," she said slowly. "It was more like when you lose the signal on the radio."

"And considering you don't have a dial you can adjust, I guess we'll just have to wait until it drifts back."

"That's a good way of putting it. Unfortunately, there's more at stake here than hearing a particular song."

"Quit pressuring yourself, Kerry. My God, you've already done the impossible. I get the feeling this is something you can't force."

"I wish it were."

"So sure of that?" He looked perfectly serious.

"What do you mean?"

He half shrugged, as if he wasn't quite sure himself, then said, "Maybe I just have this feeling that life is easier to bear when we *don't* have extra-normal knowledge."

"Paranormal, you mean."

"If you say so, Teach. But here's the thing: After what I've seen, I don't want to call it paranormal anymore. That sounds like hokum."

"Well, I seem to have a case of hokum."

He gave her a wry smile. "Not in the least. If I thought that, I wouldn't be chasing all over the county right now." Reaching out, he clasped her hand and squeezed it.

She squeezed back, grateful for his support and strength. "I had a friend in junior high school who used to have precognitive dreams. Only they weren't about little things, but about important things. Major disaster stuff, like plane crashes and earthquakes. After a while, there was no way to call it coincidence."

"That's scary."

"Well, I can't say I got scared. But I sure understood when she told me she wanted it to stop. She said she couldn't do anything to prevent it, so why know about it in advance? She said it was useless and upsetting, and she didn't want it anymore."

He nodded. "I can see that."

"The thing is, once she made up her mind that it had to stop, it stopped."

She could see him turning that over in his mind. "Interesting."

"I thought so, too. But I'll tell you, I want this to stop. Once we finish this, I want it to stop."

His hold on her hand tightened. "I understand."

"The thing is... Well, you'll probably think I'm crazy."

"If there's one thing I'm sure of, it's that you're not crazy."

"Sometimes I feel like it."

"Who doesn't?" The question carried just a hit of humor. "But what were you going to say?"

She sighed and stared down into her coffee mug while clinging to him with her other hand. "Sometimes I believe in destiny. Which is not to say I don't believe in free will. Of course I do. I don't believe that everything in life is planned for us. It's just that sometimes I think certain things are meant to be. That we're slated to have certain experiences. Destined, if you will."

"I can buy that. Some things have almost a feeling of inevitability to them. A sense that no matter what, we're going to arrive at a certain point in time and face certain issues."

"Exactly! But then when that moment or event comes, we still have to make choices."

"Yeah. The outcome isn't destined. It isn't fixed."

She looked at him. "That's it. So it's like I was meant to have these visions for some reason, that a lot of things led me here. There was no escaping it. The only question is what I do about it."

He nodded. "You could choose to go to Denver."

"Yes. That's exactly what I'm getting at. So maybe, for some reason, I *had* to experience this, but it's what I do about it that counts."

She looked out the car window, across small fields hemmed by a thickening forest. "I felt that way about the car accident, too. Maybe it was just a form of survivor guilt, I don't know. But I'd get this feeling that there was a reason. Maybe this was it."

"I can't begin to answer that, Kerry. All I can tell you is that I definitely *do not* believe that life is a random series of events without meaning. But even so, every moment of our lives we make choices. It's the choices that matter."

She nodded then took a deep drink of her coffee. "That's kind of how I feel, too. This whole thing has made me think hard about it. I mean, right after my friends died in that accident, these kinds of questions preoccupied me for a long time. But then, you know how it is. You can't operate that way all the time. Eventually you sink back into the comfort of familiarity and sort of letting life wash over you. No long-term perspective, no soul-searching questions."

"We'd go nuts if we didn't do that. Or we'd have to retreat to a mountain hermitage. Most of the time we just have to be in the moment."

At that she gave him a wry glance. "How many of us actually live in the moment, Adrian? We're always thinking about what's ahead, what's just behind. The moment is mostly that elusive point from where we look forward or back."

"True."

"Ironic, isn't it? If you think about it, we're every-where but *here*."

A quiet laugh escaped him. "You hit that nail on the head, Kerry."

"You saw my book collection. I read too much. But there's a common theme in a lot of stuff, the theme that we need to be *in* the moment if we want to be happy, not living in a future that hasn't happened yet, or a past that's done."

"Nice philosophy, except that we need to store up our acorns against the winter."

"Ah, but remember the lilies of the field..."

He smiled. "Neither do they sow nor do they reap... Yeah, I remember that. I've always loved that verse."

"Easier said than done." She looked out the window again, suddenly feeling an uncomfortable prickle at the base of her skull. "I'm tuning in. Can you drive a little farther?"

"Sure." He balanced his mug on the dash and started them down the road again.

The mug jolted and Kerry reached out, grabbing it and holding it. "I think you'd prefer the coffee in your stomach, rather than your lap."

"That's usually the way."

She didn't answer him, but instead tried to let the feeling grow in her, that sense that she knew something she couldn't quite put her finger on.

"I need to get a newer truck," he muttered. "One with better suspension and some cup holders."

She only vaguely heard him. Something was rising out of the depths of her unconscious, or whatever place those paranormal impressions came from. She tried to just let it happen, but couldn't quite prevent herself from trying to hurry it along. She said a quiet little prayer that they'd find this woman and her baby before it was too late. Just that. She wouldn't ask for any more than that.

"Stop."

Chapter 12

Adrian hit the brake and looked at her. She was still staring out the side window. "Here," she said. "Here. They're out there. All of them. They're hunting her and the baby."

"God."

"We've got to go. Here. Now."

He didn't argue. He set the brake and turned off the ignition. After radioing in to tell Gage they were stopped and where they were getting out, he gave Kerry a long look. When he climbed out, this time he reached for the shotguns. Kerry sat on the seat, seeming to have forgotten she held the coffee mugs, still staring toward a line of trees.

Reaching across her, he pulled open the glove box

and took out the ammunition. He loaded both shotguns, then stuffed his pockets with more.

Then, guns in hand, he came around to the passenger side and looked at her. "You should stay here," he said.

"You'll never find her." She put the mugs on the dash and opened the door. Sliding to the ground, she sought steady footing in the soggy ground.

He passed her the Mossberg. "Can you reload?"

She nodded.

He reached back into the cab and took out a couple more handfuls of mag shells, filling her parka pockets. Then he stuffed the ammo boxes back in the glove box and locked the truck. From the bed he grabbed a heavy backpack and slipped it on. Camping and survival stuff—in case. It was the kind of stuff a wise person always carried in the winter around here and there weren't a whole lot of daylight hours left.

"Okay. Get your gloves on, zip up and make sure you're ready."

She nodded, following his instructions.

"You stay behind me," he cautioned. "Tell me where to go, but keep a low profile, okay?"

"All right." She indicated some trees with a movement of her chin. "That way."

"Try to stay in my tracks. You'll be less likely to stumble."

The morning's sunshine had begun to give way to a gray layer of clouds, flattening the world with diffuse light. Not the best conditions.

He had to lift barbed wire out of the way. Gone were

the days of wide-open spaces, except in parks and national forests. Everything belonged to someone now, and everyone had fenced his piece of the world.

She slipped through without any trouble and he followed her with only slightly more difficulty. Then, with her right behind him he began slogging toward the trees she'd indicated.

He glanced back once and saw that she carried the shotgun carefully, muzzle pointed away and down, strap arranged to properly brace the gun if she fired. So he didn't have to worry about that. She *did* know what she was doing.

The morning's thaw hadn't been helpful at all. Ground that was usually hard had grown spongy, and only the browned grasses kept them from sinking. Still, it was a bit fatiguing, like walking in sand.

Ten minutes later they reached the trees and he paused, turning to look at Kerry. She appeared to be listening, so he didn't say anything, simply waited. As long as they had only her impressions to guide them, this was going to be slow.

"Somewhere," she whispered, as if to herself, then closed her eyes.

While she checked in to the parallel universe where things were revealed to her, he kept watch, scanning the surrounding woods with a practiced eye. Funny, he'd never thought he'd need most of his marine training again, but right now it was coming to the fore as seldom before. Patrol in enemy territory, that's what this felt like. Two killers on the loose, God knew where.

"That way," she said finally, indicating a path deeper into the woods. "She's near water."

"I think there's a stream back there."

Kerry nodded. "Do you have a map? It might help."

He turned his back toward her. "You see that little pocket on the bottom of my pack? Map and compass."

She zipped it open and retrieved the waterproofed map and the compass, then passed both to him. He opened the map, studying it for a few moments before pointing. "This is where we are. And there's a creek back there."

She leaned over, looking at the map. "How can you be sure?"

"This was the easy stuff when I was a marine."

"Oh, I almost forgot you were in the corps." That seemed to settle her mind. "After you."

Taking his direction from the map, he used the compass to keep them on course in woods that grew darker and thicker the farther they walked. At least as the woods thickened, the undergrowth diminished, providing fewer obstacles. And in the woods the ground had not thawed as much.

Until they started to climb, and rock outcroppings began to force them to divert. Adrian moved ahead confidently, though, because even without a compass he knew he could bring them to the stream. The compass just made it quicker and surer.

Water from melting ice dripped from high branches, adding an almost musical sound of "plop-plop" to the forest. Apart from a few squirrels, the wildlife had gone into hiding. Still, he knew they were being watched. Their passage wouldn't go unnoticed by nature.

Then, halting him in his tracks, a wolf coalesced out of the shadows, seeming to grow from nothing. Kerry stopped behind him and looked around him. "Oh," she breathed.

Golden eyes regarded them steadily. The wolf kept one paw lifted as if about to dart away. His coloring reminded Adrian of a husky, although the animal looked scruffier than any pet. He still hadn't finished his autumn shedding, and appeared almost moth-eaten.

Moth-eaten but powerful, the apex predator in these woods and mountains. Even bears could be taken down by hungry wolf packs.

But if there was a pack, it remained out of sight. A judgment was taking place, and Adrian waited patiently for the decision.

At last the wolf seemed satisfied, and melted back into the shadows whence he came.

"Wow," Kerry breathed. "I've never seen one in the wild before."

"Few people do. They're pretty shy."

"He didn't seem shy."

"He's probably the alpha. Has to protect the pack. I think we've been granted safe passage."

"That was so cool."

Adrian nodded, agreeing with her. But he felt his own rising sense of urgency and began to lead the way toward the stream again.

Then, seeming to come from everywhere around them,

the howls of the pack rose, an eerie harmony that could make a half dozen wolves sound like so many more. Adrian stopped again, and this time Kerry gripped his arm.

"Is that a threat?" she asked.

"I don't think so," he said after a moment. "It's probably an announcement that this is their territory. I don't think they'd do that if they wanted to attack."

"I hope you're right."

He glanced at her. "Wolf attacks on people are so rare I can't even tell you. We're more likely to get trouble from a bear."

"You *had* to say that."

"I was speaking in general. This time of year, most of the bears are in their dens."

"Asleep."

"Not quite. They can still rouse to protect themselves, but if we don't threaten them, they'd prefer to keep hibernating."

"Do we need to be quiet?"

"Why do you ask?"

"Well, I was wondering, if wolves are so shy, why do people think they're killers?"

He paused and faced her. "Myth. Legend. The rare attack on the weak and the sick when the climate was harsh. You get hungry enough, you'll attack whatever's available. Even if it's the species you domesticated into friends."

"Wolves aren't domesticated," she said.

"I didn't mean them. The wolves domesticated us, or that's what a lot of biologists think now. We fed them.

They kept watch at night while we slept. By and large, that relationship works fine. But there are exceptions...."

"Why does every good thing have exceptions?" she asked.

"Not every good thing," Adrian said with a smile. "There were no exceptions last night. And from here on out, I think we'd better be as quiet as possible. We're not far from the stream, and if those guys are out hunting, I'd rather they not hear us from miles away."

She nodded just as the wolves let out another eerie song.

Adrian leaned down to her ear. "We might not be alone."

She realized he wasn't referring to the wolves.

At once the back of her neck prickled. She gave a quick nod of understanding, and shifted the shotgun to a readier position.

It occurred to her that if the wolves were warning invaders from their territory, the warning might not be directed only at them. Now, she thought, would be a good time for a little intuition, except that she had none.

Of course. Remembering her friend who had died, she wondered, *What good is it if it isn't there when you need it?*

But that was the whole problem with the psychic thing. If it were as reliable as the other senses, it wouldn't be paranormal, would it? And people would be more inclined to believe it.

In fact, the whole world would be different, so she might as well stop complaining. Right now they had a woman and infant to find, and all she could do was pray that they'd be in time.

And keep moving. They had to keep moving.

The howls sounded again, but from a different place. The pack was on the move, too. Somewhere out there, they had found another invader. The chill that crept down Kerry's spine now had nothing to do with the weather.

When the woods fell silent again as if even the trees had frozen to acknowledge the wolves' claim of primacy, Kerry for the first time thought she heard the sound of running water. She eased forward until she walked beside Adrian and cocked her head toward the sound.

He nodded, then motioned her to step behind him again. She understood that he didn't want her to trip, but she also feared they just made a better target this way.

She whispered, "Shouldn't we spread out?"

"If you were trained. You're not."

She couldn't argue with that. What did she know about stalking killers in the woods? Not a damn thing.

The soft ground muffled the sounds of their movement, and Kerry found herself making every effort not to even let her parka rustle. The nylon, so good at keeping her warm, wanted to announce her every movement.

Ten minutes later, they were almost at the stream. The sound of running water filled the air now. Adrian motioned her to hunker down with him behind a boulder.

"Okay," he said in a whisper just loud enough to be heard over the rushing water, "we have to make some decisions here. You said the woman and the child are near water?"

She nodded, remembering her earlier impression.

"It's likely, if the killers know her and are stalking her, that they're moving along the stream, too."

"The wolves were howling to the east." She pointed.

He nodded. "The question is whether they were howling at the woman, at the killers, or at a fox. God knows."

Kerry looked around, as if she might see answers hanging from the trees like Christmas ornaments. But of course she saw nothing but tree trunks, scrub and an endless carpet of pine needles and leaves.

"Great," she muttered. "What good does it do for us to be here if we don't know what to do next?"

"That's the thing," he said. "You're going to stay behind this boulder while I go look."

"No!"

"Shh! Stay here. I need you to cover me while I go look to see if the river bank is disturbed."

At that she subsided. At least he wasn't leaving her behind out of some misguided notion of protecting her.

"I can do that," she said. "I used to be a decent shot."

"Then I don't have to tell you not to aim that thing too close to me."

"Of course not."

"If it comes to that, I'll have to protect myself. The spread on that load isn't huge, but it's enough to lay two people out if they're close."

"I know." She did. "My dad used to take me for target practice."

"Not hunting?"

"Are you kidding? You think I'd want to kill some in-offensive deer?"

A smile cracked his somber expression. "Why doesn't that surprise me?"

"My dad hunted elk and moose. He stopped hunting deer."

"Why?"

"Because I got really, really nasty about it."

"But what makes deer different from moose or elk?"

She could tell only part of his attention was on what she was saying. His eyes kept scanning their surroundings as if he had built-in radar.

"They can be mean. Besides, we had to eat."

At that she got his full attention, but only briefly. "You'll have to tell me about that some time. But right now—"

She touched his arm, silencing him. "I feel them."

"Who?"

She closed her eyes, letting the faintest whisper of in-tuition grow, nurturing it without trying to hurry it, for fear she might banish it. Adrian waited, but she sensed his impatience.

Time. Time. Time was growing short. They were getting closer. They...they...

Which they? The woman? The killers?

"They're almost here," she whispered. "Almost."

"Who?"

A different voice emerged from the woods. "Well, what have we here?"

Kerry's eyes snapped open as she felt Adrian tense beside her. She turned her head and saw a man holding a rifle pointed at them. Him. A bearded older man in camouflage.

As she felt Adrian start to move, she touched his thigh. "Behind us, too," she whispered.

"God."

"Why don't you just put down those guns," the man said, the barrel of his rifle never wavering.

Adrian tried playing dumb. "Why? Can't a man hunt anymore?"

"How stupid do you think I am?" The man turned his head and spat on the ground. "That teacher there, she reads minds. I heard all about it."

Ice seemed to encase Kerry's heart. But she knew what she had to do.

Slowly, she put the Mossberg down. Then, despite Adrian's objection, she rose until she stood, facing the man, her hands held out to show they were empty. "I don't read minds."

"Sure you do," the guy said. "I heard all about it. Even the sheriff is listening to you."

"Who told you that?"

"None of your beeswax. Now get away from that guy so I can keep an eye on you."

Kerry started to obey, but Adrian gripped her ankle, stopping her.

Adrian spoke. "You sound crazy, you know that? Mind reading? If she could do that, I'd be playing the lottery."

A branch cracked behind them, telling them where the other man was.

"I told you, woman, move away from him."

"He won't let me."

"Oh fer Pete's sake..." The man leveled his rifle at Adrian, but just as he did so, Adrian yanked on Kerry's ankle. Loss of balance sent her to the forest floor in an eyeblink. Barely did she register that she had fallen on her shotgun when shots rang out. She heard the buzz as a bullet flew by her and the *thwack* as it hit the boulder. Another bullet came from a different direction but she couldn't tell where it went. Only that the cracks of fired guns were coming from two directions.

Rolling slightly, she grabbed the Mossberg and released the safety. Pressing the stock against her shoulder while lying on her back, she raised her head to try to find the second shooter.

Even as she did so, there was another crack of gunfire. This time it was Adrian. He'd drawn his pistol from wherever he had concealed it and fired past her toward the guy who had first accosted him.

Then she saw the second man, and something took over. In an instant she sat up and aimed the Mossberg at the man, a younger version of the first. His eyes widened, and before she could pull her trigger, he dropped his own rifle.

"Don't," he said. "Don't."

She kept the shotgun trained on him.

"Watch him," Adrian said.

She glanced at him, then gasped. There was blood on his sleeve, and his face had gone white.

"Adrian..."

"Watch him, damn it! I've got to take care of the other one."

She obeyed, realizing she had no other choice. "Don't move," she said to the young man. Then her heart slammed as she recognized him. "My God, you're Tom Martinez."

He nodded, keeping his hands up.

"Why in the world are you involved in this?"

Adrian pushed himself to his feet and walked toward the other man, pistol still pointed at him.

"He's only wounded," Adrian said. "Keep your eye on Tom."

Kerry couldn't have taken her eyes off of him. He'd been her student only six years ago. A bright one. She couldn't imagine what had led him down this path.

A *snick* followed by a ratcheting sound told her Adrian was putting cuffs on the other man. Another half minute passed, then Adrian walked past her toward Tom.

"Facedown on the ground, hands behind your head," Adrian told him.

Tom didn't even resist. He did as he was told while Adrian fixed nylon flexi-cuffs at his wrists and ankles.

With both men bound, Adrian returned to sit beside Kerry, sliding down the rock as if feeling weakened. "I'm counting on you," he said.

Then he pulled out his radio and called for backup and medical aid. As soon as he got an affirmative response to the location he provided, he leaned forward.

"Get the first-aid kit out of the pack."

He still held his pistol, so she put the Mossberg aside

and did as asked. The first-aid kit was right on top, and she pulled it out.

Adrian used one hand to unzip his jacket. "Feel around in there. Top of my right shoulder. Stuff gauze into it on both sides."

She obeyed, pulling his jacket open. She had to bite her lip when she saw how heavily he was bleeding, but urgency drove her as she stuffed the wound with gauze, then reached for a second roll and wrapped it, tightly as she could, trying to make a pressure bandage.

"Thanks." For a few seconds his head fell back against the boulder. "I'll be okay. It's not as bad as it looks, Kerry. Now take care of him." He nodded toward the older man.

"No."

"What?"

"I don't care if he dies after what he did. But I'm not going close to him."

Adrian, some of his color returning, looked her right in the eye. "You're better than that."

"Wanna bet?"

But she grabbed the first-aid kit anyway and stomped over to the wounded man. Adrian had bound him hand and foot, too, but his wound didn't look that bad. At least it wasn't bleeding much. Ignoring the groans of pain that came in response to her ministrations, she put gauze around his thigh, and tightened it with a sharp jerk.

"There," she said. "More mercy than you gave your victims."

His eyes opened, and the coldness in them was

enough to make her step back. Another second of that stare sent her hurrying back to Adrian's side. He already looked almost back to normal.

"I don't believe in possession," she said when she returned to Adrian. "But whatever is in that man's eyes, it isn't human."

"Yes, Kerry, it is. It's just the worst part of us."

She shuddered. "I'd rather believe in demons."

The radio crackled to life, and the subject was dropped as Adrian guided the deputies toward them. Twenty minutes later, the first pair came crashing through the woods, their hurry making them sound like a Mongol horde.

Next to Adrian, Kerry thought, they were the best sight she'd ever seen.

Chapter 13

Once the paramedics had finished giving Adrian a temporary patch job on his shoulder, he refused to be taken to the hospital.

"We've got to find that woman and her child."

Arguments that there were now plenty of other people to aid in the search didn't deter him. Questioning of the two suspects had revealed nothing. Despite having shot at Adrian and Kerry, they insisted they'd been hunting. Tom Martinez claimed to have no idea of where his wife and child had gone. "Probably to visit a friend," he had said sullenly.

When the two men had been taken away, Adrian walked down to the stream bank and squatted. The water ran between stony banks, offering nothing in the way of tracks.

"But would a woman with a baby have walked on the rocks?" he mused.

Kerry squatted beside him. "Yes, if she didn't want to leave a trail."

He nodded. Behind them, Gage and his deputies were planning the search. They decided the bulk of them would head downstream toward the ranch.

"That's wrong," Kerry said. Leaning forward, she dipped her hand in the icy running water. At once something electric seemed to zap her.

"She walked in the water."

Adrian turned to look at her. "What?"

"Her feet are wet. She's shivering."

Kerry herself started shivering, as if she had merged with the woman in some way. "Dark. Cold. Musty. Grace..."

"Grace?"

Adrian stood up and called to Gage. "Who are we looking for?"

"Maria Martinez."

"Not Grace?"

Kerry turned in time to see Gage freeze. "The baby is Grace."

Kerry straightened and looked upstream. Then, without a word, she started walking that way. The rocks made it difficult, so without another thought, she stepped into the stream. The years of erosion had made the stream bed relatively smooth, covered in egg-sized rounded pebbles and smaller. Easier than the bank where the rocks were far bigger and less stable.

"Kerry!"

Adrian called after her, but she ignored him. She had to keep moving. Upstream. Farther. Until she reached the boulder that parted the waters. Already she could see it in her mind's eye.

Splashing behind her told her she was being followed. Her feet rapidly grew numb from the cold water, but each step seemed to bring them back to life long enough to feel burning pain.

At some level she became aware that deputies were following her, moving alongside the stream, clambering over rocks and around vegetation. Adrian was right behind her, and soon he was there to steady her with a hand on her arm.

He didn't say another word, just let her lead.

Tired. So tired. Cold. Grace. Keep her close and warm. Don't sleep.

Her eyelids felt heavy, but they weren't her eyelids. They were Maria's. Stay awake!

She didn't know if the thought was her own or Maria's and she was past caring. All she could do was hurry her step.

She'd been keeping her head down, watching her step, focusing on the inner voice. Suddenly she looked up and there was the huge boulder, taller than a tall man, dividing the waters.

Without a thought, she turned to the right and began to scramble up the bank.

"Kerry?"

Adrian was right behind her.

"Shh."

He fell silent except for the sounds he made climbing behind her. Here the slope was steep, leveling out only when they stood high above the stream. A few deputies, watching them, began to cross the stream toward them.

"Here," Kerry said. "Somewhere right around here."

Adrian turned slowly, scanning the rough, tumbled terrain.

"Maria!" Kerry called out. "Maria, we've taken Tom and Henry into custody. I'm here to help you and Grace!"

Everyone froze, listening. In the distance the wolves howled a mournful sound.

"Maria! You need to get warm. Grace can't take as much of the cold as you can!"

Silence. Then a faint voice responded. "Here."

Kerry couldn't tell exactly where it came from, but Adrian seemed to.

At once he began walking toward a rise, a tumble of boulders covered with brush. "Maria," he called gently. "Maria, I'm with the sheriff. We want to help you."

"Here," came the thin voice again.

Adrian dropped to his knees and began to pull rocks away. An instant later, Kerry joined him, her frozen hands oblivious to cuts and scrapes. Rock after rock tumbled down the slope as they were pulled free.

Then a small, dark cavern appeared. Kerry didn't hesitate, but crawled right inside.

"She's here!" she shouted the words as she crawled the last two feet to the woman and child. "It's okay, sweetie," she said to Maria. "It's okay. We're going to take you and the baby to the hospital, okay? And Tom and Henry have been arrested. Can you move?"

Maria's only answer was to hold out the bundle she clutched.

Kerry took it, and realized it was the baby. Pulling the blanket a little to one side, she saw the infant's face. Nearly white with cold, but still breathing.

At once she eased back through the opening. Adrian started to reach for the child, but Kerry shook her head. "Help Maria."

He at once crawled into the opening. Kerry struggled to open her parka with one hand, and tucked the bundled child inside, close to her body's heat. Her own feet were frozen, her hands little better, but as soon as she unzipped her parka she felt the heat rise from her torso and touch her chin. Once she was sure the child could breathe all right, she zipped it into the parka with her.

Then, slowly, she eased her way down the slope toward the approaching deputies.

"The EMTs are coming," one of them assured her.

"Good. This baby is nearly frozen."

But she herself was little better, and finally the cold took its toll on her.

Slowly she collapsed to the ground, unable to take another step.

Sitting in a heap, she began to rock back and forth, arms wrapped around herself and the infant.

Right now, she couldn't even feel relief. Maybe that

would come later, but at this moment she felt as close to dead as she had after the car accident.

Only this time she didn't see the light.

Noise filled the emergency room. From a cubicle some distance away, Henry could be heard cursing as a doctor examined his wound. Grace's thin cry intertwined with the nasty words erupting from behind a curtain.

Kerry lay on a pad that circulated warm water from her neck to her feet. A couple of thick blankets covered her, too, but she still shivered. It might have been lingering hypothermia for which they were treating her, or it might have been a reaction to events. She couldn't tell. Nor did it matter, really.

All that mattered was that there would be no more killing. Right now her heart felt light, as if she had shed a burden.

But all she wanted was to go back to a normal life. No more visions, no more fear, no more ugliness. There was, she thought, nothing more beautiful than ordinary life.

A nurse, a former student of hers, popped in to peek at her feet. "Looking good," Cheryl said. "I think you'll be out of here soon with all your parts."

"That would be nice. How are Grace and Maria doing?"

"You know I can't tell you that. Of course, I was more worried about your feet..."

Then Cheryl vanished, pulling the curtain behind her.

Sideways message received, Kerry thought. The warmth cocooning her made her body feel sleepy, but her mind still raced a mile a minute trying to absorb all that had happened. It would probably do that for days. It was the way of the mind to endlessly replay important events until some kind of organization and absorption had been achieved. At least that's what they had told her after the accident.

Closing her eyes, she let the images and feelings roll like an instant replay of the past few days. At some point she must have dozed off, because the next thing she knew, a warm, strong hand clasped hers.

Her eyes popped open and she found Adrian sitting on the edge of the bed beside her.

"Welcome back, sleepy head."

Her gaze flew to his shoulder. Beneath his torn and bloodied shirt, she saw a professional bandaging job. A sling bore the weight of his arm. Instantly she filled with relief and warmth, a different kind of warmth than the one wrapping around her frozen body. He was okay, and he was here.

"How's your shoulder?" she asked immediately.

"The guy was using a .22. Through and through, muscle tear, no major damage. I guess he was trying to avoid hitting me in the vest. Either that or he's a lousy shot."

"Thank God! What if he'd gone for your head?"

"Didn't you ever learn not to shoot for the smallest part of the body?"

Something in the way he said it made her giggle. The giggle had an edginess to it, as if the response wasn't relaxed. Too early for that, she thought.

"Your feet?" he asked her.

"Cheryl says I get to go home with all parts attached."

"That's great news!" He smiled and squeezed her hand. "Hey, Teach, it's over. You saved the day."

She shook her head. "I didn't really do anything."

"What?" He frowned. "I seem to remember you doing quite a bit."

"The visions just came. It's not like I made them happen."

"But you stuck with them. That couldn't have been easy. Then out there in the woods, you were incredible, Kerry. Incredible. I've never had a better partner."

The words warmed her all the way to her toes, even more than the heating pad beneath her. A flush crept into her cheeks, but she didn't know how to respond.

He astonished her by leaning forward and kissing her lightly on the lips. "What say we blow this joint?"

"Can we?"

"Cheryl told me to come get you."

A smile filled Kerry's face. "But Grace and Maria are okay? Nobody will tell me."

"Nobody will tell me, either, so before I came to see you, I popped in on their cubicle. Mother and child are doing very well. Scared and alone, but at least they're healthy."

"For now I guess that's all we can ask."

"No, we can ask a whole lot more. We can ask for justice. And we will," he said, taking her hand as he eased himself off the bed. "But justice takes time. For now, I'm going to ask for something else. Take me home, Kerry. Please. And stay with me."

Home had never felt so good. Despite the fact that Adrian was the wounded one, he insisted on taking care of Kerry. Pillows propped her comfortably on the sofa, a blanket covered her legs, a fire crackled in the fireplace. Darkness had fallen beyond the windows, but it was no longer a darkness that held threat.

Adrian pulled the easy chair up beside the couch so they could sit side by side, then disappeared for about twenty minutes. When he returned, it was with hot cocoa and a package of chocolate chip cookies. He put everything on the coffee table, then took a plate and arranged cookies around her mug on it.

The gesture made her smile as he handed it to her.

"I feel like a princess."

"You always should." His own smile was warm as he sat in the easy chair with his own cocoa and a stack of cookies he hadn't bothered to arrange.

"I'm glad it's over," she said, looking at her plate mostly because she was afraid to look at him. It was over, all right. And in a little while, he'd walk out of her house to return to his own home, and that would be that.

"So am I. But mostly I'm glad you're safe and there's no need to worry about those guys anymore."

"Does anyone know why they were doing it?"

Forgetting his wounded shoulder, he shrugged, then winced. "From what Gage said, they were treating it like a game. More exciting than stalking deer. Although how you can think it more exciting to walk up on unsuspecting campers and shoot them beats me."

"It wasn't the stalking," she said after a moment. "It was worse."

"Worse?"

"It was the kill. The thrill of killing a human being."

He set his mug down and twisted to look at her. "Another vision?"

"Not exactly." She shook her head and remembered. "That man's eyes. Henry, right? It wasn't about the hunting, it was about the killing. I felt it when I looked at him. Anybody can kill an animal. Not everyone can kill a human being in cold blood."

"Not everyone can kill an animal, either, but I see what you're driving at." He sighed. "Worse, I think you may be right."

"I just wish I could understand how Tom got himself involved. He seemed like a nice, ordinary kid when he was my student."

"Maybe he was, once. He wouldn't be the first person to be led astray by a powerful personality. It happens all too often. Then, once you get someone like Tom started on the path, they begin to justify it to themselves. I've seen it before, although not in a case quite like this."

"I suppose. I remember reading some psychological studies in college and coming away amazed at just how suggestible people are. It doesn't take much."

"That's one of the reasons we try to keep witnesses separated until we have their statements. Otherwise one of them could convince a dozen others that they all saw an atomic bomb explosion when all they heard was a backfire."

One corner of her mouth lifted. "A little extreme, maybe?"

"Unfortunately not. A person who assumes a position of authority can convince people to do things they'd never otherwise do. Or even change what they remember."

"I've heard that if you have ten witnesses to a crime, you're apt to get ten different stories."

"Something like that. Hell, they won't even agree on what color shirt the perp was wearing. If you start with that and someone appears to be certain that it was a white T-shirt, then pretty soon everyone else will be sure it was a white T-shirt despite the fact the perp was wearing a purple sweatshirt. It's amazing."

"Well, I guess we'll learn all about it when they come to trial."

"Or from Gage. Don't forget, I have inside sources."

"So did they," she said, shaking her head. "When we were about to leave the hospital, didn't Gage say Tom fingered Cal as the one who'd been telling him about the investigation?"

"Yeah," he said, nodding. "Gage doesn't know what to do about that. Cal and Tom were friends back in school. Cal had no idea Tom was involved. He was just sounding off to be impressive. Half the department wants to throw the book at him. The other half just wants him fired."

"I'm sure Gage will make the right call," she said. She was too tired to worry about Cal's future right now. And too worried about what was going to happen with the man who sat beside her. She was just beginning to realize that if he walked away, she might seriously want to die.

He grew serious. "How do you feel? I don't mean physically. The emotional strain has been awful for you."

"Not only for me. You were charged with protecting me. I can't imagine how rough that was for you after what happened before."

"Well..." He managed a crooked smile. "I seem to have found a partner I can trust."

Her breath caught in her throat and her eyes locked with his. The heat she saw there awoke an instant yearning in her. "You hardly know me."

"Guess what, Teach. You learn to know the important things real fast under circumstances like this. You were willing to do anything to save Maria and Grace, and you don't even know them. Do you know what it was like to follow you up that stream, knowing you were in danger of losing your feet? Or of dying from hypothermia? But you kept right on, and you didn't stop until you had that baby safe. I saw you collapse. Kerry, you were pushing forward on sheer will even before we started climbing the bank."

She colored. "What else could I do?"

"Exactly." He leaned toward her until their faces were inches apart. "I saw what you did when those men had us at gunpoint. Damn it, you were trying to protect *me*."

She shook her head. "You can't know that. Heck, I don't even remember what I was thinking just then."

"I could tell by what you did. And I can tell you right

now, I'd trust you with my life. I hope you feel the same way about me."

"How could I not? Adrian, you've been protecting me for days."

"Trying to, at any rate."

She lifted a hand and cupped his cheek. "You're a remarkable man."

He took her cocoa and cookies, placing them on the coffee table. Then he leaned in and kissed her with all the passion of a thirsty man who has found water.

"We need time," he said huskily. "I want to get to know you a lot better. I want you to know me better. But I can tell you right now, Kerry, I love you. And I don't think anything is going to change that."

"I might have annoying habits." The protest was weak, silly and an attempt to buy a few seconds as her heart lurched into her throat with a kind of fearful excitement. She wanted to believe him, but with what they'd been through, how could he be certain he wasn't just feeling some kind of aftereffect?

"You can have any annoying habit you want," he said throatily. "There's not a single thing you can do that will change my mind. I know the stuff you're made of. I trust you. And I love you."

A single tear squeezed out of her to tremble on her eyelashes. A single tear of happiness. "I love you, too," she replied, and the undeniable truth of those words filled her with an emotion that went far beyond any words. The strength of the feeling nearly squeezed the breath from her.

He kissed her again, long and deep, promises and the seeds of promises in his touch.

"I won't rush you," he said, looking deep into her eyes. "I promise I won't rush you. But I'm going to marry you."

Another feeling came to her, one of those she'd been having for days now. Her quirk. But this time the feeling was good.

"Yes, you are," she answered. "You most certainly are."

Because she *knew*. And she saw the smile on his face as he realized where her certainty came from.

Visions of destiny.

* * * * *

Mills & Boon® Intrigue
brings you a sneak preview of …

Cassie Miles's Bodyguard Under the Mistletoe

Young widow Fiona only had one thing on her
Christmas list: keeping her daughter safe. So when a
body was discovered on her property, Fiona jumped
at bodyguard Jesse's offer to stay for the holidays.
He had a stoic face, but honest, caring eyes. And no
matter how she ached to feel his toned and chiseled
arms around her, she needed the protection that
only a man like Jesse could provide.

Don't miss this thrilling new story available
next month from Mills & Boon® Intrigue.

He wasn't dead yet.

The darkness behind his eyelids thinned. Sensation prickled the hairs on his arm. Inside his head, he heard the beat of his heart—as loud and steady as the Ghost Dance drum. That sacred rhythm called him back to life.

His ears picked up other sounds. The *beep-beep-beep* of a monitor. The shuffle of quiet footsteps. The creaking of a chair. A cough. Someone else was in the room with him.

The drumming accelerated.

His eyelids opened—just a slit. Sunlight through the window blinds reflected off the white sheet that covered his prone body. Hospital equipment surrounded the bed. Oxygen. An IV drip on a metal pole. A heart monitor that beeped. Faster. Faster. Faster.

"Jesse?" A deep voice called to him. "Jesse, are you awake?"

Jesse Longbridge tried to move, tried to respond. Pain radiated from his left shoulder. He remembered being shot, falling from his saddle to the cold earth and lying there, helpless. He remembered a gush of blood. He remembered…

"Come on, Jesse. Open your eyes."

He recognized the voice of Bill Wentworth. A friend. A coworker. *Good old Wentworth.* He'd been a paramedic in Iraq, but that wasn't the main reason Jesse had hired him. This lean, mean former marine—like Jesse himself—always got the job done.

They had a mission, he and Wentworth. No time to waste. They needed to get into the field, needed to protect…

Jesse bolted upright on the bed and gripped Wentworth's arm. "Is she safe?"

"You're awake." Wentworth grinned without showing his teeth. "It's about time."

One of the monitor wires detached, and the beeping became a high-pitched whine. "Is Nicole safe?"

"She's all right. Arrests have been made."

Wentworth was one of Jesse's best employees—a credit to Longbridge Security, an outstanding bodyguard. But he wasn't much of a liar.

The pain in his shoulder spiked again, threatening to drag Jesse back into peaceful unconsciousness. He licked his lips. His mouth was parched. He needed water. More than that, he needed the truth. He knew that Nicole had been kidnapped. He'd seen it happen. He'd been shot trying to protect her.

He tightened his grip on Wentworth's arm. "Has Nicole Carlisle been safely returned to her husband?"

"No."

Dylan Carlisle had hired Longbridge Security to protect his family and to keep his cattle ranch safe. If his wife was missing, they'd failed. Jesse had failed.

He released Wentworth. Using his right hand, he detached the nasal cannula that had been feeding oxygen to his lungs. Rubbing the bridge of his nose, he felt the bump where it had been broken a long time ago in a school-yard fight. He hadn't given up then. Wouldn't give up now. "I'm out of here."

Two nurses rushed into the room. While one of them turned off the screeching monitor, the other shoved Wentworth aside and stood by the bed. "You're wide-awake. That's wonderful."

"Ready to leave," Jesse said.

"Oh, I don't think so. You've been pretty much unconscious for three days and—"

"What's the date?"

"It's Tuesday morning. December ninth," she said.

Nicole had been kidnapped on the prior Friday, near dusk. "Was I in a coma?"

"After surgery, your brain activity stabilized. You've been consistently responsive to external stimuli."

"I'll say," Wentworth muttered. "When a lab tech tried to draw blood, you woke up long enough to grab him by the throat and shove him down on his butt."

"I didn't hurt him, did I?"

"He's fine," the nurse said, "but you're not his favorite patient."

He didn't belong in a hospital. Three days was long enough for recuperation. "I want my clothes."

The nurse scowled. "I know you're in pain."

Nothing he couldn't handle. "Are you going to take these needles out of my arms or should I pull them myself?"

She glanced toward Wentworth. "Is he always this difficult?"

"Always."

FIONA GRANT PLACED a polished, rectangular oak box on her kitchen table and lifted the lid. Inside, nestled in red velvet, was a pearl-handled, antique Colt .45 revolver.

In her husband's will, he'd left this heirloom to Jesse Longbridge, and Fiona didn't begrudge his legacy. She'd tried to arrange a meeting with Jesse to present this gift, but their schedules had gotten in the way. After her husband's death, she hadn't been efficient in handling the myriad details, and she hoped Jesse would understand. She was eternally grateful to the bodyguard who had saved her husband's life. Because of Jesse's quick actions, she'd gained a few more precious years with her darling Wyatt before he died from a heart attack at age forty-eight.

People always said she was too young to be a widow. Not even thirty when Wyatt died. Now thirty-two. Too young? As if there was an acceptable age for widowhood? As if her daughter—now four years old—would have been better off losing her dad when she was ten? Or fifteen? Or twenty?

Age made no difference. Fiona hadn't been bothered by the age disparity between Wyatt and herself when they married. All she knew was that she had loved her husband with all her heart. And so she was thankful to Jesse Longbridge. She fully intended to hand over the gun to him when he got out of the hospital. In the meantime, she didn't think he'd mind if she used it.

Her fingertips tentatively touched the cold metal barrel and recoiled. She didn't like guns, but owning one was prudent—almost mandatory for ranchers in western Colorado. Not that Fiona considered herself a rancher. Her hundred-acre property was tiny compared to the neighboring Carlisle empire that had over two thousand head of Black Angus. She had no livestock, even though her daughter, Abby, kept telling her that she really, really, really wanted a pony.

Fiona frowned at the gun. *Who am I kidding? I'm not someone who can handle a Colt .45.* She turned, paced and paused. Stared through the window above the sink. The view of distant snow-covered peaks, pine forests and the faded yellow grasses of winter pastures failed to calm her jangled nerves.

For the past three days, a terrible kidnapping drama had been playing out at the Carlisle Ranch. Their usually pastoral valley had been invaded by posses, FBI agents, search helicopters and bloodhounds that sniffed their way right up to her front doorstep.

Last night, people were taken into custody. The danger should have been over. But just after two o'clock last night, Fiona had heard voices outside her house. She hadn't been able to tell how close they were and hadn't seen the men. But they were loud and angry, then suddenly silent.

The quiet that followed their argument had frightened her more than the shouts. What if they came to her door? Could she stop them if they tried to break in? The sheriff was twenty miles away. If she'd called the Carlisle Ranch, someone would come running. But would they arrive in time?

The truth had dawned with awful clarity. She and Abby had no one to protect them. Their safety was her responsibility.

Hence, the gun.

Returning to the kitchen table, she stared at it. She never expected to be alone, never expected to be living in this rustic log house on a full-time basis. This was a vacation home—a place where she and Abby and Wyatt spent time in the summer so her husband could unwind from his high-stress job as Denver's district attorney.

Water under the bridge. She was here now. This was her home, and she needed to be able to defend it.

INTRIGUE...

2 FREE BOOKS
AND A SURPRISE GIFT

We would like to take this opportunity to thank you for reading this Mills & Boon® book by offering you the chance to take TWO more specially selected books from the Intrigue series absolutely FREE! We're also making this offer to introduce you to the benefits of the Mills & Boon® Book Club™—

- **FREE home delivery**
- **FREE gifts and competitions**
- **FREE monthly Newsletter**
- **Exclusive Mills & Boon Book Club offers**
- **Books available before they're in the shops**

Accepting these FREE books and gift places you under no obligation to buy, you may cancel at any time, even after receiving your free books. Simply complete your details below and return the entire page to the address below. You don't even need a stamp!

YES Please send me 2 free Intrigue books and a surprise gift. I understand that unless you hear from me, I will receive 5 superb new stories every month, including two 2-in-1 books priced at £5.30 each and a single book priced at £3.30, postage and packing free. I am under no obligation to purchase any books and may cancel my subscription at any time. The free books and gift will be mine to keep in any case.

Ms/Mrs/Miss/Mr _____ Initials _____

Surname _____

Address _____

_____ Postcode _____

E-mail _____

Send this whole page to: Mills & Boon Book Club, Free Book Offer, FREEPOST NAT 10298, Richmond, TW9 1BR